PRAISE FOR *THE DEVIL YOU KNOW*

"An action-packed novel that starts strong and never lets up, with some twists you don't see coming."

—*Red Carpet Crash*

"The pacing is perfect, the characters' sense of urgency transferring to the readers, who will start turning pages with increasing speed."

—*Booklist*

PRAISE FOR *STORM RISING*

"Gripping and relentless, *Storm Rising* is packed with twists, action, and emotional power. Chris Hauty hits it out of the park."

—Meg Gardiner, author of the UNSUB series

"An excellent thriller perfect for our times!"

—Matthew Betley, bestselling author of the Logan West series and *The Neighborhood*

"Be prepared to stay up all night as Hayley Chill takes you deep into a conspiracy to tear the United States apart. *Storm Rising* will have you glued to the pages as you race to reach the thrilling conclusion."

—L. C. Shaw, bestselling author of *The Network*

"*Storm Rising* has all the twists and turns and breakneck pace of Hauty's earlier books but with a deeper, darker look into the soul of protagonist Haley Chill, and the soul of America, that makes this a timely and terrifying read. I didn't think it was possible, but Chris Hauty has outdone himself—again!"

—Nick Petrie, author of *The Runaway*

"Gritty and engaging, *Storm Rising* is a gripping page-turner. Crisply written, and terrifying in scope, Chris Hauty's new conspiracy thriller is a worthy addition to his excellent Hayley Chill series."

—Simon Gervais, former RCMP counterterrorism officer and bestselling author of *The Last Protector*

PRAISE FOR *DEEP STATE*

"Hayley Chill is one of those preternaturally talented solo operatives skilled in every endeavor, from her physical stamina to her administrative competence to her Jason Bourne–like cool in the face of near-death experiences. She also figures in one of the more surprising double-reverse plot twists I have seen in some time."

—*The New York Times Book Review*

"*Deep State* is a propulsive, page-turning, compelling fragmentation grenade of a debut thriller."

—C. J. Box, #1 *New York Times* bestselling author of *Wolf Pack* and *The Bitterroots*

"The plot . . . rings eerily true. . . . Will keep you turning the pages well into the night."

—Jack Carr, #1 *New York Times* bestselling author of *Only the Dead* and *The Terminal List*

"Hauty provides a fresh twist on the American patriot. Hayley Chill has what it takes to carve out her place in today's thriller scene. She's shrewd, fierce, and always lands the blow that puts her on top."

—Kyle Mills, #1 *New York Times*
bestselling author of *Code Red*

"Engrossing . . . Kick-ass."

—*Publishers Weekly*

"*Deep State* is a compelling page-turner with an unpredictable last-minute twist that will knock you off your feet."

—*Library Journal*

"With his supercharged plot and a perfectly timed, mind-bending twist, Chris Hauty becomes the latest writer to take the thriller world by storm."

—*The Real Book Spy*

"*Deep State* lets readers think they know what's going on, right up until a jaw-dropping finale. . . . [A] magnificently crafted thriller."

—*Shelf Awareness*

PRAISE FOR *SAVAGE ROAD*

"Hayley Chill is relentlessly smart and brave in this twisty, electrifying thriller."

—Karin Slaughter, #1 internationally bestselling author

"Hauty has done it again. *Savage Road* is a rocker of a novel. Whip-smart and propulsive, it dives into geopolitical cyber warfare with twists and turns you won't see coming. A must-read."

—Connor Sullivan, author of *Wolf Trap*

ALSO BY CHRIS HAUTY

Deep State
Savage Road
Insurrection Day
Storm Rising

THE DEVIL YOU KNOW

A THRILLER

CHRIS HAUTY

EMILY BESTLER BOOKS

—

ATRIA

New York   London   Toronto   Sydney   New Delhi

**EMILY
BESTLER
BOOKS**

ATRIA

An Imprint of Simon & Schuster, LLC
1230 Avenue of the Americas
New York, NY 10020

First Emily Bestler Books/Atria Paperback edition March 2024

EMILY BESTLER BOOKS/ATRIA PAPERBACK and colophon are trademarks of Simon & Schuster, LLC

Simon & Schuster: Celebrating 100 Years of Publishing in 2024

For information about special discounts for bulk purchases, please contact Simon & Schuster Special Sales at 1-866-506-1949 or business@simonandschuster.com.

The Simon & Schuster Speakers Bureau can bring authors to your live event. For more information or to book an event, contact the Simon & Schuster Speakers Bureau at 1-866-248-3049 or visit our website at www.simonspeakers.com.

Interior design by Erika R. Genova

Manufactured in the United States of America

1   3   5   7   9   10   8   6   4   2

Library of Congress Cataloging-in-Publication Data has been applied for.

ISBN 978-1-9821-7588-7
ISBN 978-1-6680-2213-9 (pbk)
ISBN 978-1-9821-7593-1 (ebook)

For Brian

Justice is indiscriminately due to all, without regard to numbers, wealth, or rank.

—JOHN JAY, THE FIRST CHIEF JUSTICE OF THE UNITED STATES

PROLOGUE

When he walked into the living room, Martin Barnes's roving gaze stopped abruptly on the exclamation point of blood splattered across the white tree skirt that never looked like snow anyway. He and his wife had purchased the condo one week after their wedding fifteen Christmases ago and augmented a collection of holiday decorations every year since. A Caribbean-themed crèche purchased in a Christiansted gift shop during their honeymoon on St. Croix. Red chili pepper string lights gifted to them by Marilyn's brother in Austin. The brass angel chime Barnes inherited from his parents. The night before Christmas, these festive adornments were a painful reminder of what was missing from the home.

Gone how long now?

Memories of his wife and sons chased Barnes from the living room, but he found no respite in the condo's narrow foyer. Dressed for work—blue business suit with a straight silhouette jacket that better concealed his service weapon—the US Supreme Court police officer paused to inspect a framed portrait hanging on the wall just inside the front door.

The photograph captured a moment of unadulterated joy during a return last January to St. Croix: the family of four arm in arm on a sun-splashed beach at the Carambola Resort, the same accommodations where Barnes and his new wife had enjoyed their honeymoon. The twins, Jeffrey and Michael—twelve years old at the time—were clad in swim trunks and shirtless, just emerged from hours in the water snorkeling and bodysurfing. Wearing one of her husband's white linen shirts over a one-piece swimsuit, a tanned and smiling Marilyn appeared to revel in the time off from work as a schoolteacher and spent with her family instead. The photo captured the mood of a joyful day perfectly, without a clue in their unclouded expressions of the nightmarish future that awaited them.

Like many others in law enforcement, Martin Barnes was a military veteran with two tours in Iraq. Yet, of all the countless missions in that hellish conflict, one resided in his head like no other. In support of a presidential directive to kill or capture Iranian nationals in Iraq, Barnes and his fellow Army Rangers entered Sadr City in a failed attempt to apprehend a wanted Shia militia leader. More than forty insurgents died in the Rangers' contested withdrawal, with zero US casualties.

Barnes could recall every second of the protracted street battle. The deafening racket of combat. Smells of blood, sweat, and the sour odor of spent gunpowder. One image, however, most frequently haunted his waking thoughts and nightmares: two Iraqi boys in a blasted-out door-way gawking at the headless body of an insurgent, freshly killed by a burst from a Ranger's M4.

In his mind's eye, Barnes saw his sons' blood-misted faces super-imposed on the two Sadr City boys. Then, in the next instant, more jarringly, he imagined the young Iraqis—covered with the insurgent's gore—standing between him and Marilyn on the Caribbean beach instead of their own sons.

Am I insane? Is this what it feels like to have lost one's mind?

Reaching for the doorknob, Barnes saw the tremor in his right hand. Sweat pricked his brow. His breathing erratic and heart rate accelerating, the plainclothes USSC police officer entertained a nagging doubt that he could accomplish the awful task demanded of him. The simple act of opening the condo's front door seemed almost beyond his abilities.

Barnes took a moment to breathe and compose himself.

Focusing on the ground at his feet, he noticed a splatter of red across the floor and on the lowest section of the hallway wall to the left.

Whose blood is this?

Jeffrey, the more cerebral of the twins, would not have risked a dash for the front door to raise the alarm. Instead, a last-ditch effort to play the hero's role would have been Michael's impulse.

Putting together the scenario in his head, a collage of supposition, recovered memory, and horror, Barnes decided the blood in the condo's entryway must belong to Michael, the bolder of his twin boys.

Nausea welled up within him.

Martin Barnes arrived at the same conclusion he had repeatedly rejected in the interminable hours since receiving his instructions.

He had no choice.

Only by irrevocable damnation would he win salvation.

Great Falls, in Fairfax County, Virginia, was twenty miles and a world away from the District of Columbia. Two-lane roads meandered through wooded hills sprinkled with multimillion-dollar estates. Ranked first by one prominent financial publication in its list of the nation's "top-earning towns," the unincorporated community was home to some of Washington's most powerful figures, including associate justice of the Supreme Court of the United States Anthony Gibbons. As a member of the USSC police agency's Dignitary Protection Unit, it was Martin Barnes's responsibility to ensure the safety of Justice Gibbons for the next eight hours.

Parking his Ford SUV inside the electronically controlled gate of the stately three-story mansion, he pulled in behind a similarly nondescript Ford SUV stopped to one side of the crushed granite driveway. Kathy Radulski, a relatively recent addition to the unit, exited the USSC-issued SUV and walked back to Barnes's window.

In her early thirties, Radulski served in Afghanistan a decade after Martin's Iraq tours. The conservative pantsuit she wore concealed neither her service weapon nor the last trimester of her first pregnancy. Barnes had relieved her on a four-day-a-week shift change for three months now. Despite their easy familiarity and habitual workplace banter, Barnes experienced the brief panic of being unable to recall her name. He lowered his window anyway; leaving it closed and refusing to speak with his fellow officer would have only raised alarm.

With a mocking grin, Radulski said, "Happy holidays, partner."

Barnes nodded his head, somewhat robotically, but could approximate a smile.

He said, "Lucky dog. Christmas Eve at home is a rarity in this business."

"I almost feel guilty. Underscore 'almost.'"

Barnes chuckled unconvincingly. "Don't feel bad on my account, lady. Remember, with great power comes great responsibility."

She grinned but was slightly perplexed. Later, in more than one of the seemingly countless interviews she would endure—with officials from USSC Police, the FBI, and the Department of Justice—a rattled Kathy Radulski will remark on Martin Barnes's failure to call her by her given name. Even then, his use of a generic appellation had struck her as wholly out of character. In every other conversation they ever had, the veteran officer had playfully mangled her last name. Radelpski. Radovich. Radinki. It was a thing.

On this day, however, it was "lady."

"How will your family ever forgive you, Barnes?"

The stricken look that flashed across his face could not be missed, not even in the half-light of the estate's tree-lined drive at six p.m. In many debriefings Radulski will mention Barnes's dramatic change of expression, too.

With a pained smile, he said, "They're happy to be rid of me."

His distress was inexplicable and raw. Then, with one last effort to keep the mood light, Radulski said with a wink, "Can't hardly blame them."

Barnes's face went blank.

"You okay, Marty?" asked a concerned Radulski.

"I'm good, friend. Just tired, I guess."

Again, failing to call her by name. As if he couldn't recall it.

Radulski tilted her head toward the mansion that loomed at the end of the four-hundred-foot drive. "He's expecting you."

"Did he offer you a hot toddy?"

She laid a hand on her belly. "Virgin hot toddy . . . so I accepted."

Radulski left his window and started walking back to her car.

Barnes called after her. "Take care of yourself, okay?"

She waved her thanks. Only after getting behind the wheel of the Ford did Kathy Radulski recognize the disturbing finality in her colleague's farewell.

The associate justice was putting a kettle on the stove when Barnes let himself in through the unlocked back door.

"Martin! Merry Christmas!"

Wearing corduroy trousers, a food-stained, blue-striped oxford shirt, and a chunky knit Guatemalan cardigan, seventy-six-year-old Anthony Gibbons's twinkling blue eyes and unruly white hair were more reminiscent of a children's television show host of a bygone era than a justice of the Supreme Court. Disarming, brilliant, and a friend to feral cats everywhere, Barnes's protectee had written majority opinions for several landmark decisions since his confirmation three decades earlier. Situated somewhere in the middle of the court's ideological divide, Justice Gibbons had joined forces with both sides on different occasions. But, much like his fashion sense, the old man's legal philosophy defied pigeonholing.

Barnes said, "Happy holidays, sir." He indicated the kitchen door behind him. "How many times have I told you to keep that door locked?"

Gibbons waved his hand, dismissing the suggestion. "Locking my doors is completely unnecessary. An armed police officer sitting at the end of my driveway is *overkill.*"

"We're honored to have the assignment, sir."

"If some fool is desperate enough to do harm to an occasionally ridiculous old man in his own kitchen, then so be it!" He retrieved a bottle of Jack Daniel's Single Barrel from the counter, held it by the neck, and, eyes sparkling, waggled it with a tempting flourish. "It's that time of year again, Martin," sang the justice.

"I have no choice but to respectfully decline your generous offer, sir. Just like I did last Christmas Eve."

With the warmth and friendliness of Gibbons's welcome, Barnes almost forgot his heinous obligation. The old man had that effect on him. Though they typically limited their conversations to trivial topics, the two men of such dissimilar backgrounds—Supreme Court justice and USSC police officer—had developed a robust and mutual affection for each other. A lifelong bachelor, Gibbons particularly enjoyed asking after his protector's sons. Not one of the twins' birthdays in the five years Barnes had been on Gibbons's detail passed without a thoughtful card and present from the old man. Marilyn always contended that the Supreme Court justice spent more time selecting the perfect items for the boys than those haphazard gifts chosen by their own father.

Puttering, Gibbons lit a flame under the kettle, his back to the USSC police officer.

"Well, I don't believe I shall allow your abstinence to prevent me from enjoying a nightcap, Martin. My niece is picking me up first thing at seven tomorrow morning. They've moved to Charlottesville. Did I tell you that? She was up visiting her sister and is kind enough to drive me both ways. Do you know who'll be following behind? Perhaps the officer can save Cindy the trouble of returning me here."

Barnes took a silent step in the justice's direction. Then another.

"I don't know, sir," he said vacantly.

Gibbons uncapped the whiskey and carefully filled a shot glass to the brim with the caramel-colored liquid.

Barnes's thoughts were a demolition derby, colliding in a jumble of indecision that paralyzed him. He hesitated, standing now only a few feet from the old man.

God! Why is this happening? Why me? There must be another way!

Gibbons turned around and was startled to see the police officer so close to him.

"Martin?" he asked, the first hint of confusion rippling across his face.

The USSC police officer thrust both hands up and forward, gripping the justice around the neck. Gibbons's shocked disbelief was brief, replaced by anguish as Barnes increased pressure on his carotid and vertebral arteries. The compressive forces generated by the police officer's throttling grip restricted oxygenated blood flow to the brain and simultaneously obstructed the larynx, inducing asphyxia. After ten seconds, Anthony Gibbons lost consciousness.

Barnes released his hands from the justice's neck and gently lowered the old man to the floor like a baby into his bassinet. He knew Gibbons wouldn't be fully brain-dead for another four or five minutes. Waiting to be certain of the justice's demise would have been the more . . . *prudent* . . . move.

But five minutes of soul-searing, shrieking self-hatred and agony? Impossible.

Reaching under his suit jacket, the USSC police officer drew his Glock, racked the slide, jammed the barrel upward into his mouth, and sent himself to an eternity devoid of light.

BOOK ONE

HIGH FUNCTIONING

CHAPTER 1

BAR BATHROOM PARAMOUR

Hayley Chill needed a drink. Having watched a burial crew put her kid sister in the ground five days after Christmas was today's excuse. Yesterday's justification had been different. Who could say about tomorrow?

She found the perfect place at the end of Third Street in West Logan, overlooking the Guyandotte River. Following the service and interment, Hayley laid low in her Chapmanville motel room for a few hours. Her needs were limited: a chair on which to sit and listen to the white noise of traffic outside on the main drag through town. Wishing to avoid well-meaning friends and grieving family members, Hayley had told no one where she was staying. The same motivation prompted her to drive ten miles south to fulfill another, more pressing necessity.

Hayley entered the West Virginia roadside tavern and paused to take stock of her refuge. Low ceiling and even lower light. A Cavaliers game on a muted television over the cash register. Murmuring patrons seated at the bar and tables, their coats and jackets hanging haphazardly from seat backs or draped over stools. The bluegrass music coming over the sound system was a pleasant surprise. Hayley also scrutinized the rows of bottles on either side of the register that were backlit to colorful effect.

Yes. This place will do just fine.

She grabbed a stool at the bar, two empty seats to her left and right.

The bartender—big, bald, bearded, and wearing an Elk River Ramblers T-shirt—responded to Hayley's predatory stare soon enough.

"Tequila," she said.

"Jose Cuervo?"

She shook her head. "Whiskey. Beer chaser."

The truth was, Hayley had been hitting the green bottle of La Gritona she'd packed in her bag pretty much all day. Tammy's overdose three days earlier was a brutal shock, only the latest in a series of traumas, but it wasn't until she had arrived in town that the full brunt of fury and grief descended on her. Returning home wasn't a trivial matter. Too many bad memories. Too much heartache. The last time Hayley saw her kid sister alive was more than six months ago, the occasion being—unironically—another overdose-induced funeral. Tammy seemed perfectly fine then, thrilled to be pregnant with her first child. Now that six-month-old baby boy had lost his mother, and Hayley, a sister she loved. At the funeral, she couldn't help but worry how long before her baby nephew was orphaned entirely, judging by the sallow appearance of Jeff, the boy's father.

What a god-awful mess.

The bartender delivered the goods. Shooting the whiskey, Hayley replaced the glass on the bar ahead of the mug of cold beer, an unmissable signal she wanted a refill. Bald and Bearded dutifully poured another. Before Hayley could lift the shot glass, the inevitable guy appeared at her elbow. Fives and ones clasped in his right hand. Requisite trucker cap. A mole on his left cheek like some John-Boy Walton come to life.

Hayley felt his gaze on her.

"What's up?" she asked with flat intonation.

Back home, Hayley had inadvertently lapsed into the soft drawl and WV dialect of her childhood.

John-Boy said, "Come from around here sounds like."

"Twenty or so miles north. Green Shoals. I moved along after high school. Doubt we ever crossed paths."

He offered his hand with a confident-bordering-on-arrogant grin. "Derrick."

Hayley pegged him for a Logan High School football star, and she wasn't wrong. Derrick Getty hadn't put on much additional weight like so many other high school jocks by their thirtieth year. Her sandy-haired barstool paramour was in excellent shape, broad-shouldered, and tall enough to seem gargantuan in the cavern-like barroom.

Hayley had noticed him glancing to his left once or twice as he spoke. Five other locals Getty's age, male and female, were sitting at a large table near the front door.

Grew up here. Going to grow old and die here.

She had managed to escape this world. Most don't.

Getty's hand was still hanging in midair. She relented and shook it with minimal enthusiasm.

"Hayley."

"Nice to meet you, Hayley."

The guy actually winked after he said her name. Bald and Bearded served up a pitcher of beer to him without having been asked. Getty made no move to return to his table.

Hayley shot the second whiskey and replaced the empty glass in the refill zone.

Her suitor responded with a low whistle of admiration.

"I can sure respect a woman who knows how to drink. Any other skills?" he asked with what he imagined was a devastating gaze.

Hayley Chill was a US Army veteran, one of the first women to earn a blue cord. Until recently, she'd been employed by a clandestine association—former presidents, ex–Supreme Court justices, retired directors from the intelligence community, and other discharged heavyweights of the US government—that called itself Publius. Not so much the deep state as a *deeper* state. Among other deeds, Hayley had saved a sitting president from assassination, stopped a massive cyberattack on the Eastern Seaboard, and helped prevent a second US civil war. Personal losses she'd suffered in the past year compelled her to retreat from further involvement with the group. Her main agenda since that self-imposed hiatus was to avoid thinking. Stop remembering. Exist barely above sentient. The alcohol wasn't an ideal facilitator of that action list, but the cost was right and it didn't leave track marks.

She held Getty's gaze with her powder blue eyes. "Got nothing for you, stud."

The former jock's grin calcified. Grabbing the pitcher by the handle, he winked at Hayley again and strutted back to his table near the door.

"Is that fucking douchebag hassling you, miss?" asked the bartender. "Rushing for twenty-two hundred yards and thirty-one touchdowns in your senior year can sure do some weird shit to a dude."

"Nothing I can't handle, thanks." She pointed her chin toward the empty shot glass. "Hit me again?"

Hayley Chill had reached that place, a kind of transcendent state. There was no stopping her now. Stripped of thought, memory, and restraint, she was on the verge of becoming pure energy.

How much loss am I expected to take?

———————————

She was washing her hands in the ladies' room when the door banged open and her wink-happy suitor entered the cramped space. The arrogant smile on Getty's face faltered for a moment in reaction to Hayley's expressionless assessment of his bold intentions. The former high school running back flinched as her right hand sped toward him. But it continued past his unguarded torso and found the latch on the door. The sound of Hayley engaging the lock was all the signal Derrick Getty needed to close the distance between them.

He put his hands on Hayley's shoulder and arm, pulling her mouth to his. Before their lips joined, however, she turned him like a failed assassin and pushed him backward into the single stall.

Dumb, dumb, dumb . . .

But action took precedence over caution. *Any* action would do.

Her finger found his belt and button fly. Straddling the toilet, the local man initially resisted Hayley taking command; never before in his countless sexual conquests had he been so wholly subordinated. But her turbo-charged authority was persuasive. Catching on, Getty relented, excited like he'd never been excited before.

———————

Unlocking the bathroom door and pushing it open, she stepped into the dimly lit barroom. Leaning against the pool table, waiting for Hayley, was a redheaded woman her age and height but at least thirty pounds heavier. Wearing a Gap sweatshirt and high-rise mom jeans, Margot Dombrowski was scowling. Hayley barely glanced at the woman as she continued toward her barstool across the room.

Dombrowski propelled herself off the pool table and into Hayley's path.

"He's in there, isn't he? You fucked my boyfriend, huh, bitch?"

Hayley wanted only to return to her place at the bar, where Bald and Bearded would have teed up the next round by now. She turned a shoulder to her accuser and tried to slip past.

The other woman cut Hayley off, grabbing her roughly by the arm.

"You little whore! We're not done here!"

Derrick Getty exited the ladies' room at the same moment that Hayley whipped her arm from the redhead's grip and shoved her backward against the pool table.

Hayley's erstwhile suitor bounded in three strides to the altercation, putting his large, athletic frame between the combatants.

"Keep your hands off her," he said, his cartoonish winks and vaudeville smirking now a distant memory.

Hayley put both hands on Getty's chest and pushed him away. The former high school jock fell backward and into the arms of his girlfriend. Reaching behind him, he took hold of a cue from the pool table. In anticipation of delivering a power stroke to Hayley's head, Getty planted his right foot forward.

She had only a second or two to act. Instincts took command.

Standing sideways, Hayley lifted the knee of her rear leg. Getty assumed she was going for his body and braced for the blow, putting all of his weight into his right, lead leg . . . exactly what Hayley had anticipated. Instead of attacking his body, however, she stomped her booted foot down on his leg just above the knee. The audible pop of rupturing quadriceps and patellar tendons preceded Getty's screams by a fraction of a second.

Pool cue sliding from his grasp as he collapsed to the floor, Getty gripped his right knee in a futile attempt to reassemble its many broken parts. The fuss he was raising wasn't wholly compatible with the jovial, tough guy image he'd cultivated since grade school. Snot dripping from his nose comingled with his tears of excruciating pain.

Hayley stood over the fallen man, the extent of his injuries all too obvious to her. Derrick Getty's days rushing on the gridiron—limited in recent years to the occasional pickup scrimmage on Sundays at the local high school—were over. With a glance, Hayley determined that Bald and Bearded was on the phone already, summoning the police. Not to worry. Witnesses would attest to her actions as being well inside the scope of self-defense.

She will be back in her motel room in Chapmanville by midnight. Getty, however, will spend the next three days in the hospital. Three surgeries to reassemble his knee will succeed to the extent that the hitch in his step is barely noticeable. Like so many pain sufferers across the nation, Getty's addiction to OxyContin will blossom into a full-fledged heroin addiction; his personal bankruptcy due to ongoing medical expenses will seem less important.

But miracles can happen, even in West Virginia. Following a second overdose in which he will be declared DOA by an ER resident late for a Friday night Bumble date, Getty will rise from the ashes of a merciless addiction. Group homes. Intense counseling. Loving friends and family members. Recovery will take a village of good intentions. By year two of his sobriety, Derrick Getty will be employed by a Richmond-based rehab center and receiving glowing tributes from coworkers and patients. Five years after his altercation with Hayley Chill at the tavern on Third Street in West Logan, Getty will be elected to the US House of Representatives for West Virginia's third district, capitalizing on his high school athletic exploits and running on a single platform of combating the opioid crisis.

Nothing of that future was apparent to Hayley at the time. Watching her bar bathroom paramour writhe on the floor, she recognized the wreckage of her present existence.

Loss upon loss.

A life without intention and headed in one direction: down.

She shrugged, aware of her intoxication for the first time that day.

Nothing new under a black sun.

CHAPTER 2

ALOHA

They called themselves the Snake Eaters.

For twenty-two-year-old Saturnino Valdés Pérez, the operation in Hawaii represented his first trip outside of Mexico. The four other men—like Saturnino, former members of the Mexican Army's Special Forces Corp (GAFE)—were experienced mercenaries whose exploits had taken them to several countries in the Americas. As the most recent addition to the unit, Saturnino accepted the hazing dealt to him by his compatriots. Such was the way of men. One day, a recruit younger than himself would join their league. Then that man would take *his* turn on the anvil.

Before his enlistment in the army, the teenage Saturnino wanted only to surf. The *palapa*-shaded beach at Playa La Ticla, an hour-and-a-half drive southwest of the family apartment in Tecomán, was his refuge from a hard life in the city. His father's unexpected death ended the teenager's love affair with the ocean. As the oldest of six children, Saturnino's role was to put food on the family table and keep a roof over their heads.

His excellent scores in basic training and an unusual proficiency on the gun range earned him an assignment to GAFE's 3rd Brigade's Rapid

Intervention Force group. There Saturnino received some of the best advanced military training on the planet, courtesy of the Mexican government's ally to the north. The US Army's 7th Special Forces Group—from which the Snake Eaters borrowed their nickname—had operated in an advisory role in South and Central America since the 1980s. The foundations of Saturnino's training, therefore, were distilled from lessons imparted by Delta Force instructors decades earlier.

The army unit's *sargento primero* was the first to depart, his reasons for abruptly leaving GAFE a mystery. Rumor suggested that Oscar Carranza went over to the "other side," selling his expertise to the highest bidder among several drug cartel suitors. No one was entirely sure what had happened to their sergeant. Then one of Carranza's most trusted men in the unit, Hector Lozano—the face of a lizard but with less heart—separated from the army and also disappeared without a trace. The Suárez brothers, Javier and Diego, were next. Finally, Saturnino left the army, too.

That was three months ago.

Reunited with trusted members of his former GAFE unit at a forest compound near Coahuayana, the young man and gifted sniper had been unconcerned that his new paymaster was a notorious drug cartel. What mattered was that he was with the top men again, former soldiers he admired. Like them, Saturnino Pérez now had money *and* respect. More money than he had ever thought existed in the world.

Walking through the terminal at Kahului Airport, on the Hawaiian island of Maui, the young cartel gunman glanced toward the others in their unit. All wore canvas pants, military-style boots, and button-down long-sleeve shirts, and in that way stood out from the locals and tourists attired in sandals, shorts, and the occasional Santa hat. Saturnino was proud of how smart he and his compatriots looked compared to the swarms of holiday travelers hurrying through the airport concourse. He and his fellow assassins were *disciplined*. Eyes looking ahead and chins slightly raised, they walked at a slower, more assured pace, each with luggage that consisted entirely of the same jet-black tactical backpacks.

We are not your gardeners.

We are not your day laborers or housekeepers.

We are the Snake Eaters.

We are the Cartel del Oeste.

Exiting the terminal, the four ex-soldiers and their commander walked into the sunshine. Saturnino paused at the curb, while the others continued to walk toward the nearby parking lot, where unknown facilitators had left a vehicle for them. He tilted his head back and allowed the sun's rays to bathe his face. Trade winds from the northeast brought cool relief. The briny smell of the Pacific Ocean—just beyond the northern end of the airport's runway—filled the twenty-two-year-old's nose, a familiar sensation from the countless days he spent at Playa La Ticla.

Since enlisting in the army four years ago, Saturnino had known only the barracks and the jungle. Though he had never confessed it to anyone—especially not the hard men who called themselves the Snake Eaters—the young gunman suffered from persistent homesickness. Not so much for the cramped family apartment in the city or his diverse responsibilities as the eldest child following his father's death. Saturnino longed for the beach. The endless waves. His not long-distant youth.

Ironic, then, that he found himself in Hawaii, world-famous for being the birthplace of surfing.

It is like . . . paradise.

Nearly nineteen feet in length, the Chevrolet Suburban SUV was big enough to accommodate the entire unit and their modest luggage; the bulk of their gear had been shipped separately to the island for obvious reasons. Hector Lozano retrieved the key fob from its hiding place under the driver's-side wheel well and unlocked the doors. As the crew's leader, Oscar Carranza, aka "El Gruñón," took the front passenger seat as his birthright. Javier Suárez and his younger brother, Diego, settled into the middle seats, while Saturnino found his place in the farthermost-rear bench seat.

Diego slapped the crew's newest recruit on the ass as he passed between the middle and rear seats. *"Don't get carsick all over me, Barbie!"*

Saturnino despised his nickname, given to him for his bleached-blond hair and green eyes. But he had learned the hard way that it was best to weather the persistent teasing in silence. The other men had made him well aware of his place among them. As the youngest, Saturnino was treated with casual disrespect; he had yet to prove himself.

Despite almost daily contact with Carranza and his crew for the past four years—first in the army and now with their hiring by the cartel—he had only the slightest awareness of the men's lives outside the unit. Diego Suárez, or "El Guasón," was relatively benign, if that was the correct word to describe someone Saturnino had witnessed decapitate a rival cartel member with a steak knife. He knew that Diego was married to the twin sister of Javier's wife and that the brothers Suárez and their families shared a rambling four-bedroom home in a suburb of Morelia. Vicious assassins by day and dedicated family men at night, Diego and Javier Suárez mercifully pulled their punches when it came to hazing the Snake Eaters' newest recruit.

Hector Lozano was Saturnino's true concern. Rumor had it that the feared sicario had been a street painter of marginal talent after finishing his formal education at the junior high (*secundaria*) level. Conscripted when he turned eighteen, he found greater success and purpose in the military than he ever had with the arts. Carranza's lieutenant was a menace of near legendary status, as lethal and unpredictable as any other assassin in Cartel del Oeste's army of killers. Fear of him was so extreme in Michoacán that most inhabitants refused to say his name out loud. Lozano lived with his mother in a modest one-bedroom apartment when not on an operation with the Snake Eaters. No one could guess what he did with the substantial money he earned as a sicario.

Lozano started the vehicle's engine. He was quietly pleased to see that the SUV had only three miles on the odometer and surmised that the faceless individuals facilitating the operation must have flat-bedded the vehicle to the airport parking lot. With a keen appreciation for competency and purpose, he took pride in killing with the same efficiency, favoring a knife over a pistol. Too often, Lozano, aka "Taliban," had seen a man (or woman) live to see another day after multiple gunshots to the body or even the head. There was zero chance of survival once a throat was slit from ear to ear. If a target had the misfortune of appearing on Hector Lozano's list, there was little hope of eluding a brutal death.

"Go to the house," said Carranza, thrusting his chin upward to signal his driver to proceed. *"The address is the only one on the navigation screen."*

Lozano said, *"Yes, sir."*

In the far back seat, Saturnino registered Lozano's deference to Carranza. Even a man as violent as Taliban feared their old sergeant.

A killer's killer. That is our commander.

If Saturnino possessed only the slightest details of Lozano's and the Suárez brothers' lives away from the cartel, he knew less about Oscar Carranza. Even in the army, their commander had been an omnipotent yet unfamiliar presence. Whether he had a family, was married or single, possessed any interests or hobbies, read books, or enjoyed music remained a total mystery. His capacity for violence was unknown, too. No one could remember Carranza raising a hand against a foe. Like a nuclear warhead, his ferocity was based entirely on his latent capacity for destruction. His savagery was wholly assumed.

The youngest sicario—if he had indeed earned that title after participating in only one assassination, an avocado grower who had refused Cartel del Oeste's extortion demands—settled into his seat as the cavernous SUV got underway. The elusive Pacific remained out of view, hidden behind a row of one- and two-story buildings to the north. But Saturnino easily imagined the scene. With his mind's eye, he watched the waves roll onto the island's north shore and seabirds swoop overhead. He could almost feel the warm sand between the toes of his bare feet.

None of the men in the Chevrolet knew the nature of their operation. Surely, death was the objective. That was what the Snake Eaters did. Their bosses gave them the names—men, women, children, it made no difference who—and they put those people in the ground. Let others harvest the fruits and vegetables, sell cars, or labor over hot grills.

Saturnino Pérez and these other hard men from the Free and Sovereign State of Michoacán de Ocampo killed for their living.

———————

The compound was at the farthest reach of Honokala Road, accessed by Ulalena Loop at mile marker 3 on the Hana Highway. Behind tall wooden gates opened by an entry code included with directions found in the glove compartment, the single-story main house sat to the rear of a gloomy clearing carved out of the rain forest. Waves that crashed against the rocks at Waipio Bay—less than a half mile distant—could be neither heard nor seen from anywhere on the property. A five-acre lot in the semirural setting assured privacy.

Lozano parked beside a second, identical Chevrolet Suburban in the circular gravel drive. Like any newly arriving tourists on the island, the cartel assassins piled out of their vehicle and assessed their surroundings. Glimpsed through a hectic stand of rainbow eucalyptus, thatch screw pines, and koa trees—all wrapped in maile and leie vines—was a secondary structure constructed of cinder block and seemingly half-buried in an adjoining hillside.

Carranza led the men up the half dozen steps to the porch of the main house. Consulting the instruction sheet left for them, he punched a six-digit code in the keyless door lock and was rewarded with the satisfying sound of a metal bolt retracting. The four other men followed their former army sergeant inside.

Lozano found the nearest light switch and illuminated the home's interior, a necessity despite the noon hour. The furnishings were thoroughly utilitarian. Saturnino Pérez guessed that the house had been vacant before the men's arrival and equipped solely with items of their most basic needs. All traces of the previous occupant (and certainly all personal decor) had been removed, no doubt by the same anonymous team that would eradicate every residue of their stay after the mission's completion. The morose rain forest beyond its walls underscored the home's dreary ambiance, suggestive of a low-budget vacation rental.

Since turning off the highway—perhaps too grand a word for the twisty, two-lane, sixty-four-mile road that led from the "bright lights" of Kahului to the island's remote eastern end at Hana—not a single word had been exchanged among the five men. Experience had taught them to wait for orders from their commander. Standing five feet, eight inches tall, the former Mexican Army sergeant was in no way defensive about his short height or pockmarked face. Though he would never confide such intimacies to the others, the lesson drilled into a teenage Carranza by his military-minded father was that the accurate gauge of a man is measured neither in inches nor by conventional attractiveness. Physical strength wasn't a factor, either. What made a man a meaningful presence in the world, according to Arturo Carranza, was his intelligence, will-power, and a capacity for cruelty.

On his fourteenth birthday, two weeks following his father's talk, Oscar Carranza used all three qualities to outwit and murder a man twice his age. A police sergeant in his home city of Uruapan had attempted to coerce the teenager's cooperation informing against a neighborhood meth-amphetamine dealer who occasionally paid Carranza a few pesos to serve as a courier. Faced with the choice of arrest or execution by the street gang, the fourteen-year-old created a third option: luring the policeman to a des-olate location on the outskirts of town and putting a bullet in his head with a Texas-manufactured ghost gun. Athletically inclined in his youth, Car-ranza was no gangster at the time. But his father's lesson had not been lost on the boy; cunning and a commitment to survival were paramount.

He stopped inside the door and allowed the other men to explore the dimly lit house as he scanned the interior, searching for something. His men, alert to their sergeant's every mood, barely breathed lest they incur his wrath.

No one in the crew—not even their commander—knew the precise details of the operation.

He found what he was searching for on the coffee table in the living room, a modest manila folder containing a thin sheaf of papers, maps, and photographs. Carranza sat on the couch and began reading. The other men stood at a respectful distance, waiting to hear his report.

Carranza took several minutes to examine every page, reading some sections twice through. Finally, the former army sergeant looked up from the folder, regarded his men with a neutral expression . . . and said nothing.

None of the men had ever visited any Hawaiian island before today. The nature of this next operation had been a source of fierce speculation among them . . . except for Carranza, who was above idle gossiping. Javier Suárez—known as "El Greñas" for his slick-downed, shoulder-length black hair—couldn't contain his curiosity. Perched on the balls of his feet, his hair in a ponytail that belied a fearsome reputation for enthusiastic torture, the cartel soldier asked in his native (and only) language, *"Will it be like the last one, Commander?"*

Oscar Carranza considered the question for a moment.

Intelligence, unstoppable willpower, and unbridled cruelty . . . all of these attributes would be required to complete the mission outlined in the paperwork he held in his hands.

"Sí y no," he said.

CHAPTER 3

LIKE THAT MOVIE.
YOU KNOW THE ONE
I'M TALKING ABOUT.

The morning after the funeral, Hayley left her motel room in search of a much-needed cup of coffee and found Andrew Wilde sitting in the metal patio chair next to the door. The man who recruited her for the deeper state wore a crisp blue suit and white shirt, the same as every other time they had met in person. The colors were a startling contrast to his perpetual—if slightly orange—tanned complexion. Fifty years old but fit as a triathlete half his age, Wilde exuded a blasé attitude. As a rule, he didn't rattle. Conspiratorialism was his religion.

Hayley couldn't guess her immediate supervisor's background except for some vague history with US military special forces. In Iraq? Or was it Sudan? Wilde never said one way or another. Her surprise finding him outside her room was exceeded only by her displeasure; another operation for Publius was off the table.

"My *siblings* don't even know where I'm staying," she said.

"Seriously?"

Wilde couldn't fathom Hayley would doubt his ability to locate her no matter where she tried to hide.

With a moment's reflection, she concurred. Hayley had yet to discover the furthest boundaries of the deeper state's resources. Did Publius have agents and sympathizers at all of the government's intelligence agencies? How many pairs of eyes did Wilde have on *her* at any given moment? Though Hayley's cell phone utilized two operating systems for complete data separation—one a particularly robust version of Android and the other a third-party, stripped-down OS—she had to assume her superiors in the organization were still able to monitor her every phone call, email, and text.

These suspicions, verging on paranoia, might have been answered eventually if she still worked for the deeper state. Which she did not. Not anymore. Four months ago—one week following a miscarriage that coincided with the conclusion of her last mission—Hayley sent Wilde a terse, unequivocal text message: No more.

Hayley gave the country everything but her life, and barely avoided that ultimate sacrifice.

To Andrew Wilde sitting outside her motel room, she said, "Do I have to tattoo it across your forehead, man? I quit."

He folded his hands behind his head, seemingly without a worry in the world. "I remember the good old days when it was always 'sir' this and 'Mr. Wilde' that. What happened to that young, bright-eyed soldier who was the epitome of army values?"

"The deeper state recruited her."

Ignoring her taunt, Wilde ran down the list. "Personal courage. Duty. Respect. Selfless service. Honor. Integrity. And loyalty."

Hayley felt blood rushing to her face.

"You're questioning my loyalty . . . *sir?*" she asked, casting the last word as an epithet.

"No one in the organization doubts your loyalty, Chill, or any other aspect of your character or skill set. That's why I'm here."

"A new op? I told you. I'm done with all of that."

The confident half grin on Andrew Wilde's face irked Hayley. She quickly calculated the damage she could inflict to his jaw with a well-placed, Thai-style roundhouse kick. Dislocation, for sure. Outright fracture? A definite possibility.

"C'mon, let's go get that cup of coffee you clearly need," said Wilde.

They shared a table at the Tudor's Biscuit World off Crawley Creek Road. At half past six, the franchise was otherwise deserted.

Hayley grimaced after sipping her coffee.

"Good?" asked Wilde, fucking with her.

"It's coffee."

He couldn't have cared less. "Sorry about your sister."

Knowing better, Hayley waited for the chaser.

Wilde said, "That poor kid. Your nephew."

"What about him?"

"In terms of your brother-in-law's legal troubles. Maybe you haven't heard? Given your carousing last night, I mean."

Hayley flinched. With sudden horror, she realized the previous night's activities were a total blank.

Another blackout episode?

Desperate to hide the alcohol-induced gap in her memory, Hayley played along.

With an abashed grin, she said, "Well, you know me, sir. Just blowing off a little steam."

Watching her closely and gauging her reactions, Wilde said, "The police stopped Jeff on the way home from the services yesterday. Crossing the double yellow line. He failed a field test and the one back at the station. A search of his car turned up enough pills to elevate charges to possession with intent to distribute."

Hayley hadn't known, of course. She wondered if Wilde had orchestrated the bust.

He said, "We can help Jeff. Publius takes care of its own . . . That is, those in the family."

Her silence opened the door wide to Wilde's pursuit.

"Your brother-in-law needs treatment, Chill, not one to fifteen years in Huttonsville. And little Tommy needs a father."

Her sister had named the baby after their dad, whose ghastly murder in the past year represented another hole blasted through Hayley's heart.

"Enough."

One word delivered like a threat. Her nephew's well-being was the only thing that mattered in Hayley's life now.

What would April Wu say about her return to duty? Discussions with Hayley's fellow deeper state operative and only-friend-in-the-world regularly lasted late into the night, protracted bull sessions in which April typically played devil's advocate. Hayley suspected her friend would be supportive of any adventure beyond the four walls of her apartment near Logan Circle.

Sensing victory, Wilde said, "This is like that movie. You know the one I'm talking about."

She had no response to the non sequitur.

Holding both clenched fists over the table, Andrew Wilde pulled them to his chest and delivered the infamous line of film dialogue with gusto. "'Just when I thought I was out, they pull me back in!'"

Hayley, one day removed from burying her youngest sister, was not amused.

"Respectfully, sir, cut the shit. Why are you here?"

Wilde said, "Anthony Gibbons."

"What about him?"

"You mean besides being choked to death by the USSC cop on his protective detail?"

Hayley said, "I figured there was more to it than the headline. What's the real story?"

"FBI is investigating. The cop—Martin Barnes—left no suicide note. Nothing on his phone or home computer indicates a desire to kill his family and a Supreme Court justice."

"The family's been located?" asked Hayley.

"No sign of them yet. But there was blood evidence in the home, belonging to the wife and one of the sons. Police and feds are looking for them."

"No bodies mean they could still be found alive."

"Sure, they could," said Wilde without conviction.

"So, if this is all a matter of a crazed cop going on a murder spree, what does that have to do with Publius?"

"You didn't hear me say anything about 'crazed.'"

"Do you think someone has called open season on Supremes, sir?" asked Hayley.

Wilde knew that he had Hayley's full interest now. That he had won, once again.

"I don't think anything. At least, not until you tell me what I *should* be thinking."

"Okay. I'm guessing my job is to stick close to a justice. Provide an extra layer of protection. But how do you know which one is the next target?"

"Political extremists on both sides are keen to manipulate the court's ideological makeup. The FBI and Homeland Security keep tabs on conspirators and nutcases of every stripe. There's always plenty of chatter and outright threats, but nothing that's ever been acted on."

"Until now."

"Perhaps. Publius has access to reports going back three years. We're analyzing them."

Hayley said, "Justice Gibbons was a centrist. His rulings were difficult to predict one case to the next."

"Correct. Nobody knows if the threat is a one-and-done or something entirely different. The Marshals Service has taken over protection responsibilities from the Supreme Court Police. They've already put details on the eight remaining justices."

Hayley said nothing, waiting for the bottom line that Wilde was sure to draw.

"The people we work for will sleep better with the awareness that Publius has an agent on each of those units."

"Where am I going, sir?"

"We're still sorting that out." He paused, then said, "Not everyone in the organization is one hundred percent on you these days, Chill."

"Eighty-five percent?"

"Don't flatter yourself."

Wilde slid out of the booth. They were still the only customers.

"My brother-in-law, sir? Slap on the wrist and out. Back with Tommy."

Wilde ignored the reminder. "You know the film I was talking about?"

"Yes, sir. *The Godfather*."

"Part three. Now, that was a movie." Wilde headed toward the door, saying over his shoulder, "I'll be in touch. Try to get back to DC without getting thrown in jail."

Hayley was almost glad she couldn't remember activities last night that were arrest-worthy.

Wilde stopped and turned, leveling his index finger at her. "And let's watch that drinking, you copy?"

Hayley responded with a contrite nod, enough of a commitment for Wilde to continue to the door. She faced forward again and saw April Wu sitting at the table where Andrew Wilde had sat only moments earlier.

"What an *asshole*," said April.

Hayley grinned, grateful to see her friend in whatever state of ethereal existence.

Months earlier, April Wu succumbed to injuries suffered in the line of duty. Her spectral visits with Hayley began shortly after her untimely demise in a GW Hospital bed. A close relationship—one that included all aspects of their rivalry, respect, and affinity for each other—was able to continue, if wholly on April's terms.

Whether a real ghost, a figment of Hayley's alcohol-fueled imagination, or her ersatz Jiminy Cricket, April's wraithlike form came and went as she pleased. Dead, but not gone. Not by any stretch.

And yet, representing yet another loss in Hayley's truly horrific year.

She swung her legs out from under the booth. "Let's get out of here."

In the beginning, Hayley was understandably disconcerted by April's "resurrection." Once she had recovered from the initial shock of those random appearances, her attitude shifted. As a covert agent for Publius, Hayley was essentially shorn of close friends, romantic relationships, and family. Yet, regardless of whether April Wu was actually a ghost or simply Hayley's conscience speaking, the deeper state operative grew to appreciate not only her friend's company but also her counsel, however snarky.

They had first met as agent candidates at the deeper state's secret training site in eastern Oregon. It was rivalry at first sight, broken bones and bruised egos the immediate by-product of their competitive dynamic. April and Hayley were the top-scoring recruits—whether male or female—in nearly every possible category. But the West Virginian claimed the ultimate prize of their epic contest, selected over all others to lead Publius's first operation. April Wu eventually forgave Hayley for besting her in that regard; the ache that would never diminish, not even in death, was her unrequited love for the blond-haired, blue-eyed freak of nature.

Propped up against flimsy motel pillows, April—doomed to wear the same canvas cargo pants, dark T-shirt, and army pullover for eternity—lay on the bed and watched Hayley gather her belongings.

"How was he?" asked April.

"Who?"

"Derrick 'Look at Me I Was a High School Football Star' Getty. Remember? The dude you hooked up with in the bathroom of Tavern Dismal on the oil-slicked banks of the River Superfund."

Blank-faced, Hayley said, "Oh."

"You don't remember any of it, do you?"

"That's what I have you for."

April wasn't about to allow Hayley to shrug off the incident.

"Bullshit. I can tell you're freaked out. This is the second blackout in one month."

Hayley rolled her eyes, but didn't dispute April's accounting.

"Andrew Wilde is right about at least one thing. You're hitting the bottle too hard."

"Give me a break."

"Seriously. How else to explain last night?"

"Oh, is Casper jealous?" Hayley instantly regretted the crack. "Sorry."

April, unfazed, waved off the apology. "You know, one of the nice things about being dead is that the difficult emotions you had as a living person are flattened out. Less jagged. You don't cry. Don't laugh or cum. Everything is just kinda..." She searched in vain for the appropriate word.

"... dead?" asked Hayley.

"Yeah. Like with really good dope, I feel no pain."

Now it was April's turn to regret her choice of words, these in particularly bad taste the day following the funeral of Hayley's sister.

"Sorry," she said. "Drugs bad."

Hayley shrugged it off. Her meager belongings packed, she was ready to head out.

April asked, "So you're back in the warm embrace of the deeper state? Good."

"Good?"

"Hayley Chill needs a mission like a fish needs water to breathe—"

"Wait..."

"Work with me here. Andrew Wilde, monumental tool that he is, has delivered just the medicine that you need."

Hayley said, "I didn't know I was sick."

"What you have, you never know you have. A symptom is the pronounced lack of objectivity."

"I... what?"

April said, "You need to get busy, dummy. Get out of your head. Save the world."

"Look who's talking."

"What do you know about this side of the mortal divide? I could be partying over here like it's Rome 99 BC."

"Whatever. After this operation—when I know Jeff and Tommy are squared away—I'm done for good."

"Right. I'm calling bullshit on that, too."

"Call it whatever you want. I get my hands on one little psychotropic pill and you're history."

"You wouldn't dare!"

Hayley turned for the door. Glancing over her shoulder, she saw that April had vanished. Her friend could show up during the long drive back home to DC, or be waiting for Hayley at the condo, sitting on the couch and thumbing through a copy of the latest *Atlantic* magazine. Then again, April might not resurface for another week or two. There was no telling when or where she might choose to haunt Hayley again.

Exiting the motel room, Hayley unlocked her car and tossed her bag into the back seat.

Has someone declared open season on Supremes?

Did she care if someone was attempting to manipulate the Supreme Court's ideological tilt? Hayley could remember when she used to give a shit about such things. Not too long ago, she would have charged into a hail of gunfire to protect the integrity of the nation's highest court. Until recently, Hayley had lived by one inflexible code: support and defend the Constitution of the United States or die trying. But would she still swear to that oath?

Pausing beside her car, Hayley Chill felt the ground spin under her feet. The confidence she had feigned for April's benefit evaporated, replaced by dizzying insecurity.

Experiencing a surge of vertigo, she willed herself to get behind the car's wheel. Washington was seven hours away. Hayley pressed the ignition, shifted gears, and drove. Her mind enveloped in fog, she could manage only these functional simplicities. Foreseeing the long drive home, Hayley had severe doubts that she could make it. Unless she made a quick stop. Just a miniature or two. Whiskey or tequila, it made no difference. A quickie there in the parking lot of the package store. Another for the drive back to DC.

Hell, I don't have a problem with alcohol.
She only needed a little something to sharpen her senses.

————————

As the team's youngest member, Saturnino was given the task of driving back to the airport to pick up gear shipped separately to the island. On the island for slightly less than twenty-four hours, he didn't mind this lowly assignment. While the others traipsed through the forest to set up surveillance microphones and cameras on the property's entire perimeter—sweating in the afternoon heat and drenched by intermittent rain showers—Saturnino enjoyed the Chevrolet's blasting air conditioner and acquainted himself better with the island's north shore.

Of particular interest were the surf breaks.

Before leaving Mexico, Saturnino had researched Maui's offerings. Anyone who ever surfed a wave in their life had heard of the infamous break at Pe'ahi, known worldwide as "Jaws." Anxious to catch a glimpse of the iconic spot on his drive back to the airport, Saturnino was disappointed to see nothing of the ocean at mile marker 13, where descriptions on the Internet had suggested he would find the turnoff. Continuing a few more miles west, however, he was treated to an expansive overview of Ho'okipa Beach Park. On the eastern end of the break, two dozen surfers were working a three-to-four-foot swell. Windsurfers dominated the waves at the western point.

As he maneuvered the twisting highway at a reduced speed—stopping even for a few minutes to observe the local surfers in action was unthinkable—Saturnino snatched repeated glances in the beach's direction. How he envied the tanned, blond-haired gringos unloading boards from the tops of their cars parked along the road. The ocean! The waves! The sun shining on the water! Inadvertently brought back to the carefree days of his youth, Saturnino's heart ached as he wondered if that life was irrevocably lost.

An impatient driver behind him snapped the cartel assassin out of his sentimental brooding.

How could he be so foolish?

I am Saturnino Pérez, newly minted soldier for the Cartel del Oeste. I am a Snake Eater, a killer who would kill again.

Ho'okipa behind him, the young sicario focused again on the road ahead. As he drove into funky Paia, a town that stubbornly clung to its hippie past, Saturnino could see aircraft landing at Kahului Airport five miles east. One of those planes had just delivered a crate he was to retrieve and return to the compound on Honokala Road. Saturnino assumed the shipment would contain the weapons and tactical gear required for an operation finally revealed to the crew by their taciturn commander. Though he was new to this world, Saturnino believed their mission to be diabolical even by Cartel del Oeste's standards.

None of the men could say whether they were working for their bosses back home in Michoacán or if an anonymous, well-paying client had hired the crew as contractors. What difference did it make? They would perform their jobs with unquestioning obedience. By God's grace, they would survive and return to Mexico richly rewarded for their efforts. If they had the misfortune of being killed or, worse, arrested by the North Americans, Saturnino and the others had every assurance their families would receive the hundreds of thousands of dollars promised them . . . as long as they completed mission.

———————

The carton was large, with markings that suggested it contained a newly purchased, full-size GE chest freezer. An employee of the airfreight service, Juan Menotti, operated a forklift to load the enormous box into the back of the Chevrolet. Even with all the rear seats folded down, the massive package barely fit inside the vehicle. To Saturnino's surprise, the forklift operator was also from Mexico. With the loading operation completed, the two men paused at the driver's door for a friendly conversation under threatening clouds that rolled in from the northeast.

"Your boss is a good one?" asked Menotti.

Saturnino's instructions were to retrieve the crate and return immediately to the compound. But the cartel gunman was young and curious; he never imagined he would visit Hawaii. He had so many questions. The airfreight service employee seemed friendly and without suspicion.

Saturnino made a gesture with his right hand that suggested "so-so."

He said, *"A rich Californian. Hardly ever comes over. Maybe twice a year."*

Menotti, in his mid-thirties and boasting an impressive array of gold-capped teeth, nodded knowingly. *"That's good. Very good!"*

"I only arrived last week. Are there many of us here?" asked Saturnino.

"Yes, yes! Very many!" said Menotti. *"Doing the real work, of course. Making the beds. Cleaning the floors. Tending to the machines."*

And killing when the killing needed to be done, thought the newcomer.

"Many Mexicans live on Maui, my friend," said Menotti with pride. *"More than native Hawaiians. Truly, it's paradise! With your crazy hair, you'll fit right in!"*

Saturnino responded with a sheepish laugh, self-consciously running his hand through his unruly blond mane. Though it had been years since he last rode the waves at Playa La Ticla, he resumed dyeing his hair after leaving the army. Naively or not, the cartel gunman was determined to make the "surfer" look his signature.

Menotti looked over his shoulder, checking for any sign of his supervisor, then turned back to Saturnino. "See you around, huh?"

The younger man said, "Okay," revealing the extent of his English.

Steering the Chevrolet out of the cargo facility south of the main terminal and into light traffic on Haleakalā Highway, Saturnino felt unsettled as he imagined the other man's comparatively simple life. Though he earned more in a single day than Juan Menotti probably made with a year's salary at the airport, the young sicario felt an unexpected surge of self-recrimination and regret. He could not help but envy the humdrum predictability of driving the bright yellow forklift from tarmac to loading dock, over and over again, five eight-hour days a week. Then home, perhaps to a loving wife and children.

As rain began to fall and the windshield wipers automatically sprang to action, Saturnino pulled himself out of this indulgent daydreaming. The turn for the highway to Hana was just ahead.

Back home in Michoacán—where he was recognized by all as an assassin for the Cartel del Oeste—Saturnino was the object of respect and fear. Here on Maui, he was just another shuffling Mexican, with head bowed and a dirty neck.

Driving at high speed, the SUV's big twenty-two-inch tires spraying standing water on the pavement, he prayed he hadn't dallied too long at the cargo facility. Had Oscar Carranza or the bosses in Morelia installed listening devices in the Chevrolet? The brief conversation with the airport worker was enough to earn Saturnino a bullet in the back of the head.

Maybe continuing to dye his hair surfer blond wasn't a good idea after all.

CHAPTER 4

Z GAME

For as long as she could remember, Hayley Chill ran. Whether for fun, exercise, or emotional release, running was a wellspring of orderly calm in an otherwise chaotic life. Until this past summer, she ran miles almost every day and in any weather. Since her miscarriage four months ago, however, Hayley had been unable to muster the motivation needed to lace up her running shoes and hit the pavement. In fact, she hadn't done very much of anything except maintain a constant alcohol-induced, low-grade buzz designed to numb a harsh residue of painful emotions and memories.

But today was different.

Her baby nephew needed her. If anyone could be counted on to answer the clarion call of familial responsibility, it was Hayley. She was determined to recapture a semblance of physical fitness.

Having returned to her DC apartment on P Street near Logan Circle last night from Tammy's funeral in West Virginia, she stayed up more than two hours paying bills and returning emails. A sense of newfound purpose and accomplishment energized Hayley in a way she hadn't experienced in weeks. Despite a wavering loyalty to Publius, she could commit herself fiercely to an operation that would ensure her nephew's well-being.

She woke up before sunrise. Wearing running shoes and clothes that emphasized function over appearance—shorts and top from Target—Hayley took the stairs down to the street level and jogged out of the lobby, heading south on Ninth Street. The cold, winter air hit her lungs with a shock. She quickened her pace, anxious to feel the first beads of sweat. Her normal route was a warm-up run to the National Mall, followed by three or four laps around the park at variable speeds. Hayley could complete a four-mile circuit around the mall in twenty minutes or faster when she was in shape.

She wasn't stupid. After an extended break from regular exercise, Hayley knew today would be a challenge. Maybe only twice around the mall would suffice for a first time out. She had no idea when exactly the deeper state wanted her for the operation to protect a yet-to-be-named Supreme Court justice. Hayley imagined she had at least a week to get into decent shape, two weeks if she was lucky.

In her late twenties and carrying only an imperceptible amount of body fat, Hayley's arm and leg muscles retained their sharp definition. She expected to be ready when Andrew Wilde called with orders.

Hayley had this.

Except . . .

Before she had run the roughly one and a half miles from her apartment to the Smithsonian Natural History Museum, she was out of breath. Every step was a struggle, calves twitching with the earliest tremors of cramping. Throughout her life—as a kid in Green Shoals, in the army, and even during her tenure working in the White House—Hayley maintained an elite level of conditioning. Strenuous exercise was as much a part of her daily routine as eating.

Hayley was flummoxed as she plodded past the Lincoln Memorial and turned west toward the distant Capitol Building. How could she feel so thoroughly defeated by a modest run she had effortlessly completed countless times in the past?

Is it the booze?

Hayley dismissed the possibility. She hadn't been drinking *that* much. Wondering if perhaps she was sick with the flu or some other transitory illness, the deeper state operative stopped running and walked another twenty yards to a bench. She couldn't have been less surprised to find the specter of her good friend and fellow Publius agent waiting for her there.

"My god, what a pathetic display of physical fitness," said April Wu. "I can't believe you ever beat me at *anything*."

Hayley plopped down on the opposite end of the bench from her friend and began a series of stretches—half pigeon, seated warrior and twist—to work some looseness into her leg and torso muscles.

"Lot of attitude for a dead girl," she said dryly. "Why don't you go haunt someone else for a change? An old boyfriend who deserves tormenting maybe."

"Who's to say I don't? You have no idea what I do when I'm not around here riding your ass."

"I figured you just slunk back to your crypt. Or posed for Halloween decorations."

A tourist family taking in the sights at sunrise gawked at Hayley, who appeared to be talking to herself.

"Go jump off the Washington Monument, why don't you?" April yelled after the visitors from Missouri.

Hayley had to grin. Despite her friend's lacerating sarcasm and judgmental nature, no one had her back more faithfully than April Wu.

"So . . . ?" Hayley didn't know why her friend had chosen this particular moment to appear. Not that April always needed a good reason to show up unexpectedly. Her visitations seemed to occur in those in-between moments in Hayley's daily life. While driving. Or eating a meal, which would otherwise be passed utterly alone. Instead of checking her cell phone, as most people did in these extra minutes, she had the apparition of her closest friend for a diversionary pleasure.

April said, "I came to see you off."

"I probably won't be leaving for another week, weirdo. Andrew Wilde is still sorting things out."

April shook her head. "First thing tomorrow, dork."

"Wait, what? You can do that?" a pleasantly shocked Hayley asked.

"The perks are *unbelievable.*" April grinned slyly. "Two words. 'Aloha, mahalo.'"

Hayley grimaced. "Hawaii?"

"You're going to need your A game. Seriously. You'll be joining Justice Fischer's protection detail. She has a second home on Maui."

Hayley knew about Fischer's place in Hawaii, having researched all the remaining eight justices the night before. Anita Fischer was her *last* choice.

"Fuck."

"You know, most people would be overjoyed with the prospect of Hawaii for the holidays."

"It's New Year's Day. The holidays are over."

But Hayley's mind was elsewhere, wondering why Publius would send her to a backwater like Maui. Hawaii was a theme park. Now that she had committed to a final operation, Hayley wanted to be at the center of the action. Did Andrew Wilde and his superiors in the deeper state think so little of her operational readiness? She wanted to quit Publius on her terms, not suffer the indignity of a demotion.

Receiving her orders from the ghost of her dead best friend seemed only another indication of her fall and dissolution.

I really have to stop drinking.

Hayley had attempted to quit booze a half dozen times in the past four months.

She felt the phone secured to a FlipBelt vibrate.

Checking the caller's identification and connecting, she said, "Mr. Wilde."

He was in his car, driving southeast on Massachusetts Avenue.

"You're not home." His brusque demeanor was on-brand; whether the fate of Western civilization was at risk or he was ordering lunch, Andrew Wilde's tone of voice never much changed.

"Out for a run, sir."

"Tell me where you are and I'll pick you up. We have to talk. Matters have accelerated. You're leaving tonight on the red-eye."

Hayley glanced at the other end of the bench and saw that April had disappeared without her promised goodbye.

You're going to need your A game.

Given her destination, Hayley figured her Z game would do just fine. She said, "I can meet you at Fourteenth and Constitution."

"Good."

Andrew Wilde was about to disconnect the call when he heard Hayley's voice again.

"Pack light, sir? For warm weather."

Thoroughly jaded and rarely surprised, Andrew Wilde realized that his troubled covert operative still could impress even him.

"Yeah. How did you know?"

Hayley ended the call, satisfied she had scored a point.

CHAPTER 5

DIABÓLICO

Fourteen-year-old Bodhi Wilson emerged from the water at Ho'okipa on Monday, January 2, after a ninety-minute wing surfing session that had started in the half-light of dawn. With increasing wind speeds later in the day, surfers, kiters, and windsurfing rigs would share these same waves in a high-speed ballet as intricate as onstage at London's Royal Opera House. By unwritten rules, however, mornings were reserved for board surfing only. Bodhi—born on Maui and having spent at least part of every day of his young life at Ho'okipa—was granted unique privileges. As long as he gave surfers the right-of-way, he was met with benign indifference. Having transitioned from surfing to wind whacking the previous summer, the eighth grader was already an expert with the inflatable wing and hydrofoil board setup. Staying in his lane was not a problem.

His dad picked him up a little before eight and dropped him off at the house on Laenani Street in Haiku, a twelve-minute drive from Ho'okipa. With the resumption of classes after the winter holiday recess, the school day's starting time was pushed back an hour. For a water and wind fanatic like Bodhi, taking advantage of the late start with a quick sail was a no-brainer. Thirty minutes to shower, get dressed, and grab a quick breakfast left him just enough time to walk a block to Kokomo Road and catch the school bus.

Bodhi's mom, Janet, stood in the open front door as her husband, Taylor, paused to allow their eldest to pile out of the Ford pickup and retrieve his gear from the cargo bed. Husband and wife—college sweethearts who moved to the island a day after graduating from Fresno State sixteen years earlier—conversed through the open passenger-side window.

"Don't forget. Toohey's. At seven," said Janet with a flat expression.

His hair still wet and board shorts clinging to his thighs, Bodhi jetted past his mom and disappeared inside the house. Behind the Ford's steering wheel, Taylor stared straight ahead. His stiff grimace would be familiar to anyone who had caught their spouse in a marital transgression. The dalliance with a young clerk at an organic grocery in nearby Paia had lasted exactly two weeks. He couldn't articulate why he had indulged in the long-simmering temptation. Discovering the affair by virtue of a text notification from the young woman on her husband's cell phone was the shock of Janet's life. She'd assumed the man—her best friend for the last twenty years—was incapable of betrayal of this magnitude.

Unable to meet his wife's withering gaze, Taylor stared out the windshield and said, "Seven. Toohey's." Dropping the truck into gear and heading off to a residential construction project in Lahaina was sweet relief.

Janet returned to the kitchen, where her youngest was finishing a stack of cornmeal pancakes, and checked a wall clock. The sound of a hallway bathroom shower running clued her to Bodhi's progress.

"Hurry up, Finn," she said to the ten-year-old, then exited the kitchen and approached the bedrooms at the opposite end of the ranch-style home. Before Janet arrived at the bathroom, she heard the water shut off. Supplementing the family income as a medical transcriptionist and anxious to get her workday started, the harried mom banged on the door anyway.

"Five minutes, Bodhi. I'm way too busy today to drive you."

The fourteen-year-old emerged with a bath towel wrapped around his waist.

"Five whole minutes?" He guffawed. "I've got this."

"Prove it," Janet said, unimpressed.

She reversed course to finish the boys' lunches while Bodhi darted into his bedroom.

When the oldest boy entered the kitchen, he had exactly sixty seconds to eat his breakfast before it was time to leave for the bus. Finn was already waiting by the door with his pack strapped to his back. The bag drooped nearly below his butt, heavy with the extra weight of a copy of *Gray's Anatomy* gifted to him by his uncle. Finn had decided months earlier he wanted to be a doctor . . . and typically didn't allow anyone to forget that fact.

"Bodhi! *Come on!*"

Ignoring his younger sibling, Bodhi casually wrapped two pancakes around scrambled eggs. Janet was at the sink, cleaning up.

"Dad barely said two words in the car this morning. What's going on between you two?"

An avid surfer, one-time Maui County lifeguard, and two-time winner of the 9.9-mile channel swim between Lanai and Maui, Taylor Wilson had the hard-won respect of locals and Native Hawaiians alike, enough to have earned the appellation of "waterman." Bodhi adored his father, who had taught the teenager everything he knew about the wind, weather, and ocean. By any measure, Dad could do no wrong.

"Time's up," Janet said, deflecting the difficult question. "Go!"

Pancake burrito in hand, Bodhi headed toward the front door, backpack slung over his shoulder.

Moments later, Janet backed away from the kitchen sink and retreated to the living room, where she could watch her two sons heading up the block to the bus stop. The meeting with her husband at a local burger joint—a confrontation Taylor reluctantly agreed to—was entirely her idea. But, having won that concession from him, Janet was experiencing a secondary wave of anxiety and unsettledness.

What exactly did she want out of this difficult conversation with her husband? There had been no substantive discussion between them since she had discovered his by-then terminated dalliance; ironically, the young woman's text Janet had inadvertently found was a plea to resume their affair. In the thirteen days since that awful moment, the Wilsons had rarely spoken except for the most practical reasons. Consulting with her closest female friends, Janet didn't know if she wanted to "work things out" with a regretful Taylor or banish him from the family home. Time would tell. Everything depended on the course of their talk later that evening.

The idiot better not be late.

"Certain types of tumors can grow teeth."

Bodhi and Finn stood at the southwest corner of Uakoko Place and Kokomo Road, facing north in the direction their school bus would be coming. They considered themselves fortunate to be among the last students to be picked up on the route, a geographical happenstance that bought them a few extra minutes in the morning and the earliest drop-off after the school day's end.

Sullivan Academy was a scholastically rigorous institution, non-denominational, and expensive. With only a few hundred students enrolled, grades K thru 8, the Wilson boys represented a small percentage of children on full or partial scholarships. Drilled into both boys by their parents was the absolute necessity to take full advantage of this educational opportunity. Gifted with many glowing attributes, Bodhi and Finn were among the top handful of students in their respective grades.

Bodhi was unimpressed by his younger brother's startling medical declaration, only the latest in what seemed like a million. Watching for the bus, he asked, "No kidding?"

"And hair!"

"Amazing," said Bodhi, unamazed.

"They're called teratomas and they typically form in *testicles*."

"Now you've got my attention."

Without missing a beat, Finn said, "I heard you ask Mom about Dad and her. Are they getting a divorce?"

"*No*, dummy." Bodhi regretted talking to his mom within earshot of Finn. "Why would they go out for a 'date' tonight if they were getting a stupid divorce?"

The logic seemed suspect to Finn, who didn't share his brother's athletic abilities, but made up for that inequity with precocious brain power and intuition.

"I guess," he said dubiously.

Their school bus appeared from below the rise of Kokomo Road.

"Just never mind. Everything's okay," said Bodhi with less conviction than he had hoped to feign.

Saturnino was in the second vehicle with the Suárez brothers, long-haired Javier behind the wheel and wisecracking Diego riding shotgun. They had been following the yellow bus for thirty minutes, picking up the school vehicle early in its route farther east. The other Chevrolet, with Carranza driving and Lozano his passenger, had just dropped into position in front of the bus after it made its last scheduled stop on Kokomo Road.

Their operational plans, which the team had developed and fine-tuned in the time since arriving on the island, pinpointed three locations along the remainder of the bus route as prime opportunities for interception. With everyone linked by communication headsets, Carranza in the lead vehicle would announce which location—depending on real-time contingencies—to utilize. If none of the three locations were deemed advantageous for the mission's success, Carranza would abort the operation and they would try again tomorrow. Dressed in black fatigues and T-shirts, the men had selected light weapons from the veritable arsenal contained in the crate that Saturnino had retrieved from the airport. Handguns were more than enough firepower to get the job done given their targets.

The first possible location was less than two minutes from the stop where Saturnino had seen the two boys climb aboard the bus at the intersection of Kokomo Road and Uakoko Place.

Carranza's sharp command crackled over his headset.

"Ninety seconds."

Javier looked into the rearview mirror and saw no traffic following them. *"All clear, Commander."*

From their vantage point approximately fifty yards behind the lumbering school bus—a 2012 IC CE Series with a thirty-five-passenger capacity—the Suárez brothers could see the lead Suburban accelerating far ahead of the target vehicle, disappearing around the bend in the road at Haupoa Place. Homes with well-tended lawns lined either side of Kokomo Road. The gunmen had driven the entire route before dawn. Saturnino remembered how quickly the landscape would transform when the bus made a right turn onto Kaluanui. That road led into a thick stand of rain forest, with little traffic and no houses for more than a mile.

The first intercept location was a thousand feet after the right off Kokomo, where Kaluanui reversed its direction nearly one hundred eighty degrees. Saturnino knew Lozano would stop the lead Suburban just past the turn, with a view of the road ahead. Following the bus, the Suárez brothers and Saturnino would have an unobstructed view of the road behind them. Stealth was a critical component of the operation, and other vehicles intruding on the scene would complicate matters exponentially.

With analysis of the plan and layout of the first location, Carranza calculated their exposure's duration at twenty seconds. The former army sergeant had assessed that other places risked even more extended periods of possible inadvertent intrusion by witnesses. For that reason alone, Carranza felt the first location was the best of the three preselected sites.

The men in the follow vehicle watched the bus slow and then turn right onto Kaluanui Road. They made the same turn approximately fifteen seconds later as the rain forest closed in from both sides of the narrow two-lane road, still slick with the previous night's rain.

"Clear ahead," said Carranza over the radio.

Javier Suárez checked the rearview mirror, as he had done before making the right turn. *"Clear behind."*

There was a brief pause.

Carranza's voice came through the headsets. *"We do it here."*

Five seconds later, the men in the follow vehicle saw the brake lights on the school bus illuminate as it squealed to an abrupt stop at the hairpin turn.

Javier pulled up to the right side of the bus's rear bumper and slammed on the brakes. Saturnino and Diego Suárez exited their vehicle, Glocks in hand, and rushed to the front of the bus. They found the doors open and Lozano on the first step inside. He was pointing a Browning .45 at the bus driver's head. Carranza remained behind the wheel of the lead Suburban stopped in front of the bus at the apex of the hairpin curve. Saturnino could hear the wheels of the follow vehicle spinning in acceleration as Javier Suárez reversed away from the bus's rear end.

To the gringo driver, Lozano said, "Go there." He waggled the end of his big Browning in the direction of a gravel turnoff on the left side of the road in case his heavily accented English wasn't clear.

Standing at the bottom of the steps, Saturnino could hear the screams and sobbing of children.

So it begins.

The bus driver, long-haired Gilbert Reedy, was relatively new to Maui, lured from Oregon seven months earlier by the promise of year-round warm weather and north shore surfing. Despite unambitious life goals, he took his job seriously and avoided marijuana on school days. But with his lanky frame, James Blake concert T-shirt, ratty board shorts, and mandatory reef sandals, the twenty-five-year-old seemed a less-than-formidable adversary for the professional killers from Mexico.

His head bobbed repeatedly, telegraphing his cooperation.

Twelve seconds had elapsed since the men had stopped the bus at the hairpin curve on Kaluanui Road.

Four seconds earlier, Carranza had driven the lead SUV several feet forward, clearing the way for Gilbert Reedy to ease the school bus up a one-lane gravel road to his left. Javier followed close behind. Then

Carranza reversed direction and backed into the narrow lane. On foot, Saturnino and Diego Suárez brought up the rear.

Twenty-one seconds after the school bus and SUVs had stopped, there was no sign of the vehicles or their occupants on Kaluanui Road. It was as if the looming rain forest had swallowed the auto caravan whole.

Saturnino walked the length of the stopped bus to the open doors. Behind him, both drivers of the SUVs stayed in their vehicles. The unit's newest recruit didn't see Lozano and assumed he was dealing with the driver inside the bus. Diego was only a few steps ahead, about to climb aboard the school vehicle. Glock held down at his side, El Guasón was atypically somber. Wearing his sicario face, he climbed aboard the bus.

Then it was Saturnino's turn.

Inside, the youngest Snake Eater found a chaotic situation. Nearly all the children were wailing, terrified by the sight of the armed trio who had commandeered their school bus. Saturnino, of course, had been fully apprised of the operation. He knew that children—some as young as seven—were their target. It was common knowledge back home that when it came to the drug cartels in general and Cartel del Oeste in particular, no act of violence was out-of-bounds. Young or old. Male or female. *Everyone* was fair game.

But Saturnino's short career as an assassin-for-hire had been limited to assisting in a single execution of a grown man. Contemplating an operation involving children in the abstract was one thing. To come face-to-face with a bus of terrified children was another. He froze at the top step, unable to continue forward to his assigned position at the back of the vehicle.

Lozano, keeping control of the adult driver, noticed the newest recruit's hesitation.

"Move, dammit!"

Saturnino blinked and briefly imagined the punishment he would incur should he fail in his duties: he would likely beg his torturers for a quick and more merciful death. Pushing past Diego Suárez at the front of the bus and holding the Glock high for maximum effect, Saturnino strode the length of the vehicle, past the terrified children cowering in their seats. He was nearly to his assigned position in the far back when he noticed the two boys occupying the second to last seat on the right-hand side of the bus. What caught his attention was their preternatural calm. Every other child on the bus was sobbing—some loudly, others softly. Not these two.

Saturnino recognized them as the last two kids to catch the bus. The older boy, thirteen or fourteen perhaps, seemed unusually composed. His consoling the younger one—a sibling, maybe—was no doubt responsible for that child's remarkable poise.

Who are these two that they are so special?

Lozano's sharp command cut through the racket of the children's outcry.

"Pendjo!" he shouted. *"It's time!"*

Yanked out of his paralysis, Saturnino obediently turned, shuffled backward to the terminus of the aisle, raised his pistol high, and fired two shots, piercing the vehicle's roof. The gunshots had the desired effect of absolutely cowing the already traumatized children.

Carranza had assigned Diego, who possessed the best command of English, the task of communicating to the kids.

His accent thick and nearly incomprehensible, he said, "Everyone . . . off the bus and into the vehicles on our exterior."

The schoolchildren sat frozen in their seats for a long moment, too frightened to respond to Diego's commands. Exasperated by the delay, Lozano spewed a stream of arcane obscenities in Spanish.

The older boy at the back of the bus shot to his feet and said, "Everybody! We should do what they say. Leave the bus, nice and easy."

Assured by their classmate's composed authority, the hysterical kids regained a semblance of composure, stood, and quietly filed off the bus.

Saturnino's initial suspicions were confirmed. The older boy in the second to last seat was someone to keep his eye on.

This one has ice water instead of blood in his veins. Like a sicario, perhaps even more than me.

CHAPTER 6

DIEGO'S STORY

Two Months Ago—Day of the Dead

*I*n the name of the Father, and of the Son, and of the Holy Spirit. Amen. Bless me, Father, for I have sinned. It has been over twelve years since my last confession."

"Why so long, my son?" asked the old priest, his unshaven chin barely visible behind the metal screen.

Kneeling in the dim confessional, Diego shrugged. *"Life, Father. My responsibilities are many."*

"One should never be too busy for the care of one's soul. A strong and vibrant faith in Christ will make your secular burdens lighter. You are a family man?"

"Yes, Father."

"You are faithful to your wife and treat her with respect?"

"Yes, Father."

"That's good. Children?"

"Four young ones, Father. All are healthy, thank God."

"Thank God, indeed." The priest paused to blow his nose, then said,

"Tell me your sins, my son, so that you can begin your absolution and restore the presence of Jesus in your life."

Fireworks in the street shattered the sanctuary's tranquility and echoed off the stone-block walls. Diego snuck a peek at his wristwatch.

He said, *"Father, I have committed mortal sins. They are of a grave matter."*

"Tell me your sins, my son. Perhaps they are not as bad as you think."

"I have committed murder, Father."

The priest fell silent. He stymied a yawn that threatened to crease his face.

Diego continued. *"I have killed many people, Father. Fifteen or more. One just last week. And other even more terrible things."*

The priest understood what sort of man was sitting on the other side of the confessional's metal screen.

"Father?"

The old man chose his words carefully. *"I understand your trepidation, my son. Mortal sins are of a grave matter."*

"But . . . can God forgive me?" asked Diego.

"Everyone can receive the Act of Contrition."

"For any sin?" asked Diego, grateful for the anonymity provided by the confessional. Not because he had admitted to capital murder. Most everyone in his hometown knew what he did for a living. His position within the Cartel del Oeste had earned him their terrified respect. Here, in the confessional, Diego was anxious to keep private his vast relief that he might yet avoid eternal suffering in Hell.

The priest said, *"God will forgive any sin. But the penitent must live a life in which his love of God and neighbor is expressed by his present actions."*

"Oh, I will, Father . . . eventually."

The old priest took a moment to summon his courage, no small endeavor considering the situation.

"You must do better than that, my son."

Diego had been understandably nervous coming into the confession. Having received the answers he had wanted, he felt more relaxed now.

He could be El Guasón again. The Joker.

"Or, maybe God can do better, Father."

"G-G-God—"

Diego interrupted the priest's stammering protest. *"Perhaps if He shone His light just a little brighter into my heart, then I wouldn't be compelled to do such terrible things."*

The sicario checked his watch again. Having stepped away from spending precious minutes with his family during the Day of the Dead celebrations in the plaza, Diego was anxious to get back.

"My penance, Father?"

The old priest's voice lowered, as if ashamed.

"Are you sorry for the sins you have confessed?"

"God be my witness, I am sorry for these and all of my sins."

"Your penance is to say five Hail Marys," the priest said without enthusiasm.

Surprised, Diego asked, *"Is that it?"*

"A prayer of contrition is expected."

Diego didn't bother to close his eyes or bow his head. *"My God, I am sorry for my sins with all my heart."* He stopped, forgetting the next words of prayer.

"In choosing . . ." prompted the priest.

"In choosing to do wrong and failing to do good, I have sinned against you whom I should love above all things." He glanced at his watch again, cutting to the chase. *"In His name, my God, have mercy."*

The priest sighed and remained silent.

"Do not disappoint me, Father," said Diego, both lighthearted and threatening.

"Through the ministry of the Church may God give you pardon and peace, and I absolve you from your sins." The priest made the sign of the cross as he finished a prayer of absolution. *"In the name of the Father, and of the Son, and of the Holy Spirit. Amen."*

He heard footsteps and the church's doors opening before he finished.

CHAPTER 7

SOMETHING EVIL

Hayley had never been to Hawaii. In fact, she had never traveled outside the continental United States before landing at Kahului Airport. How popular media depicted the archipelago was the sole basis for her understanding of the Aloha State. Though an avid student of history, she had no awareness of the islands' past prior to statehood. Hawaii was a vacation destination, not reality. By her estimation, a landmass of almost eleven thousand square miles of extreme biodiversity was little more than a backdrop for a beer commercial.

Strolling through the airport concourse, Hayley grimaced at the wall-size advertisements for helicopter tours and other vacation activities. No other place that could call itself the United States of America seemed more unlike the tree-covered mountains of West Virginia. Hayley had confirmed every prejudice she possessed regarding Maui within minutes of her arrival. She couldn't imagine that anything of actual consequence ever happened there.

Leaving the airport terminal, Hayley avoided the tram to the car rental center and walked the short distance instead. Newly arrived passengers hell-bent on squeezing every second from their pricey vacations jostled with one another for a place in line at their respective rental agencies. The weather conditions, with a consistently high temperature of eighty-two degrees and balmy trade winds, seemed cartoonish after having left a Washington, DC, that was preparing for the first significant snowstorm of the winter. Hayley, wearing a female FBI agent's unofficial uniform of chinos, navy-blue polo shirt, and running shoes, felt as if she had landed in a tropical theme park.

None of this is real.

That impression shifted when she stepped to the counter with her carry-on roller bag. The female rental agent, a Native Hawaiian in her mid-thirties, was red-eyed and experiencing some emotional distress.

"ID, please," she said with difficulty.

Hayley handed over her driver's license.

The agent tapped the keyboard connected to her terminal, on the verge of tears.

"Ma'am?" asked Hayley.

"I'm sorry." The agent shook her head and tried to power through her emotions and process the rental.

"Please. Take a minute. I can wait."

The agent glanced toward a supervisor at the other end of the counter and then focused on her computer again, shaking her head.

"If you don't mind my asking, what's wrong?" asked Hayley. "Is there something I can do to help?"

The rental agent continued to type as she said, "You haven't heard, I guess."

"Heard what, ma'am? What's happened?"

"The children . . . eighteen kids . . . taken this morning," said the agent, her voice catching repeatedly. "Vanished without a trace."

The woman began to sob openly. Hayley looked and saw the agency's office supervisor scowling in their direction.

Turning to the agent again, she asked, "Kidnapped?"

The woman nodded, struggling to compose herself. "My sister's youngest is one of the missing."

Hayley looked up and down the counter and noticed that all of the agency representatives appeared similarly anguished. Opposite them was a growing crowd of newly arrived vacationers wholly oblivious to the emerging crisis on the island. Their impatience to get into their rental cars matched the stress and despair of the local workers in intensity.

The agent returned Hayley's driver's license and an envelope containing her rental agreement.

"Aisle B, stall twelve."

She somberly accepted her paperwork, catching the woman's gaze. "Thank you. All of you . . . you're in my thoughts."

She strode to the doors leading out of the rental center, keeping her head down and canceling the tourists' exasperated faces from her consciousness.

Hayley dumped her roller bag in the back seat of her rented Kia Soul and got behind the wheel. She lifted her shirt, clearing a Glock 19 nestled in a Tactica "belly band" holster. One of the perks of her Publius-provided cover as an FBI agent had been the ability to keep the weapon on board her flight. Her usual carry method back home in DC was inside the waistband, but her attire mandated by Hawaii's warm weather precluded the layering necessary to conceal a weapon. Having never worn the belly band holster, Hayley was surprised by how comfortable it was even while sitting in the car.

She drew the Glock, confirming a round was in the chamber and the mag fully loaded.

The rental agent had made an impression on Hayley.

Maybe I was wrong about this place.

The original plan had been to check into her hotel and head out to Fischer's home—located on Maui's mostly undeveloped northwest coast—in the morning. But the kidnapping, while unrelated to her operation, had unsettled Hayley. What good was she sitting in a hotel room? April Wu's spectral visitations had had the effect of awakening certain unexpected sensitivities in Hayley. Though her friend and fellow Publius operative hadn't made an appearance in the previous twenty-four hours, Hayley felt another presence on the Valley Isle.

Something evil is here.

Hayley's route took her through Kahului, a town of thirty thousand. With shopping malls, office complexes, and light industrial parks, the municipality could pass for any back on the mainland. Few tourist attractions or large hotels existed within its borders. Unable to shake a feeling of tenuousness and uncharacteristic disquiet that had plagued her for weeks, alcoholic fortification seemed, operationally speaking, to be a good plan. Hayley stopped at the first liquor store she passed and emerged a few minutes later with a bagged bottle of inexpensive tequila. She took a quick get-my-head-in-the-game nip and placed the bottle in the glove compartment.

She followed Kahului Beach Road out of town, where it narrowed to two lanes with a rapid change of scenery. Once past Waiehu Beach, retail locations disappeared, replaced by mountainous rain forest to the left and the ocean blue to the right. Hayley felt as if she had entered another world. Kahekili Highway—too grand a designation for a narrow, twisting roadway that changed direction every few hundred feet—climbed higher into the island's rugged northwestern terrain.

Hayley was grateful that traffic was relatively nonexistent, limited to the residents of this isolated area of the island. At times, a light pickup truck or decade-old Japanese SUV would appear suddenly on her bumper, pressing for the right-of-way. On those occasions, she would take advantage of the rare pullout rather than suffer the annoyance of an impatient local driver tailgating her. As she drew closer to her destination, astonishingly, the route ahead was even more treacherous. Two lanes of traffic became one, with no room to spare on either side. Hayley crept at increasingly slower speeds around these blind turns, mindful of a sheer drop of hundreds of feet to the ocean below.

What do you do when you need a carton of milk?

Finally, the landscape opened. A Dodge Durango parked at the gated driveway on her right signaled that she had completed the semi-perilous drive, though no house was visible from the road. Surveillance cameras stood sentinel on either side of the gate. Hayley assumed more cameras were positioned in the surrounding woods.

Stopping beside the SUV and lowering her passenger-side window, Hayley addressed the two USMS deputies sitting in the front seat.

"Aloha," she said.

Irony had been her intention, but self-consciousness was the result.

The two men looked down at Hayley from their slightly elevated perch in the bigger vehicle.

"Can I help you?" the bald one asked without enthusiasm.

"FBI Special Agent Chill." She presented her credentials.

There was no reaction from either man. They had been expecting her arrival. Also apparent was an undercurrent of hostility.

What is this? Because I'm a woman?

Hayley knew that the US Marshals Service was predominately male as a federal agency. The Honolulu field office had *zero* women on its operations staff. Of course, the two deputies' attitude could be due to a jurisdictional beef. Who was to say?

One thing was certain: at least some of the personnel on the protection detail were not happy about Hayley's participation.

The bald deputy marshal pressed a button on a remote clipped to the sun visor without a word of acknowledgment or welcome. The formidable metal gate swung open. Shifting her rental car into drive and glancing into the rearview mirror, Hayley pretended not to notice his sarcastic wave.

The gated entry at the road was the sole means of accessing the estate. Hayley took stock of the property's stark isolation and high defensibility as she followed the long, curving driveway through the property; sea cliffs at the opposite end of the property were as good as a medieval castle's fortifications. Any incursion besides using the guarded driveway was impossible short of a helicopter assault or HALO drop.

The main house was as dramatic architecturally as its surroundings. Hayley had never seen a private residence like it. Sited at the terminus of a long promontory, surrounded on three sides by a stand of windbreaking Norfolk Island pine trees, the two-story house of wood, glass, and brushed steel was both grandiose and accommodating of its natural surroundings. Though the structure was built in the last decade, judging by its high-end building materials and sleek lines, it paradoxically projected a sense of ancient origin. Had it ever *not* stood above the Makalina Ravine? A blending of contemporary and mid-century modern that suggested a Japanese sensibility, the home's design was clean, uncluttered, and utterly private. Utility and guest buildings that Hayley had passed on the way down from the main road were out of sight, as were any houses on neighboring properties.

Four vehicles were parked at the end of the driveway, three late-model SUVs and a Tesla connected to a charger cable that unspooled from a panel discreetly mounted on the side of the house. Hayley's humble Kia Soul seemed out of place in these environs. Turning off the ignition, she popped open the glove compartment, her hand hovering above its lowered door. Would a quick nip from the squat bottle of Espolòn be such a bad thing? As she lifted the bottle for a satisfying, tide-me-over slug of tequila, a middle-aged, dark-complected man wearing Dickies duck shorts and a matching desert khaki-colored short-sleeve work shirt walked past behind the car, carrying a long-handled hoe over his shoulder.

Fuck!

Hayley recapped the bottle and stowed it again in the glove compartment. Then, still fretting over the maintenance man's untimely intrusion, she slammed the glove compartment closed and exited the car. Terry Shaw was waiting on the front porch for her, a tall, tanned man in his mid-thirties.

"Agent Chill," he said neutrally. Shaw had done his best to quiet the grumbling among the other deputies on the protection detail, but he wasn't happy about the FBI agent's intrusion, either.

"Deputy US Marshal Shaw, I presume."

They shook. Hayley felt his eyes bore into hers with a frank appraisal. His lack of reaction did not answer whether she had passed this initial assessment.

"Welcome to paradise," said Shaw, trying hard not to make it sound like a threat.

"Is it?" she asked with an edge to her voice.

"Depends on the person, I guess."

"Justice Fischer?" asked Hayley, nodding toward the house behind Shaw.

"Down below. Swimming." He cocked his head with a sarcastic tilt. "That's where you come in, isn't it?"

Anita Fischer had made no secret of preferring at least *one* female on her around-the-clock protection detail. And, meaning no disrespect to the US Marshals Service, the justice wanted that female to be an FBI agent. Terry Shaw and other DUSMs most definitely took offense. None of their complaints, of course, were articulated outside of their firmly closed circle.

"I'm more than an exercise buddy, Deputy Shaw."

Ignoring the sharp bite of Hayley's reminder, he indicated the front door. "Let's go inside. I'll give you the lay of the land before Marlin returns."

Hayley followed him to the massive steel and glass door that pivoted off-center rather than swing open on hinges. "Marlin is your code name for Justice *Fischer?*"

He shrugged. "Not all of us DUSMs went to college like you brilliant FBI agents."

On Shaw's heels, Hayley recalled the DC scuttlebutt that suggested personnel at the USMS carried a chip on their shoulders, no doubt due to their reputation among other federal law enforcement and intelligence agencies as knuckle draggers. She had always written off such harping as intragovernmental shit talk. But, given the fact that Terry Shaw had referenced a possible disparity in education achievement within minutes of meeting her, Hayley was now inclined to give those rumors more credence.

She was surprised to find four people who were *not* with the protection detail inside the sleek entry hall setting up for what appeared to be a party or social event. Shaw read her startled expression.

"No one told you?" he asked. "Marlin is getting married tomorrow."

"With every Supreme Court justice essentially under protective lockdown, you're hosting a *wedding* for your protectee tomorrow?"

"You've never met Justice Fischer, have you?" asked Shaw.

"Not in person, no."

"There have been one hundred and fifteen Supreme Court justices in the history of the United States. Seven have been women, and none of them got there by being shy or retiring types."

Hayley said, "All true, but that doesn't explain why you're allowing her to host a wedding ceremony during an active threat watch."

Shaw felt his patience draining away like water through his cupped hands. He endeavored to keep his temper in check; the young woman who stood before him undoubtedly had influence back in Washington that he decidedly did not possess.

She's DC . . . and I'm La-La Land.

Adopting a conciliatory tone, Shaw said, "The house and the property are secure, as you've witnessed on your drive down. Guests and hired staff will be limited and completely manageable."

Hayley stared at Shaw with skepticism intact.

Trying again, he said, "We have the situation under control."

"Why would the situation be anything less?"

The woman's voice came from the opposite end of an entry hall.

Anita Fischer, a forty-five-year-old associate justice of the Supreme Court, stood just shy of five eight, her damp red hair unruly after being freed from a swim cap. Trim and architecturally shouldered, Fischer retained the same physique she had as a varsity swimmer at Stanford. Daily exercise, a vegan diet, and a fierce drive were the reasons for the justice's athletic physical fitness, all the more impressive given the demands of her professional achievement.

Hayley Chill, of similar iron discipline, intelligence, and build, liked her at first sight.

"Is there a problem, Terry?" asked Fischer.

"This is Special Agent Hayley Chill, ma'am, just arrived from DC."

"Ah, yes. Excellent. In case I'm attacked by a white shark with radical ideological beliefs. A nationalist sea snail, perhaps. All kidding aside, they can be deadly, you know. A leopard conus can reach nine inches in length. The Hawaiian word for them is *poniuniu*. Pick up a striated conus shell on the beach and the snail is still inside? Oh, boy, watch out! One zap from that little sucker can cause respiratory failure. Potentially deadly."

Hayley offered a respectfully bowed head. "Madame Justice."

Fischer rolled her eyes. "Please. That makes me sound like the protagonist of a Sam Peckinpah movie or Marvel superhero. 'Anita' will suffice, Hayley . . . if I may be so bold."

"Thank you, ma'am, and congratulations," said the deeper state operative, who wouldn't address a Supreme Court justice by her first name at the point of a gun.

Fischer glanced toward the hired staff busily preparing for the next day's ceremony.

"Ha, yes! Thank you!" she responded with zero blushing.

Fischer had known her fiancé for less than a year, and together they made the decision to tie the knot only two weeks ago. Close friends had made no secret of their disapproval of the wedding. A decade older than Fischer, Lachlan Morris was a celebrated journalist-turned-author with fleeting appearances on the *New York Times* bestseller lists. His impact on the nation's current zeitgeist, however, was significantly less than that of a Supreme Court justice.

For most of Anita Fischer's professional life, she had been too busy—and too emotionally inept, perhaps—for deep romance. Lachlan Morris scrambled that all-encompassing devotion to her legal career. With their first date, his raconteur's charisma, non-reactionary politics, and rugged, Marlboro Man good looks bowled her over. Morris made her laugh, and given the stresses of her lofty judicial position, that ability was *everything*.

They decided to get married at the start of their stay on Maui. Undoubtedly, the dreamy, paradisiacal nature of the island—and Fischer's serene refuge there—played a role in the decision. She couldn't remember who brought up the idea first. No matter. Since giving Morris her yes, the youngest justice on the United States Supreme Court had never been happier. In her heart, Anita Fischer knew the truth: marrying Lachlan Morris was the right choice.

"Ma'am?" prompted Shaw, snapping Fischer from her momentary reverie.

"Oh, sorry." She let loose a delightful trill of self-deprecating laughter. "Just look at me! I'm a perfect nut these days."

"Will it be a . . . large gathering?" Hayley asked both Fischer and Shaw.

Fischer said, "The security situation has given us the perfect excuse for keeping it a small affair. A few friends from here on the island. My sister will parachute in for the requisite twenty-four hours. And no one should be surprised if Lachlan's crazy uncle makes an appearance, on the lam from his latest marital debacle. I'm sure we'll soldier on somehow, despite the obligatory lockdown . . . and this ghastly kidnapping."

Neither Fischer nor Hayley noticed the cloud that came over Shaw's expression.

"Where is Mr. Morris presently, ma'am?" asked Hayley.

"Holed up at the Ritz-Carlton in Kapalua, working on his opus about the Clintons. We thought we would opt for the traditional route and deny him the sight of his betrothed before the big day. Do you know the origin of this bizarre tradition? Comes from the days of arranged marriages and deals made between the fathers of the bride and groom, who may have *never* laid eyes on each other before the ceremonial union. Can you imagine?"

"I guess that explains the veil," said Hayley.

Fischer's eyes widened, impressed. Her conversations thus far with her USMS protectors had been less than illuminating.

"Why yes," said Fischer, turning a mock accusatory gaze on Terry Shaw. Though the justice's teasing was meant to be good-natured, he felt ganged up on by the two women. The DUSM shed defensiveness like dandruff.

"I don't know much about veils and wedding stuff. Sorry, ma'am."

Given his closed-off and mostly self-contained nature, the women couldn't have known the cause of Shaw's muted emotions. Should they have intuited he knew most of the children who had vanished without a trace that morning? Perhaps. All of the missing children were the sons and daughters of Shaw's friends and neighbors. Though the USMS field office was on Oahu, Shaw had lived on the Valley Isle for the last ten years. His wife, Marie, was a painter who preferred the funkier, more artistic vibe of Maui's north shore and upcountry. Sharing the cost of a three-bedroom apartment in Honolulu with other DUSMs made it possible for Shaw to split his time between the two islands.

"What measures will be in place tomorrow?" Hayley asked, oblivious to his distraction.

News of the wedding ceremony was yet another disturbing revelation. Was Publius aware of this avoidable breach of security protocol? Perhaps the additional jeopardy posed by the event explained why she was selected to assist with Anita Fischer's protection detail. But why wasn't she informed if that was the case? Hayley briefly considered the idea of contacting Andrew Wilde in the hope that someone with sufficient influence could exert pressure on Fischer to postpone the wedding.

Hayley couldn't shake her intensifying uneasiness, a sense of impending disaster, and not one based solely on the children's disappearance. The exotic unfamiliarity of the place—a tropical island in the middle of a vast Pacific Ocean—was like a mental cough syrup that left her feeling slightly woozy.

Addressing Fischer, Shaw said, "Being a relatively long-term resident of the island gives me a unique perspective on the situation, ma'am. I won't be surprised if I know some of the folks helping out tomorrow. Besides our USMS detail, we'll have people from the Maui Police Department on the road controlling access and such." Then, with painfully obvious insecurity, he added, "And there's Special Agent Chill from the FBI, of course."

Fischer said, "Now, now, Terry, don't be weird."

Shaw grimaced his apologies as he checked his vibrating phone. "Excuse me for a minute."

"And *I* need to get into some dry clothes." Fischer strode off toward another part of the house. She really did seem to be enjoying life.

Shaw waited until his protectee had left the area, then turned away from Hayley and exited through the front door, taking his call on the front porch.

Hayley watched Shaw as he talked on the phone, his anxiety plain now for her to see. She upbraided herself for not fully appreciating the implications of Shaw being a Maui resident and recalled the visible anguish of the car rental employees. Was the call in regards to the missing schoolchildren? The deputy's tense behavior now had a good explanation.

My god, what if his kid is among the missing?

Shaw's phone conversation lasted less than a minute. When it was apparent that he had disconnected, Hayley joined him on the porch.

"Everything all right?" she asked, keeping her tone of voice neutral.

Shaw glanced toward an ocean that stretched to the horizon. A line of clouds marched in formation twenty miles out, dropping a gray curtain of rain that spun off an incidental rainbow. Somewhere unseen, wild chickens clucked.

"It was nothing. Family stuff."

His answer confirmed what Hayley feared.

She said, "I heard about the situation in town. I . . . I can't imagine what you must be going through."

"My wife and I don't have children, Agent Chill."

Shaw fell silent for several long seconds, staring again at the sea, sky, and distant clouds, but seeing nothing. Finally, he said, "I know these kids. *Personally* know them. Marie's best friend has two . . . missing."

"I'm so sorry."

Hayley could see that the DUSM felt crushed by pressing professional duties and those on the home front. And she could relate to that feeling.

"Go home," she said. "I'll stay here with Fischer. You've got the two men at the gate."

"It's okay. I'll finish my shift. But you should get some rest after your flight. Tomorrow will be a long day."

Hayley realized that this was going to be the way between them. The not-so-quiet competition reminded her of April Wu. Was everyone in this business a stubborn hard-ass?

She decided not to play the game.

"Okay. I'll head off. See you here bright and early tomorrow morning?"

"Zero five thirty."

Despite her compassion for the guy, Hayley was relieved to go. The situation at Fischer's home, for now, appeared secure. She decided against contacting Andrew Wilde, perhaps due partly to her sympathy for Shaw's situation. Hayley reminded herself to cut the DUSM as much slack as possible. Anticipating the likely difficult times ahead, her mind went directly to the bottle in the Kia's glove compartment. A sting of tequila in her throat. The subsequent white flash across her consciousness.

Within minutes, safely down from the western reaches of Kahekili Highway and back in town, Hayley pulled over to the shoulder to have just that.

CHAPTER 8

GRENADE

He arrived home a few minutes before nine. Marie had long since eaten dinner and cleaned up the kitchen. After retrieving a beer from the refrigerator, Shaw found his wife in her studio behind their ranch-style home on Lia Place in Haiku, an unincorporated community a few miles inland from the north shore and folded snugly in the rain forest.

An oil painter who worked typically on big, three-by-four-foot stretched canvas, Marie Walker refused to indulge "tropical" motifs in her artwork. Instead, graduating from UCLA's arts program a dozen years earlier, she embraced an inclination for darkly expressive figurative painting. A current series composed of headless bodies, contorted by extreme emotions and mysterious circumstances, was representative of this career-long exploration of brutal emotions. Working from her imagination and dream life—never utilizing a photograph or live model—Marie painted as a form of exorcism, off-loading imagery that would otherwise torment her if unrevealed in her art. She sold through a gallery in Paia often enough to outearn her husband's USMS salary.

Shaw stood in the doorway and watched his wife paint.

"Does it help?" he asked.

"A little." After a pause, Marie added, "Not much."

"Same with me. I thought maybe work would be a distraction." He sighed, then took a pull off the beer. "Fat chance."

Seated on her work stool, Marie studied the half-finished canvas. The female torso, arms flailing, was a haunting image.

"What's Janet saying?" asked Shaw.

"She's devastated, Terry. Paralyzed with fear. Not saying much," said Marie with an edge.

Realizing that she was punishing her husband entirely without cause—that her terror had drop-kicked her emotional equilibrium—Marie put down her brush and rotated to face Shaw.

"I'm sorry."

Standing, Marie accepted with relief his long embrace.

"It's okay," he told her.

She took a step back. Shaw offered his beer, which Marie gratefully accepted.

"I tried calling Taylor. Didn't pick up," he said, watching her take a long, satisfying swallow of cold pilsner.

Marie wiped her mouth on her paint-splattered sleeve and handed the bottle back to her husband.

"On top of what they were *already* going through? This will crush them."

Shaw brooded a moment, wanting to take care with what he said next. Taylor Wilson was a good friend. The two couples typically shared a meal at least once a week. Shaw had been blindsided by his pal's admission of an attraction to the "checkout girl," as he called her. He was even more surprised when Taylor followed through with that flirtation. The revelation of his transgression and its aftermath not only impacted the Wilsons' marriage but also their close friendship with Terry and Marie. Conversations had become strained. Alliances scrutinized.

And now *this* nightmare.

"We'll be there for our friends, Marie. We're going to do everything we can for them."

This idea seized her. Of being of some help. In whatever way.

Almost manically, Marie said, "We should go over there."

"Now? It's after nine."

The fact that they were childless—Marie unable to conceive—made Shaw aware of the inequities between the two couples. Bodhi and Finn's kidnapping now made that imbalance much worse.

"Let's call," he suggested as an alternative.

"Call?" she said, as if describing a fourth-place finish in a five-person race.

"I'm due back at work at five a.m. Fischer's getting married tomorrow, remember?" asked Shaw, getting no sympathy from his wife. "They might want to be left alone, for all we know."

Marie turned her shoulder to him, reaching for a cleaning rag.

"Well, you stay home, then, and get some sleep. I'm going." Off his plaintive look, she said, "Don't worry about it, Terry. You're good."

But Shaw knew he wasn't "good." He wouldn't be in shouting distance of good until all of the missing kids were returned home unharmed.

Mute, he watched Marie clean up. Shaw imagined accompanying his wife on this mission of mercy. As a couple, they would go to Taylor and Janet Wilson's home and mouth the appropriate words. They would say, "Whatever we can do to help." Or, "Everything will be all right, I'm sure." And perhaps, "We can't imagine what you two must be going through."

As hard as he tried to resist the gravitational pull of the tragedy, Shaw felt as if he were hurtling pell-mell into its maw. His job with the USMS seemed almost a distant (and relatively pleasant) memory as he followed his wife out of the art studio and into the kitchen. He could only wish the potential assassination of a Supreme Court justice under his protection was his only concern.

He nodded when Marie looked at him.

"You're right. We should go over there."

No big shock, but the youngest kids were having the most challenging time. Bodhi Wilson had hoped that the one adult among them, their bus driver, would have been of more help. Nicknamed "Gekko"—the under-ten children being big fans of the PJ Masks animated universe—for the green T-shirt he wore nearly every day, Gilbert Reedy endured the first hours of their collective captivity curled up on the floor in a fetal position. That left Bodhi and Makana Murty, the only other fourteen-year-old in the group, to keep things under control until help arrived.

Inside the SUVs, the men had given them hoods to put over their heads. Bodhi estimated the travel time in the vehicles from Kaluanui Road to their ultimate destination as having been approximately thirty minutes. Once at that location, the men ordered the hooded children and their bus driver out of the vehicles. Judging by the drive's duration and smell of ocean brine in the air, Bodhi guessed they were on the north shore and east. Near Waipio Bay, perhaps. Without the hood over his head, he could have confirmed their location by the outline of the hills.

They walked hand in hand across what felt underfoot to be open ground. There were plenty of stumbles and falls. But working together—and prodded by their one captor designated to speak—the kids made their way without injury. Waiting for further instructions from their abductors, Bodhi heard the squeal of door hinges. Only after the kidnappers marched them all inside and the door closed were the children free to remove their black hoods.

The true nature of their makeshift prison was something of a mystery.

The undivided room—about fifty by ten feet—had a concave roof of corrugated steel painted white and a poured-concrete floor. If Bodhi had to guess, he would say they were being held captive in some type of bomb or hurricane shelter. The kidnappers had modified the reinforced steel door to be locked from the outside. Mattresses and blankets lay in piles at the rear of the room. Illumination came from three light fixtures mounted on the ceiling. Large cartons of Lunchables and bottled water occupied three locations in the shelter, the small kitchen at the chamber's midpoint being otherwise bare.

Bodhi and Makana had inspected every detail of their lockup once they got the younger kids settled down. Plying the eight- and nine-year-olds with S'mores Dippers and Dirt Cake went a long way to calming tattered nerves and bought the older children time to assess the situation. Bohdi's ten-year-old brother acted as an intermediary between the two age groups, someone who could speak the younger kids' language and thereby gain their trust. As blond-haired as Bodhi was dark, Finn rose to the occasion within the earliest minutes of the ordeal.

The two fourteen-year-olds conferred with a modicum of privacy near the door. Glancing over his shoulder at the others, Bodhi said, "As long as we can keep the treats coming, I think we're kinda good."

"Thank God for Cookie Dunks," Makana said wryly.

Bodhi liked his fellow eighth grader and had since kindergarten. Makana was also a passionate surfer; it would be impossible to tally the number of hours the two had spent on the beach together as little kids. Last year, in seventh grade, Bodhi began to experience an added dimension to his affinity for the tall, dark-haired Makana. This first-in-a-lifetime romantic tension was not lost on her. A stolen kiss at sunset on the sand at Ho'okipa resolved the issue. Whether Makana wasn't ready yet for such business or simply didn't feel "that way" about her childhood playmate was immaterial. To the relief of both teenagers, their friendship survived the mini-drama.

"What is this place?" asked Makana.

"Bomb shelter, I think," said Bodhi.

In 2018, authorities sent an alert to every cell phone on the Hawaiian Islands warning of an imminent ballistic missile strike. Residents awaited the impending nuclear attack for thirty-eight nerve-racking minutes before state officials admitted the warning was a false alarm. Nine years old at the time, Bodhi remembered the incident well, his first awareness of weapons with the potential for ending human civilization. A curious child, he asked endless questions about nuclear devices and the threat they posed. In those conversations, his father discussed the existence of private shelters and showed the boy photographic examples. Since the kidnappers' bunker was partially buried in a hillside and therefore susceptible to flooding, Bodhi assumed that protection from hurricanes couldn't have been its intention.

Well, we're pretty good down here if there is *an actual nuclear attack.*

He chose not to share this glimmer of a silver lining with his friend.

Their phones, of course, had been confiscated by the armed men. Neither of them had wristwatches.

"How long do you think we've been in here?" he asked.

"Couple hours?" guessed Makana. "Have we been kidnapped? My parents don't have any money."

If Bodhi had to guess, he would say that his parents didn't have much money, either.

"Do you think these guys . . . ?" Makana couldn't finish her question.

"They want money. Why else take so many kids at once?"

Though he had spoken with what sounded like complete confidence, privately Bodhi wasn't entirely sure what to think. He'd read newspapers and seen reports online of terrible things done to children. Of disturbing conspiracy theories.

Could those diabolical schemes be real?

Makana said, "They have guns, Bodhi. They can do whatever they want with us."

Her anxiety was contagious. Despite his natural composure, Bodhi now suffered from the same fretful emotions. With a glance toward Gekko and his pronounced state of uselessness, he realized that the younger kids were *his* responsibility.

Held captive in a subterranean prison by armed men who spoke in short bursts of rapid-fire Spanish, he felt a creeping panic overtake him. What helped was remembering an observation his father had made when first taking a frightened five-year-old Bodhi beyond the breakers on a surfboard.

Watch the water. Know the ocean. Stay in the moment.

To fear the thing was to be defeated by it. Anticipate failure and failure is what you will get. With twelve-foot waves commonplace in the winter, surfing at Ho'okipa could be a terrifying experience for a novice. However, by remaining calm and staying observant of ever-changing nuances in wind, current, and wave, Bodhi was able to avoid getting crushed. Be present. Don't panic. Avoid emotional extremes. These lessons were applicable outside of surfing as well.

Fear was the enemy. Knowledge was a weapon.

The sound of scuffling outside the door signaled that the men with guns were returning.

Makana gasped, her voice seizing in her throat. Behind them, a few of the younger kids began to cry. The door opened, into the room.

Shaw waited in the car while Marie continued to console Janet Wilson, the two women standing on the Wilsons' front porch. It was nearly midnight. He was due back at the Fischer estate in five hours. The DUSM doubted he would be able to find much sleep before then, his mind in a low-simmering boil. Ninety minutes in the company of the bewildered, terror-consumed parents of Bodhi and Finn Wilson had been psychological torture for even Shaw, despite his tours in Afghanistan. His buddy Taylor's transformation from a good-natured, boisterous general contractor to an emotionally hollowed-out automaton was a sight that would haunt Terry Shaw for the rest of his life.

The street was slick from rain showers that blew through Maui almost nightly. Shaw listened to the racket of trilling insects and invasive coqui frogs—all sounds of the rain forest encroaching on the small subdivision in which the Wilsons lived—and breathed in thick air infused with the mingled scents of night-blooming jasmine and plumeria trees.

How long the women would continue to talk was anyone's guess. Closing his eyes, Shaw pantomimed sleep in the hope that such playacting would provide some minimal benefit.

His vibrating phone ruined even those slight chances.

Shaw retrieved his phone and saw that the caller was his younger brother back in the States.

"Kinda late for you."

"Hi, Terry."

The voice was male, middle-aged. Texas accent, maybe. Not his brother.

"Who is this?" asked Shaw.

"You can call me 'Joe.'"

"Why are you calling from this number?" Then, sharper, "Where's Jake?"

"Your brother? Home in bed, I suppose. We cloned his cell number to call you. But none of that makes any difference. Are you paying attention, Terry? The information I'm about to tell you is very important."

Something in the caller's easygoing tone—his total control and mastery of the situation between them—sold Shaw on that statement's truth.

This guy is no joke.

"Are you still there?" asked Joe.

"Yes."

"We have those kids, Terry."

"Repeat that."

"The schoolkids that disappeared—there in your slice of paradise—we took them."

Shaw unconsciously gripped the steering wheel tightly with his free hand, his gaze darting to his wife standing on the porch with Janet Wilson.

"We took them, okay? And now we have them," said Joe.

"I understand." Shaw's voice became more accommodating. Conversational. A chat between two old friends. "What do you want, Joe? I know a lot of parents who are desperate to get their kids home in their beds."

"Great news, Terry. You can make that happen. Only you can help."

"Okay. Tell me what you need, friend."

"Believe me when I say this: everything depends entirely on *you.*"

"Understood. Tell me what you want!"

Shaw hadn't meant to raise his voice. He knew that he had to maintain control of his emotions.

Seconds ticked past in silence.

Oh, God! What have I done?

Shaw asked into the void, "Hello? Joe?"

"Kill her, Terry. By any means you like, Justice Anita Fischer must die."

Shaw sat still, the insect noise outside the open car window washing over him. His gaze remained riveted on the two women on the porch.

"Did you get that, Terry?"

"You're crazy," Shaw said evenly. He considered the possibility of running a *57 trace on the call. Then, stalling for time, he asked, "Why do you want Justice Fischer dead?"

Joe said, "No point in tracking this number, Terry. It'll only show that Jake called you. Having heard about the kidnapping, he was worried about his big brother on the island. The two of you talked for a few minutes. And that was it. No one will ever be the wiser."

Shaw was beginning to appreciate the skills of the people he was dealing with. The children's abduction wasn't the impulsive work of amateurs. So he absolutely needed to be alert and keenly observational regarding everything about the phone call. What "Joe" said. How he said it. Any sounds he might discern in the background.

Calmly, Shaw said, "I'm not going to kill the person I've sworn to protect."

"That or having the deaths of eighteen sweet kids on your head, Terry." Joe paused, his smirk transmitted over the phone line. "Somehow worse when none of them are yours, isn't it?"

"Let's meet in person and talk about it."

Joe didn't even deem this stalling effort worth a villainous guffaw.

"Act fast, Deputy. Those kiddies are scared half to death, and for good reason."

Shaw felt a wave of revulsion rising within him.

He said, "This isn't going to work."

"Tell no one, Terry. Not your wife. Not your fellow DUSMs or local police. Don't say a word to that pretty, young FBI agent who just arrived on the island, either. We'll know if you do, believe me. And that'll mean killing time. Dead kids time, Deputy. Don't test us on this, please."

"Joe—"

"That's enough for now. You know what you have to do. Eighteen innocent children for one lady judge. I think that decision is what they call a 'no-brainer,' am I right?"

His thoughts in a jumble, Shaw said nothing in response.

Joe said, "In the future, I'll only communicate with you via text. Like our chat now, also untraceable."

Shaw continued to remain silent. His reactions couldn't keep up with the noose that Joe was progressively tightening around his neck.

"I know everything there is to know about you, Terry. You're a good man. Solid, dependable, and none too bright. I'm positive you'll do the right thing."

Joe disconnected the call.

Shaw stared at the phone in his hand as if it were a grenade with its pin pulled.

This goddamn thing has delivered my death.

Crickets, night birds, and frogs raised their ruckus outside his window, unseen in the darkness. Rain fell in a sudden downpour. Marie turned away from a long embrace with a distraught Janet Wilson, dashed down the steps, and jogged toward Shaw waiting in the car.

Maui Seaside on Kaahumanu Avenue was a conventional two-story hotel a single block up from Kahului Harbor and with a good view of Pu'u Kukui's summit to the west. Kaahumanu was a busy six-lane divided thoroughfare that served as the best route for travel to the northwest coastline and Fischer's estate. Hayley was fortunate to have found lodging at the Maui Seaside, rarely available during the high season and a bargain at four hundred fifty dollars a night. Despite the expected reimbursement by Publius, Hayley was nevertheless pained to sign the room rental agreement for a final cost of over three thousand dollars.

She sat outside on the small patio off her room, overlooking the pool. The harbor and mountainous northwest coastline to her right were illuminated by the reflected light of a three-quarter moon. The date was

January 3. A few minutes after midnight, the air temperature was a pleasant seventy-one degrees. One of the countless wild chickens that inhabit Maui wandered past, heading in the direction of the sliver of beach on the property's northern perimeter. Hayley had witnessed the colorful birds everywhere, which were the ancestors of domestic chickens (or so a local had informed her) freed or intentionally released in the aftermath of Hurricanes Iwa and Iniki.

With no natural predators on the island.

A paradise for chickens, then, if not for humans. How safe was a Supreme Court justice where eighteen schoolkids could disappear off the face of the earth?

She poured another couple ounces of tequila into the hotel-provided plastic water cup. Replacing the bottle on the ground next to her chair, Hayley saw April Wu in the room, sitting on the corner of the bed and apparently watching the muted television.

She knew her friend couldn't possibly be watching TV. Ghosts don't *need* television.

"C'mon, get your ass out here."

April stood and joined Hayley on the porch, sitting on the other available patio chair.

"Thought maybe a low-grade buzz would've kept you at bay tonight," said Hayley.

"How do you know it's not your 'low-grade buzz' that has you seeing things?"

"Well, then . . . Cheers." Hayley took another sip of caramel-colored alcohol. "You know about the lockdown wedding?"

April nodded and said, "Love can be blind . . . and very, extremely stupid."

"What about this kidnapping business on the island? Any spectral insight to that?"

"You think I'd tell you if I did?"

"Well, do you?"

"I come to hear your confessionals, slugger, not to hand over a cheat sheet."

"You told me about Wilde's intentions in sending me here."

"Don't confuse your own good intuitions with my giving you the answers for questions you don't even have yet."

"What?" asked Hayley.

"Never mind. How about you? You going to bone that hot DUSM?"

"Christ, April!"

"Well, it wouldn't exactly be out of character."

Hayley emitted a low groan. April's visitation notwithstanding, she felt painfully alone and couldn't shake the feeling that she was an alien in this place. A paralyzing diffidence threatened to replace the trademark zeal that once energized her every waking minute. Before her last mission, in which she had suffered significant personal loss, an unshakable conviction to preserve and protect the US Constitution perpetually inspired the West Virginian to action. That ambition was her guiding light. But now?

Hayley was an operative who could scarcely operate.

Sitting in a hotel patio chair and quietly sipping tequila from a plastic water cup—the harbor waves gently lapping against a sandy shore less than a hundred yards from where she was seated—she had lost sight of that beacon. Perhaps irretrievably.

Her motivation to do what was best for her motherless baby nephew suddenly seemed pedestrian compared to her previous endeavors, failing to provide her the necessary boost. Would Hayley have what it took to overcome the obstacles and hostile threats she feared would reveal themselves with daybreak? Could April Wu be of some help? What else is a spectral best friend good for, if not solitary counsel and consolation?

She stared into her plastic water cup, the last sips of alcohol yet to be consumed. Indulging a rare moment of confessional honesty, Hayley said, "The thing is, I don't know exactly what I'm doing here . . ."

There was only silence in response.

Hayley looked up and saw that April had vanished. As was her wont.

BOOK TWO

DENIAL

CHAPTER 9

DAY TWO

Shaw managed to sleep a couple of hours at best. Tormented by a cascade of questions, he moved to the couch so as not to keep Marie up. Analyzing his phone conversation with the purported kidnapper, Shaw realized he had neglected to demand proof of life. Perhaps Joe had no connection to the children's disappearance whatsoever. What if the call was a fiendishly clever attempt to exploit a wholly separate criminal plot? That possibility offered little solace. What chance was there that the conspirators would go away if he opted to defy them? Some mysterious cabal had picked him to murder a sitting justice on the US Supreme Court. Failing one effort, they would undoubtedly try another.

Abandoning all hope for more sleep, the DUSM got up from the couch and went barefoot into the kitchen to make some coffee. It was a few minutes after four a.m. Sand on the tile floor reminded him of the walk on the beach he and Marie had taken on New Year's Day. Since their earliest time together, a stroll before work or at sunset was time they both cherished. Sometimes they talked. Sometimes they enjoyed the silence. Always, though, they walked hand in hand.

They met eleven years ago. Marie and three girlfriends were visiting Oahu from the mainland. Shaw was assigned to the Honolulu field office, finishing his first year with USMS. On that fateful Sunday, Lanikai Beach drew them both with its isolated but accessible white powdery sand and calm waters protected by an offshore reef. Desiring time away from her boisterous posse, Marie caught a bus from Waikiki for the hour-and-a-half trip to Lanikai. Meanwhile, Shaw tagged along with a couple of guys from the office for a lazy day at the beach. Renting a kayak for an hour cruise out to one of the small uninhabited islands offshore, Marie battled shifting winds a few hundred yards from shore. Shaw, as her would-be savior, swam out to help. Never the strongest of swimmers, the DUSM was utterly exhausted by the time he reached the kayak. In the end, Marie did all of the "lifesaving," with Shaw holding on to the kayak as she paddled it back to the beach.

They took their first beach walk that day, replicated several hundred times since.

The iconoclastic painter and laconic deputy marshal made an unlikely pair. But beneath those superficial labels were deeper affinities; the couple complemented one another in a dozen different ways. A generous helping of Marie's impulsiveness softened Shaw's analytical side. Conversely, her exuberance could be alienating without his steadying hand. She didn't give a goddamn who looked askance at her involvement with a deputy with the US Marshals Service. He dared anyone to say an unkind word about the barefoot young woman from California who was a registered member of the Green Party. At the end of her scheduled vacation in Hawaii, Marie flew back home to Los Angeles and made every necessary arrangement to end her residence there. Within a month, she was back on Oahu and searching for a place to share with Shaw. A year later, the newly married couple moved to Maui and the house on Lia Place in Haiku.

Waiting for the coffee to brew and staring absently out the over-the-sink window, Terry Shaw recalled those first days on the island with Marie and wondered how he could *not* tell her about the phone call. From the beginning, they had shared every detail of their daily lives despite wildly divergent professions. He never embraced the stereotype of a hard-boiled cop who refused to divulge work issues to his spouse. More surprisingly, Marie welcomed Shaw's commentary regarding her art-work. They were partners in every way possible. Concealing "Joe's" coercionary phone call from her was inconceivable.

Shaw depended on his wife for her unconventional and creative problem-solving. Marie would know what to do. She could find a way out of his predicament that he wouldn't perceive in a thousand years of trying.

On the kitchen counter to his left, the coffee maker finished gurgling.

"I couldn't sleep, either," said Marie from the doorway.

Snapping from his reverie, Shaw turned.

Tell her.

Tell her now.

"I'm sorry," he said.

"Don't apologize. Wasn't your fault."

How could they possibly know if I only told her?

Shaw said, "Go back to bed. I'm going to pour a cup of coffee and take off. Won't hurt to get up to Fischer's a little early."

"Who could go through with a wedding ceremony on a day like this?"

Marie didn't have a political bone in her body. But her husband had confided in her a few stories of his protectee's imperious and sometimes capricious ways. On the other hand, Terry Shaw's wife was always a little relieved when his duties were limited to Fischer's protective detail instead of more dangerous responsibilities. Chasing down and appre-hending federal fugitives on the Hawaiian Islands could be dangerous work, and Shaw had fought enough gun battles in his USMS career to give his wife nightmares.

"It's another world over there, babe," he said, referring to the Fischer estate. "Perched on that rock, you can forget the rest of the planet exists."

"Exactly."

Shaw didn't want to argue the point. But, like everyone else in Maui's upcountry and north shore, the stress caused by the children's disappearance had eroded charitable feelings. Everyone was angry. A common and unspoken sentiment held that frivolity was forbidden until all of the kids were safe and sound. The inevitable invasion by intrusive news media on this second day of the crisis would only exacerbate these tensions.

I can't tell her.

This is my burden to bear.

With the realization that he couldn't take Marie into his confidence, Shaw experienced the pulverizing weight of his isolation. Of course, Anthony Gibbons's murder at the hands of the USSC police officer on his protection detail was front and center in Shaw's mind. And here he was, next in line to be smeared with the same infamous label: assassin.

"I should get going."

Marie approached, wordless, and offered her open arms. A grateful Terry Shaw welcomed her comforting embrace. If only he could remain in this familiar moment forever . . .

If only I didn't have to feel so fucking alone.

―――――――――

Hayley's first act of the new day was to empty the rest of the tequila into the bathroom sink. Only an inch or so remained in the bottle, but the gesture represented a significant decision: She would stop drinking. Today. For real. Though she understood that the positive effects of newfound sobriety would take time to reveal themselves, her push-ups, sit-ups, squats, and side-straddle hops that followed the ceremonious disposal of alcohol felt strong and purposeful. A page was conclusively turned.

Showered and dressed, Hayley stepped out the door at precisely five a.m. after securing her Glock in the belly band holster. Drive time to Fischer's estate on the northwest coast was twenty-five minutes. Not expecting to find any local cafés open at this early hour, Hayley assumed there would be coffee at the house.

My shit is straight . . .

Or was it?

Pausing on the walkway outside her hotel room, a self-aware Hayley sensed that her typical intensity and focus were lacking. A passionate appetite for action had been integral to all of her achievements since leaving home soon after high school graduation. Whether graduating from the US Army's earliest gender-integrated basic training, finding success as an amateur boxer, or with her improbable missions for the deeper state, Hayley was a locomotive of determination. Adversity couldn't stop her. Avoidance of pain was not a factor.

To jump-start that formidable power of concentration in critical moments, she had developed the ritual of gripping a sharp stone tightly enough to produce small lacerations in her hand. Only with that ceremonial sacrifice would she feel prepared.

There is nothing to fear. Blood has been drawn. Now I can fight.

Scanning the sidewalk for a suitable talisman, Hayley retrieved a jagged rock from the pavement next to her rental car's front tire. She closed her fist around the stone and squeezed it with all of her strength for twenty seconds, ignoring the stinging pain radiating from its jagged edges.

I'm back on track.

The time of heartache and loss is over.

I can do this.

Hayley wanted to believe that she had put all ambivalence and emotional numbness behind her. She craved to feel like herself again.

Unfolding her grip on the stone, the deeper state operative was stunned to see there were no cuts in the palm of her hand. She had failed to draw ritualistic first blood.

Fuck . . .

The sky still dark in the predawn, Terry Shaw turned right on Kauhikoa Road. A left would have taken him to Hana Highway, his usual route to make the fifty-minute drive to Fischer's home. But his early start afforded him some extra time and he wanted to drive by the mobile command set up in Makawao, the closest town to where the school bus was found. The detour would take him only a few minutes out of the way. Compelled to see for himself police efforts to resolve the crisis, Shaw desperately wanted to believe there was another way to bring the children home.

Besides the death of Anita Fischer.

After a few minutes of driving south, Shaw entered Makawao, a charming no-stoplight town of seventy-five hundred souls and the geographical center of Maui's upcountry. Though sunrise wasn't for another hour, Shaw found cars stopped two and three deep at the four-way intersection of Makawao and Baldwin Avenues. Police vehicles, private cars, and the expected television trucks lined the road. Pedestrians stood in worried clusters, waiting for the latest news. Shaw had never witnessed a similar level of activity in town, even on a Saturday afternoon in the high season.

He had heard that local law enforcement and the FBI had set up mobile command units at Makawao Park, the town's recreational facility formally known as the Eddie Tam Memorial Center. Once west of Baldwin Avenue, Shaw could see the glow from the floodlights that illuminated the parking lots and ball fields. Two Maui PD officers stood in the middle of the two-lane road directing traffic at the facility's entrance, where more pedestrians maintained their silent vigil.

As traffic slowed to barely ten miles per hour a hundred feet from the turn into the park, Shaw saw his friends Taylor and Janet Wilson standing in the scrum of anxious onlookers. The distraught parents of Bodhi and Finn had told Shaw and Marie the evening before about their multiple interviews with the investigators. As of midnight, the authorities offered no new information, leads, or motivation for the children's abduction.

Seeing Taylor and Janet again only a few hours later, Shaw assumed they had managed to find even less sleep than him. Though Janet's face was buried in her husband's shoulder and her expression obscured, Taylor Wilson's grief was on full display. The DUSM felt his stomach twist. He knew the truth . . . and the truth was torture.

Stuck in the jammed traffic at the turn for Makawao Park, Shaw heard his phone thrum on the passenger seat. Glancing down, he saw that he had received a new text from Joe.

Shouldn't you be heading straight to work?

Stunned, he realized that whoever was behind the conspiracy had somehow inserted malware into his phone, a device that was the nexus of Shaw's work and personal existence. They would know where he was, with whom he communicated, and what was said.

After a digital life span of precisely ten seconds, the text message disappeared entirely from the screen.

His phone vibrated again with the arrival of a second SMS.

Don't do anything stupid, Terry. ALWAYS keep this phone turned on and in your possession at ALL times.

The driver behind Shaw tapped his car horn to prompt some movement from him; the road ahead had cleared.

Shaw kept his foot on the brake, paralyzed by the latest communications from the children's abductors.

Anguished parents and other concerned local inhabitants standing on the shoulder of the road at the park entrance turned to stare at the stopped SUV.

Inside the vehicle, Shaw watched the second message disintegrate in a swarm of diminishing pixels . . . into nothingness.

Another SMS was transmitted. A photo this time, of the missing schoolchildren in a dimly lit, cavernous room. Alertly, Shaw pressed buttons on either side of the phone to capture the image. Navigating to his photos folder, he clicked on the saved screen capture and was frustrated to see the image was completely blurred out and utterly useless.

Then another text message arrived . . .

Do it TODAY, Terry. At the wedding. Kill her and the kids go home.

The driver behind hit his horn again, this time more impatiently. Shaw looked up from his phone, his focus shifting to the pedestrians gathered at the driveway entrance. His eyes locked on Taylor Wilson, whose two sons were in the photo's foreground that had briefly appeared on Shaw's phone. Janet Wilson also stared at him with a mixture of profound grief and desperate hope.

Was Shaw bringing them new information? Did he have answers not in his possession only a few hours earlier? In the kind of crisis that had engulfed the Wilsons, no cause for hope was too outlandish or unlikely. To abandon all faith was to pitch headlong into an infinite abyss of despair.

The cruel irony that he *did* have vital information regarding the children's disappearance did not escape Shaw. But sounding the alarm, however cautiously, was unthinkable. He could not imagine a reality in which he was responsible for those kids never coming home.

There's got to be another way.

Taking his foot off the brake and accelerating at a fast clip, Shaw proceeded west on Makawao Avenue, spurred by the devouring eyes of Taylor and Janet Wilson standing on the side of the road. Checking the rearview mirror, he was thankful that his friends had vanished in the gloom of the predawn.

CHAPTER 10

MATA POLICÍA

Bodhi woke from a dream of wing-surfing at Ho'okipa. Of the ocean and taking flight, propelled by wind and wave. The dream was so vivid he could almost feel the sting of salt water in his eyes, smell the Pacific brine. Waking in the subterranean chamber with seventeen other child hostages, the ever resilient fourteen-year-old shook off a moment of depression and focused again on getting his younger brother and the other kids out of their dire predicament.

The Wilson boys had claimed floor space close to the door. Given a shortage of sleeping pads, they fashioned a bed out of flattened cardboard from one of the food cartons. Most of the other kids slept at the rear of the long room, on the other side of the kitchen area. Makana elected to stay with the larger group, giving comfort to younger children. Three boys from Finn's class chose to sleep close to the Wilson brothers. Gilbert Reedy, the only adult among the hostages, had taken refuge under a small kitchen table that he draped with a blanket for a modicum of privacy.

Throughout the long night, the intermittent sobbing of the youngest kids had awoken Bodhi. Finn, of course, slept soundly. He stirred now, though, somehow sensing his older brother's wakefulness. With eyes opened, the ten-year-old pushed himself halfway up to a sitting position and looked around the room, then turned back to Bodhi.

"Still here?" he asked.

"Still here."

Finn rolled over on his back, folding his hands beneath his head.

He asked, "What time is it?"

"Not sure. Feels like six o'clock."

"What does six o'clock feel like?"

Bodhi was an infinitely patient big brother. With a sibling as precocious as Finn, patience was a necessity.

"It feels like . . . this."

Finn smiled.

"No, *this* feels like Christmas morning."

"Seriously?" asked Bodhi.

Nodding, the younger Wilson boy said, "Kinda. In a way. Know what I mean?"

"Uh, not really."

Though unfailingly optimistic, Bodhi couldn't see how their dire circumstances compared to his favorite holiday.

Finn said, "When something really bad happens in the movies, parents who are fighting or getting a divorce *always* stay together by the end."

"Hate to break it to you, little brother, but this isn't a movie."

"Just wait and see. Mom and Dad are a *lock*."

"Well, we have to get out of here first, right?"

"I guess so." Then, with more conviction, Finn added, "Yeah. Let's get out of here first."

The other kids near them had roused themselves.

"I'm hungry," said one.

"I gotta pee," said another.

The third boy was too sleepy to say anything.

To Finn, Bodhi said, "Take care of these guys, okay? I'm going to talk to Gekko."

THE DEVIL YOU KNOW

The younger Wilson boy nodded and led his three buddies away. Bodhi could see that the group at the other end of the chamber was stirring, too. He caught Makana's eye and gestured to her.

They met in the kitchen area.

"How'd it go?" Bodhi asked.

Makana shrugged, valiantly keeping up a tough facade. "The younger kids are having a tough time. They're homesick . . . and scared."

Bodhi gestured toward Gilbert Reedy's lair. "Let's talk to him."

"Sure. Good idea."

Together, they squatted, their faces only inches from the cloth curtain. Bodhi rapped his knuckles on the tabletop.

"Gilbert?"

For a moment, there was no response. Then . . .

"Go away, kid."

The bus driver's voice was hoarse, shredded by the last twenty-four hours of stark terror.

Bodhi said, "Gilbert, we need to do something to get out of this place. *You* need to do something."

"I don't have to do anything," said the man hiding under the table.

"C'mon, Gilbert," cajoled Makana. "Just come out and talk to us."

"C'mon, Gilbert," repeated Bodhi.

After a brief pause, the bus driver crawled out from his hiding place. Eyes hollow, gaze fixed, and facial muscles in a kind of pre-death rigor mortis, Reedy was suffering the stress of the hostages' collective ordeal poorly.

The two teenagers confronting him exchanged a worried look. Should they have just allowed Gekko to remain in his curtained hidey-hole?

The role of hostage was a bad fit for Reedy, who avoided physical confrontation from the earliest age. An only child of husband-and-wife dentists, Reedy came to Maui from gray, rainy Portland, Oregon, ostensibly to surf, but possessed neither the skills to be any good nor the diligence to develop them. Until the masked men commandeered his bus, he spent the majority of his waking hours smoking pot and playing video games with a few other amiable fuckups like himself. An inevitable repudiation by his frustrated parents required the minimal salary provided by driving a Sullivan Academy school bus.

"What?" Reedy asked sullenly of the two teenagers before him. He followed that question with a glance toward the younger kids, whose proximity (and youth) seemed a burden to him.

"These guys are the real deal, Gilbert," said Makana.

"All the more reason to stay under this table," responded the bus driver.

Keeping his voice low, Bodhi said, "Look, we can't assume the police are going to rescue us."

"What exactly do you propose that I do?"

"Not *you*, Gilbert," said the older Wilson boy. "*We.*"

Makana looked at her friend in surprise.

Bodhi was calm but emphatic, in total command of his emotions. There was no sign of a nervous grin or misplaced confidence. He had the same mindset when paddling out into chest-high breakers or before an algebra exam—respect for the challenge at hand and a resolve to meet it head-on.

"We'll make our prison a fortress."

Saturnino didn't like the way Taliban had been watching him since the school bus takeover, like a half-starved dog gawking at a slab of red meat. He worried his nemesis would kill him on the spot if not for Oscar Carranza's ironfisted control over the unit. The Suárez brothers gave Saturnino a difficult time, too, but limited their abuse to verbal cruelties. Hector Lozano's intentions came from a much different place, as if he wanted to annihilate the younger man.

All but Javier Suárez, outside standing guard at the bomb shelter entrance, were gathered in the large living room of the main house. Carranza sat at the long dining table opposite the kitchen doorway, tapping the keyboard of a tablet computer. Diego Suárez occupied an easy chair beside a television, scrolling aimlessly on his phone. Lozano sat in the middle section of a couch, laying claim to the entire piece of furniture and daring anyone to join him.

Saturnino had entered the room from the kitchen moments earlier, bringing in a tray of sandwiches he'd prepared. Cooking for the others was yet another of his humiliating duties. True to form, Lozano watched the younger man's every move, forcing air through his nostrils like a frustrated bull. Only Saturnino knew the reason for Taliban's antagonism toward him. Though Lozano had shown no interest in the younger man while both were in the army, that dynamic dramatically changed once Saturnino joined Cartel del Oeste's ranks. Lozano made his furtive desires evident one rainy night in a Morelia safe house and was rebuffed by a frightened Saturnino.

To breathe a single word of the encounter was unimaginable. Not even Carranza could save the newcomer if he made such a mortifying accusation.

Lozano's constant glowering was blatant enough to be noticed by the others. Glancing up from his phone, Diego gave Taliban a quizzical look. *"What's your problem, man? Has it been too long since you last killed someone?"* To Saturnino, he said in reference to Lozano, *"You would think he had sated his thirst in Las Tinajas."*

Saturnino found the younger Suárez brother's barb amusing, but refrained from smiling. He didn't want to think about Las Tinajas. Now was too soon to joke about what had occurred there.

Lozano said, *"As if it was any of your business, cocksucker."*

Diego's propensity for jokes may have seemed to diminish his menace, but the number of dead bodies left in his wake would suggest otherwise. Lozano's vulgar insult was an unforgivable transgression. The cartel gunman could not let such an affront pass without a response.

The light went out in Diego's eyes as his hand moved to his waistband, where he kept a Glock.

"Shall I make it my business, brother?"

Both men leaped to their feet, drawing their weapons, stopped short only by a sharp command from Carranza. *"Enough!"*

Lozano gestured toward Saturnino.

"This one is soft, Commander! He froze on the bus. He's useless!"

The other men's eyes fell on the newest recruit like scalding water. Saturnino realized that a critical moment in his nascent career as a hired gun was at hand. Carranza's approval was as important as having a heartbeat.

Simultaneously earning Lozano's eternal enmity was an unfortunate consequence.

Saturnino said, *"Commander, this is an obvious lie. I followed orders to the letter!"*

Carranza relished his role of ultimate authority, though his stern expression revealed no pleasure. His control over other men was more satisfying than sex or food. How many men could boast of having the absolute obedience of hardened killers?

The former army sergeant regarded Saturnino through hooded eyes. He had heard his phone on the table rattle with the arrival of a text message, but kept his gaze locked on the largely untested sicario, the one the others called Barbie.

"We'll see who is lying soon enough."

Lozano appeared satisfied with Carranza's response. By Taliban's reckoning, their commander could do no wrong.

Diego, not one to hold a grudge, sat back down and resumed gazing into his phone. *"A bad liar only needs to be a good killer, eh, kid?"*

In no mood for jokes, Saturnino did not respond. Leaving the platter of sandwiches on the coffee table, he retreated into the kitchen.

Their internal divisions settled for the moment, Carranza glanced down at his phone and saw the notification of a text received. Opening WhatsApp, he read a message composed in Spanish.

Hello, Oscar, this is Joe.

Carranza texted his response. Sign?

The King is dead.

The former army sergeant had no more awareness of "Joe's" identity than Terry Shaw. His client was nothing more than a series of these SMS messages, a dozen or so of the thirty trillion sent over the Internet every year. The texts could be originating in China or from the house next door. Who was to say?

He answered with the countersign. "Long live the King."

Joe texted, How are things there?

Good. Awaiting instructions.

Is your location secure?

Yes, answered Carranza.

Good. You have the required supplies?

Yes. We have all that we need.

Your men are trustworthy? Adequate to the job?

Carranza glanced over his shoulder toward the kitchen door, where he heard Saturnino cleaning up. Yes. Of course.

Good. We are doubling the money we agreed to pay you.

OK.

Is it? I must know that you are satisfied in every possible way.

Yes. We're fine here.

Good. Keep your phone close.

I will.

The pockmarked sicario stared at his phone, waiting for the next message from Joe. Exhibiting this deference was a trial. He was unused to subservience. Even back home in Mexico, Carranza was known for his refusal to exhibit undue admiration for the cartel's bosses. At an early age, the former army sergeant learned that respect, like love, was a commodity too easily traded. But something about these messages had unnerved him. Joe's anonymity and elusive quality had rendered him godlike. Untouchable.

Several seconds passed. Then . . .

There's something I need you to do right now. Is that okay?

Carranza responded immediately.

Yes.

―――――――――

Javier Suárez stood up from a folding chair in front of the bomb shelter's door. The rest of the kidnapping crew approached at a fast walk. Oscar Carranza was a step or two in the lead, with Hector Lozano on his heels. Diego and Saturnino Pérez brought up the rear.

All wore grim, now-is-no-time-for-fuckery expressions.

All were armed.

"What's up?" asked Javier Suárez, cradling an AK-12 rifle.

Carranza stopped at the door and gestured at it with the FN semi-automatic in his right hand. Known colloquially as a *mata policía* ("cop killer") for the armor-piercing 5.7×28-millimeter ammunition it fires, the Belgium-manufactured Five-seveN was El Gruñón's signature weapon. Having put a bullet in the heads of at least three police officers back home, the gun in Carranza's hand had more than lived up to its street nickname.

"Open it," the former army sergeant ordered his man as he rolled the watch balaclava down over his face.

While the other men similarly masked themselves, Javier Suárez inserted a key into the two heavy-duty padlocks and pushed on the imposing four-inch-thick cement and metal door.

The door opened only an inch or two and then was stuck, clearly barricaded from the inside. Diego stepped forward to help his brother, and together they dislodged the several chairs and boxes the hostages had placed in front of the door.

The schoolchildren cowered at the far end of the narrow room, with the oldest kids positioned as their vanguard. Carranza led the masked gunmen inside and almost instantly registered that the sole adult was missing. Barely pausing, he kicked the draped kitchen table up and over, revealing the crouching bus driver.

Unsheathing a large knife, Lozano stepped forward and yanked the bus driver upright by his hair. Maintaining his grip on a mewling adult hostage, he thrust the knife handle-first toward Saturnino.

Lozano said, *"Barbie does it."*

The youngest children were wailing. The older boy took a step forward, his fists balled.

"No!"

Carranza pivoted, putting the end of the FN's barrel an inch from the teenager's forehead. He didn't need to say a word for the boy to back off.

Saturnino felt the others' eyes on him. This was his test. Did he have the balls? Was he a man who could kill on command without hesitation?

The shrill cries of the children were like the seabirds taunting him.

His hands stayed down at his sides.

Without a second's delay, Lozano brought the knife up in a sickening flash and sliced off the whimpering man's left ear as if cutting a leafy strawberry top, all captured on the cell phone held by Diego Suárez.

The children yowled as blood bubbled from the open wound and down the side of their bus driver's head.

For a brief moment, the man didn't recognize his own maiming. In those few moments, he only heard a disconcerting and wholly unfamiliar gurgle of fluids inside his skull.

Of a void where one shouldn't exist.

Then came the pain, and he screamed, too.

CHAPTER 11

LOZANO'S STORY

EL SOL DE MORELIA

Monday, March 28, 2022

20 people die in armed attack at illegal cockpit in Zinapécuaro Single gunman approached the unlicensed event to attack the attendees

*T*he Attorney General of the State of Michoacán reported that during the night of last Sunday there was an armed attack at a cockfight pit in the municipality of Zinapécuaro, which caused the death of 20 people, so far. According to the agency, the incident occurred at a venue in the community of Las Tinajas.

"At this time, personnel from the Michoacán Prosecutor's Office are traveling to Las Tinajas, municipality of Zinapécuaro, to investigate a report of aggression perpetrated during the illegal cockfight," the agency wrote through its official networks.

The Prosecutor's Office specified that there were 16 men and 3 women who died from the rain of lead at the clandestine event, while another woman lost her life hours later in a hospital. It was reported that illegal rooster fights were taking place at the site of the attack.

Regarding the attack, the Prosecutor's Office indicated that one subject armed with a semiautomatic rifle arrived at the scene and fired at the people attending the illegal event. The attacker escaped in a vehicle whose characteristics have not yet been identified.

On the other hand, personnel from the institution located more than 100 7.62-caliber shell casings, which were collected at different points in the building, and secured 15 vehicles at the scene.

State and federal security elements implemented an operation in the town of Las Tinajas in Zinapécuaro after the murder of 20 people recorded this Sunday night, said the Ministry of Public Security (SSP).

In a statement, the unit indicated that they intensified security measures to find the whereabouts of the man responsible for the violent acts. A spokesman for SSP said he believed the attack was instigated by "revenge" by one cell of Cartel del Oeste against another.

"It was a massacre of one criminal group by one sadistic criminal," said President Andrés Manuel López Obrador in a news conference.

The SSP, the Secretary of National Defense, and the National Guard maintain land patrols and surveillance operations in the municipality and its surroundings.

In addition, in the neighborhoods, towns, roads, and highways of Zinapécuaro, they carry out the same operation to deter any crime. In the area where the events were recorded, the Michoacán Police guard the area with the State Attorney General's Office (FGR).

The unit reported that other attendees of the illegal cockfight were injured, but were taken to hospitals in the region, while the Expert Services Unit carried out corresponding investigations.

This is the second massacre recorded this year in Michoacán.

CHAPTER 12

FROSTY

Watching the wedding ceremony—held outdoors with the Pacific as its backdrop and twenty or so family and friends in attendance—Hayley guessed that Anita Fischer's white chiffon, off-the-shoulder dress cost more than she earned in a year. Did it irritate her that the salt-and-peppery groom pulled off both "carefree" and "dapper" in a short-sleeve linen shirt and matching cotton trousers? Or that Fischer requested guests and staff alike to wear white? Only she and the DUSMs on the protection detail, including Terry Shaw, were breaking the color protocol by adhering to their customary chinos or jeans and dark-colored polo shirts. Hayley had overheard one of the young caterers complaining about a last-minute scramble to find white pants.

She felt the welcome glow again, having ferreted out a bottle of scotch in the kitchen pantry. Three long, hard pulls and a deliciously warm sensation of potency surged through Hayley. Gone was the pain in her head that had throbbed to a persistent beat. Jangled nerves and jittery muscles had calmed the fuck down. And the sheen of sweat that had coated her entire body since her latest attempt to go cold turkey? Evaporated.

Again in alcohol's warm embrace, she could barely recall her hours-old resolution to quit.

Standing at the porch railing to keep a close eye on the Maui-style nuptials below, Hayley felt her body becoming hers again. To stay strong, however, she estimated a return to the pantry was needed in an hour or so.

Hayley focused anew on the task at hand.

Stay frosty. Eyes peeled.

Despite this effort to concentrate, fantasies involving alcohol intruded on her consciousness, unwanted but mouthwateringly pleasant. As the bride and groom exchanged vows within her earshot, Hayley imagined she was at Fox & Hounds, a favorite dive bar back in Washington. She could almost hear the delicious rattle of a single, large ice cube in the tumbler filled nearly to the brim with reposado, feel the sting in her throat as she took a sip, and the bloom of fire that would envelop her every cell.

Maybe that pantry visit would need to be made in the next thirty minutes.

———————

What are you waiting for? Do it.

Joe had sent the text a few minutes earlier while Shaw was up at the gate checking in with local law enforcement stationed there. Reading the message, the DUSM felt as if he'd been gut-punched. They were watching him. Here at the Fischer estate. *Now.* Shaw was currently positioned under a Norfolk pine fifty yards from the ceremony. Only Hayley Chill, the interloper from DC, ignored his warning to stay out of sight and remained obtrusively positioned on the porch. What was she trying to prove, anyway? Her excessive vigilance—becoming more evident by the minute—struck Shaw as extreme even by FBI standards.

Having been declared man and wife, the newlyweds kissed enthusiastically as the officiating minister in a white Makapu'u Hawaiian shirt looked on with a benevolent grin. The seated guests applauded and hollered their approval as Shaw briefly entertained a homicidal fantasy. Who could stop him if he left his position under the tree, walked to where his protectee and her new husband were being ushered to a dramatic overlook by a professional photographer, drew his service weapon, and put two slugs in her head? Hayley Chill? Would he then put the gun to his head or wait for the FBI agent to finish the job?

Screw that.

There had to be another way forward besides a Hobson's choice between killing his protectee and the death of eighteen schoolchildren. A third option *had* to exist. But if he somehow blew it—by making the wrong move or spooking the kidnappers—how would he ever be able to live with the deaths of those kids on his conscience?

———————

Poking her head inside the door to ascertain the location of the guests and catering personnel, Hayley felt a small measure of relief. Everyone but Fischer, her new husband, Lachlan Morris, and the USMS protection detail were safely contained within the confines of the home's first floor. Unconvinced by the thoroughness of Shaw's vetting of guests and temporary staff members, Hayley preferred to keep eyes on everyone. She couldn't shake the paranoia induced by Anthony Gibbons's strangulation at the hands of a United States Supreme Court police officer.

The most trusted are those who must be most feared.

Turning around and walking to the porch rail again, Hayley saw Terry Shaw approach from the tree line on the west side of the property. What good were the USMS deputies positioned so far away from their protectee? If one of the guests or caterers pulled a well-hidden knife or gun, how would they stop an attack from a hundred yards out? Emboldened by the alcohol she had consumed in the pantry, Hayley pretended not to hear Shaw when he instructed the protection detail to stay out of sight during the ceremony—despite the request coming from Fischer herself.

Good thing, too, because how else could she have seen the gun if she wasn't alert and doing her job?

———————

Having spent more than six months every year for the past decade in Mexico, Joe Gunn was entirely comfortable in most any situation south of the border. Yet, despite that familiarity—which included a reliable fluency in Spanish—he gripped the steering wheel of his rented Mercedes with an unconsciously white-knuckled anxiety. His apprehension had nothing to do with the fact that he was about to sit down with Rafael Hernández, one of the chief lieutenants of a notorious drug cartel boss; in truth, he enjoyed the company of remorseless men with a propensity for extreme and sadistic violence. Instead, Gunn's trepidation came from a more mundane source; it wasn't every day that a vicious drug cartel entrusted you with the secure transportation of a quarter billion dollars of its money.

The drive to San Andrés Coru from the airport in Morelia—where he had arrived by a Learjet 60 chartered by one of the dozens of shell companies in Oakvale Pharmaceuticals' control—was estimated to take two hours. The road was good and Gunn could take the rented Mercedes to triple-digit speeds when traffic allowed; his contacts had assured him that local police needn't be a worry.

The landscape between Morelia and Pátzcuaro was arid and haphazardly developed. Farther west, however, Federal Highway 14D was more scenic, with rolling, forested hills and well-tended ranches. The air that poured through the open driver's window was redolent with the scent of Michoacán pine and reminded Gunn of his native Bastrop County in Texas. Once free of the clutter of trailer-hauling semis festooned with Spanish-language advertisements and Mexican corporate logos, the indifferently handsome, middle-aged Gunn could almost imagine he was driving south on State Highway 71 bound for La Grange.

San Andrés Coru, a town of twenty-five hundred, spread across the forested valley to the west of the highway. A narrower road—a hundred feet beyond a ramshackle tire repair shop and under the pedestrian bridge—dropped down into the center of town, defined primarily by two small grocery stores. Driving the length of the community took less than a minute before Gunn was once again motoring through an undulating countryside of woods and avocado farms. The road was more potholes than actual pavement and barely wide enough for the produce trucks that frequented it. A cemetery with decaying aboveground crypts served as a reminder that the afterlife was, indeed, little more than a disintegrating eyesore.

At half past four in January, the sun was nearly set.

Obscured by brush and its macadam all but obliterated, the turn-off from the farm road was easy to miss. Gunn put the Mercedes SUV into reverse and came back to it. Three light-duty pickups blocked access twenty feet up the entry road, and the armed men standing guard were sound evidence that he had arrived at his destination. Gunn pulled in behind the last truck. Three gunmen came to his window with weapons leveled.

Handing over his passport to one of the men, the North American said in his journeyman Spanish, *"I am Joseph Gunn. Mr. Hernández is expecting me."*

The frowning cartel gunman carefully compared the passport photo to the Mercedes' driver. Satisfied, he gave the document back to Gunn and signaled to the other men to allow the visitor to pass.

Descending the hillside, Gunn saw that the avocado orchards suffered from severe neglect. Several trees had died, with native grasses and vines reaching their lower branches. Farm machinery rusted where long-disappeared ranch hands had abandoned it. Gunn passed ten bodies in a field as he crossed the small valley and climbed a small rise opposite, the heavily rutted farm road snaking its way toward the main house. He barely glanced in the corpses' direction.

On the home's elevated patio, men with guns and military-style combat gear waited.

Gunn was searched, of course, as was his rental car. Marched up steps leading to the compound, he sensed the cultivated valley behind him and, farther east, the sleepy town of San Andrés Coru. All of that was in the past. The present was entirely different. Gunn had entered another existence—as if set adrift on a dark and uncharted ocean—and was wholly at the mercy of its ancient forces. Still, the North American did not feel offended or repulsed. On the contrary, Gunn marveled at the essential, raw human inclinations that could foment such a place.

My God, this is true beauty.

The number of armed men present in the compound suggested to Gunn that the derelict avocado farm was the cartel's temporary command post. The camp would exist here for three or four days and then move on, leaving dozens of putrefying bodies in its wake. A commotion on the other side of the main house—missing all of its windows and doors, the roof half caved in—could be heard from the front-side patio. Through the blasted-out openings in the walls, Gunn saw a large group of gunmen gathered in a debris-strewn central courtyard.

His escorts wordlessly signaled to him. Following them as they walked through the ruined farmhouse, Gunn gestured forward, toward the gathering of men, and asked, *"What's this?"*

"Hostages from an arcade in Uruapan, controlled by Los Viagras," said the gunman next to him, referring to a rival, upstart cartel.

"So . . . ?"

"So now the games begin," the gunman said with a grin that wouldn't look out of place on a Boy Scout.

They stopped on the outer edge of the crowd that formed a rough circle at the courtyard's center. Two hostages stood in the middle of the makeshift arena, one Mexican and one foreigner. Both hostages showed signs of severe beatings and faced each other from a dozen feet apart. The shouting of the spectators made it difficult for anyone—hostages and cartel gunmen alike—to hear an obese man playing the role of referee.

Unslinging his AK, the self-designated judge fired a burst into the air over the heads of the mob.

"Silence, assholes!"

The effort won some measure of quiet from the spectators. Gunn, wearing a business casual ensemble of dark khakis and a matching short-

sleeve linen shirt, looked to the other side of the spectator circle and recognized his diminutive host, Rafael Hernández, standing on an elevated
planter with four sunglass-wearing bodyguards. The fiftyish cartel hon-
cho caught sight of his guest among the ragtag crowd of gunmen draped
in military garb and nodded his greetings. Gunn smiled winningly in
return as if seeing a client across a hotel lobby hosting a business conference.

Having won the attention of the boisterous audience of gunmen, the
referee gestured to the ground and addressed the two terrified hostages.

"Combatants, choose your weapons!"

At his feet was a flaming antique gas blowtorch and a lightweight
chain saw of recent manufacture. The crowd hollered and laughed, fully
anticipating the macabre spectacle to come.

For Gunn's benefit, his escort explained, *"They fight to the death. The
winner is offered the position of sicario."*

"And if he refuses the offer?" asked Gunn.

"Tortured until dead," the gunman said with an indifferent shrug.

The hostages regarded the demented gladiatorial weapons in disbelief, drawing verbal abuse from the raucous mob. Looking down at
the scene from his perch, Hernández clapped in apparent appreciation.
Gunn was intrigued. He had never before witnessed a fight to the death
between a chain saw and an antique blowtorch. Without invitation, he
pushed his way through the throng to the first row of spectators.

The sandy-haired foreigner at the arena's center looked to the spectators and locked his gaze on the incongruent sight of Joe Gunn, who
possessed the good looks and snappy attire of a syndicated game show
host on a tee box at the Riviera Country Club.

"Help me," he said plaintively, his accented English betraying Australian origins.

Gunn smiled as the fat referee stepped forward and delivered a slap
to the Australian's cheek.

"Choose, you dog!"

Still, the Aussie hesitated, staring at the chain saw and blowtorch
in horror. The other hostage had gathered his wits enough to under-

stand he might increase his odds of survival by taking the first choice. He stooped to retrieve the chain saw from the ground, an "in-tree," gas-powered Stihl with a relatively compact fourteen-inch guide bar. The battered Mexican revealed his status as a common laborer by starting the tool and revving its engine without the need for instruction.

The baffled Aussie squatted beside the blowtorch, a one-hundred-year-old brass Clayton & Lambert with a pint-size canister reservoir. Tarnished and dust-covered, the device's operation defied him. After assessing that the priming flame had been lit long enough to heat the burner assembly, one of the gunmen knelt down and pumped the pressure into the brass tank. He then indicated the turning knob protruding from one end of the burner unit.

"Here. Turn here," the gunman said in heavily accented English.

Twisting the knob, the Australian hostage accomplished the most immediate task; a blue flame burst eight inches from the opposite end of the brass nozzle with a miniature roar. He took hold of the blowtorch's wooden grip handle and stood erect.

Gunn watched as the two hostages circled each other, armed with their respective weapons. This period of inactivity allowed for the spontaneous betting that erupted among the spectators. Favorites emerged and most money seemed to be on the Mexican hostage, his Stihl chain saw deemed the more effective weapon in close-quarters combat. Or perhaps the Australian's tentative nature swung the odds in his opponent's favor. It made no difference to Gunn. He elected not to gamble on the fight's outcome, satisfied enough with the novel brutality of the contest.

The two combatants alternated feints, using these early moments to become more accustomed to their respective weapons. Then, sensing his opponent's reluctance, the Mexican struck first, lunging at the Aussie and delivering a glancing but still devastating blow to the sandy-haired man's torso. Blood gushed from the gash inflicted by the revving chain saw and soaked the Australian's filthy T-shirt. But coming so close to his adversary opened the Mexican to a counterattack and the Aussie seized that opportunity, sweeping the orange and blue flame across the other man's right arm.

With both combatants wounded, it was clear to all present that the contest would be brief; neither hostage could afford more delay and risk total incapacitation. Emboldened, the Australian waved the blowtorch wildly in his opponent's direction—dodging the Mexican's thrusts with the chain saw all the while—and managed to scorch the other man on his face, chest, and upper legs.

From his vantage point in the first row of spectators, Gunn could see droplets of gasoline leaking from the blowtorch's rickety plunger. He noted with fascination that, as the tide shifted unmistakably in the Australian's favor, the sandy-haired combatant took some relish in inflicting injury to his opponent. Having sustained several horrific burns, the Mexican was fighting a purely defensive battle against the increasingly aggressive Australian.

Slashed across both hands by the blowtorch's hissing flame, the Mexican could no longer keep hold of the chain saw and he dropped it to the ground. He fell to his knees and slapped at his burning clothes with already ruined hands.

"May God save me!"

Some in the mob of gunmen implored the Australian to finish off his opponent. In a frenzy, the sandy-haired foreigner was happy to oblige his supporters. Standing over the defeated man, the Aussie raised the brass, fire-spewing blowtorch in preparation for delivering a final, prolonged application of three-thousand-degree flame to the Mexican hostage.

The plunger's antique seal, having failed with all of the jostling, released the reservoir's contents on its user's head, igniting in the next second, and transforming the presumed victor into a human tiki torch. Frantic to extinguish the conflagration that engulfed the upper half of his body, the Australian staggered in one direction and then another—arms flapping like a flightless bird—before falling to the ground and writhing in agony.

With singed hands, the Mexican combatant grabbed his weapon and stood. Revving the Stihl's motor, he bent over the burning man and ended his misery by chainsawing off his head.

Gunmen settled their bets. The dazed Mexican, horridly scorched but no longer a hostage, was led away for much-needed medical attention. Having enjoyed himself immensely, Gunn felt a need nonetheless to attend to business and pushed his way through the lingering throng to greet his host. He was due back in Los Angeles by nine thirty to pick up his daughter from water polo practice in Thousand Oaks.

Hernández climbed down from the concrete planter and extended a hand to his visitor from the north, saying in nearly accent-free English, "Welcome, Mr. Gunn."

"Joe," he corrected the cartel boss. "Good to finally meet you in person, Commander."

"How did you find our little entertainment? Better than Netflix?"

"I'm more of a HBO Max man myself, but yes, just spectacular," said Gunn with the easy grin that had gotten him far in life.

"You can understand why our leader can't be here to meet you? Your Justice Department has been extraordinarily aggressive in their pursuit of 'El Mencho.' I myself haven't sat down with him face-to-face in six months."

"Not a problem, my friend. I spoke with him on the phone just yesterday."

"Good," said Hernández, gesturing. "Follow me."

Trailed by the bodyguards, the cartel boss and Gunn walked across the courtyard and climbed crumbling stairs to a second, smaller house situated on a higher embankment. This structure was in better condition than the main house, with nearly all its windows intact. Hernández led the way inside, where underlings had scavenged a few pieces of dusty furniture for his use. A satchel was open on the wooden desk, along with a laptop and satellite phone. Hernández sat in the chair in front of the leather bag. Gunn took a seat across the desk from him.

The cartel man retrieved a small device from the satchel and placed it on the table between them. Black and roughly the size of a car remote, the hardware wallet stored private keys necessary for accessing online cryptocurrency accounts in an offline environment.

"Last I checked, two hundred and seventy-four million dollars in Bitcoin, as discussed," said Hernández.

"And you leave it unguarded?"

"Here is safe, my friend. 'Here' is safer than you can possibly imagine."

His four bodyguards arrayed at all four corners of the room seemed strong evidence of the fact.

Gunn said, "The other matter, then."

Hernández shrugged. "Our men are not performing to your satisfaction?"

"No problems so far. My concern is their ability to keep their mouths shut after the operation is completed."

The cartel leader's demeanor mimicked the compassion of a well-compensated undertaker.

"Truly, on the island they have found what will be their eternal paradise."

Wanting absolute clarity, the North American asked, "Carranza and his men will never leave Hawaii?"

Hernández nodded. "An asset is already in place to make their 'retirement' a certainty."

Gunn looked askance toward the bodyguards.

"No need to worry, friend. My sons are unquestionably loyal."

Only with a second look did Gunn recognize the physical resemblance of the four young bodyguards with their father. Satisfied by these assurances, he reached across the table to take the hardware wallet.

Hernández stopped Gunn's hand before it reached the device.

He said, "No matter what form this money takes—crypto, heroin, or bank shares—it's still El Mencho's money, yes?"

Gunn strategically deployed his trademark grin once again. "Always and forever."

He was in the car and speeding east toward Morelia five minutes later.

—————————

Hayley Chill glanced in Shaw's direction as he approached the steps leading up to the front porch, then returned her gaze to the bride and groom posing for photographs precipitously close to the cliff's edge. Three steps backward and it was a hundred-foot drop to the rocks below. In Hayley's opinion, that proximity to accidental fall was an unnecessary risk. And why did the male photographer continually glance in her direction? She had noticed the man—mid-thirties, bearded, exceptionally physically fit given his profession—furtively checking her out since he had arrived at the estate.

The dread she had felt within her earliest minutes on the island— ignited by news of the local schoolchildren's abduction—still smoldered. Throughout her life, Hayley's intuitions had provided an infallible early-warning system of impending disaster. Ignoring these hunches, she learned, was unwise. Though the scene at Justice Fischer's home could not have seemed more harmonious on the island's Instagram-worthy northwest shore, the deeper state operative sensed that danger was close.

Or was she being paranoid? Second-guessing herself was an unfamiliar and potentially debilitating obstacle to doing her job. Hayley was desperate to hold her center.

She focused again on the newlyweds and their photographer, wiping her consciousness clean of distracting thoughts.

Stay frosty!

"Are you okay?"

Terry Shaw's voice drifted up to her from the bottom step. She would've looked at him—answered with some taciturn quip—were it not for catching sight of the outline of a pistol's grip underneath the back flap of the male photographer's jacket.

Keeping her eyes on the photographer, Hayley said, "I'm good."

Reading her gaze and its direction, Shaw looked over his shoulder to where Fischer and her new husband were posing for the squatting wedding photographer.

"What?" he asked, not reading anything amiss in the mundane scene. With no response, Shaw prompted, "Hayley?"

She didn't hear the first question. Not the second one, either.

The photographer stood and simultaneously pushed back his jacket, retrieving the object that had aroused Hayley's alert suspicion.

Taking hold of the black pistol grip, the dark-suited man swung his hand around toward the newlyweds.

Hayley was sure now. She knew what she was seeing.

"Gun!"

She flew down the steps, past a startled Terry Shaw, and ran the fifty feet across the yard to near the cliff's edge, bringing down the startled photographer with a flying tackle that nearly took them both over the precipice. Spreading her body across the man, Hayley immobilized his gun hand in her vice grip. Fischer and Morris, alarmed by Hayley's shouted warning and violent takedown of the photographer, had retreated half the distance to the house.

Shaw was on the scene within seconds. His perspective standing over Hayley and the photographer gave him an unobstructed sight of the pistol grip–mounted, small-body Sony camera in the man's right hand.

"What is wrong with you? Someone get this maniac off me!" shouted the wedding photographer, a world-class amateur bodybuilder who admittedly got much more than he had bargained for when stealing flirtatious glances at the blond, blue-eyed FBI agent throughout the day.

Shaw bent over and tried to extricate the man from Hayley's hold.

"Let him go, Hayley."

She maintained her control over the photographer, lost in the conviction of her scrambled perceptions. Convinced the threat was real.

"It's a camera, for Christ's sake! Not a gun," said Shaw. He had no problem taking the camera from the photographer's loosened grip and brought it into Hayley's sight line.

"See? Only a *camera*."

She did see now. Pushing off the man, Hayley sat on the ground, her hands laying purposelessly in her lap. Grass stains on her khaki pants were the only badges of her effort. Those and her abject humiliation.

Staring at the photo equipment that Shaw held up for her—and an alarmed Anita Fischer—to see, Hayley felt nothing.

CHAPTER 13

THIS MUST BE THE PLACE

Do it.

Shaw ignored the text. Following Hayley Chill's eviction from the property, the head of Fischer's protection detail could momentarily pretend her unprovoked attack on the newlyweds' photographer was the worst crisis he would face that day. Was she inebriated? Shaw wasn't sure. But, somewhat grotesquely, he was almost thankful that Chill's bizarre behavior had the effect of briefly displacing a much graver anxiety.

A second text, received three minutes after the first, was a sufficient reminder of his awful dilemma.

Do it. NOW.

Shaw was up at the road, having just watched Hayley roar off in her rental car less than five minutes after her humiliating conduct.

What are you waiting for? Get down there and KILL HER.

Jesus Christ!

The DUSM glanced toward the scrum of local law enforcement and fellow deputy US marshals stationed at the entry gate. Just how close was he being watched? And by whom? One thing for sure was that Shaw

couldn't afford to ignore Joe's texts any longer, given a third that immediately followed the first two . . .

NOW, Terry. Or we start killing kids NOW.

———————

Down below, at the house, the party was in full swing. The just-married
couple, all smiles and kisses, were roundly feted by their more than
slightly buzzed guests. While Lachlan Morris was indeed one happy
groom—no doubt, his celebratory mood fueled by several flutes of
Larmandier-Bernier Terre de Vertus brut—Anita Fischer's happiness
was both sober and profound. Whether receiving a steady stream of
heartfelt congratulations from guests or dancing with her new husband,
the Supreme Court justice radiated joy. Few would easily associate this
new bride with the stern woman draped in a black robe who sat on the
nation's highest court of law.

Like the three other deputy marshals positioned throughout the first
floor, Terry Shaw endeavored to keep his presence as discreet as possible.
Standing next to the stairs leading up to the primary bedroom, he could
keep eyes on every guest inside the house. DUSMs were stationed either
on the porch or in the kitchen and dining room areas, which were popu-
lated solely by service and staff. Unlike the other men on the protection
detail, Shaw was on high alert . . . for all the wrong reasons.

He felt his phone vibrate inside his pocket and assumed it was notification of yet another text from Joe, making seven messages since the first
he received while escorting Hayley Chill off the premises. Each was an
ever more strident command to murder his protectee or else.

Shaw watched Fischer's every move as she pinballed from one guest
to the next. Could he do it? Could he kill her? Committing the act seemed
impossible, whether in front of the assembled wedding guests or during
an opportune moment of privacy if she ducked into the downstairs guest
bathroom. But each vibration of his phone suggested another agonizing
step closer to the violent death of a child hostage.

Lachlan Morris and Fischer were arm in arm now, laughing gaily in response to a joke the journalist-turned-author had just dispensed for the enjoyment of a handful of white-attired guests surrounding them. Shaw's misery knew no bounds as he looked on, the weight of his Glock snug in its side holster suddenly feeling like ten pounds instead of the manufacturer's specified thirty-four ounces (loaded). The absurdity of Hayley Chill's false alarm seemed a distant memory; Shaw could only wish she had been right.

As much as he was reluctant to admit it, had the wedding photographer *been* a second assassin, all of his worries would be over.

Then it was no small horror that Shaw saw his protectee untangle her arm from Morris's embrace and turn in his direction. Ignoring the pleas of her tipsy guests, Fischer walked directly toward the DUSM, clearly intending to converse with him.

He felt as if he could barely draw a breath. Killing her would be a trivial matter of drawing his weapon and shooting her in the head at point-blank range. A round in his own head and his agony would be over.

"Tell me I'm not embarrassing myself, Deputy. Am I being too silly?"

Do it.

"N-no, ma'am. You're doing fine."

Do it NOW.

Quizzical, she studied his face.

"Are you okay, Terry?"

He realized he was sweating, BBs if not bullets.

Wiping his forehead with the back of his hand, Shaw said, "Fine, ma'am."

Fischer frowned playfully, not believing him for a second. "It's been a long day, but not more so than for you and the other men on the detail."

NOW, or we start killing kids NOW.

"Not a problem, ma'am."

Fischer glanced over her shoulder at the people milling about the elegantly decorated great room and then turned back to Shaw.

"We're all so good here. Our guests have drunk so much champagne they couldn't hurt me if they had been secretly hired to do so. Go home."

He realized he could never shoot his protectee while she was facing him. Looking him in the eye. Had Justice Gibbons's USSC protector throttled him from behind? At that moment, Shaw felt his phone vibrate again in his pocket with the notification of yet another text.

He decided he would kill her when she turned to walk away. He would shoot her in the back of the head.

"I appreciate the offer, ma'am. Believe me, I do. But that's simply not possible." He tried to smile, but mostly failed. "We'll be fine."

Satisfied she had given it the old college try, Fischer grinned and shrugged. The justice, acting more like a girl at her sweet sixteen party, raised her right hand and waggled her fingers as a goodbye and turned to rejoin her guests.

With his left hand, Shaw started to lift the bottom of his polo shirt while reaching for the holstered Glock with his right.

Anita Fischer stopped, pivoting to face him again. Off guard now, Shaw dropped both hands limply to his sides.

"Was Hayley all right? I feel so badly for her. Will she be in terrible trouble back in DC?"

Shaw stood before her, immobilized and dumbstruck. There was no denying Fischer's genuine concern for the young FBI agent. Despite it being her wedding day, the woman still had enormous compassion for the people whose duty it was to serve and protect her.

"I'm not sure, ma'am. I'll follow up."

Fischer reached out and took Shaw by the hand.

"You're a good man, Terry. Thank you . . . for everything."

Leaving Fischer's estate, there were only two directions to travel. Driving west meant five miles of navigating a treacherous single-lane road and hairpin turns, a route that had defeated countless tourists over the decades. Turning east meant a shorter and less daunting drive back to Kahului. In a blinkered rage, Hayley elected to turn right, driving west at speeds that exceeded the posted limit by margins bordering on lunatic.

She blew through the resort areas of Kapalua and Kaanapali, blistered the highway above Lahaina, and whipped past the lighthouse at McGregor Point, somehow—miraculously—unseen by local highway patrols. The kamikaze run continued up the switchback-laden road leading to the top of Haleakalā, the massive shield volcano at the island's center, in a tire-squealing, hard-braking fury ride that Hayley managed to finish without killing herself or anybody else. Sundown approaching and emotions spent, she parked and walked a few of the trails at the volcano's summit, oblivious to the wind and cold at a ten-thousand-foot elevation. No thoughts or introspection had accompanied her at any point of this pell-mell vehicular dash halfway across the island to its highest peak. Hayley Chill, on autopilot, was nearly non-sentient.

What she remembered next was the sound of vigorous knocking at her hotel door. Hayley awoke on the floor of her room, got to her feet, and silenced the pounding by opening the door. Shaw regarded her with a clinical dubiousness that caused her to cringe inside.

Oh, God, what have I done now?

The awful realization landed on her like a cartoon anvil from a miles-towering height. She had no recollection of the previous hours, her last memory being her arrival at the Fischer estate early that morning. That's all.

In those seconds, neither Shaw nor Hayley said a word. Her only consolation was that the DUSM had no power to read minds.

Finally, Shaw said, "I thought I should . . . check in. See how you were doing."

"Thanks."

What else could she say?

"You were in some kind of state leaving the property."

"Yeah . . . well . . ." Her words drifted, lost in the ether. Prodding, Hayley asked, "Pretty bad, right?"

"Pretty bad."

"I guess that's it."

"Sorry, Chill. My hands were tied. As the detail's supervisor, I had to make the report."

Something I did was bad enough to alert Washington.

Hayley didn't want to check her phone for messages from Andrew Wilde. Not ever again.

Needing to look at anything other than a disheveled and miserable Hayley Chill, Shaw glanced at his wristwatch.

"Well, I should be getting home."

While resentful of her intrusion, Shaw could not deny a drudging respect for the woman. And sympathy. He had done his part to ensure she hadn't killed herself on the road into town. Time to go.

He said, "Good luck."

Hayley gripped the door for support. "Thanks, Shaw."

She closed the door as the DUSM turned back toward his SUV, the engine running for a quick getaway.

Hayley could finally face the truth regarding her disorderly and miserable hotel room.

This must be the place.

Anyone would know rock bottom when they saw it.

The unavoidable call with her deeper state supervisor had provided the basic facts regarding the debacle at Fischer's home. Shaw had contacted superiors at USMS headquarters in DC. Communications were exchanged between that agency and the FBI. Hayley's cover withstood the initial buffeting caused by the dustup, but Andrew Wilde deemed it necessary to order her return home, anyway. Arrangements were made for a return flight to Washington in the morning.

Stepping outside for air after the difficult phone conversation, Hayley was unsurprised to find the ghost of her dead friend sitting in one of the patio chairs next to the door. Since her untimely demise, April Wu had made it a habit of showing up in Hayley's more problematic moments, like flies to raw meat. The current situation could not have been much worse. Everyone back at the Fischer estate had wanted to understand how she could mistake a Sony camera for a handgun. Several missing ounces from a gifted bottle of eighteen-year double cask Macallan single malt in the pantry wasn't overlooked, even by a busy Supreme Court justice. On her wedding day.

"Welp, I bet we'll never get that guy to shoot your wedding," said April.

"At this point, I'm fairly sure you're the only idiot I could convince to marry me, and you're not even real."

April said, "Let's go for a walk."

———————

In his car, Shaw avoided traffic stacked up in Paia by taking the bypass road to Baldwin Avenue and driving to Makawao before doubling back north into Haiku. The message he had been anticipating since leaving Fischer's estate arrived as he turned onto Lia Place. He was surprised Joe took so long to reach out again.

I knew you wouldn't do it.

Parking in front of his house, Shaw stared at his phone as it thrummed with the notification of another message, one with a video attached. Then, reaching across the dash, he retrieved a second phone from the glove box and navigated to its camera app before playing the video message on his work phone.

Filming with the backup device, Shaw viewed a video of the schoolkids—Bodhi and Makana in the foreground—confined in a dimly lit, narrow room with cinder-block walls painted an institutional gray. The camera angle shifted to their bus driver as unseen hands hauled him to his feet. The audio-free video focused on the adult hostage's head moments before a knife was brought close to it.

The video ended abruptly, replaced by a text message.

Consequences, Terry.

Shaw continued to record with the backup phone as the SMS followed the texted video into digital oblivion. He waited for additional messages, but none were forthcoming.

The misting rain had ceased. Shaw scrutinized the quiet neighborhood a second time, seeing only shadowy grass lawns, picket fences white as tombstones, and the dark facades of lurking ranch-style homes. No place in the world seemed more removed from the trauma of recent hours than Lia Place, his tranquil refuge from the storm.

Flipping down the mailbox door, he reached inside and his fingers found a fleshy object. Retracting his hand as if from an unexpectedly hot oven, Shaw crouched to peer inside the mailbox.

His home's mailbox.

Nestled on a stack of mail and in a dollop of blood, he saw a severed ear.

Leaving the mailbox ajar, Shaw sprinted for the front door. He pushed it open without the benefit of a key—not unusual, as he was continually on Marie over her insistence of leaving it unlocked—and charged into the dark, silent house.

Could the ear signal another reason his wife failed to answer his repeated phone calls?

"Marie!"

Shaw didn't wait for his shout to echo back to him, hurtling through the living room and into the dim kitchen lit only by appliance LED lights, then out the wide-open back door to the bonus room in the home's rear, where low light spilled onto the scraggly backyard grass through a second open door.

He entered the art studio like a gust of wind.

Turning to face him—headphones clamped over her head—Marie looked up from her drawing pad with mild annoyance over her husband's brash entry, blissfully unaware of his dilemma.

His slow-motion tragedy-in-the-making.

A final message of the night arrived minutes later, while Shaw was removing all traces of blood and flesh from his mailbox:

The next ear will be a small one.

Sitting in the living room with Lozano and Javier Suárez, Saturnino listened as the older, more experienced gunmen discussed his failure to take a knife to the bus driver's ear. Lozano had his opinion on the matter, of course.

"*This little shit. If I were in charge, I would have gutted him on the spot. Give the kiddies a show. Why not? The blond cocksucker is useless!"* said Lozano, as if Saturnino—seated only a few feet away—wasn't even present.

Javier said, *"But you're not in charge, so let it go."*

Indeed, Saturnino expected to be killed for his refusal to disfigure the bus driver. A cause for optimism, however, was that the order to sever the hostage's ear had come from Hector Lozano and not their commander. Taliban had no authority over the other men in the unit. Any sway he might hold over Saturnino and the Suárez brothers was purely through intimidation. If Lozano wanted something from the younger man, it was up to him to take it. Or for Saturnino to have the balls to stop him. Carranza, who considered himself above such petty nonsense, meddled in the squabbles between the men in his command only if necessary.

Why *did* Saturnino refrain from slicing off the hostage's ear? He brooded on the question as the other men dissected his character. Poverty, the entrenched socioeconomic class distinctions endemic to Mexico, and limited educational possibilities contributed to Saturnino's decision to join the military and then the cartel. Now he was having second thoughts. Had he made the right choice?

Am I the same as the others?

His first and only murder was in some ways an accident, provoked when a ranch owner pulled a shotgun from behind the door when Saturnino came to collect the cartel's monthly tribute. The confrontation had been a matter of either him or the other man dying that day. Afterward, he felt nothing, experiencing an almost dissociative state devoid of remorse or regret. At the time, that lack of emotion had convinced Saturnino he possessed what it took to join the fraternity of hard men. He assumed the killing and torture that were the tradecraft of cartel foot soldiers would come even more easily with time and frequency.

Taking the schoolchildren as hostages had upended those assumptions, undermining his confidence. When his nemesis, Lozano, ordered him to take a knife to the bus driver's ear, Saturnino froze, paralyzed by the children's screams. Given an opportunity again, he must act with strength. Otherwise, he was a dead man.

But what was the likelihood of another opportunity to prove himself? The Cartel del Oeste was not known for doling out second chances. His fate rested solely with Carranza, who had driven off earlier in one of the SUVs. Where he went was anyone's guess. In all matters concerning Carranza, the other gunmen presumed nothing.

In response to Javier Suárez's comment, Lozano turned his head slightly and spit on the floor.

He said, *"Fuck you and your whoring mother. You've always had soft eyes for that prick. Is he sucking your cock? Is that why you're so tender for him?"*

Guns were everywhere. On the table and chairs. Held casually in hand. So many guns and all the more noticeable when the two sicarios went silent as the room was infused with a new, even uglier tension.

Javier didn't look up from browsing the Mercado Libre shopping website on his phone. After a long pause had elapsed, he said, *"You have the reputation, my friend. No one in Michoacán will disagree. Taliban is feared for good reason. But mention my sweet, God-fearing mother again and they will be the last words you ever speak."*

Lozano didn't have to reach for a weapon.

Angling the Mossberg 590M Shockwave shotgun with box magazine in his lap so that the barrel pointed at Javier, he said, *"Your—"*

The whirring sound of the front gate's motor drifted through the open windows. The three gunmen fell silent, leaving their seats and taking cover until they could identity their visitor. Seeing one of the SUVs rolling up the drive wasn't enough to relax their vigilance. The three men lowered their guns only when they saw their commander exit the parked vehicle and approach the house.

Carranza had refused to delegate to any of his men the task of delivering the ear; he couldn't say why, but something about body parts excited him. Parking up the block from the gringo's house, he had approached the mailbox in darkness and silently deposited the bloody hunk of flesh inside. Turning back for the SUV, the former army sergeant recalled the Spanish version audio message from his old AOL account—"¡Tienes e-mail!"—a memory he realized dated him. Who lived at the address and why his client had demanded the ear be taken and left in the mailbox was unknown.

Entering the safe house following his errand, Carranza read the room. *"What is it?"* he asked.

The ready smile on Javier's face was authentic as Astroturf. *"Just chilling, Commander."*

Carranza wasn't fooled. His eyes went from one man to the next in search of the truth.

Saturnino found it difficult to control his emotions under his commander's scrutiny. The long hours without any reaction from Carranza had left the young sicario's nerves frayed. What would be his fate?

With a ramrod-straight back, Saturnino said, *"Sir, I apologize if I failed you today. I promise I won't let it happen again."*

Carranza seemed uncomfortable with the younger man's slavish declaration. In truth, he had made his decision within seconds of Saturnino fleeing the bomb shelter.

Gesturing with a dismissive wave of his hand, he said, *"Fail me? I didn't order you to cut off the bus driver's ear. That was Lozano's task alone."*

Saturnino was visibly relieved.

Javier Suárez shot a triumphant look at Lozano. To Carranza, he asked, *"What next, then, Commander?"*

"Nothing further tonight. You . . ." Carranza looked at Saturnino, seemingly unable—or unwilling—to call the youngest sicario by name. *"You take the next shift outside. And no sleeping or you truly will be sorry."*

"Yes, Commander!"

Saturnino hustled across the room and disappeared into the kitchen, where a back door provided access to the property's rear yard and the bomb shelter beyond.

Carranza turned to retreat to his sanctuary in the house's primary bedroom. Lozano followed, catching up with him in the bedroom's doorway.

"The boy is soft! He's a danger to us all!"

Carranza hated this aspect of many duties.

He said, *"What do you expect me to do?"* His voice was calm, with a hint of impatience.

"Say the word. I'll put him down like the dog that he is."

"How many hostages do we hold? Eighteen? Nineteen? Children, yes, but nineteen! And only five of us."

The one they called Taliban fell silent. He had made his pitch.

Lozano was his most valuable weapon. Carranza needed him.

He said, *"All in due time. We have no idea of what the future holds. But I swear, I will not forget the boy's disrespect. Before we leave this island, you will have your moment."*

She followed April's lead as they strolled west on Kaahumanu Avenue, a busy four-lane divided highway.

"Want to talk about what happened today?"

"Not really," said Hayley, her voice barely registering above the whoosh of passing traffic, but defiant nonetheless.

"Let's anyway."

"I took a bite of the shit sandwich. What else is there to say? Thought I saw a gun and tackled the guy. Excuse me for giving a goddamn."

"All of that is beside the point, dork. What *really* happened today was full-on, alcohol-induced blackout."

"C'mon. I took maybe the equivalent of two drinks out of that bottle," protested Hayley.

"And we know from past experience that sometimes it only takes one drink for you to forget whole stretches of a day."

Hayley felt a flush of anger come to her cheeks.

Which infuriated her even more.

"Who asked you for your opinion anyway?"

"My opinion? How about Andrew Wilde's thoughts on the matter? Or Anita Fischer's. Ask anyone in your orbit. I don't think you'd be going home tomorrow if your life wasn't a thermonuclear clusterfuck. And how exactly is that going to play out for your baby nephew? You think the mysterious hands in the deeper state are going to be so eager to keep your hapless, opioid fiend of a brother-in-law out of jail after you flamed out here on Maui? What if someone actually does put Fischer down? What if you're the one asshole who could have saved her?"

April paused long enough for her vicious soliloquy to sink in and then asked, "Tell me again, dork. How's that drinking thing working out for you, huh?"

Hayley's nonanswer was answer enough. Still resistant to fallibility or the need for change, she followed in lockstep as her friend turned right at Central Avenue and continued walking north.

"Something you get in the afterlife? Perspective. Fuck tons of perspective. What else is death good for but the ability to look back and witness the wreckage of your life. Of the decisions not made. Of denial and fear of change. I can see it all from my vantage point. Believe me, I've got nothing but time . . . and perspective."

They approached a two-story structure. Most storefronts on the block were dark and their parking spaces empty. However, light and signs of activity emanated from the first floor of 70 Central Avenue. A misty rain had begun to sweep across the north shore, the wind pushing the shower with surprising force.

Pausing, April said, "Hayley Chill, superwoman. Unstoppable. Relentless. The almighty defender of the US Constitution and hero to presidents. First in her class at Publius U. And maybe . . . just maybe . . . not on top of her shit as much as she thinks."

A man in his twenties with long hair, holding a Styrofoam cup in one hand and a lit cigarette in the other, stayed dry in the doorway of the modest storefront where Hayley and April had stopped.

What he saw: a young blond-haired woman with blue eyes who had been battered by one day in a lifetime of trauma and loss. And alone.

"We're just getting started. Care to come in?" asked the man with the cup of lukewarm coffee, gesturing behind him to a gathering of the similarly afflicted.

Hayley nodded only just a little.

CHAPTER 14

¿QUÉ ES ESTO?

With Lozano's menacing presence like torture by suffocation, Saturnino was relieved to escape the confines of the main house. The rain clouds had moved south, leaving the sky awash in stars. The young sicario drew a deep breath, the scents of Maui's upcountry bringing him instant rejuvenation. Like an aromatherapy miracle cure, the eucalyptus and salty sea spray–infused breeze lifted his mood considerably from the throat-constricting panic he had been experiencing only moments earlier.

Had he cured himself of his self-doubts? Would Carranza and the others ever trust him, no matter how he performed in the future? Considering these questions, Saturnino had to laugh. But, of course, nothing had changed. Carranza only granted him a temporary amnesty. All that mattered was what *he* was to learn about himself. In the hours to come—here on this island—Saturnino would know for certain if he was worthy of these hard men.

Cradling a Kalashnikov in his lap, Diego Suárez sat in an easy chair he had dragged from the main house to the small cement pad at the bomb shelter's threshold. With Saturnino's approach, he stood and stretched, holding the rifle like a marching band baton twirler. At thirty-four, he had begun to think that he might be getting too old for the work of a cartel gunman. Unfortunately, the needs of his growing family undermined his efforts to save enough money to quit. Pressed for the truth, he would admit that he enjoyed the camaraderie of his fellow assassins and his singular role as prankster. In the typically mirthless world of drug cartels, El Guasón (the Joker) had few competitors for the title.

"My God, this ass of mine! It could use a good massage. What do you say, Barbie? Give these cheeks a vigorous rub down, would you? I'll pay handsomely for an enthusiastic effort."

Saturnino took no offense, retorting, *"Lozano is the man for that job. He'd do it for free, too."*

Diego laughed and frowned simultaneously.

"Be careful, kid. Taliban takes scalps like most of us take a shit."

The unit's newest recruit shrugged as if unconcerned by his rift with Lozano.

Diego said, *"I saw our commander return. What's the latest?"*

"Who knows? He told us nothing more than he had to, bro."

Diego said, *"One brother is plenty enough for me, 'bro.'"* He handed off the AK and started back toward the house.

Loud knocking on the door from the inside stopped both men. The muffled voice of one of the older children was unmistakably distressed.

"Hello! We need help! One of the little kids is sick!"

More pounding on the door followed.

"Please, help! We're not messing with you!"

Saturnino traded a long look with Diego Suárez, who pulled a Glock from his waistband. The younger man gripped the Kalashnikov, pointing it at the door.

Bodhi didn't think it could have gotten much worse inside the bomb shelter in the minutes after Gilbert Reedy—calling him Gekko now felt utterly wrong—was attacked by the knife-wielding kidnapper. In response to the bus driver's mutilation, every one of the younger kids utterly lost it. Not that Bodhi hadn't been terrified, too. He was standing next to Gilbert when the assault occurred, his shirt stained with the guy's blood.

All the gunmen left the bomb shelter immediately following the attack, taking their grotesque trophy with them. Having watched enough television shows and movies, Bodhi assumed the kidnappers had cut off Reedy's ear as proof of life. That the Mexicans hadn't selected the kids for mutilation was small comfort. The incident proved the gunmen were capable of extreme violence.

Makana and Finn stood by, ready to help, as Bodhi rendered rudimentary first aid to the maimed bus driver. He was surprised at how easily he was able to get control of the bleeding. Removing Reedy's T-shirt, Bodhi used it as an effective compress. Within minutes, the flow of blood from the gaping wound stopped. Makana helped to rip the shirt into a long bandage that Bodhi tied around the bus driver's head.

That task completed, Finn and Makana paused to regard his handiwork. Reedy explored the improvised bandage with both hands.

He said, "Feels weirdly not too bad."

"The ear doesn't do a whole lot other than direct sound into the external acoustic meatus," offered Finn.

Makana reacted—understandably—with surprise to the younger Wilson's knowledge on the matter, prompting some explanation from Bodhi.

"Finn received a copy of *Gray's Anatomy* for Christmas. Says he's going to be a doctor."

Finn said, "Otolaryngologist, actually."

Makana was incredulous. "I don't even wanna know what that is."

In doctorly fashion, the future ear, nose, and throat man asked, "How are you feeling, Gilbert?"

The bus driver, undoubtedly in a state of shock, dutifully played the role of patient. "I'm okay."

Bodhi glanced over his shoulder at the other kids huddled at the rear of the bomb shelter, a blubbering and wailing mass of twelve-and-unders.

He said, "Finn, get Gilbert on his back and elevate his feet."

"Who's *Gilbert*?" asked the younger Wilson boy.

Bodhi gave his brother an annoyed look. Then, gesturing toward the bus driver, he said, "Cover him with a blanket and keep him comfortable. Makana and I are going to help the other kids."

Finn was happy to hone his doctoring skills on the injured Reedy.

Hours passed before Bodhi and Makana managed to calm the other children, aided by a numb resignation that set in among them. The youngest kids, ironically, seemed the best adapted to handling the situation. They even began to make up simple games to pass the time. The tweeners—the ten-, eleven-, and twelve-year-olds—had a more challenging time coping with their ongoing ordeal. Refusing food and water, these children fell into a kind of submissive inertness, sleeping all day regardless of the time.

Makana was first to notice Myles Spenser, a shy and quiet kid who typically kept to himself, acting more furtive than usual. Then another ten-year-old sitting on the floor next to him cried out, "Gross! What's wrong with his arm?"

The commotion drew Bodhi to the rear of the bomb shelter, where he found Makana squatting next to an extremely pale Myles. His left arm was shaking uncontrollably, jerking back and forth with spastic violence. The other kids gawked from a safe distance, some of them losing control of their emotions all over again. Finn pushed through the crowd to join his older brother standing over Makana and Myles.

"Focal seizure," the younger Wilson brother remarked dispassionately.

A frightened Myles gawked at his quivering left arm as if it were attached to someone else's body.

Bodhi spun and dashed to the other end of the bomb shelter and began pounding on the door.

"Hello! We need help! One of the little kids is sick!"

He paused for a moment, waiting for an answer, then hammered on the door again with his fist.

"Please, help! We're not messing with you!"

Behind him, Bodhi could hear the frantic cries of the younger kids and Makana's frustrated efforts to do something to help Myles.

Open the door. Open the door, please.

As if in response to his telepathic commands, Bodhi heard a key inserted into the lock. The door pushed open, revealing two kidnappers— only one wearing a mask—with weapons raised and peering inside the dimly lit bomb shelter.

"One of the kids is sick! He needs to see a doctor!"

Both kidnappers stared at the fourteen-year-old uncomprehendingly.

"Médico?" asked the gunman without a mask, his black hair glistening with product.

"Yes! Yes, *médico!*" Bodhi gestured toward the rear of the bomb shelter. "It's Myles! He's having some kind of seizure!"

The Mexicans stood and gaped at the boy, unsure what to do next.

Bodhi waved the men forward, saying, "Come! He needs help!"

The man wearing a mask took a step forward, glancing toward his compatriot for permission.

Bodhi boldly grabbed the armed man by his arm. "Yes! Please hurry!"

Keeping his rifle lowered and in a firing position, the masked gunman ventured into the bomb shelter. His compatriot covered him with his drawn handgun.

Bodhi led them toward the rear of the long, narrow room, shooing away any stray kids in their path. As the younger children cowered at the farthest end of the room, the masked kidnapper stopped where Makana continued to comfort Myles, whose arm continued to shake violently.

The black-haired man stared, his face flattened with bewilderment. "¿Qué es esto?" he asked his masked compatriot. *What is this?*

Saturnino's stomach knotted; he knew what was wrong with the boy. His younger sister, Rosa, was similarly afflicted. Growing up, when the necessary medicine was too expensive, Saturnino witnessed dozens of similar spectacles.

"*Epilepsy,*" he said.

Diego was annoyed more than anything else. "*No!*"

Saturnino nodded gravely. "*A mild attack. But he wouldn't be shaking like this if he took his medicine. If he doesn't get the necessary pills, the attacks will continue. Grow worse.*" He paused, then said, "*He will die.*"

The older boy—the brave one who didn't rattle and who demanded they come inside—was shouting something that neither Saturnino nor Diego Suárez could understand.

"*What should we do?*" asked Diego. "*Should we alert El Gruñón?*"

Saturnino knew only one thing for sure: they must *not* summon Oscar Carranza.

In the hours and days to come, the youngest sicario wondered if it was this moment in the bomb shelter—watching the tremors in the child's arm quake and then gradually subside—that his life took a new and inevitable course.

"*No,*" he instructed Diego. "*You see? The boy is better now.*"

———

Shaw didn't tell his wife about the severed ear.

Marie had wondered, of course, why he looked the way he did. Why was he so upset? Standing in the doorway of her studio, Shaw gaped at her as if she'd risen from the dead. He evaded her inquiries regarding his raw emotional state, laying it off to the long workday and unresolved crisis in the upcountry.

His calm assurances were a facade. Pure evil had come to his doorstep, delivering the severed ear of Gilbert Reedy. Without much additional effort, the kidnappers could have taken from him everything that mattered. Shaw couldn't imagine a universe in which his wife was seriously hurt or killed.

The kidnappers' message was crystal clear: we are watching you and can destroy you at any moment.

"You connect with Janet today?" he asked, striving for normalcy.

Marie nodded. "She's a wreck, of course. Did you hear about Akoni Murty?"

Shaw steeled himself for what he assumed would be more awful news. "Makana's older brother."

"He attempted suicide today. Blames himself for what happened to his kid sister."

"*What?*"

"Akoni was too hungover to drive Makana to school. That's the only reason she was on the bus yesterday."

"Going to be okay?"

"Yeah. His mom heard something and went to Akoni's room to investigate. She was able to cut him down in time." She paused, then added, "Made the noose from a bathrobe belt."

Marie took pride in a lifelong resiliency that helped her survive a physically abusive father and near poverty imposed on the family after his death in an automobile accident. More than most people in their social set, her childhood was one of unrelenting hardship. But that upbringing, Marie believed, was a forge that had only hardened her. Made her stronger. Nevertheless, the children's kidnapping had deeply rattled her. In the glare of those events, the dark, Gothic nature of her paintings now struck Marie as pretentious and callow.

Tears welling up from an untapped spring, she said, "One of those kids has epilepsy, Terry. He's going to die without medication. I mean..." Marie searched for a way to express the fears gripping her. "... that's a *fact.*"

Shaw couldn't recall the last time he saw his wife cry. She wasn't the type. Tonight, however, there was nothing else to be done except shed tears over the pain their community was suffering. He went to her, dropped to his knees, and put his arms around her waist. Marie's grief was his to bear. And it crushed him. Like Akoni's suicide attempt. The parents of the missing children. And the kids.

God, those poor kids.

What unimaginable hell were they enduring?

All of that and, of course, the severed ear.

If his wife had any idea how close evil had come to their doorstep, how would she cope then?

Listening to Marie quietly weep, Terry Shaw steeled himself. He had failed once to act. He would not fail again. At the next possible opportunity, he would kill Anita Fischer.

One life sacrificed for so many.

No, not one . . .

Two lives.

Despite the late hour, Hayley found all the supplies she needed at a Walgreens two blocks from her hotel. Another woman at the meeting—a schoolteacher with two decades in the program—had given Hayley a list of provisions she would need for the first hours of her recovery. A bag of miniature Snickers bars. Trident chewing gum. B-complex tablets. Vitamin C. Zinc. And Mountain Dew.

Lots of Mountain Dew.

She said nothing during the meeting. Her initial reaction after sitting down in one of the few unoccupied chairs was probably not unique:

Oh, my God, is this some kind of cult?

But within minutes, that initial skepticism was replaced by relief. Never a joiner, Hayley could not deny her unexpected connection with the twenty men and women seated in the dreary storefront. From wildly disparate walks of life, they had all come to the same harrowing realization that they had no power over their addiction to alcohol. With the support found in rooms like this one, however, dedicated participants in the program had a shot at rebuilding their lives. Despite the harsh overhead lighting, cracked linoleum floor, third-hand office furnishings, and cheerless art framed on the walls, Hayley found a home.

With the meeting's conclusion, the high school teacher approached Hayley as the other participants, already familiar with one another, chatted and slowly made their way to the door. During the meeting, Susan described the difficulties she was experiencing because of the children's abduction. She taught at a public school miles from the one attended by the missing kids, but appreciated the bonds between a teacher and her students.

Now she wanted to know if the gathering had helped the newcomer. "Yes," said Hayley. "Thank you."

Having stayed silent during the meeting besides introducing herself, she felt compelled to offer more to an openly compassionate Susan. Unable to speak with total honesty given her role as a deeper state operative, Hayley recounted stories of her hardscrabble childhood, her father's murder, and the loss of family and close friends to opioid addiction. Her miscarriage only months earlier was a more recent emotional trauma. Though no barometer existed for inclusion, she was an obvious candidate for the benefits and support the program could provide. So, armed with Susan's list of helpful supplies to get through the early days of her sobriety—and a promise to keep coming back—Hayley headed for the door.

With a clearer mind and calmer spirit than she possessed only a few hours earlier, she had decided against getting on a plane tomorrow morning as ordered by the deeper state. If Andrew Wilde judged her incapable of protecting Anita Fischer from potential assassins, she would remain on Maui to help bring the missing kids home safe and sound. Scores of volunteers were searching every corner of the island. Joining in that effort would be better than cutting and running.

She accepted the inevitability of jitters, muscle spasms, headaches, and night sweats that had accompanied earlier attempts to go cold turkey. Nevertheless, her resolve was ironclad: Hayley would never take another sip of alcohol. There would be no going back to the old ways. The bingeing and bashing. That life was over.

Unloading her supplies in the hotel room, Hayley formulated a plan to rise before dawn tomorrow and go for a long run. A knock at the door prompted her to check her watch. Was it Terry Shaw checking on her again? Almost ten o'clock? Hayley retrieved her Glock and, holding the weapon behind her back, went to the window and peered through the parted curtain.

She saw a black SUV idling in a parking space beside her Kia. Whoever had arrived in the vehicle was out of her sight line.

Hayley shifted a few feet to the door. "Yes?" she asked in a loud voice.

"It's Anita, Hayley. Can I come in?"

Hayley flipped over the swing bar lock and opened the door wide, revealing Anita Fischer wearing a belted silk sheath dress, braided leather slide sandals, and a cardigan draped over her shoulders. The retail cost of the Bottega Veneta intrecciato leather tote she carried would buy three of the Glocks like the one Hayley held behind her back. Casual yet effortlessly stylish, Anita Fischer exuded an air of intellectual competence despite the late hour.

Arrayed directly behind her were three scowling deputy US marshals, who maintained a tight phalanx around their protectee.

"Ma'am?" asked Hayley, perplexed.

Fischer glanced over her shoulder as she entered. "I'll only be a minute, okay, fellas?"

Unhappily, the DUSMs turned their backs to the room and maintained their vigil from outside.

Hayley closed the door and waited for the older woman to announce the reason for the highly unexpected visit.

Fischer's eyes fell on a "12 Questions" pamphlet and items from the pharmacy Hayley's new AA friend had recommended.

"Ah!" she exclaimed knowingly. "I'm just shy of my twentieth year. I take it you're newer to the program?"

Chagrined, Hayley said, "A couple of hours in."

"That explains an awful lot about today's . . . shenanigans." Fischer smiled sympathetically. "Bravo for taking the first step. I'm sure Lachlan won't mind his depleted stock once he knows it went to such good use."

Hayley was typically all business. "Ma'am, what can I do for you?"

"On my wedding night, do you mean?"

"Leaving that unsaid, yes."

"Lachlan fell asleep an hour ago. Dear man, he 'celebrated' himself into a state of complete exhaustion. I, however, have a stack of

opinions to read in the next twenty-four hours and one to start draft-
ing before we return to Washington. I'm afraid this will be a working
honeymoon for me."

Fischer sat on the bed and pointed at a chair in the corner of the
room.

"Sit, please."

Hayley sat.

"It's easy to forget we're people, you know, under those scary black
robes. When we come down from our perch? We have personal lives just
like everybody else." Fischer had to smile at what she said. "Well, a just
slightly warped version of everybody else perhaps."

"I understand, ma'am."

"My friends think I'm crazy to have married him. But you know
what? I've worked nonstop my entire life. Since I was old enough to pick
up a pencil, I've pushed as hard as possible to accomplish each and every
one of my life's goals. Believe it or not, I dreamed of being a Supreme
Court justice when I was eleven. Now I have a new goal, Hayley. To
really *love* someone, with the same fierce devotion that I've loved my
career."

Fischer couldn't possibly know how much Hayley Chill related to
those words.

"Yes, ma'am. I know a thing about a drive to succeed, too. The gravitational pull is pretty intense getting out of West Virginia."

Fischer nodded, sensitive to their character similarities as women
who had sacrificed for their ambitions.

She said, "Among the many calls and messages of wedding-related
congratulations, I did receive one of particular note. Not because it came
from a former president of the United States. I collected three of those
in total, and one from the current resident of 1600 Pennsylvania Avenue.
Perks of the job, I suppose, but I'm neither naive nor narcissistic enough
to believe those felicitations are anything but obligatory."

"Copy that, ma'am." Hayley already had an inkling of what would
come next, but let the other woman confirm this hunch.

"Nice man, this ex-president. Enjoying his retirement in Texas.

Pretty decent painter, if you like portraits. Could be a lot worse, right? Quite a fan of yours, too. Enough to gift you with a fancy gun?"

"Custom 1911 pistol, ma'am."

"I'm more of a Sig Sauer gal myself."

Hayley was surprised that the Supreme Court justice knew the German gun manufacturer from sauerkraut.

Reading the younger woman's expression, Fischer said, "Long story. Another time. Anyway, your superfan POTUS had heard about your little misadventure at the house today—I don't want to know how—and your subsequent dismissal from my protection detail."

Fischer paused here with a bemused expression.

"Not every day I have a former leader of the free world calling me on behalf of a thirty-year-old FBI agent. A bureau associate deputy director? Maybe."

"I'm twenty-seven, ma'am."

Fischer regarded Hayley through slotted eyes.

"And you're no FBI agent, either."

"No, ma'am."

"Your Texas friend feels very strongly that you should remain with me for the time being. What do you think about that?"

"Ma'am, my superior—"

Fischer cut her off.

"Forget what he said. The big dogs want differently. *I* want differently, Hayley. The ocean's a treacherous place," she added pointedly.

While thinking about those missing kids and how badly she wanted to help them, Hayley said, "Of course, ma'am. I'd be honored."

CHAPTER 15

RULE OF FOUR

P assing through the gates at Hidden Hills, a community thirty miles west of downtown Los Angeles, Gunn mulled over his asking price. Would he demand one or two million dollars from his boss in exchange for the hardware wallet good for unlocking the cryptocurrency belonging to the Cartel del Oeste? Responsibility for transporting the device and laundering its contents was made significant not by the amount—a quarter billion dollars wasn't real money in this day and age—but because of the people involved. If the drug profits somehow disappeared without a trace, both he and David Barrett, CEO of Oakvale Pharmaceuticals, would be assassinated before the week was over. God knows what would happen to their families.

No doubt, Gunn was entitled to hardship pay. The question was, exactly how much?

The original problem had been an issue of liability. Oakvale Pharmaceuticals, where Gunn served as head of corporate security, had been sued in California state court for failure-to-warn and design-defect claims on a generic drug of its manufacture. There was no doubt that the anti-inflammatory pain reliever caused serious side effects, including necrosis of the skin, toxic epidermal necrolysis, and Stevens-Johnson syndrome. However, AP's legal team was able to transfer the case to federal district court, which found for the defendant on a ruling that held the company could not be liable for damages under a state law that conflicted with federal statutes.

With careful analysis of the sitting justices, Oakvale's cadre of lawyers anticipated a reversal in the Supreme Court. Opening the generic drug manufacturer to tens of billions of dollars in liability claims, the case posed an existential threat to the company. Therefore, keeping it off the court's calendar was an absolute necessity. Without Justices Fischer and Gibbons—both of whom were likely to rule against Oakvale—the number of justices required under the "rule of four" to grant a writ of certiorari could not be met. In the unlikely event that the court delayed a decision until new justices were confirmed, the expected nominees selected by a pro-business, regulation-wary POTUS were deemed "friendly" to corporate defendants. The lower court's ruling would almost certainly stand.

Connecting the shocking deaths of two centrist justices with Oakvale's legal troubles would seem improbable: the drug liability case was one of dozens under consideration by the court. In the country's current politically polarized climate, suspicions would fall instead on nefarious actors with purely ideological agendas.

By Gunn's reckoning, the corporation's continued existence depended on its head of corporate security, not its CEO. He had conceived the entire operation—conspiring with Cartel del Oeste to knock off two US Supreme Court justices in exchange for laundering the drug cartel's ocean of cash—and supervised its rollout. Only seven years earlier, the LAPD unceremoniously fired Gunn over a domestic violence beef. He shed that life like a snake does its skin. Remarried and sharing custody of his two teenage kids, Oakvale's head of corporate security was ready to kick a new life into hyperdrive.

So far, his plans had gone off without a hitch.

Pulling into the driveway off Long Valley Road, Gunn parked in front of his boss's "neo-Georgian inspired," six-bedroom, eight-bathroom home. Despite it nearly being midnight, David Barrett was waiting on the front step of the entry portico. Wearing sandals, jeans, and a Lacoste polo shirt, the boyishly handsome CEO was understandably nervous, contrasting with Gunn's poised calm.

Barrett came to the driver's window of the 7 Series BMW before his head of security could open the door.

Lowering the window, Gunn asked, "Is there a problem?"

Barrett gestured behind him toward his ridiculously opulent house. "Family's asleep. You know how it is, Joe."

As if he's ever invited me into his house or introduced me to the wife and kiddies.

"Sure, I do, Dave. Unbelievably difficult finding a little privacy with only nine thousand feet to spare."

The CEO laughed unconvincingly. "How'd it go down there?" he asked.

"Good. Interesting place."

Barrett knew well how "interesting" Mexico could be, having two factories south of the border that necessitated a steady stream of payoffs to political figures and various authorities. Gunn was the conduit of those bribes, a responsibility that put him in direct contact with the shadowy figures in the country well before Oakvale's current legal jeopardy.

"Yes. You got the money, I take it?" asked Barrett.

"I want two million, Dave."

As if asking for a drink of water. Or the time of day. Like two million dollars was nothing to Oakvale's CEO.

Which it was.

Barrett didn't need too much time to consider just how dependent he was on his head of corporate security.

"Okay."

Gunn smiled.

He said, "Things look good in Hawaii. Very good. The issue will be resolved soon."

Barrett was relieved to hear this report. But . . .

"The thingamajig? The hard wallet?"

"Hardware wallet, Dave. Our new investors expect a big share of Oakvale's Mexico operations for their money. By this time next year, they want control of *all* of our facilities south of the border. That means laundering another tranche of the same amount in six months . . . and another two million finder's fee for me."

"Yes, yes. I understand. But—"

"I don't have the device, Dave. You do."

Barrett was understandably confused.

Gunn said, "I didn't want to hold the damn thing any longer than I had to. Imagine the trouble if I misplaced it. Those cartel boys don't play games, I can tell you that."

"Where is the . . . hardware wallet, then?" asked Barrett.

"In your daughter's room. You'll find it in a little glass-topped jewel case on the bookshelf. Unless she found it and plugged it into her Mac-Book, which would be a very bad thing."

Barrett's alarm caused his eyes to widen like a silent movie star's.

"But . . . how . . . ?"

"Had a little time before picking up Juliet from water polo practice."

The CEO glanced over his shoulder at his twelve-million-dollar Hidden Hills estate home, which bristled with more surveillance and security infrastructure than most banks, and wondered how Gunn evaded a system he had no involvement in setting up.

Gunn shifted his BMW sedan into gear. "Don't worry about how, Dave. Just take it as confirmation that I know what the fuck I'm doing."

Bodhi could hear one of the younger kids at the other end of the room whimpering, in the grip of some bad dreamscape worse than their collective reality. He guessed the time to be around two or three a.m., based on nothing more than a feeling of the dead of night.

He was long past worrying about his own survival; most important to Bodhi was getting his brother, Finn, home safely. The other kids needed him, too, especially Myles and some of the younger children who were having worrisome issues with their emotional health. None of the hostages wanted to eat another morsel of the packaged snack food provided by their kidnappers. And Bodhi didn't even want to think about his parents' suffering.

Stay focused. Fix what is within your power to control.

He sat up from the bed he had fashioned out of flattened cardboard.

Bodhi recalled Myles's seizure and the two kidnappers who had come into the bomb shelter in response to his pleas for help. Why had one of the gunmen entered without wearing a mask? The other man would have reminded him if he had merely forgotten his balaclava. There was only one explanation: hiding their faces was no longer necessary because the hostages would never live long enough to identify them. Bodhi forced himself to accept the brutal reality that their kidnappers intended to kill them all once their usefulness ended.

"What are you thinking?"

Makana had crawled closer from her cardboard bed on the opposite side of the narrow room. They kept their voices low, not wanting to disturb the others.

"I was thinking we have to get out of here. We can't wait to be rescued."

Bodhi kept thinking about the two men. Why had the one man kept his face covered? What did *that* imply?

"I think so, too," said the girl. "It's up to us."

"The guy with the mask. He seemed to keep the other one calmed down."

"Yeah. He seemed cool, right?"

"Yeah," said Bodhi. "Kinda."

Like reading the ocean's surface before paddling out, the fourteen-year-old assessed the conditions of their captivity and started working on a plan.

CHAPTER 16

CARRANZA'S STORY

Psychiatric Outpatient Clinic
Military Base, Region XII, Zone 21
Morelia, Michoacán

Date of Exam: 7/11/2020
Time of Exam: 4:12:35 PM

Patient Name: Carranza, Oscar
Registration No./Rank: C38953194/Sergeant

History: Sgt. Carranza is a widowed 38-year-old man. He has complaints of persecution by National Defense personnel and others outside of the military community.

The following information was provided by:
  Sgt. Carranza
  Sgt. Carranza's Mex Army peers and superiors

Sgt. Carranza presents symptoms of persecutory delusional disorder, precipitated by the trauma of his wife and son's deaths in a vehicular accident last year. Symptoms of his delusions began over a period of months. He believes his family is still alive.

Current Symptoms: Sgt. Carranza reports that his appetite has decreased. Significant weight loss of twenty pounds has occurred. He reports the weight change as occurring over the last three months. Because he believes his family is alive, he reports no depressive symptoms and attributes his weight loss to increased physical exercise. He reports fear of being conspired against by his superiors and peers within the military and by members of his community.

Suicidality: He denies suicidal ideas or intentions. Denial is convincing.

Prior Depressive/Manic Episodes: He reports that his failure to achieve his youthful aspirations in the arts instigated a long depressive episode that was alleviated after conscription by the military.

Severity/Complexity: Based on the risk of morbidity without treatment and his description of interference with function, severity is estimated to be high.

Sgt. Carranza has symptoms of delusional disorder. Delusional disorder symptoms have been present for months. Delusional disorder symptoms are occurring daily. He has frequent verbal altercations with superiors that have resulted in official reprimands. Difficulty sleeping is occurring. There is difficulty falling asleep.

Symptoms/Associated Signs and Symptoms: He reports paranoid delusions of persecution. He reports hallucinations involving his wife and son, who he reports as being alive. While no ritualistic acts of violence are reported, he presents obsessive ideation of violent acts of a sadistic nature.

Past Psychiatric History:

Withdrawal History: There is no history of Sgt. Carranza having experienced withdrawal from any substance.

Psychiatric Hospitalization: Sgt. Carranza was psychiatrically hospitalized for a period of two weeks following his failure to enter art school.

Suicidal/Self Injurious: Sgt. Carranza has no history of suicidal or self-injurious behavior.

Addiction/Use History: Sgt. Carranza denies any history of substance abuse.

Psychotropic Medication History: Psychotropic medications have never been prescribed for Sgt. Carranza. Past psychiatric history is otherwise negative.

Social/Developmental History: Sgt. Carranza is a widowed 38-year-old man. He is Mexican. He is agnostic.

Relationship/Marriage:
Sgt. Carranza is a widower.

Children:
Sgt. Carranza had one child, Hector, deceased.

Barriers to Treatment:

Psychological: Severe delusional disorder is a barrier to treatment success. Psychological problems will be addressed via treatment plan. (Severe delusions.)

Patient's Goals: "I want a discharge. They have it out for me."

Family History: Father known to have delusional disorders and consistent suicidal ideation.
    Mother thought to have depression.
    Sister known to have anxiety.
    Family psychiatric history is extensive. Father underwent psychiatric treatment and hospitalization, which impacted his immediate family. Father committed suicide when patient was sixteen years old.

Medical History:

Adverse Drug Reactions: List of Adverse Drug Reactions:
    (1) Added ADR to Penicillin, Reaction(s) = Respiratory Distress, Status = Active

Allergies: Sgt. Carranza reports no known allergies.

Compliance: Sgt. Carranza reports intermittent compliance, stating that army doctors "are trying to kill him." Patient is noncompliant with medication orders.

Clinical Exam: Sgt. Carranza presents without outward emotion, is attentive, groomed and attired per army regulations. He speaks at a normal rate, volume, and articulation and is lucid and spontaneous. His body posture is erect and agile. Facial expression and general demeanor are alert but outwardly inexpressive. He denies having suicidal thoughts. Associations regarding his family and fellow military personnel are illogical. He reports delusions of persecution. He reports visual and auditory hallucinations. He reports homicidal ideas and intentions. Cognitive functioning and fund of knowledge normal. Short- and long-term memory are functional. Capacity for abstract and arithmetic calculations are normal. Insight into problems is poor. Judgment appears poor.

Diagnoses:
Delusional dysmorphophobia, F30.2 (ICD-10) (Active)
Histrionic personality disorder, F60.4 (ICD-10) (Active)
Antisocial personality disorder, F60.2 (ICD-10) (Active)

Instructions/Recommendations/Plan:
Hospitalization is recommended because patient is impaired to the degree that there is severe interference with interpersonal/ occupational function. Medical discharge is recommended.

Psychopharmacology
Psychiatric Hospitalization
Supportive Therapy

Start Clozapine 200 mg PO QAM x30days
30 (thirty) None refills (Delusional Disorder)
Start Ambien CR 10 mg PO QHS x30days
30 (thirty) None refills (Insomnia)

(Office / OP, New)
Maj. Jesus Andino, MD

By: Maj. Jesus Andino, MD
On: 7/11/2020 4:12:35 PM

BOOK THREE

ROCK BOTTOM

CHAPTER 17

SHALLOW GRAVE

Shaw knew how he would kill Fischer. Unsurprisingly, giving the justice a quick and painless death was his goal. The sooner, the better. Also critical was a foolproof and efficient manner in which to off himself. Thank God he wouldn't be around to see if the kidnappers released the hostages after their demands were met. But Shaw was those kids' only hope. Unless he acted today, one or more of the children would be dead by nightfall.

Marie was up earlier than normal. Did she intuit that today was special? Shaw found her in the kitchen after he emerged from his shower and dressed for work. The clock radio on the counter—a vintage Panasonic RC-6015 "flip" clock he had inherited from his grandparents and painstakingly restored in their memory—showed two minutes past five. She poured him a cup of coffee she had just brewed. Shaw smelled the fruity aroma of Kona beans. At twenty dollars a pound, the coffee was for "special" occasions. The last time Marie had made him a cup was on his birthday.

Shaw was dumbfounded, momentarily forgetting the dread with which he had awoken.

He asked, only half-jokingly, "It's not our anniversary, is it?"

"After the last few days, I thought it was time to treat ourselves. Simple pleasures, right?"

God, I love her.

A blanket of gloom fell heavier on Shaw, realizing the consequences his actions today will have on Marie.

She read his mood, if not his thoughts.

"What is it? What's wrong?"

Can't stumble now. Push through it, Shaw.

"The whole thing, baby. You know? Don't worry, though. I'm fine." Off her dubious expression, Shaw added, "I'm trying."

He never ate much for breakfast, but Marie insisted her husband sit while she made some scrambled eggs for both of them. Shaw tried to take his thoughts away from maudlin observations—*the last breakfast I will share with her, the last kiss*—but found it impossible not to dwell on the finality of these moments.

The notion had not escaped Shaw that Joe was behind the murder of Justice Gibbons on Christmas Eve by US Capitol police officer Martin Barnes. That shocking crime and the disappearance of Barnes's wife and two sons was attributed to the disgraced cop. The media accepted as fact that Barnes had "snapped." Shaw wondered if investigators would make the same assumption about him. Sitting at the kitchen table and watching Marie prepare their food, he hated the idea that she would live with that disgrace. For her sake, Shaw decided to leave the secondary phone with which he had started recording Joe's self-destructing text messages in a safe place. He didn't want the truth revealed immediately, lest the kidnappers kill their hostages. Indeed, any other consideration must be secondary to saving the children's lives.

They ate in near silence, both refusing to acknowledge the evil that had descended on their community. Whatever talk passed between them was limited to the humdrum details of their household and the weather. Shaw did not mention the future, even ignoring Marie's attempt to discuss a long-planned trip to the mainland in the spring. Unfortunately, he wasn't *that* good of an actor.

Shaw had resolved to make his departure quickly, without undue ceremony or emotion that might further arouse his wife's suspicions. Fat chance of that once he laid eyes on Marie for what would be the last time.

"What's wrong?" she asked again as he held her tight and kissed her hair, then her face.

He said, "Nothing."

And "I love you."

It was time to leave. Shaw turned and walked to the car parked at the curb. The sun wouldn't rise for another ninety minutes.

––––––––––

During her predawn run, Hayley felt a glimmer of what she remembered as her former self. A familiar lightness of step. Her lungs were unencumbered as they ballooned with air. Leg, arm, and back muscles loosened as she broke a sweat—a limbering helped in no small part by the humidity of Maui's consistently balmy climate.

She ran for the sheer pleasure of the act. As if in a trance. Without thought.

Leaving her phone in the hotel room was a singular act of rebellion. That minor transgression was underlined and written in bold when she returned to find the device vibrating irritably on the nightstand. Andrew Wilde, of course.

"Certainly wasn't my idea," he said without prelude or hello. "You staying on. Who's next on your takedown list? The guy who mows the lawn?"

"With your satellites, sir, I thought you'd know there is no lawn to mow at the Fischer residence."

"Powerful friend you have in the former president, Chill. Screw up again, and he'll make for a powerful enemy."

And since Hayley had this powerful friend in the deeper state, she didn't give a damn what Wilde thought.

"Was there something else, sir?" she asked.

Five thousand miles from his operative's hotel room in Kahului,

Andrew Wilde sat in his home office in the furnished condo he had leased only a few weeks earlier. He didn't expect to stay long, his lengthiest tenure in any residence for the last decade being no more than six months. No personal objects or decorations were anywhere in evidence. The salt and pepper shakers in the kitchen came with the other furnishings. Wilde had moved in with his clothes and a toothbrush. An odd existence, but such was the price of dedication to the deeper state. It was a quarter past eleven in the morning. He had no life outside of Publius. Despite the prickly attitude he put forward to his first, active operative, Wilde recognized his bluster was only cover for a paternalistic infatuation with Hayley Chill.

She was the closest Wilde would ever come to having a daughter, engendering the kind of emotion that made the man feel exceedingly and uncomfortably vulnerable. If being a brusque asshole kept their interactions well between professional white lines, then brusque he would be.

"I've got new information on the murder of Justice Gibbons."

"Yes, sir?"

"They found the bodies of Barnes's wife and kids. A bird-watcher stumbled on a shallow grave at Sky Meadows State Park in Fauquier County, Virginia. An hour west of DC."

"Okay." Hayley was busily computing how exactly this news impacted her assignment with Fischer.

"Martin Barnes didn't kill his family."

"How do we know that for a fact, sir?"

"What was done to these people before their deaths. No one tortures their own kids like this, not even cops who 'snap.'"

"If Barnes didn't kill his family, who did?"

Wilde already had his supposition and waited for Hayley to catch up. The connection dawned on her soon enough.

"Whoever wanted Gibbons dead took them to coerce Barnes. One Supreme Court justice for the price of his wife and two kids."

Wilde said, "Organ harvesting is a known signature of Mexican drug cartels, monetizing their hostages in ways beyond the original demands for ransom."

Hayley upbraided herself for not seeing it more clearly sooner.

Terry Shaw practically performed a jig on my grave when I was booted off the unit. The other DUSMs, too. They all have connections to the missing schoolkids. Any of them could be compromised.

"Sir, we need to check in with the family members of the deputies on Fischer's protection detail. All of 'em. All shifts."

"Already in process, Chill. Our people posing as telemarketers will call their homes once it's a reasonable hour out there."

"What about rotating them out, sir?"

"You're obviously referring to the kidnapped schoolchildren over there. As far as we've determined, none of the DUSMs have people among those missing."

Which prompted an eye roll from Hayley.

People?

"Sir, this is a very tight-knit community. Self-contained. There's only one decent grocery store in the upcountry. Everyone knows some-one with a missing kid."

"USMS is aware of the situation. But personnel are limited. Replace-ments will need to be flown out. It's going to take some time. Remember, other justices could be at risk."

"The missing kids. It would be one hell of a coincidence if the kid-napping isn't connected to a threat against Justice Fischer."

"Calm down. Everyone on this side understands the urgency of the situation."

She wondered what he meant by "side," but let it go.

"Sir, has news of the Barnes family been suppressed? If whoever is behind this knows we've connected Gibbons's murder to the school bus takedown, the ransom threat is neutralized. They'll kill those kids."

"We're not brainless, Chill. An FBI team replaced local authorities within an hour of the bodies' discovery. The detective team that made the initial identification is solid and keeping their mouths shut. Beyond that, it's strictly limited to need to know."

"Good."

Wilde said, "Less than ten people in the country know about this.

We're counting on you to keep Justice Fischer safe until Publius can make arrangements to move her to a secure location back here."

"Wait a minute . . . What? You're picking Fischer up?"

"Of course we're moving her. We can't wait for USMS to get new people on the ground. She's not safe there."

Hayley struggled to keep her emotions in check. "Shipping Fischer off to the mainland unexpectedly is a death sentence for those kids, sir."

"Maybe, maybe not. What I do know for certain is that an FBI jet will be landing on Maui in five hours and Fischer will be on board when it takes off twenty minutes later."

Why argue with him?

"I'm leaving now, sir. I'll be on-site at the Fischer residence in twenty-five minutes."

A pause stretched before Wilde spoke again.

"You sure you're up for this, Chill?"

"Yes, sir."

"These other . . . issues?"

Hayley said, "Resolved, sir. Good to go."

"Keep me posted."

She was behind the wheel of the rented Kia Soul and on the road for Fischer's estate five minutes later.

———————

Saturnino was awake when he heard Carranza using the bathroom off the primary bedroom. The youngest sicario wasn't in the habit of sleeping more than four hours in normal times. But nothing was normal about the last few days. Lying on the couch in the living room, Saturnino had passed much of the night with his hands folded beneath his head, staring up at the unpainted wood tongue-and-groove ceiling. The constant racket of coqui frogs kept him company through the long hours of darkness, a metronome to his swirling thoughts.

His deliberations ran the gamut, from recollections of his younger sister and her epilepsy, to family outings disrupted by a seizure, the trips to emergency rooms, and of his parents teaching him at an early age what to do to help his sibling if she fell ill while they were away from home. These memories and more like them defined much of his childhood and homelife. All members of the family were on guard, perpetually crouched in anticipation of the next medical crisis.

And now this kid in the bomb shelter. Saturnino's father had drilled into him what would happen to his sister if she went without her daily medication. The end would come fast.

The end would come ugly.

They might as well kill the kid now. Put him out of the physical misery that was sure to come; the boy was as good as dead anyway. Same with the others. All the hostages shared the same incontrovertible fate: none would leave the compound alive. Diego Suárez had told Saturnino the previous night, before they went into the bomb shelter, that there was no reason to wear a face covering any longer. The decision had been made. Who knows by who or where? Or even when. Perhaps there had never been any intention of releasing their hostages.

Before they opened the bomb shelter's door, Saturnino had decided to pull the balaclava over his head anyway. Was it shame? Or perhaps he had something less than ironclad confidence in Carranza to get them off the island and back home to Mexico. Maybe both motivations compelled Saturnino to keep his face hidden from the hostages.

After two hours of sleep, Saturnino sat up in anticipation of the other men appearing in the living room. The sun had yet to rise, but he stood—fully dressed, having removed only his shoes for bed—and walked through the open doorway that led into the kitchen. Getting the coffee started, among many other trivial duties, was Saturnino's responsibility.

Carranza entered the kitchen only a few minutes later, followed by his shadow, Hector Lozano, Browning .45 in his right hand.

The former army sergeant said, *"Leave that for now. Follow me."*

Saturnino immediately turned away from the counter and fell into step behind the two men as they trooped into the living room. Diego Suárez was already present and waiting by the door. Like the others, he was armed.

Carranza gestured at Saturnino's shoes on the floor next to the couch. *"Hurry. We're going outside."*

As the others clomped out the door, Saturnino quickly pulled on his high-top sneakers and, without bothering to lace them up, grabbed a Glock from under the couch pillow and hurried to catch up.

Carranza and Lozano led the way toward the bomb shelter at the rear of the property. Sitting in the chair at the door, Javier stood as the other men approached. He held the AK-12 at ready.

Saturnino jogged to fall in line with Diego Suárez, half-breathless. *"What's up?"* he asked.

"New orders."

The youngest sicario reacted with the surprised concern of the rankest civilian.

Diego frowned. *"What the fuck? Don't let the others see you whimpering like a little girl."*

Saturnino attempted to effect the dead-eyed gaze he knew to be the trademark of cartel hit men and managed to appear even more clownish.

Diego shook his head in bewilderment, judging the younger gunman as a lost cause. To deflect his annoyance, he checked the magazine of a Glock he held in his right hand.

They stopped at the bomb shelter door, waiting for their commander's instructions.

Carranza said, *"Taliban takes one ... An older kid. The others will raise all hell."* Looking each of his men in the eye, he added, *"You know what to do."*

Saturnino was the only one to pull a balaclava down over his head, drawing a sharp look from his commander. He reluctantly removed the covering and stuffed it in a pocket.

With a nod from Carranza, Javier Suárez stepped forward and unlocked the twin padlocks.

CHAPTER 18

SK8-HI

The bomb shelter door blew open with no warning and the men entered like windblown debris. Most of the children inside the cinder-block warren awoke with a start and howled in unison, terrified by the shadowy figures crowded in the doorway. The sole night-light in the kitchen area at the room's midpoint illuminated the squirming, twisting youngsters as they withdrew in a pitch retreat to the unreliable sanctuary at the rear wall.

Bodhi, Finn, and Makana scrambled to their feet and formed a defensive line, separating the younger kids behind them from the gunmen. Even the head-bandaged Gilbert Reedy had fled to the shelter's rear as the kidnappers advanced.

As the men drew nearer, into the light cast from the kitchen area, Bodhi looked for the kidnapper who had kept his face covered the day before. He was a possible ally—seemingly the most humane and approachable of their abductors—and the fourteen-year-old was determined to exploit that opportunity. But all of the five men were without masks and shared similar builds. Bodhi despaired he would be unable to identify his potential ally again, but then he glanced down and saw a familiar pair of worn-in Vans Sk8-Hi brown sneakers.

With his dyed-blond hair, the kidnapper wearing the skateboarder kicks stood out dramatically from the other men. He was also younger and didn't possess quite the same aura of menace. If not for their present circumstances, Bodhi would have pegged him as one of the itinerant surfers who showed up on the island for a season or two before moving on.

The kidnappers' intentions were unclear. They had paused at the room's midpoint, speaking to one another in their native language.

"Hey!" Bodhi said, gesturing at the blond-haired man.

The youngest kidnapper ignored Bodhi. Then, after a brief pause, a gunman with a polecat-like face stepped forward and clamped his grip on Makana's arm, saying something in Spanish that Bodhi didn't understand.

While the other men formed a phalanx on either side, the feral kidnapper began to drag Makana toward the door. Bodhi threw himself at the armed men.

"Let her go!"

A gunman with long, slick-backed hair violently pushed Bodhi, who fell on his ass. But the teenager bounced to his feet again like an inflatable clown punching toy, taking hold of Makana's free arm.

"Stop! Take me instead! Take me!"

Alarmed by his older brother's offer to exchange himself for Makana, Finn propelled himself into the fray, his wail merging with screams from the rear of the room. Rattled by the asylum-like racket, the kidnappers struggled to maintain control of the situation.

One of the men barked into the ear of the ferret-faced kidnapper, who released his grip on Makana and lunged to take hold of Bodhi.

Finn tackled his brother around the legs and held fast. It took two of the gunmen to pry the ten-year-old loose and keep him held down until Bodhi was led out of the room.

The fresh air was a relief after being cooped up for so long in the crowded, poorly ventilated bomb shelter. Bodhi filled his lungs with the familiar fauna-scented oxygen as the feral kidnapper hauled him to the one part of the cinder-block wall that protruded from the hillside. Glancing to his left, he could see the hills to the south rising above the trees and confirmed his earlier estimation that their location was on private property at Waipio Bay. Years spent on a surfboard waiting for a wave had given Bodhi a deep familiarity with the ragged profile of the north shore topography.

The gunman was close enough for Bodhi to smell the sour-sweet tang of his budget deodorant. Feeling the cold metal of a gun barrel pressed to the side of his head, he looked forward, past the other gunmen arrayed in front of him. Did he register the cell phone held out to record his execution? Probably not, because the predawn gloom nearly swallowed up that pinch of artificial light.

Confusion rose like bile. Bodhi had yet to fully process the mash-up of events from the last few minutes. Struggling to focus his thoughts—to dampen a rising panic—he recognized the inevitability of his death.

All sensory information withdrew from his consciousness, replaced by memory.

Of his younger brother, Finn.

His parents.

The ocean's wind and waves.

Of sailing.

Flying.

———

With Fischer's wedding ceremony over and done with, Terry Shaw found a quiet and much more normal scene at the estate's entry gate the following morning. Only the lone USMS SUV with two of his fellow deputies presently stood sentry. As supervisor of the protection detail, Shaw knew Anita Fischer and her husband were alone at the house. Jeremiah, the estate's maintenance man, wouldn't report for work for another hour. Fulfilling the kidnappers' demands would be a trivial matter of aiming his gun from point-blank range at Anita Fischer and squeezing the trigger.

Shaw stopped next to his colleague's SUV pointed in the opposite direction and rolled down the window.

"Busy night?" he asked the agent in the passenger seat. His name was Malcom Esposito. He and Shaw played golf every month or so, badly.

"After Marlin's midnight visit to that squirrely FBI agent back in town? Clear sailing."

Fischer going into town last night was news to Shaw. Even more unexpected was the justice's visit with Hayley Chill.

"What was that all about?"

Esposito rolled his eyes, grimaced, and indulged nearly every other facial tic to express his annoyance. "Hell if I know, boss. Bottom line, Special Agent Chill is back on the detail."

"Who says?" Shaw asked angrily.

My God, she might be at the house right now!

Esposito shrugged. "Marlin?" He was one of the marshals who had accompanied Fischer to Hayley's hotel.

"The protectee doesn't make these decisions, Espo. Headquarters does."

"And HQ *did*. Guess you didn't read your emails this morning?"

Shaw muttered an obscenity, staring absently out the windshield.

Esposito said, "Don't sweat it, chief. I haven't seen hide or hair of her since last night. With her friends in high places, she can roll in whenever she wants."

Relieved, Shaw shifted the vehicle into drive, but kept his foot on the brake for one last word with his USMS colleague.

"Do me a favor, Espo. She shows up, don't let her come down. We don't need a loose cannon on-site."

"C'mon, Terry." He had no desire to catch any shrapnel from Shaw's squabble with the Washington-based FBI agent.

As he took his foot off the brake and slowly moved forward, Shaw said, "This is on me. You're in the clear."

The quarter-mile gravel road—descending the hillside in three long switchbacks to the bluff and house below—required undivided attention navigating. When a text message arrived from Joe, Shaw retrieved his phone from the seat next to him and glanced quickly at the screen. Snapping a photo of the image with his other phone was out of the question.

He saw: a close-up of one of the child hostages, Bodhi Wilson, with a gun held to his head, an old Browning .45 by the looks of it.

The image gradually disappeared from the screen as Shaw gawked at it, the SUV coasting down the grade. He felt the left front wheel bump and, looking up, registered that the vehicle was veering off the narrow, sloping gravel road.

Throwing the wheel to the right, Shaw dropped the phone. Once he had averted disaster and steered the SUV onto the road again, Shaw braked and put the transmission into park. He found the phone on the floor under his feet and flipped it over to view the screen again . . . as a second image dissolved.

Shaw wasn't sure how long he remained like this, seated behind the wheel of his stopped vehicle and staring at the phone in his hand without really seeing it. For less than thirty seconds? Or did his immobilization persist for minutes more than that? The SUV's six-cylinder engine thrummed. An ocean breeze from the northeast streamed through his still-open driver's-side window.

If he had any doubts he could execute his protectee, that worry was dispelled by the image of Bodhi Wilson with a .45 pressed to his head.

Now a much deeper horror settled on Shaw, the sensation of suffocating inevitability that had effectively robbed him of all free will. In those long seconds, he realized that this inexorable compression of his waking consciousness would stop *after* he was dead, reduced to a lump of insentient organic material on a coroner's examination table.

Terry Shaw wanted the torment to be over.

And had only one way to end it.

CHAPTER 19

ANITA FISCHER MUST DIE

S he headed west on Kahekili Highway, pushing the rental car to its engineered limits. The twisting two- sometimes one-lane road, with a nearly continuous sheer drop-off on her right side, was unsafe at speeds above twenty miles per hour. Hayley drove much of the route at nearly double that rate. Her luck held up until she was a half mile from Fischer's gate, when Hayley rounded a hairpin turn and nearly collided with the rear end of a cargo van picking its way through the vertigo-inducing course.

Fuck! Get out of the way!

The van's driver, lacking telepathic powers, continued to putter along at fifteen miles per hour and ignored one turnout and then a second.

Hayley flashed her lights without achieving the desired result. Swinging the Kia into the incoming lane, she sped even with the van as both vehicles approached yet another sharp curve. Clearing the turn, Hayley saw a compact pickup coming in the opposite direction and swung the rental car back into the right lane, the Kia's rear bumper kissing the cargo van's front end. The two other drivers laid angrily on their horns as Hayley sped into the next inevitable hairpin turn, tires squealing.

The turnoff for Fischer's estate and the USMS vehicle posted there came within sight, less than two hundred feet away. Again, she felt a familiar tremor. Pausing in the middle of the road, Hayley retrieved her phone. Andrew Wilde.

"I'm at the house," said Hayley without preamble, the words coming in a rush.

"Everyone checked out. All family members accounted for."

"It's a *very* tight-knit community, sir. Every man on the protection detail has a close connection with one or more of the missing kids."

"We're still running checks on service staff, Chill," Wilde said dismissively.

"Would you bet the house on a house cleaner pulling a trigger on your target, sir? The deputy marshals are armed and *trained*."

"Point taken."

"Yes, sir. I've got to get down there."

"Do that. Hold down the fort until the FBI team arrives on the island. I'll text you their ETA."

"*Real* FBI, sir?"

Hayley heard Wilde guffaw before he disconnected the call.

Seconds later, she pulled next to the SUV and lowered her window.

"Who's down there?" she asked Malcolm Esposito.

"Shaw."

The DUSM's demeanor bristled with hostility. Hayley wondered again if the conspirators had compromised more than one of the deputies.

"Open the gate, please."

"Sorry. Can't do that."

Esposito frowned as he spoke, hating the position his chief had put him in.

Fucking Shaw.

Hayley gripped the Kia's steering wheel instead of reaching through the window and putting her fingers around Esposito's neck.

"DC cleared me for your detail, deputy. Open the goddamn gate."

In her impatience with the DUSM, some West Virginia had crept back into Hayley's speech pattern. Made no difference, however. Esposito's lower lip bulged. He shook his head and said nothing more.

Hayley popped her door open and strode across the open ground to the gate, daring the deputy marshals to shoot her in the back.

Watching her clamber over the barrier from their SUV, the two DUSMs mulled their response.

Esposito asked, "Should we stop her?"

His partner didn't have to give the matter a moment's thought. "Did you see her tackle that wedding photographer? No way, dude."

The driveway was a little less than a half mile long. Hayley was still loose and warmed up from her run an hour earlier. The sun had risen high enough to the east to illuminate the hills behind her. As she ran down the dirt-and-gravel road, Hayley decided it might be smart to have a plan.

Stop Terry Shaw from killing Justice Fischer.

Stop the kidnappers from executing their hostages.

Great. Now I have a plan.

Hayley kept running.

Shaw heard Fischer knocking around upstairs in her bedroom suite as he entered the house through the back door.

Here. In the kitchen. This is the best place.

From experience, he knew his protectee would come here first after descending the stairs. Lachlan Morris would sleep in, no doubt, at least for another hour. Fischer's new husband had indulged his passion for expensive wine throughout his wedding day and well into the night.

He won't be any problem.

Shaw stood in the middle of the expansive chef's kitchen and considered where he should place himself. Would a seat at the center island be the most natural location? Or should he stand by the sink? What would he say to Fischer, if anything, before killing her? Realizing how nervous he was, he had to remind himself to breathe. Perhaps he was overthinking the situation.

It'll all be over soon.

The justice wouldn't be surprised to see him. Since the beginning of the enhanced protection detail, Shaw was always the first DUSM to arrive on the premises. Fischer had found Shaw waiting on the porch that first morning and encouraged him to come inside even if she wasn't yet downstairs . . . *with* the proviso that he get the coffee started.

His protectee was like that. Anita Fischer was the friendliest and most accessible of any judicial dignitary for whom Shaw had worked. Despite his wife's misgivings regarding "Marlin," he couldn't deny his affinity for the Supreme Court associate justice.

But Shaw didn't much feel like getting the coffee started for Fischer on this particular morning. He didn't want to dwell on how strongly he considered his friendship with her.

Shaw had thought a *lot* about his method of assassination. Of course, he read several news reports regarding the other murdered Supreme Court justice. Martin Barnes strangled Justice Gibbons, a particularly painful and grotesque way to die. Shaw wanted to give Fischer a painless death. Like he had envisioned yesterday during the wedding reception, he would shoot her in the head from behind. Fischer would never know what hit her.

One of the stools at the kitchen's center island, he decided. He would sit there and—

"You're here bright and early."

Fischer's arrival in the kitchen took Shaw by surprise, what with his back turned to the open door at that end of the room.

"Ma'am. Good morning," he said, instantly feeling idiotic.

The justice scrunched her face in reaction to his befuddlement.

"You okay?"

Shaw nodded, wishing he were seated on the stool so he could have watched Fischer's approach through the doorway. He stood in the middle of the kitchen, paralyzed. A memory of the photo that Joe had texted him minutes earlier continued to haunt him. That poor Wilson kid!

Rage rose within him. Helplessness, too.

"I thought we had a deal," said Fischer with mock severity as she walked to the counter.

"Sorry, ma'am."

His feet remained planted in place, as if submerged in concrete.

Shaw put his hand to the holstered gun under his shirt now that Fischer's back was to him. She wasted no time retrieving a canister of ground coffee from the cupboard. With pedestrian tastes when it came to her morning caffeine, a cheap automatic coffee maker was her brewing method.

"I need to wake up Lachlan somehow. Howitzer maybe? He's catching a plane for Honolulu at eleven," said Fischer.

Shaw drew his Glock 26 and kept the gun down to his side as he pivoted and approached his protectee.

Do it.

"You might wonder why my new husband is abandoning me less than twenty-four hours after exchanging our vows. Excellent question. Something about his editor. I don't know. It's just as well, really. I have a veritable Mount Everest of work to get through in the next four days. My dear beloved *swears* he'll return in time for dinner."

Less than three feet separated them. Shaw raised the Glock so it was only a few inches from the back of Fischer's head.

Do it!

His finger left the guard and settled lightly on the trigger . . .

Shaw felt a presence behind him and turned his head slightly to look over his right shoulder, while the gun remained pointed at Fischer's occipital bone.

Hayley Chill, hyperventilating, stood in the doorway, a Glock in her outstretched hand and trained on Shaw. He swung his gun around in a silent, fluid ballet move until it notched the approximate location between Hayley's blue eyes. A preoccupied Fischer continued to prep the coffee maker, oblivious to the stalemate playing out behind her back.

She said, "If you ask me, married life isn't all that different from the one I had as a single, fun-loving associate justice of the United States

Supreme Court. Still making my own coffee. Still spending the majority of the day at my desk."

Shaw and Hayley stared at each other, without expression, OK Corral style.

Originating from the depths of the DUSM's consciousness—a place colloquially known as the "heart"—relief escaped Shaw's mouth in the form of a barely perceptible sigh.

After a few beats of this mute confrontation, they lowered their weapons in unison and holstered them.

Having flipped the power switch on the coffee maker, Fischer turned and was pleasantly surprised to see Hayley standing in the kitchen doorway. Her smile was wide and genuine.

"Ah! The cavalry has arrived!"

"Yes, ma'am."

Fischer looked from Hayley to Shaw, detecting the diminishing electrical charge of tension between them.

"What's going on?" she asked.

"DUSM Shaw is still getting used to a woman on his detail, ma'am."

"Caveman," Fischer scolded with comic admonishment.

Having approached the abyss, only to step back from it at the last moment, Shaw could neither speak nor move a muscle.

"No worries, ma'am," said Hayley. "Give him time. He'll come around."

"I certainly hope so."

Fischer headed toward the opposite doorway. "I'm off to extricate that husband of mine from bed. Wish me luck. I don't think he's going to like it one bit. Both of you, be prepared to come up, guns drawn, to protect me from his wrath."

In an instant, she was gone, leaving Shaw and Hayley alone in the kitchen.

The DUSM finally found the power of speech.

Morose and defeated, he said, "We are so fucked."

Hayley didn't share his fatalistic outlook on the situation. Running had always been her wellspring, the springboard of many inspirations. Her sprint from the highway to the house was no exception.

"Not necessarily," said Hayley, aware of how little time they had to act.

The grass was wet and refreshingly soft under Bodhi's bare feet. With a glimmering of the sun's rise filtering through the tree canopy overhead, he watched the gunmen confer among themselves. The ferret-faced one, who had put a gun to the teenager's head, released his grip on him and joined his cohorts in their barking, angry chatter. They had no concern that Bodhi might try to escape. How far could he go before one of them shot him dead?

Bodhi was alive. That's all that mattered. Once they put him against the concrete wall, he thought it was all over. Not once before in his young life had he thought of death as a thing that would happen to *him*. Even in the worst moments in the ocean—when Bodhi wiped out on the big winter waves that crashed against Maui's north shore—did he imagine the possibility of his life's end.

The moments against the wall outside the bomb shelter were nothing like Bodhi's near-drownings. Instead, he had experienced a wholly different level of terror, one that crushed every shred of hope. His kidnappers had achieved the dubious distinction of embodying a graver threat than even the mighty Pacific Ocean.

Bodhi refused to cry. Having watched innumerable depictions of facing death with dignity in countless television shows and movies—whether from Lord Shen in *Kung Fu Panda 2*, A.J. in *Armageddon*, or Daniel Craig's James Bond in *No Time to Die*—he simply closed his eyes in a courageous acceptance of his fate. The memories of a rich life, however abbreviated, replaced his perception of the hard men and their unintelligible babble. Terror gave way to acceptance, which yielded to gratitude.

Then . . . nothing.

Bodhi opened his eyes again after several moments standing with his back against the rough concrete wall and saw that his kidnappers had decided on a different course of action.

He would live, at least for now.

———————

Hector Lozano wasn't thrilled to be denied his pleasure. As his cohorts observed, too much time had passed since his last kill. Putting a bullet through the kid's skull would've been a sweet indulgence indeed; his calm acceptance of death had infuriated Taliban to no end. Lozano was mere seconds from squeezing the trigger and blasting the brat to nothingness, when Carranza barked an order for him to stop after having snapped photos of the event with his phone.

"That's enough!"

Lozano kept the big Browning .45 to the kid's head. *"What? You don't want this one dead?"*

The other men were also confused, but their commander's sometimes erratic behavior was familiar to them. The best strategy was to not question Carranza's abrupt changes to a plan. Instead, simply obey and move on.

"I want him alive . . . for the other thing."

To Saturnino, these words were only the source of more confusion. What "thing"? Though he was secretly relieved to avoid witnessing the cold-blooded execution of the child, Saturnino feared what his commander might have planned for their hostages.

But Lozano and the Suárez brothers had taken part in kidnapping the American housewife and her two sons, unlike Saturnino. So they knew exactly what Carranza had in mind.

Diego Suárez was chagrined to hear the news and said, *"That's a lot of 'donors,' Commander."* He dared not protest more.

But Lozano wasn't so inhibited. He wanted a more immediate thrill. To Carranza, he said, *"The client requested execution photos, not proof of a threat of execution."*

Saturnino watched as the stoic boy opened his eyes, obviously surprised to be alive. Once again, he found himself in frank admiration of the teenager's courage.

Carranza rebuffed his subordinate with a glower. Releasing his hold on the child hostage, Lozano went to where the others were standing, to plead his case.

"We need them all, Commander? How do we even get the product off the island?"

Carranza wasn't in the habit of explaining himself to his men. But the audacity of his plan was apparent even to him. Who would attempt such a thing? Selling the hostages' body parts tripled the pay they would receive from the cartel for merely kidnapping the children. They would not only be able to purchase bigger and better homes for themselves but for their parents and grandparents, too. Harvesting organs from all nineteen hostages would bring substantial wealth.

"I've made all of the arrangements. We need only the largest cooler available and twenty or twenty-five pounds of dry ice. A broker will pick up the shipment from the airport," said Carranza.

The men reacted with a grim silence. Between them, the Suárez brothers had killed many men and women. Children, unfortunately, had been the unintended casualties of a few of these operations and the brothers had blotted the guilt from their daily thoughts and dreams. But *this* new plan of Carranza's was a whole other scale of depravity. A line they didn't even know existed was their destiny to cross.

Despite these misgivings, refusing to obey their commander's orders was not a consideration. They had become accustomed to the cartel's extreme violence in the past; they hoped that this new business would also become a matter of routine.

Saturnino felt numb. He looked again at the teenager standing against the concrete wall. The boy was looking down at the ground, his bare feet digging into the spongy turf soaked from the previous night's rain. Watching this simple act of distracted gratification, Saturnino recalled similarly taking pleasure in the feel of his bare feet burrowing into the warm sand back home in Mexico at Playa La Ticla. The gesture resonated with Saturnino in a deeply disturbing way. He wanted to believe he was like the other men. That he was, like them, a Snake Eater.

Terry Shaw followed Hayley outside onto the porch. Walking down steps to a landing atop a narrow ridge that plunged at its terminus into the rocks and surf, they found all the privacy the following discussion required. The morning was windless and a glassy ocean stretched out before them, a serene backdrop that belied the gravity of their situation.

Shaw tried to push past an overwhelming sense of fatalism . . . and failed.

"They'll kill them. Those kids are dead."

"They won't, Shaw. We'll stop them."

"You'll report back to Washington. The whole FBI circus will descend on this place and the kidnappers will execute their hostages and melt into the local population."

Choosing her words carefully, Hayley said, "I'm not going to report back to DC."

Shaw didn't speak for a moment, regarding her with a quizzical expression.

She was unlike any FBI agent he had ever met. He recalled that none of his contacts with the bureau could place her.

"Who are you?" he asked.

Then, "*What* are you?"

"Nothing you've ever heard of," said Hayley.

He was hardly satisfied with her response.

"Look—"

She cut him off. "We don't have time to argue about it, Shaw. At this minute, a private jet is heading to Maui to take Anita Fischer off-island. We both know what'll happen to those kids then."

Whisking the justice off the island was news to Shaw.

"But . . . I would've been notified of any plan to move her."

"The mutilated corpses of Martin Barnes's family have been found.

Select officials within USMS and the FBI understand now that Barnes was coerced. That puts every DUSM on Fischer's protection detail under suspicion of being similarly compromised. Independently of the private jet coming here, your agency is sending replacement teams."

"Then who's sending the fucking jet?"

Hayley's silence was loud and clear.

"That which shall go unnamed," said Shaw, answering his own question.

With a resigned sigh, he acknowledged his subordination to Hayley, who had more than earned his respect in the last thirty minutes.

"When does the jet arrive?" he asked.

Hayley glanced at her watch. "Four hours, max."

Shaw was a proud man. But the strain of shouldering the burden imposed on him by the mysterious Joe had made him more malleable. He could be more honest with himself now, admitting his nearly total reliance on the young woman with almost otherworldly powder blue eyes. Her weird, alien-like resolve.

"So? What's the plan?" he asked.

"Anita Fischer must die," said Hayley, unintentionally echoing Joe's exact words.

CHAPTER 20

NAKALELE POINT

L achlan Morris came downstairs dressed and ready for his day trip to Oahu. Wearing a white Loro Piana unconstructed linen sport coat and navy-blue seersucker trousers with "no sock" leather driving moccasins and tortoiseshell sunglasses folded over the neck of his striped polo shirt, he was the picture of a former journalist and successful author. With the help of a ghostwriter, his first-draft manuscript reexamining the scandalous second term of President Bill Clinton had passed muster with Rebecca Finch, his editor at Simon & Schuster. The best years of Morris's brief journalistic career spanned the Clinton administration, and a handful of blockbuster revelations he unearthed for the book were cause for his publisher's giddy excitement.

Vacationing in Honolulu with her family, Morris's editor had invited both him and Anita Fischer over to Oahu for the day. No doubt relieved the risk she had taken purchasing the book off a three-page proposal had seemingly paid off, Finch wanted to hand-deliver her editorial letter. To celebrate the occasion, she suggested a lunch at La Mer, one of that island's finest restaurants. Genuinely swamped with work, Fischer begged off, but encouraged her new husband to go without her.

"Now, *that's* the look of a successful author. Carl Bernstein, watch out."

Fischer stood with Hayley, Shaw, and a second DUSM, Michael Ford, in the foyer as Morris, tanned and carrying only a few extra pounds on an otherwise athletic, six-foot frame, finished descending the stairs and joined them.

"Please. If Rebecca was anticipating even a quarter of Bernstein's numbers from my book, she would've sent over a private jet," said Lachlan with modesty that was transparent as glass.

Fischer shook her head with equally mock disapproval. "Let's have none of that, thank you. No husband of mine will be anything short of a *New York Times* bestselling author." Aware it had been years since Lachlan had made that paragon of lists, she added, "Well, *USA Today* would do."

Hayley and the DUSMs stood by patiently as this newlywed banter played out.

"I detest abandoning you like this, darling," said Morris, putting his hand to her face, oblivious to his audience in the way only celebrities and the very rich can effect. His celebrity was a thing of the past and he didn't have a fraction of his wife's net worth, but Morris's ability to fake it was just one of his many personal traits that captivated Fischer. He truly was a delightful diversion from the mountains of paperwork on her home office desk.

"Oh, at our age, we're hardly Romeo and Juliet material. Besides, flying to Oahu trailed by my wonderful bodyguards would cost a small fortune." She planted a quick kiss on her husband's lips. "Go. Be feted."

With a winking glance toward the well-armed protection detail, he said, "Well, I *suppose* you'll be in good hands."

Turning to face Fischer again, he leaned in for a longer and more soulful kiss than the first. Then, breaking off their embrace and looking her very much in the eyes, he said, "Stay safe. See you at dinner."

He strode across the cavernous foyer and disappeared out the door with nothing but his car keys in hand.

Fischer stood motionless for a beat, seemingly plotting her next move. To no one in particular, she said, "I think I'll go for a quick swim before settling down for work."

Shaw appeared surprised by her announcement. "Ma'am?"

"It's like a lake out there. The perfect day." Fischer gestured toward Hayley, adding, "And, plus, I have my swim buddy. That's why we dragged her all the way out here, isn't it?"

"Justice Fischer—"

She cut off Shaw and touched Hayley lightly on the arm, asking, "You brought your suit?"

Hayley seemingly had no opinion one way or another regarding their protectee's impulsive decision. "In the car, ma'am."

"Great!" Fischer said brightly. "Let's get to it."

They regrouped at the top of the stone steps that descended from the bluff to a small pocket beach the size of a tennis court. Above them, Jeremiah, the maintenance man, trundled past behind the wheel of the loud Kawasaki Mule, a gas-powered utility vehicle, and disappeared from their view. Absent that noisy distraction, the view was breathtaking.

Fischer led the way down to the beach, wearing sandals, a one-piece Speedo swimsuit, and a robe. Hayley followed, barefoot and wearing a black front-zip one-piece suit. Both women had slung towels over their shoulders. Bringing up the rear, wearing their street clothes, were the two DUSMs, Shaw and Ford.

At daybreak, the ocean had been extraordinarily calm. But a robust northeast wind had grown stronger and now the water surface was an undulating mass with the occasional whitecap. The fringe reef a hundred yards from shore that ran the length of the island's north side protected the little beach from big rollers, but a pronounced tidal surge roiled the water at the sand's edge.

"Ma'am, I'm not so sure about this," said Shaw as he arrived at the bottom step and gazed out to the ocean.

"Ridiculous. I'll have you know that I attended Stanford on a swimming scholarship." Fischer removed her robe, retrieved a pair of goggles from a pocket, and kicked off her sandals. Dropping her towel on the sand, she dashed into the water as she pulled the goggles over her head, barely breaking stride to high-step over the undulating swells.

"Hell," said Hayley. "She really isn't kidding around."

"Better get in there after her," said Shaw.

Tossing her towel to the ground, Hayley followed Fischer into the water without the benefit of goggles. The two deputies, feeling somewhat useless, could only stand on dry land and watch as the women swam away from the beach.

———————

Minutes later, a concerned Michael Ford stood on the water's edge, staring out to sea.

"Why are they out so far?" he asked without looking to Shaw, who stood next to him and kept watch on the two swimmers near the reef a hundred yards out. "Aren't they a little close to those breakers?"

Ford brought a pair of binoculars to his eyes and focused them on Fischer and Hayley. "Why do they have to be so far out?" he asked again, with obvious irritation and anxiety.

Shaw retrieved his phone from a pocket. "Fuck it. I'm calling it in."

Ford kept glass on the women and said, "Napili Fire Station has a boat."

"But a Jet Ski can get over that reef, though."

"Jet Ski will take too long to get here. The MFD boat can put rescue swimmers in the water on the other side of the reef."

Michael Ford, like Shaw, was a resident of Maui but lived in Lahaina, a world away from the upcountry. Despite the ocean's proximity, Ford avoided any water that couldn't be contained in a tall glass. His passions were Harley-Davidson motorcycles, cooking, and bird-watching. Terry Shaw had always appreciated Ford's levelheadedness and frictionless ego. By the estimation of everyone working out of the USMS office in Honolulu, he was a reliable and competent deputy.

Shaw nodded and dialed the three-digit emergency number.

"Shit."

"What?" asked Shaw.

"A big wave. I don't see Agent Chill."

Shaw looked to where he last saw the women. Only one head was above water, moving swiftly to the west in an apparent lateral current.

"I see one swimmer!" Shaw announced.

Ford kept watch with the binoculars. "Fischer. Did you get through to MFD?"

The call connected at that moment.

Into the phone, Shaw said, "Yes, Operator, this is Terry Shaw, with the United States Marshals Service. I'm reporting two swimmers in distress. Hakuhee Point, just east of Mokeehia Island."

"She's up. I see Hayley." Ford pointed with one hand while keeping the glass on the water.

Holding the phone to his ear, Shaw looked in the direction his partner indicated and saw a swimmer maneuvering to escape the impact zone of the rollers breaking over the reef.

Ford shifted the binoculars to his left.

"They're separating. Fischer is caught in that lateral current, moving west."

Shaw listened to Ford with one ear and the emergency operator with the other. Then, into the phone, he said, "Two swimmers. Hakuhee Point. One swimmer in distress is a VIP, understand? We need boats and people out here, stat!"

Ford continued to pivot, turning the binoculars farther and farther west.

"I'm going to lose sight of her. She's moving past the ridge." A beat, then Ford said, "I've lost her."

———————

Hayley stayed in the water, searching for Fischer until a rescue swimmer from the Napili station boat ordered her onto his board and carried her back to the pocket beach. Wrapped in a towel, she met Shaw and other authorities at the top of the steps.

Before he could say a word, Hayley asked, "Anything?"

Shaw shook his head. "Between MFD, Ocean Rescue, and private citizens, we've got probably fifty boats on the water between here and Nakalele Point looking for her."

One of the patrol officers from MPD snorted and said, "If the tide sweeps her past Nakalele, the next stop is Molokai."

The crack drew a sharp look from Shaw and everyone else standing in earshot. Hayley saw April Wu—hair unkempt and wearing her after-life uniform of cargo pants, dark T-shirt, and army pullover—standing at the back of the scrum of law enforcement and public safety authorities. With her inscrutable expression, the ghost of Hayley's only true friend in the world was not a welcome sight.

The deeper state operative turned to accept the medical examination of a female EMT. Shaw appeared at her elbow.

"Are you okay?" he asked. "You were out there a long time."

All eyes were on Hayley. Many were accusatory. Her job was to protect an associate justice of the Supreme Court and she had failed. She had lost Fischer.

"I'm fine," said Hayley, her emotions in check.

Shaw said, "Lot of people want to talk to you. If you think you're up to it."

"I'm good. Let me get dressed. Then they can ask all the questions they want."

Without waiting for Shaw's lead, Hayley turned and walked on shaky legs up the slight rise to the main house. Glancing over her shoulder, she was relieved to see no sign of April Wu in pursuit.

————————

Bodhi, sitting with Finn near the bomb shelter door, heard the commotion at the rear of the chamber and pushed to his feet to be of assistance.

Of course, all the other kids were wildly relieved when he rejoined them, none more so than his younger brother. Bodhi was surprised—and maybe a little bit thrilled—by Makana's emotional response to his return. Their tearful reunion was more motivation for him to be a leader and engineer their escape. Even Gilbert Reedy deserved salvation. Everyone was counting on him, and Bodhi was hell-bent on deserving their faith and trust.

Arriving at the shelter's rear, Bodhi discovered Myles Spenser in the grip of a second and much worse epileptic attack. In the clonic phase of a grand mal seizure, the contortions of his face and limbs would have been a disturbing experience for adults to witness. The kids looking on with horror and repulsion collectively withdrew, leaving Bodhi and then Makana to give assistance to the stricken boy.

"What are we supposed to do?" asked Makana. "Shouldn't we put something between his teeth? A piece of wood?"

Unsure, Bodhi didn't answer immediately.

"No, that's just a myth," said Finn, coming up from behind them. "He won't swallow his tongue."

"What do we do for him, then?" Bodhi asked his brother.

"There's not a lot you *can* do except maybe place him on his side. You know, to keep his airway clear. But don't try to hold him down or stop his movements. Just . . . let him ride it out."

Makana, already on her knees beside Myles, maneuvered him onto his side. The seizure continued.

Bodhi spun around and, pushing his way through the younger kids watching the scene unfold from a distance, ran to the door. He pounded on it with both fists.

"Help! We need a doctor! Please!"

Bodhi waited a moment. With no response, he banged on the door again.

"Open up, goddammit!"

Hearing activity on the other side, Bodhi stepped back as the door opened. He was relieved to see the blond kidnapper, regardless of the assault rifle he cradled in his arms.

"Please, we need a doctor! One of the kids is having another seizure. This one's much worse."

The gunman took a few steps into the bomb shelter, but paused before venturing farther. He made no move to aim his weapon at Bodhi.

"Can you get us a doctor, please? *Médico?*"

Ignoring Bodhi's request, the kidnapper gestured for the teenager to walk ahead of him. The kids parted to allow their kidnapper an unobstructed view of their sick classmate. Only the sounds of the boy's involuntary snarls and guttural buzzing broke the tense silence. Stopping ten feet from where Makana was crouching beside Myles, the blond gunman looked on without emotion.

Saturnino had seen an attack like the one afflicting the kid plenty of times. Before his parents could afford the medication, his sister, Rosa, suffered in the same way and almost died on two occasions.

This one will die, too, but not this morning. His attack is almost over.

Saturnino watched as the sick boy gradually stopped shaking and jerking around.

Sleep will be a welcome relief. He'll be okay, for now.

Turning around and walking back to the door, Saturnino was confronted by the stoic hostage who had impressed him from the beginning, reminding him of his younger self. Even though Saturnino didn't know what the teenager was saying, the boy's strategy to ally with him was completely transparent. If Saturnino were in the kid's place, he would do the same. Without resources and at an overwhelming disadvantage, selecting a potential confederate from among the kidnappers was a good plan.

Appeal to the most like-minded kidnapper. Make yourself something other than a victim. Establish any commonality.

Even though Saturnino recognized the boy's agenda precisely for what it was—a last-resort effort to avoid his dark fate—he was compelled to admit that the plan was working.

CHAPTER 21

HOW COMPLETELY
FUCKING CONVENIENT

Standing in the foyer of Fischer's house, Shaw watched Hayley Chill's interrogation by investigators from the Maui Police Department. Agents with the FBI field office in Honolulu and his boss, J. P. Stevens, the United States marshal for the District of Hawaii, were landing at the airport this minute, and he couldn't help feeling sorry for the woman.

It was going to be a very long day for Chill, he mused.

It's going to be a very long day for both of us.

Shaw felt his phone thrum, and, turning away from the gathering in the living room, he was surprised by the caller's number. What happened to communication by text only? Of course, the presumed drowning of a US Supreme Court justice was news bound to travel quickly.

"Yes?" He had walked out onto the porch for some privacy.

"Are you bullshitting me, Terry?" asked Joe.

"What're you talking about?"

"You think I'm fucking around? Are we playing games here?"

"Calm down. I presume you're talking about Fischer having gone missing."

"Presumed drowned. How completely fucking convenient."

Shaw said, "If you think—"

Joe interrupted him. "Yes, I think you're jacking with us. I *know* you're jacking with us, you ridiculous fuck."

Shaw noted the plural "us." Joe, or whatever his name was, had never used the pronoun before. Another clue.

"What can I say? Fischer went into the water, which she does almost every morning she's on the island, and didn't come back. There's practically an armada out there right now, looking for her."

"Well, for those kids' sake, you better hope they find the fucking body."

Joe hung up.

With the call's unceremonious end, Shaw drifted back into the foyer. He was worried about Joe's loss of temper. Would he soon be receiving another photo of a hostage's execution? His eyes swept over the men and women gathered in the living room, Hayley Chill at their center, patiently and methodically responding to their questions.

———

Done with the call, Gunn sat down in time to watch a girl from Calabasas foul his daughter and steal the ball without a whistle from the referee. Briefly entertaining the notion of descending to the pool deck to punch out the inattentive ref and bounce his head off the concrete, he decided to focus his anger on the DUSM instead.

What were the chances Anita Fischer had drowned?

Googling on his phone, Gunn found an article from *Maui Now* that reported eighteen ocean drownings in Maui County alone. Between 2007 and 2016, the number of fatalities was a whopping one hundred seventy-six. It wasn't entirely out of the question, then, that Fischer had succumbed. But Gunn needed a body. He needed proof.

David Barrett wouldn't be a problem. Given the outrageous illegality of their plan to save the company, the Oakvale Pharmaceuticals CEO wholly relied on Gunn's discretion. Consequently, the lowly corporate security office held the true power in this relationship. For the remainder of his life, and probably beyond, Joseph Gunn would have Barrett, a billionaire many times over, in his pocket.

Gunn's real worry was the Cartel del Oeste. He held no such sway over those sadistic thugs. If the operation on Maui went sideways—or if the cartel's money stashed in Oakvale's accounts at Queensgate Bank in the Cayman Islands was eventually compromised by the feds—the Mexicans would force-feed Gunn his own spleen.

God only knew what those maniacs would do to his daughter.

Fischer's accidental death was not a contingency Gunn had considered in his planning. If Shaw had faked Anita Fischer's drowning, what was his goal? To buy time and locate the kids? The hostages' rescue would remove all leverage Gunn held over the DUSM. Ordering the gunmen to execute their hostages in response to Shaw's subterfuge would achieve the same result.

As he watched his lithe thirteen-year-old daughter—too slight, really, for the rough-and-tumble sport of water polo—emerge from the pool following her team's loss to the much more athletic Calabasas team, Gunn realized he had few options. Mulling it over, he waved away another parent who was approaching to bitch about the team's poor effort in the pool.

He needed to send Terry Shaw another message. Something more impactful than a severed ear.

Gunn recalled his recent trip to Mexico and the exciting things he saw there.

Leaving his seat in the bleachers to bring his daughter her towel and some consoling words, he dialed another number on his phone.

———

The late-afternoon sun bathed the Maui landscape—whether rock cliff, swaying palm, or fast-food restaurant—with a golden glow. As Hayley drove east on Kahekili Highway and dropped into a bustling Kahului, she struggled to shake off a blanket of fatigue that had descended on her on the twenty-minute drive from the Fischer estate. No one was exactly blaming her for the probable drowning of an associate justice of the US

Supreme Court, but nor were the authorities involved exactly not blaming her. Hayley had been chosen—or so her cover story told—for her swimming skills. So, what the actual fuck happened out there?

Glancing in the rearview mirror, she saw April Wu in the back seat.

"How you feeling, champ? Like a new woman?"

Hayley understood that her ghostly companion was referring to her nascent sobriety and not the exhaustion prompted by the harrowing day she had just endured.

"The stupid has started to lift . . . I think."

"You *think*?"

A discernable rebalancing of her mental equilibrium had been nearly instantaneous since quitting alcohol, and Hayley wasn't embarrassed to admit it.

Or that April was an agent of change.

"Thank you, by the way," said Hayley.

"What else are dead friends for?"

Despite her premature demise, April seemed to be positively joyful.

Glancing in the rearview mirror, Hayley gave her a quizzical look.

"You're in high 'spirits.'"

April groaned. "Har, har," then said, "I'm just enjoying this. So, sue me."

Hayley looked forward, navigating the Kia through increasingly heavy traffic. She wondered which part of her present circumstances brought April so much happiness. Was it her newfound sobriety or receiving blame for the apparent drowning of her high-profile protectee?

Lifting her gaze to the mirror again, Hayley saw that her friend had vanished.

Entering the hotel's parking lot and finding an open spot in front of her room door, Hayley clocked the groundskeeper from the Fischer estate, Jeremiah, sitting in a chair outside the door next to hers. A Hawaiian Jack Reacher, his six-foot-six frame and unsmiling presence struck her as sufficiently intimidating.

The car parked, Hayley exited and approached the silent Maui native.

"Seriously? The room next to mine?" asked Hayley.

Jeremiah, as was his custom, said nothing, but only gestured to the door to his right. The room's curtains were fully closed.

Hayley gripped the knob and pushed the door open.

The middle-aged woman swathed in a blanket pulled from the bed sat on one of two chairs in the room. Bare legs protruding from the bottom of her wrap, she appeared upbeat despite her humdrum surroundings.

"Be a doll and get me some clothes, would you?" asked Anita Fischer.

After she changed into a pair of Hayley's decidedly un-Fischer-like khakis, budget running shoes, and men's navy West Virginia Mountaineers T-shirt, they ate take-out mochiko chicken from Tin Roof Maui that Jeremiah had picked up for them.

The television was on with the sound muted, tuned to CNN, which ran wall-to-wall coverage of Fischer's shocking death.

"Believe me, I almost did drown! Swimming back to shore was extraordinarily difficult, and this from someone—"

Hayley finished for her. "—who went to Stanford on a swimming scholarship."

"Seriously? I've said that before?"

Hayley rolled her eyes . . . and changed the subject. "Jeremiah was there waiting for you?"

"Next pocket beach over. We took an overgrown animal track in the ATV, up the next ridge to the westernmost corner of my property. He had left his pickup parked on the side of the road."

"The FBI and MPD will want to talk to him," said Hayley.

"Jeremiah is Native Hawaiian. Believe me, the authorities will get nothing from the man he doesn't wish to give them."

Hayley nodded, studying the older woman. "How are you, ma'am? You still okay with all of this?"

"If I can do *anything* to save those kids' lives, then I'm good." Her eyes drifted to the flat-screen TV bracketed to the wall, displaying a video of Lachlan Morris arriving at the Maui airport an hour earlier.

With MPD patrol officers shielding him from a press of reporters and camerapersons, Fischer's new husband appeared visibly distraught. Walking from the airport terminal door to a waiting SUV at the curb, he kept his eyes glued to the ground, ignoring questions shouted to him by the vociferous reporters.

Fischer said, "Oh, God, the poor man. That was my first thought when you and Terry sprung this crazy scheme on me: Lachlan!"

"I understand, ma'am. But we can't take the risk of expanding our circle beyond the four of us," said Hayley, referring to herself, Shaw, Fischer, and Jeremiah.

Fischer brooded a moment, then asked, "And how long must we keep this charade going?"

"Twenty-four hours, ma'am. Forty-eight, max."

"We won't make many friends with this stunt, you know. Imagine how much money the authorities are spending to locate my waterlogged, crab-bitten corpse."

Hayley said nothing, but regarded Fischer with that flat, blue-eyed stare that had unnerved plenty of other contrarians in her past.

"Okay, the children." Fischer bobbed her head in resigned acceptance. "Maybe folks won't be so angry with us if we indeed help get those kids back home, safe and sound."

"Yes, ma'am," said Hayley, ignoring the conditional wording of the older woman's statement. She checked her watch. "I should get going. Bleeding minutes just sitting here."

"Right. Of course. That's my job. Sitting here, I mean." Fischer looked around the less-than-stupendous accommodations, already bored. She had been a woman of constant activity and accomplishment all of her life, no matter the scale of a particular goal. Now circumstances beyond her control had condemned her to do absolutely nothing in this 330-square-foot hotel room. "I'd *kill* for the papers sitting on my office desk."

"I'm afraid that would be impossible, ma'am. Dead justices don't write Supreme Court opinions."

"No, they don't, do they?"

"Maybe Jeremiah can get some books for you to read? Are there any novels you've wanted to dig into?"

"*Novels?*" Fischer asked as if it were a word for hard-core pornography.

"Anything you want, ma'am. We can probably find it for you."

After a moment's thought, the older woman said, "I've always been curious about that Potter fellow, funnily enough. But, of course, never had the time."

Hayley stood. "Shouldn't be too difficult to find."

CHAPTER 22

WAIPIO BAY

Makana and Bodhi faced each other, separated by ten feet of open ground and holding new Emerson flipper knives in their right hands. With a bowie-style blade, the knives had been fished out from the weapons crate and shipped to the island in conjunction with the men's arrival. Neither of the teenagers conveyed any semblance of combativeness however, much to the displeasure of their kidnappers directing the scene from a short distance away.

The designated gladiatorial arena was an open area that abutted the rain forest and the southernmost end of the property. Makana and Bodhi were equal parts confused and scared. Did their kidnappers *really* expect them to go at each other with combat knives?

The man who seemed to be the kidnappers' leader barked at one of his minions—a jokester habitually grinning—who stepped forward with a pistol and put it to Makana's head.

In his heavily accented English, he said, "Fight or die, sweetie."

Makana valiantly strove to fight off tears and lost that battle.

The gunman pressed the pistol's barrel harder against her temple, pushing her into a half-crouch.

"Fight! No cry!"

"Stop it!"

Bodhi sprang forward with his knife and slashed at Makana's tormentor. The razor-sharp blade of the Emerson grazed the gunman's face, leaving an angry red line the length of his right cheek that immediately sprouted droplets of blood.

The ferret-faced gunman who had threatened to execute Bodhi that morning was recording the scene with a cell phone. He laughed at the teenager's knife attack on his cohort—drawing a sharp rebuke from the gang's apparent ringleader—and stopped filming. For obvious reasons, the video wasn't supposed to include the kidnappers.

Wiping his fingers across the wound and then checking them, the injured gunman, enraged by the sight of his blood, was no longer smiling. Without thinking, he raised the handgun to shoot Bodhi in the face.

Another harsh word from the gang's leader stopped him from squeezing the trigger. Cursing, the bloodied man reared back and brought the gun around, smashing Bodhi in the head.

The teenager fell facedown on the ground and received a vicious kick to the ribs from his assailant. Bodhi stayed prone in the mud with his arms folded beneath him, steeling himself for the next kick. Before the gunman could deliver another blow, Makana threw herself on him, holding the flipper knife to his throat.

Tough kids, mused Saturnino Pérez as he and Javier Suárez rushed forward to stop the girl from making stew meat of Diego's throat.

Carranza put himself between the enraged Suárez brothers and the two child hostages. Saturnino put his hands on the girl, but not before she had managed to cut Javier. Lozano couldn't stop smirking, his enjoyment of the mayhem understandable; he was purely a spectator.

Bleeding from the face and neck, the injured Diego raged like a bloodied bull in the ring.

"*I don't care about your plan to cut them up for parts! I will kill them now! First one and then the other!*" he shouted at his commander, who continued to protect the two hostages with his body.

Bodhi remained on the ground, Carranza's foot planted on his back. The former army sergeant had taken the knife off the boy a moment before.

Like Lozano, he had thoroughly enjoyed the boy's knife attack on the Suárez brothers as a spectator sport. Violence attracted him, especially committed on anyone he deemed was out to get him. And Carranza was fully convinced by now that Diego and Javier were conspiring malcontents. He considered killing Diego on the spot for his bold disrespect of him. Superiors in the cartel dared not raise their voices against Carranza, let alone the men under his command.

For a moment, hostages and kidnappers alike waited to see what the bullet-headed cartel commander would do or say. Even Lozano was breathless in anticipation of Carranza's reaction to Diego's affront.

Todo a su debido tiempo.

All in good time.

His eyes reduced to angry slits, Carranza crouched, took hold of Bodhi by his shoulder-length hair, and slashed down with the flipper knife, carving a neat line in nearly the identical place where the teenager had cut Diego Suárez.

Blood seeped from the wound in profuse droplets. Makana screamed.

Bored now with the whole affair, Carranza pointed the knife at Lozano.

"*Film him, idiot.*" Swinging his arm around and down at the bloodied boy sprawled on the ground. "*Quickly, then lock them up again.*"

The former army sergeant pivoted and strode off, heading toward the house.

Diego Suárez snorted and spat in the direction of the boy. He left the scene, too, as Lozano stepped forward to film a short clip, recording the boy on the ground. His bloody face.

Terry Shaw's career with USMS was in the toilet. As head of Fischer's protection detail, he was responsible for her safety and welfare. A meteor could zap the justice and superiors would still harshly review him for failing to maintain situational awareness of the space rock hurtling Earth's way. Had Fischer slipped in the shower and broken her neck, they would blame him for not being in the stall to catch his protectee at the last possible second.

Though boats and Jet Skis were still on the water at sunset, searching for Fischer, Marshal Stevens sent Shaw home anyway. The interviews had lasted for hours, with various departments and their officials relentlessly grilling Shaw and Ford. Every minute the DUSMs were on-site was examined and picked over. Who had agreed to allow Fischer to enter the water? Why wasn't Maui Ocean Rescue alerted earlier? What precisely had the deputies done to assist their protectee once they noticed possible trouble? The questions were endless. Counting even her long hours in the water, Hayley Chill had gotten off easy.

Following an afternoon of back-to-back interviews, Shaw fought an urge to shout in his interrogators' faces, "Anita Fischer is alive and well, thank you very much. You can find her at the Maui Seaside Hotel in Kahului." He proclaimed no such truth, of course. Instead, the DUSM dutifully and calmly responded to every inquiry, leaving out only the parts that would endanger the kidnapped children of the island's upcountry.

Shaw had gone along with Hayley's crazy idea primarily because he could not come up with a better plan. Compared to killing Fischer and then himself, he had to admit she had devised an intriguing alternative. Presenting the scheme to Fischer after she came back downstairs from getting dressed and before Lachlan Morris had emerged, Shaw was hardly surprised by his protectee's receptiveness. Fischer's independent streak and creativity were qualities that had most impressed him.

He called Marie during a short break between interrogations. His wife heard there had been an accident and that Fischer was missing, of course. Shaw received her sympathy in near silence, then explained that he would be getting home late that night, if at all. He didn't need to worry about Marie asking too many questions. Shaw experienced a modest degree of guilt, though. His wife would feel bad for him, her compassionate side working overtime. There was nothing to do about any of that now. Getting the kids home, safe and sound, would solve *all* of these problems.

Driving east, Shaw avoided the hotel where Fischer was holed up, not wanting to bring undue attention to her location. Instead, he bypassed Kahului on Airport Road with a plan to meet Hayley in the Walmart parking lot at Pakaula Street. Minutes from that destination, he heard a familiar electronic chime. Retrieving his phone from the passenger seat next to him, he saw a text from Joe.

I want a body, Terry. Give me a body or I start MAKING my own.

Shaw was moving at a fast clip; memorializing the text and any to follow while driving was nearly impossible. Traffic in the lane beside and behind him, however, blocked access to the shoulder. He spun the steering wheel, swinging his SUV into westbound lanes and threading oncoming traffic to a chorus of angry car horns. Arriving safely—somehow—on the north shoulder of the highway, Shaw slammed on the brakes and retrieved the backup phone as Joe's text was disappearing on his primary device.

He was ready, though, for the video that came next. Pressing play, Shaw watched images of Bodhi Wilson sprawled on the muddy ground. Shaw assessed that the cut on the boy's face was made by a knife. The bloody wound on the side of his head appeared to be blunt force trauma.

The video clip was short, only five seconds in duration. Once it ended, the image on Shaw's phone screen dissipated and then disappeared altogether. He immediately reviewed the recording of the video he had made on the second phone, having the luxury now of pausing and repeating playback.

With the fifth viewing, Shaw saw a detail he had missed earlier. Despite the video's brevity, Bodhi moved slightly during the snippet. Shifting his body, the teenager exposed the wet ground directly underneath him where he had positioned his hands.

Pausing the video, Shaw brought the phone close to his face and studied the image. He wasn't mistaken. Letters were crudely drawn in the muddy ground just over Bodhi's hunched shoulders, forming a faintly legible word.

WAIPIO

CHAPTER 23

HAWAIIAN PLATE, GJE631

Hayley sat behind the wheel of the parked Kia Soul at Walmart, in a section closest to the entrance off Pakaula and within spitting distance of a Panda Express that shared the same lot. Terry Shaw had texted that he would be arriving at exactly five minutes after six; he was now a minute and a half late. She didn't appreciate the delay. Hayley needed to know her partner would be reliable in all aspects of their operation, large and small.

Then again, Shaw required the same of her and Hayley hadn't been exactly a monument of dependability. How was the DUSM to know she had turned the corner on her drinking? How was *she* to know? Twenty-two hours of recovery and Hayley was feeling the full effects of withdrawal. Head and muscle ache. Irritability. General jitteriness. But, as she had confessed to April earlier, the stupid had lifted. Though she still fell short of operating at full capacity, Hayley was confident she would perform when the time came.

She checked her watch for the third time in as many minutes.

Where the fuck is he?

Her gaze fell on a young guy coming her way from across the parking lot. Dyed-blond hair, stocky build, and dark complected, the man was most notable for the humongous, newly purchased ice chest perched precariously on top of his cart. Hayley had to chuckle at his attempts to keep the cart moving in the correct direction while simultaneously preventing the 150-quart Coleman cooler from sliding off.

Pausing to fish a key fob from his pants pocket, the blond man—Latino and not Native Hawaiian, Hayley decided—continued to maneuver the shopping cart toward the black Chevrolet Suburban parked across the aisle from Hayley in her Kia. She watched as he lifted the cargo door, slid the cooler off the cart, partially into the SUV's rear, and opened the lid. Next, he transferred what might have been thirty or forty pounds of dry ice from the shopping cart into the cooler. His task complete, the blond Latino shoved the cart away and leaned into his vehicle.

He emerged, a pistol in his hand briefly visible before he stuffed it in the waistband of his jeans and pulled his shirt over the weapon.

No one was around to see the man arm himself . . . except Hayley, who had frozen at the sight of the handgun.

She watched the man walk back toward the store entrance, a fabric object stuffed in his back jeans pocket Hayley guessed to be a black balaclava.

Drawing the Glock from her belly band holster, she checked the chamber, racked the slide, and rechecked the chamber. Seconds later, Hayley was out of the Kia and following the young Latino man with dyed-blond hair across the Walmart parking lot from a distance of about fifty yards.

Saturnino Pérez could not bear to see the little kid suffer any longer. Haunted by the suffering of his younger sister with the same affliction, he was determined to help the epileptic hostage. The contradiction in his actions was obvious. On the one hand, he had facilitated the commander's plans to harvest organs from the hostages by purchasing the necessary supplies, e.g., cooler and dry ice. At the same time, Saturnino was taking a grave risk in securing medication that might alleviate the boy's seizures.

Totally fucking weird.

Nevertheless, Saturnino felt a sense of purpose and strength that had eluded him since arriving on the island as he strode toward the big-box store. Helping the epileptic boy connected him strongly to his life before joining the cartel. The plan had come to him while gathering the supplies that Carranza ordered him to purchase. Saturnino didn't consider the possibility of failure or putting the larger operation at risk. He felt inordinately calm, as if he could bend reality to his will.

In the aftermath of the failed gladiatorial contest between the two oldest children, existing tensions between the Snake Eaters had only increased. Would they complete the operation and escape the island undetected? Saturnino's fatalism, common in his world, held that what happened would happen regardless of his desires. Whether he lived or died was for God to decide. Saturnino was similarly at the mercy of the cartel's whims. He would do as his superiors ordered.

But helping the epileptic child was wholly *his* decision.

Striding into the brightly lit Walmart, Saturnino experienced the luxurious swelling of pride as he walked with purpose toward the rear of the store, where he had previously determined the pharmacy to be located.

He knew what he had to do.

———

Terry Shaw pulled into the Walmart parking lot and saw the maroon Kia Soul, in the exact location they had agreed to meet. But Hayley wasn't sitting behind the wheel. Nor was she anywhere in its proximity.

Shaw debated what to do. He was keen to tell Hayley about the clue that the Wilson boy had managed to convey in the hostage video. "Waipio" had to be a geographical reference to Waipio Bay, on the island's north shore and not far at all from Haiku. He was anxious to act on the information.

But where the hell was Hayley Chill?

Pulling into an available space next to a hulking Chevy Suburban, Shaw exited his vehicle and headed toward the store's entrance.

The Walmart was moderately busy, shoppers having just gotten off work and buying only targeted items. Few seemed to be browsing, eager to get their errands completed and return home in time for dinner. Saturnino walked past racks of new men's and women's clothing and continued into the home goods section of the store. He could see the pharmacy at the end of one long aisle. Several customers stood at the high counter, conferring with white-jacketed pharmacy staff or waiting for them to fill prescriptions.

Saturnino continued walking, steering clear of the pharmacy and pausing now and then to inspect an item for sale. Timing was important, as was the location. He wanted to be close to the pharmacy, but not too close. The fewer shoppers he encountered in the area, the better. Earlier, when he had purchased the cooler and dry ice, Saturnino made a sweep of the entire store. He memorized the location of security cameras and emergency exits. The lone security guard—armed with a Glock 19— never left his position at the front of the store. No one gave Saturnino so much as a second look.

In the middle of the store, Hayley kept the young Latino guy in eye-sight and waited for him to indicate his intentions. For the moment, he appeared to be shopping. She pretended to do the same.

Her phone thrummed. Hayley half turned away from her target, but kept him in the corner of one eye as she spoke into the phone.

"Hello?" She hadn't recognized the number.

"It's me," Shaw said as he passed through the entrance.

"I'm in the store."

"So am I. What're we doing here? I thought we were meeting in the parking lot."

Hayley didn't know how to explain what she was doing.

"I'm following a guy."

"What do you mean you're 'following a guy'?"

"My age. Latino. Five ten maybe. Dyed-blond hair. I watched him drop off items from the store in the back of his truck, then grab a gun and come back inside with a balaclava in his back pocket."

Shaw stopped just past the checkout area and looked in all directions for Hayley. "Half the dudes in here probably have a gun under their shirt. Where are you?"

Seeing that the Latino guy was on the move once more, Hayley started following him again.

"I'm in household goods, center aisle parallel to the checkout registers."

Shaw moved vaguely in that direction, but his shuffling gait betrayed his impatience with what he considered a waste of precious time.

"Joe sent another text and video." He paused, his excitement getting the better of him. "One of these kids was able to reveal their location in the video, Hayley."

She heard this revelation, momentarily forgetting about the blond Latino man.

"*What?*"

Hayley stopped in her tracks and looked back in the general direction of the store's entrance.

Shaw was striding aimlessly through the carousels of men's shirts halfway across the store from Hayley.

He said, "Waipio Bay, just off the Hana Highway. Maybe eight miles east of Haiku."

Hayley pivoted again and saw that the armed man had left the main aisle.

Torn by indecision, she was momentarily—and uncharacteristically—paralyzed.

"Hayley?" asked Shaw.

She reversed direction and started walking back toward the front of the store.

"Coming."

Hayley hadn't gone more than a few steps when gunfire from somewhere in the store behind her changed everything.

An aisle with shelves of paper goods was more than adequate for his needs, with no other shoppers in sight and within proximity to the pharmacy. Saturnino stopped and pulled the Glock from his waistband. Checking again for witnesses, he pointed the pistol at the ceiling and squeezed the trigger four times.

The booms of gunfire were sufficiently deafening, producing almost immediately the desired screams of unseen shoppers in adjoining aisles.

Saturnino stuffed the pistol back into his waistband and waited.

The sound of gunshots from deeper in the hundred-thousand-square-foot store froze Shaw in his tracks. Shoppers and employees in his vicinity rushed for the doors, most screaming. More people streamed in that same direction from elsewhere in the store. The sole security guard was nowhere in sight, presumably one of the first persons to flee given his post near the doors.

Jogging in the direction where he'd heard the gunfire, Shaw stuffed his phone in a pocket and drew his Glock, holding it upright with both hands and pointing it toward the ceiling. The sight of the weapon prompted several customers in his vicinity to assume he was the gunman—or the "active shooter," as television news and dramas had trained them to think—and incited a second round of hysteria.

Shaw ignored the commotion and, assessing the threat level of every person he encountered, began his approach toward the rear of the store. He hoped Hayley Chill wasn't dead.

Saturnino counted to fifteen, then walked to the farthest end of the aisle that terminated at the rear of the store and eased his head out for a look left.

The pharmacy area was deserted.

He stepped out and fast-walked toward the area, stopping short of the counter, underneath a security camera bracketed to the wall and trained on the pharmacy service area. A tall cylinder container held numerous walking sticks and canes for sale.

Saturnino drew one of the canes from the display, swung it at the camera, knocking it from its perch, and then vaulted over the counter.

From his sister's history with epilepsy, he knew what medication she took as a treatment for her seizures. Suspecting that the brand name might be different in the US, he had checked the Internet before arriving at the store for the generic name: levetiracetam. Scanning the shelves behind the pharmacist's counter, Saturnino was relieved to discover the drugs arranged by their generic names in alphabetical order.

Forty-five seconds after pumping four rounds into the store's ceiling, Saturnino had the pill bottle in hand. As he left the storage area and moved toward the rear of the pharmacy, he swept his arms across the shelves and spilled hundreds of pill containers onto the floor in his wake.

———

Hayley had walked to the far end of the central aisle—against the stream of fleeing customers in the opposite direction—without seeing the gunman. Then, doubling back, she checked each aisle another time. The store had become strangely quiet in the next seconds after the gunfire and initial screaming of customers.

Hayley found no shooting victims in her search.

Pausing at the entrance to the aisle for paper towels, napkins, disposable diapers, and other paper products, she took note of the holes in the ceiling directly overhead. Moving down the aisle, she heard a clatter of hard plastic being struck and then fall to the floor.

The pharmacy!

She reached the end of the aisle and, Glock ready, navigated the corner, swinging the pistol around.

A security camera lay in pieces on the linoleum floor. Hayley could hear more noise coming from behind the pharmacy counter. She approached silently, gun ready. Before arriving at the counter area, a louder racket emanated from inside the pharmacy.

Hayley eased around the wall at the end of the counter and saw the gunman exiting through a rear service door. She leaped over the counter and pursued her target, almost losing her footing on the spilled pill containers and their contents.

At the door, she waited for a beat, then yanked it open, ignoring the shout from Shaw behind her to stop. Instead, she stepped outside—into the gathering darkness of the Maui night—leading with her gun.

———————

Shaw pulled open the delivery door at the rear of the pharmacy. Hayley was on the ground about thirty feet away, between two cars in the parking lot. He ran to her, scanning the area for her assailant, and, crouching, saw that she was bleeding from her head.

The DUSM began to check her for other injuries or possible gunshot wounds. He found none.

Hayley's eyes fluttered open.

"Don't move," he told her.

She sat up anyway.

"Your phone," she said accusingly. Shaw had told her that the kidnappers' malware almost certainly compromised his device.

He gestured toward a pocket.

"Been carrying my personal phone. Left the corrupted one in the car."

Relieved, she said, "We've got to get out of here."

The sound of sirens fast approaching came from three different directions.

"Are you crazy? MPD is going to want your statement. *And* you're going to need to get checked out by an EMT."

"I lost him, Terry. Stupidly. He was just some stupid kid, ripping off the pharmacy for OxyContin probably. It was dumb to go after him. Even dumber to let him get the jump on me. But we can't stay. The cops will keep me here for hours."

Shaw couldn't dispute her reasoning.

"You sure you're okay?"

"I'm okay enough."

Hayley accepted a hand getting up on her feet.

Her head cleared somewhat on their walk from the rear of the massive store to the lot on the western side, bordering Pakaula Street. With every step, she silently upbraided herself. Why had she let herself be distracted by some strung-out dude in a Walmart parking lot? What was with this "save the world" complex of hers? Who did she think she was anyway, Joan of Arc? Superwoman? Maybe not all of the stupid had lifted after all.

Approaching the area where they had left their cars, Hayley gestured toward the empty space next to Shaw's SUV.

"He was parked there, in that space. I watched him from my car across the aisle," she said, pointing at her Kia rental.

"Black Suburban?" asked Shaw.

"Correct. Hawaiian plate, GJE631."

"You wrote it down?"

"I didn't need to write it down. I *saw* it," said Hayley, in the next instant regretting the arrogance of her comment.

"You . . . saw it?"

Wanting to move past the topic, Hayley said, "I'll call in an anonymous tip to local police. Let's get moving."

CHAPTER 24

LEVETIRACETAM

With their third night of captivity, Bodhi and the other child hostages had lost any sense of reality other than their soul-sucking, alternative existence inside the increasingly dank bomb shelter. Time had little meaning. Acute stress suppressed appetites. Hope felt like a relic from ancient times, but the struggle continued. They had survived another crisis and lived to see the next hour of imprisonment.

Bodhi's plan to make an ally out of "Malibu"—their nickname for the blond gunman—had failed to gain traction. Seconds earlier, the blond kidnapper had unexpectedly unlocked the door to drop off supplies and rebuffed the fourteen-year-old's persistent attempts to communicate. Stern and silent, he pushed the cardboard carton containing six one-gallon plastic bottles of Ice Mountain spring water into the room with his booted foot and shut the door in their faces.

Bodhi had miscalculated; Malibu was no different than the other kidnappers. They needed a new plan.

The important thing was to keep trying.

Bodhi's most immediate worry was Myles. The ten-year-old had failed to recover from his second—and far worse—seizure. Having stopped eating, the boy accepted water only with prodding from Makana. Even the youngest schoolchildren understood that Myles was very sick. Bodhi was concerned a third episode might kill him.

Deadlifting the carton of spring water from the floor, Bodhi carried the box to the kitchen area, where Makana was prepping dinner for the younger kids. In a noble effort to break up the monotony of meals that consisted solely of the prepackaged Lunchables, she and Finn had opened all the cartons and customized their offerings. A mini hot dog removed from its bun and wrapped in the extra cheesy pizza was an early favorite. Mashing up the nacho and cheese dip with a Ham & American Cracker Stacker produced a surprising melody of textures and tastes far more interesting (and delicious) than the original, unaltered meals. Adding Airheads candy to the Capri Sun drink was Finn's culinary contribution, making him a hero among the youngest hostages.

"Hey, MK," said Bodhi, greeting his good friend, who he had faced off armed with a combat knife only an hour earlier.

Makana glanced at him while she continued to fill disposable bowls and plates with her latest concoction. A nasty red line stretched from Bodhi's ear to the corner of his mouth where Carranza had cut him. The hematoma on the side of his head was the size and shape of a halved hard-boiled egg. Yet, despite these injuries, Bodhi's eyes were bright and his facial expression encouraging.

"Hey." Regarding his facial injury, she said, "Well, you'll always have a conversation starter."

"Won't we all."

Makana tried to smile but just couldn't.

"When will this ever end?" she asked.

"Soon, I promise." Bodhi sounded confident. Like he *knew*. "Tonight is our last one in this . . . fucking . . . bomb shelter."

Makana had never heard her friend use an obscenity before. Plenty of their classmates liberally sprinkled their conversations with such words, but not Bodhi Wilson. He did not need the tribal affirmation afforded by such linguistic behavior. Dropping an f-bomb underscored the confidence he had in his prediction. Makana luxuriated in her friend's conviction. At no point in their ordeal had she needed this sort of encouragement more.

She even managed to smile.

"I believe you."

She lifted the flap of the carton containing the spring water and extracted one of the gallon bottles. In the process, a small plastic container fell out of the box—a pharmaceutical manufacturer's white "packer" pill bottle.

Makana retrieved the bottle from the floor and shook it, producing a reassuring rattle. She read the label.

"Keppra?"

Ten-year-old Finn had wandered over.

He took the bottle from Makana and studied it with clinical detachment.

"This stuff is like a first-line treatment for kids with epilepsy."

"How the hell would you know that?" asked Bodhi.

His brother shrugged.

"I asked our patient."

———————

After dropping his work phone off at home in Haiku, Shaw and Hayley drove the roads and narrow lanes just north of the Hana Highway for more than two hours, well into the night. Huelo Road and up Door of Faith. Backtracking to the highway and taking the right turn at Ulalena Loop to Waipio Road, only to double back to Honokala and a long, looping route to Hoolawa. They drove up Loomis, a narrow lane that paralleled Hoolawa Stream, and returned to the highway to check out Honopou Road. Any roads farther west wouldn't be associated with Waipio Bay, so Shaw retraced all of the routes they'd already driven. They saw nothing amiss. There was no sign of the kidnappers or their hostages.

Few streetlights illuminated these dark lanes. Most of the homes in the affluent and sparsely developed area were hidden behind tall fences and gates. The futility of the exercise was dawning on Shaw. What were they expecting to accomplish by driving these roads anyway? If the FBI or MPD were involved, they could go door-to-door and interview the inhabitants of the two hundred or so residences in Huelo, as the area was known to locals. Helicopters could join the search. But an official operation of that scale—involving dozens of uniformed investigators—would put the kids at grave risk.

"How much longer do you think we should stay out here?" he asked Hayley, sitting in the passenger seat and gazing out her open window. Into the darkness and its shadows. They hadn't spoken in the last fifteen minutes.

She also recognized the ineffectiveness of prowling the narrow, unlit roads off Waipio Bay without canvassing residents. But Hayley didn't want to return to the hotel, where Anita Fischer would expect results. She was no stranger to tough predicaments. The trick was to replace fear and panic with mule-strength persistence.

From a tumble of thoughts—and a day that seemingly began eons ago—Hayley snatched random, near-term memories. A satisfying run through the heavily scented, thick air of predawn Maui. Walking in Fischer's house moments before Terry Shaw's attempt to kill her. Plunging into the ocean and the luxurious sensation of seawater on her skin. Hours of interviews after Fischer's presumed drowning. All of these recollections and more flickered past her active consciousness like an old-time kinetoscope.

Hayley experienced an odd and deeply unsettling feeling as if she were an impassive voyeur of someone else's life.

The image of the blond Latino guy snapped into focus. His gigantic cooler. Dry ice.

Hayley's gift of an extraordinary memory encompassed eidetic—unusually vivid retention of visual images—and an echoic registry that enabled her to recall audio events. Even more unique was her ability to meld disparate memories, whether an image or sound, that would otherwise defy meaningful connection.

That instinct that compelled her to recall her last conversation with her superior in the deeper state, Andrew Wilde.

They found the bodies of Barnes's wife and kids. Buried in a shallow grave at Sky Meadows State Park in Fauquier County.

Hayley continued to gaze out her window as if putting herself into a trance.

What was done to these people before their deaths. No one tortures their own kids like this, not even cops who "snap."

Somewhere someone was calling her name. Hayley ignored the faint sound of Shaw's voice. She was almost there. Almost had grasped some truth . . .

Organ harvesting is a known signature of Mexican drug cartels, monetizing their hostages in ways beyond the original demands for ransom.

"Good God . . ." she said as the pieces fit together, the full realization falling on her like an animated safe.

"What is it?" Shaw's voice lifted Hayley from her reverie.

"The gunman at Walmart. He's one of the kidnappers."

"What?"

"I told you they found that USSC cop's family, right? The one who killed Justice Gibbons. The wife and two sons were mutilated. Organs harvested."

"Repulsive." Shaw still didn't make the connection. "What's that got to do with the shooter at Walmart?"

"He bought this huge Coleman cooler and probably forty pounds of dry ice. I saw him load it in his car with a case of drinking water."

Shaw saw it now. The evil that they were facing. He braked on the dark and deserted lane, unable to process the revelation and drive simultaneously.

"Holy shit." Then came a moment of relief. "Thank God you didn't call in the plates."

"Can you run 'em?" asked Hayley.

"We don't want to alert anyone at my office *or* the bad guys. Running a license plate on the down-low isn't possible anymore, not even for USMS. You need a 'friend' at the DMV, which I have."

"Good."

"Going to have to wait until tomorrow morning. I don't have the guy's cell."

But one detail was bothering Shaw.

"What is it?" asked Hayley.

"What'd he go back in for? Why take the gun in there—create a diversion and risk arrest—just to score some Oxy? Doesn't add up."

"I only assumed he hit up the pharmacy for opioids. Maybe he was going after something else."

"Like medicine," guessed the DUSM.

"One of the kidnappers might be hurt or sick."

A long moment stretched into silence. Shaw was brooding.

Hayley, as was her wont, got there first . . .

"Or one of the kids."

"Myles Spenser," said Shaw.

"What about him?"

"Severe epilepsy. The morning they were abducted he forgot to bring his daily meds."

Hayley nodded, her hunch confirmed. All of them.

"How much do you want to bet once the pharmacy completes their inventory, the only medication missing is for seizures?"

"But why steal medication for a hostage while you're getting supplies to carve them up for their organs?"

Hayley hated to state the obvious because what she was about to say was so . . . fucking . . . wicked.

"*Live*-stock, Shaw."

———————

Javier said, "*You want them alive, but you also want them out.*"

Saturnino sat in the living room with the Suárez brothers. Carranza was in his room. Lozano stood guard at the bomb shelter. They all sensed the endgame was near. Their commander had said as much. One more night, he assured them. The job would be finished. Closing down the operation on the island meant dealing with the hostages. The "harvesting," Carranza called it, prompting a chuckle from his loyal sidekick, Lozano.

Then home. To Mexico. And much wealthier for their troubles.

Diego and Javier Suárez had participated in the operation in Virginia, similar to the one in Hawaii but on a smaller scale. Breaking into the policeman's home while he was away and abducting his wife and two sons was a trivial matter. Operating on US soil, however, increased the stakes. Bribery would not have prevented long imprisonment had they been apprehended, as was possible in Mexico.

"Their abduction wasn't without complication. The oldest boy resisted. We were forced to knock him and the mother around a bit before winning their . . . cooperation," admitted Diego.

Saturnino didn't need to hear about the abduction. He was curious about the other part.

"And later?" he asked. *"When it was time to go."*

"Ah, Barbie wants to know how we carved them up, brother," Diego said, smiling. *"Have you ever butchered an animal, surfer boy? A goat, perhaps? A frog in high school biology?"*

Saturnino glowered, impatient with Diego's teasing.

Javier said, *"Stop, little brother. He wants to learn. And we'll need his help tomorrow. All of us will need to be involved in finishing the job. There're nineteen hostages. Nineteen!"*

Diego Suárez let out a low whistle. All kidding aside, the task before them seemed distasteful even to him.

Candlelight flickered against the walls, the only illumination in the room. A boisterous wind had picked up outside, the branches of over-hanging trees thrashing the house's windows. Saturnino perched on the edge of his seat, a willing audience. The older Suárez brother was a gifted storyteller with an excellent memory for detail.

CHAPTER 25

JAVIER'S STORY

Ten Days Earlier . . . Christmas Day

We brought the hostages to a safe house about fifty miles west of DC, a split-level brick home on ten acres surrounded by thick woods. The windowless basement—with an enclosed storage room—was more than adequate to confine the two boys and their mother. Gagged and chained to the basement floor, our hostages made no fuss. It was almost possible to forget they were even down there!

"Ever the taskmaster, our commander ordered us to maintain an around-the-clock guard, just as we have done here on Maui. We took turns, with four-hour shifts sitting in a chair in front of the storage room's padlocked door. Otherwise, for two days we did nothing but eat and sleep. There as here, only the barest furnishings were provided by unknown facilitators. Despite our isolation, El Gruñón forbade anyone from venturing outside in the daytime. When Lozano was on guard duty, I played cards with my brother. We were bored, of course, but that unpleasantness was eased by our anticipation of a generous payday once the job was completed.

"We knew that our next stop would be here, in Hawaii, where neither Diego nor I had ever visited. Our commander assured us that Maui was exactly like Cabo San Lucas—all beaches and gringos—and our anxieties vanished. In years past, we had vacationed in Baja with our families and enjoyed immensely our time there. You know, Barbie, that our wives are twin sisters and we all share the same big house in Michoacán? No? I can see the jealousy in your face! Anyway, it was welcome news when El Gruñón announced that he'd received orders to eliminate the hostages. We were one step closer to returning home. But before we could kill the policeman's wife and sons, there was still much more to do—what he referred to as work no registradas en libros . . . off-the-books.

"Since leaving the army and joining forces with our former sergeant, we have participated in many kidnappings. Too many to count! Avocado farmers, rival cartel soldiers, journalists, and wealthy civilians—were all targets for abduction. The motivations for taking a hostage were equally diverse. Sometimes it might be for revenge. Other times there was the need to send a message or simply to terrorize an obstinate community.

"Our first victim—an incorruptible policeman in Talpa de Allende— fetched a payment of seventy-five hundred dollars from his terrified family. On orders from above, we killed the man and buried his body in the pine-covered mountains above town. Such a waste. It was our commander's vision that saw the potential for further profit beyond the ransoms paid by the hostages' families and business associates. Do you recall the reports from years ago that authorities in our state arrested members of the Knights Templar on suspicions that their network was kidnapping children to harvest their organs for the black market? I believe this is how Oscar Carranza got his devilish idea. Without telling the bosses, he made inquiries. A few days later, when we received orders to undertake the next kidnapping—our target, the pesky gunman of a rival cartel— El Gruñón was prepared. Or, at least, so he thought.

"I was assigned the role of surgeon because I received the best grades in high school. Lot of good those classes did me—my first attempt to harvest our hostage's liver, pancreas, heart, and kidneys ended in a complete failure. The second and third attempts didn't go much better. Even when I could find my way around the inside of a torso and extract the correct organs, the *process of removal and transportation had damaged the tissue so badly that the buyer refused delivery. Our ambitions exceeded our skills by a comically wide margin.*

"With practice, however, I improved my technique, due in no small part to tutorials we found on a medical school website. We determined the best range of temperature—between one and four degrees—for preservation and limited our harvest to the kidneys, the simplest organ to extract and the most robust. Focusing solely on that organ produced much better results. With our fourth and fifth efforts, Carranza received fifty thousand US dollars for the two sets of well-preserved and viable kidneys, money that we split among ourselves.

"Hand it to our commander to strive for more than perfectly adequate, Barbie. In conversation with his overseas middlemen, Carranza learned that a pair of corneas could fetch fifty thousand dollars on the black market. And skin, too, was a highly valued commodity. Both were far easier to preserve and transport than a kidney or other internal organs. Soon enough, our focus was on those two items—eyes and skin—for harvest.

"By the time we arrived in Virginia, we had refined our side hustle. As usual, our commander assigned me the task of surgeon, but ordered Diego to observe my techniques so that he might develop the same skills. Our equipment consisted of a plastic bucket, turkey baster, a forty-eight-quart cooler, twenty-five pounds of dry ice, one roll of wax paper, a combat knife, soup spoon, and a dermatome. What is a dermatome, Barbie? Imagine an adjustable wire cutter for slicing cheese. Once I got the hang of it, this extraordinary tool made the job much easier.

"In Virginia, we entered the storage room in the basement prepared with a cotton cloth and a six-ounce plastic bottle of diethyl ether. Held to the woman's face, the anesthesia worked beautifully. The two boys, of course, protested as their mother was released from her chains and removed from the room. Lozano's assistance was most beneficial on this occasion.

"Our commander had prepared the dining room table for the operation, draping it with a bedsheet and readying the ice chest for the product. Mindful of my brother's orders to develop his own skills, I had him cue up the cadaver dissection lab videos on a laptop. Confident that we had perfected our proce-

dures sufficiently, El Gruñón ordered me to collect the kidneys in addition to the corneas and skin.

"The hostage was unconscious, stripped naked, and lying on the dark-colored sheet. Diego stood at the ready with the ether should the need arise for additional anesthesia. I made my first cut, starting at the woman's sternum and stopping at a point just below her belly button. Slicing through layers of fat and abdominal muscles required repeated strokes until I succeeded in exposing paper-thin fascia. Plenty of blood oozed from these initial incisions without a cauterizing tool commonly found in a hospital operating room. Diego suctioned up a sizable portion of the fluids with the turkey baster and squirted them into a plastic bucket at his feet. The iron smell of blood filled our nostrils.

"Slicing through the fascia exposed a nest of intestines. From experience, I knew to avoid piercing that ropy tangle. Doing so in the past released a horrendous smell that drove all of us from the room. In the Virginia basement, I made no such error. Gathering both small and large intestines in my hands, I placed them intact on the tabletop. With that mess removed, the kidneys— shaped exactly how you would imagine, Barbie, like an oversize bean—were revealed on either side of the spine.

"In past efforts, I had cut the fascia-wrapped artery and vein attached to the organ without prior preparation. Given the subsequent uncontrolled bleeding, the hostage quickly expired. I learned, therefore, to clamp the artery strand with a garbage bag twist tie. By utilizing this technique, only a trickle of blood seeped from the end of the compressed strand when I cut the kidney free. Handing it to our commander, he secured the organ in a ziplock bag and carefully placed the package in the ice chest.

"Observing the hostage's shallow breathing, El Gruñón shouted, 'You're losing her!'

"Certainly, I couldn't help feel a slight resentment toward our commander's tone of voice. I was, after all, the doctor. Nevertheless, I quickened the pace of my labors. Harvesting the cornea from an eyeball far exceeds the limitations of my rudimentary tools, not to mention my skills. Therefore, our buyers requested that we collect the entire eyeball—'enucleation' being the medical term for the procedure, Barbie—which thankfully is a trivial matter.

I instructed Diego to hold the hostage's eyelids as wide open as possible and extracted the eyeball with a kitchen spoon. All that remained of the task was to detach the optic nerve and muscles with my knife. The entire procedure took less than two minutes. El Gruñón, clutching the plastic bag containing the hostage's eyes, was impatient for me to finish. 'Hurry! The skin next!'

"*I responded to his barking command without comment and retrieved the dermatome tool from my doctor's bag. Once again, my prior experience came into play. I had learned the best locations for a productive harvest of skin were the back, thighs, and buttocks. Women and the young were the better candidates—less hair, of course. Mastery of the dermatome tool required some practice. Good thing there was never a shortage of hostages back home to perfect my technique. By the time we arrived in Virginia, my abilities, if I must say so myself, rivaled those of any certified plastic surgeon. Though the procedure took several minutes, I collected four and a half square feet of skin. At twenty-eight dollars a square inch from our buyers, the haul was worth almost twenty thousand dollars!*

"*Diego asked, 'I trust the operation was a success?'*

"*Okay, I laughed. Ever the joker, my brother. In that moment, I remembered that it was Christmas Day. Involuntarily, my thoughts went back to our families in Michoacán. I recalled the holiday celebrations in the years preceding this one. Our children carrying candles as they sang and walked around the house like Mary and Joseph, asking for shelter. The fireworks after Misa de Gallo at midnight on Christmas Eve. I swear, Barbie, I could almost taste my mother's red pork tamales. The delicious champurrado that my wife, Isabella, makes every year for everyone, so wonderful on a cold December night.*

"*Burdened by these memories, I turned to Diego and said, 'I need a break, brother.' But our commander thought otherwise. Placing the woman's eyes in the ice chest, he said, 'No break. The two kids next. Then you can rest.'*"

BOOK FOUR

WITH A CLEAR MIND

CHAPTER 26

NOTHING IS AS IT SEEMS TO BE

At exactly 6:30 a.m., Hayley knocked on the door of the room next to hers. She hadn't gone out for a predawn run, mindful that she now represented the entirety of Anita Fischer's protection detail. Instead, after snagging two hours' sleep, Hayley had sat at the picture window in her room and kept watch on the walkway outside. From that vantage point, she observed the semi-wild chickens hunting for grubworms in the lawn that ringed the pool and two feral pigs trotting across the parking lot under a moonless sky. Other than those docile beasts, Hayley witnessed no other intruders on the hotel's premises in the long hours before dawn.

She had briefed Andrew Wilde in a lengthy and often contentious phone call that ended just moments earlier. Naturally, her superior was incensed that Hayley and her USMS "boyfriend" had essentially kidnapped a US Supreme Court justice. How could she be confident that Terry Shaw wasn't still compromised? By taking such an unorthodox action, Hayley put Publius on a collision course with the mandates of *legitimate* US federal agencies, i.e., the FBI and the United States Marshals Service. But with the justice's present location unknown, what would the deeper state gain by recalling Hayley and shutting down her rogue operation? Doing so would only imperil Fischer all the more.

After firm assurances from Hayley that she had things under control, Wilde grudgingly allowed her twenty-four hours to rescue the kidnapped children before he made his next move. Taking the win, Hayley was tactful enough to refrain from stating the obvious: Wilde had no "next move." As far as the USMS or any other federal agency knew, the Supreme Court justice had drowned. Until a body was recovered, the only authorities with an active role in the situation were Maui County's Department of Fire and Public Safety.

Fischer opened her door a few inches and then wider once she saw Hayley on the threshold. Walking into the room, the deeper state operative found the television tuned to a cable news channel. Coverage of Fischer's presumed drowning and its political ramifications continued to dominate all news broadcasts.

The justice muted the television's audio and returned to sitting on the edge of her bed. Dressed in Hayley's clothes and without makeup, Fischer had lost much of her magisterial gravitas.

"How are you faring, ma'am?" asked Hayley. "Enjoying the books?"

The first two volumes in the Harry Potter series sat on the bedstand. Jeremiah, Fischer's trusted maintenance man, had found the paperbacks at Walgreens and brought them around late last night.

"Oddly, yes. A fabulous escape from my present reality. And I so love Harry's wonderful humility."

Hayley nodded and smiled politely. She had never read the series, much to the dismay of April Wu, who had been an acolyte. At ten years of age—when most readers first discovered their love of all things Hogwarts—Hayley was shoplifting books like *The Girl with the Dragon Tattoo* and *Team of Rivals*, Doris Kearns Goodwin's revelatory nonfiction account of Lincoln and his cabinet. Though her childhood was difficult, Hayley wasn't the type of child who preferred to escape reality. She demanded more from a book if given her precious time. After reading these purloined volumes and others like them, Hayley typically returned them to a store's shelf in near-pristine condition. No book would have lasted long in the family home, where phone directories, shopping circulars, and free newspapers were regularly burned in the woodstove when kindling ran short.

Why the hell am I thinking about all of that now?

Hayley refocused her thoughts on present matters.

"Can I get you something to eat, ma'am? I'll be heading out soon."

Before meeting Shaw, she wanted to drive the roads at Waipio Bay again. Time needed to be spent in Paia, too—the nearest commercial center—in hopes of spotting the blond-haired kidnapper. Hayley would have liked nothing better than to repay him for the knot on the side of her head. Though less than thirty-six hours had elapsed since she quit drinking, Hayley felt stronger and more like her old self by the minute.

"Jeremiah promised to bring something by seven," said Fischer. "With all this lying around, I'm not exactly hungry."

"Okay. I'll be leaving once he gets here, ma'am."

"You're concerned about the prospects for finding the children," said Fischer, pointedly not a question.

Hayley hadn't expected this level of perception from Fischer, wildly underestimating the diverse talents of the youngest woman to win confirmation to the United States Supreme Court.

"We have a license plate and description of one of the kidnappers. Something to go on, at least."

Fischer was genuinely encouraged. "That's great!"

"We'll see," said Hayley without enthusiasm.

As she turned to leave, Fischer said, "I need to see Lachlan." Her tone of voice left no room for negotiation. "I want to show my husband that I'm okay."

Hayley asked, "Ma'am?" She was stalling for time.

"I watched another interview with him on CNN. And others, too. Fox. MSNBC. The BBC. Lachlan's devastated, Hayley. In unimaginable pain."

"Ma'am, expanding those in the know beyond the four of us would expose those kids to enormous risk."

"You work for someone, correct? Whatever agency or shadowy

group that utilizes your services—you have a boss. Did you inform that superior of my current status and whereabouts?"

"Only your status, ma'am," admitted Hayley reluctantly.

"So, that circle of trust is somewhat wider than you suggested . . . seconds ago."

"Ma'am, the people I work for—"

"—can't be any more trustworthy than my husband," interjected Fischer.

"Getting Mr. Morris here securely will require time and energy that we could otherwise apply to finding the hostages, ma'am."

Anita Fischer had to admire the younger woman's stubborn resistance. But that appreciation went only so far. Witnessing her husband's torment had been unbearable. Lachlan's broken emotional state, as evidenced in his tearful interviews on television, was such that she feared he might harm himself.

She said, "Sneaking him in and out will cost only a couple of hours, at most. Let's get it done, Hayley."

Shaw found his wife in her studio after his morning shower. On days he wasn't on Oahu, Marie's habit was to linger in the kitchen and chat before he headed out for the day. Shaw recognized in his wife a shared eagerness to lose oneself in work.

Does she blame me for Fischer's drowning, too?

He stood in the open doorway of the studio, coffee in hand, and watched her paint. Marie knew he was there but continued to stab at the canvas with her brush.

Shaw admired Marie's shoulders and lean arms—beautifully revealed by the loose-fitting tank top she wore—as she labored. He had *always* appreciated this view of his wife. Not since he met her on the beach more than a decade earlier had he desired another woman. His aching adoration of Marie had increased until that sentiment seemed to be something bigger than love.

"I'm leaving," he said to her back.

"Okay." Marie remained facing her work in progress, an extravagant depiction of two nude human forms of indeterminate gender as they became ravens and took flight into a dark, forbidding sky. With tones of gray and charcoal black, the painting captured perfectly the evil forces that had descended on the island.

"Are you angry with me?" Shaw asked, though he knew he should be going.

Marie put down her paintbrush and swiveled on her work stool to face him. "Yes—for not telling me what's going on."

Shaw had told her nothing of his and Hayley Chill's ruse. For all Marie knew, Anita Fischer was dead. Her unavoidable assumption was that her husband was a professional embarrassment, soon to be demoted. Or worse.

He burned with the desire to tell his beloved wife about Joe. That Fischer was alive and well. And that their friends' kids still faced grave peril. Desperate to confide in Marie the unremitting fears that had haunted him since learning of the connection between the children's abduction and his job protecting the Supreme Court justice, Shaw remained mute lest he blurt out the truth.

His phone vibrated in his pocket.

Hearing the device, Marie picked up her brush. She had given him the chance to level with her, and he refused . . . again.

Before returning to her canvas, she said, "I've waited all of this time since this awful business began. But I won't wait forever, Terry. I can't."

"Understood," he said. Then, "I love you."

She paused for what seemed like an eternity to him, then said, "Love you, too."

Curt.

Reluctant.

Shaw returned Hayley Chill's call from the car.

Anita Fischer's demand to be reunited with her husband, however briefly, wasn't a huge surprise. But that didn't mean Shaw hated it any less.

He turned the ignition, eager to get underway. Then his phone thrummed again.

"You're fucking with me. I know it."

Joe Gunn was pacing the corridor outside his boss's office at Oakvale's headquarters in Calabasas. He hadn't intended to keep breaking protocol, but the evolving situation required speaking directly with the DUSM. Two hours ahead of Shaw in Hawaii, he kept his voice lowered due to the level of activity on the executive floor.

He asked, "Drowned while swimming in front of her own house? Give me a break."

"I thought you were only going to text after our first call," said Shaw with a practiced casualness.

Gunn had instructed Oscar Carranza—who he only knew by his nickname, El Gruñón—to send the USMS deputy photographic proof of a dead hostage and was baffled by Shaw's insolence.

What the hell is going on over there?

The corporate security officer suspected the cartel gunman was fucking with him, too.

Gunn said, "You're bullshitting me, Shaw!"

"Justice Fischer is presumed drowned. With the assistance of US Coast Guard assets, Maui County's Department of Fire and Public Safety continues to search the waters along the island's north coast. Those efforts switched from rescue to recovery at zero six hundred hours today."

The DUSM's dispassionate tone of voice—as if releasing the blandest official statement to the press—infuriated Gunn more.

"Then you better goddamn pray they 'recover' her body soon."

Gunn disconnected the call.

The circumstances of Fischer's disappearance and Shaw's recent change of attitude were a concern. Though monitoring the USMS deputy's malware-infected phone had revealed nothing untoward in his communications and movements, Gunn strongly suspected that Shaw was playing him.

He entered the CEO's office suite, rebuffed the gatekeeping secretary's protestations, and blew into David Barrett's lair without bothering to knock on the solid walnut door.

The handsome, auburn-haired chief executive officer of Oakvale Pharmaceuticals was in a meeting with his vice president of marketing. One look at Gunn's expression prompted Barrett to turn to the other exec and ask, "Give us a minute, Carol?"

Once she was out and the door closed behind her, Gunn said, "I'm going over there."

"Hawaii? Is that wise?"

"Of course not. It's *necessary*."

Despite his elevated station in the corporation's hierarchy in relation to the security officer, Barrett shriveled in Gunn's presence.

"When?" he asked.

"Now."

"Okay. This drowning business, it's—"

Gunn turned, heading back to the door. "Never mind why or what, Dave. Just order up the jet."

In their conspiracy to launder cartel money while simultaneously staving off financial ruin by manipulating the makeup of the US Supreme Court, Gunn had always endeavored to play the game while "seeing three moves ahead." He had no choice. Failure of any one element of the plot would cause the entire scheme to collapse. Having witnessed first-hand how the cartel dealt with enemies at its stronghold in San Andrés Coru—the gladiatorial combat with blowtorch and chain saw difficult to forget—Gunn was understandably keen to see events unfold as intended.

———

The last time they had laid eyes on any of their kidnappers was when Malibu dropped off the carton of drinking water. Not coincidentally, the previous night unfolded without incident or drama, easily the best of their captivity. Everyone slept reasonably well. Myles was improving, with no adverse reaction to the medication and seemingly protected from further seizures. The older kids joined with the youngest in a made-up game that combined elements of I Spy with My Little Eye with charades. Corny but fun. Makana's concoctions in the kitchen rose to new levels of silliness and were surprisingly delicious.

The kids felt more optimistic, but none more so than Bodhi. If Malibu was willing to smuggle much-needed medication to his hostages, it seemed reasonable to expect more help from him. Indeed, Bodhi dared to hope he might assist in their escape. Imagining the sunny morning on the other side of the bomb shelter's cinder-block walls, the older Wilson boy experienced a surge of buoyancy.

We might just get out of here alive yet.

Another reason to hope ignited when Gilbert Reedy emerged from his self-cocooning not long after the kids rose from their makeshift beds. Head wrapped with the bloody homemade bandage, the only adult among the hostages got to his feet and shuffled to the kitchen, ignoring the stares of his young charges. Until now, Bodhi had witnessed the bus driver's rare excursions from his blanket refuge only in the middle of the night when Reedy assumed the children were fast asleep.

What prompted Gekko's incremental return to normalcy if not a belief they were nearing the end of their collective ordeal? Bodhi approached the bus driver, anxious to solicit his cooperation in their possible escape from the fetid bomb shelter.

"Gilbert! Hey, man, how are you?" The fourteen-year-old worried this overt cheeriness might be too much. He was overcompensating for the lingering bitterness engendered by Reedy's maiming; after all, it was Bodhi who had convinced the bus driver to participate in their earlier resistance effort that got his ear sliced off.

Reedy barely mumbled in response. Avoiding the teenager's eyes, he pawed through the big box of Lunchables. Bodhi persisted.

"You want Makana to fix you up with something a little customized, Gilbert? A little Lunchable razzmatazz?"

Another grumble and shake of his head signaled that Reedy wanted no further association with his fellow hostages, despite their tender ages. The bus driver retrieved one of the snack boxes and returned to his blanket refuge. Bodhi grabbed him by the arm.

"Wait!"

"*What?*"

"I just want to talk to you for a minute," he said, a plaintive tone creeping in from the edges of his voice.

"About what?"

Bodhi could now see that inspiring Reedy to join their cause was futile, but was committed to trying. Against his better judgment, he exposed his burgeoning optimism.

"One of the kidnappers is on our side, Gilbert. He can help us escape."

The bus driver sneered. "No one will help us."

He turned to face the other kids, who had looked up from their diverse activities, drawn by rising voices.

"We're going to die," said Reedy.

The room was hushed now. For better or worse, the bus driver had the floor now. He had *everybody's* attention.

Articulating every syllable, he said, "THEY ... WILL ... KILL ... US ... ALL."

Silence followed Gilbert's shrill declaration. Satisfied that he had made his point, the bus driver continued to his spot on the floor, squatted, and yanked the blanket over his head.

———————

Shaw pulled over and stopped at the passenger drop-off curb of Kahului Airport. He looked at Lachlan Morris in the seat beside him and held out his hand, palm up.

"Phone, please, sir."

The DUSM's work phone was in the trunk. Shaw still didn't know if the malware installed on the device only betrayed his location and communications or was also able to hijack audio and camera capabilities. No reason to take any chances.

"Seriously?" asked Morris. "I turned it off when we got in the car, as you requested."

At half past nine in the morning, the once celebrated journalist and sometimes bestselling author was feeling the harsh effects of insufficient sleep, exhaustion from multiple televised interviews, and the shock of losing his wife of fewer than two days. As a result, his coping skills were at a low ebb.

"Dead serious, sir. With the SIM card inserted, bad actors can still track the device even when it's powered off. Just easier if I hold on to the phone."

"What is this all about anyway? I have a right to know."

"I'm sorry, sir. All of your questions will be answered soon, I can promise you that."

Morris relented. "Fine. What are my instructions again?"

"Take the tram back to the rent-a-car facility." He indicated the light rail line across the street from the terminal. "Go to the parking area for Budget, stall J7. Get in the car and you'll be driven to the ultimate destination."

"Ridiculous," muttered Morris. Nevertheless, he donned sunglasses and a Washington Nationals baseball cap and, with a modicum of stealth, exited the car and walked across the street to the tram.

———————————

Hayley was sitting behind the wheel of another Kia Soul, exactly like the one she had turned in twenty minutes earlier. She had told the rental agent that her previous vehicle was making "funny noises" under the hood and was quickly provided with a replacement. The quirky, boxy Kia was growing on her, and Hayley considered replacing her BMW Mini she had back home in DC with a used Soul.

The passenger-side door opened and Lachlan Morris climbed in.

She and Morris had barely interacted on his wedding day. Of course, he remembered Hayley for her infamous takedown of the innocent photographer.

"Oh, it's *you*."

"Sir, if you don't mind getting in the back seat?"

Making no secret of his exasperation, Morris exited the front of the car and got into the cramped back seat. Hayley checked the enclosed parking garage in all directions for law enforcement or media presence. None was in evidence.

With Morris ensconced in the back seat, Hayley turned the ignition. Before she reversed out of the parking stall, she had one last request for her aggravated passenger.

"And, sir, if you would please lie down on the seat."

Morris gaped at her, incredulous. "You must be joking!"

If pressed, Hayley would have most likely admitted the tradecraft wasn't sophisticated. But what more could she expect with so little time to prepare . . . and Morris's recalcitrance? However improvised, she was confident that these simple measures, while annoying, would preserve the secrecy of Anita Fischer's status and location.

Hayley merely stared at Lachlan Morris and waited for him to comply.

Defeated—and his curiosity piqued by these cloak-and-dagger measures—he scrunched down and laid himself across the car's back seat.

Hayley got underway, vigilant for any vehicles following her out of the car rental center and onto Airport Road.

"How long is this going to take?" asked Morris, his mood not improving.

"Not long, sir. Approximately eight minutes."

She had other concerns besides her passenger's impatience. Shaw had connected with his contact at DMV an hour earlier and determined what they expected: the plates on the Suburban at Walmart came back as stolen. Hayley's description of the blond Latino dude was all they had to go on. With a sense that they were running out of time, Shaw lobbied hard to get the truck and suspect descriptions out to law enforcement agencies currently on the ground.

He's wavering. The pressure is getting to him.

Hayley recognized that Shaw had shouldered the burden of nineteen lives for several days. Unsurprisingly, he was primed to throw all caution aside and seek reinforcements. She needed to talk to him, convince him that they must hold off communicating with the police or FBI. Give them more time to think. And maybe get lucky.

"This better be worth it," grumbled Morris from the back seat. "My wife died yesterday, remember?"

"Understood, sir."

"*You* were in the water to protect her. *You* were brought in *exactly* for that purpose."

"Yes, sir."

Hayley wanted to tell him that she was sorry for his loss, but hesitated to do so because (a) Morris had suffered no such loss, and (b) he was being a jackass about it.

So, she said nothing.

"This is just great," said her passenger, plumbing new levels of self-pity.

Hayley saw the hotel halfway up the block and was grateful that her ordeal was almost over.

Ten minutes.

That's how much time she intended to give the newlyweds. Ten minutes and not a second longer.

She knocked on the hotel door. After twenty seconds, she rapped on it again but more emphatically. Fischer opened the door. Looking past her, Hayley could see Lachlan Morris sitting on the bed. Stunned to silence and staring at the floor, he was immobile. His new wife, however, was smiling as she regarded Hayley Chill.

"Thank you, dear."

"You impressed upon Mr. Morris the need for his absolute discretion, ma'am?"

"Yes, of course. Lachlan wants a safe resolution to this hideous kidnapping as much as anyone."

Hayley nodded. "We should be going then, ma'am. I'll be running him back up to the house."

"Do your thing, by all means. And thank you again."

Having been genuinely concerned for her new husband's mental and emotional well-being, Fischer's gratitude toward the younger woman was enormous.

Hayley only nodded in response.

Fischer turned toward Morris.

"Lachlan . . . ?"

He stood and shuffled to the door. As a journalist, Morris had covered wars and assassinations. He watched a space shuttle disintegrate in the blue Texas sky and was at Ground Zero for the World Trade Center's collapse. But nothing had prepared him for the shock of seeing his wife alive again.

His gaze had no focal point, roving fitfully. But that emotionally overloaded distraction found its center when Morris looked into Hayley's eyes and held fast on them.

Finally, he said, "My deepest apologies, Agent Chill."

Twenty-four hours after Fischer had disappeared in the waters below her bluff-top estate, local news trucks and other journalists were still camped out at the gate. A quarter mile in either direction, driveways and turnouts had been similarly commandeered by shiny vans, rental cars, and police cruisers.

As she slowed for the last hairpin turn before Fischer's address, Hayley looked at Morris sitting in the front seat beside her.

"Let's just get down to the house. No involvement with any of this business here," she said, gesturing to the gathering media swarm.

Morris nodded with a slightly bemused expression on his face that worried Hayley.

This was a mistake.

The newspeople saw Morris sitting in the front passenger seat of the rental Kia before it had reached the turnout for the gate, where a crowd of curious bystanders blocked the way forward. They scrambled like bees out of a disturbed hive.

Hayley was forced to stop. Photographers and camera operators trained their lenses on Morris. Reporters clamored for his attention.

Where the hell is Terry Shaw? Someone should be controlling this madness.

She tapped the horn and eased the rental car forward. The scrum refused to give way. Reporters, in a frenzy, mobbed the car's passenger side.

"Mr. Morris, any comment regarding your wife's disappearance? Has the Coast Guard provided any new information?" shouted one reporter.

"Lachlan, where exactly were you when Justice Fischer drowned?" yelled another.

"What are you feeling right now, sir? Can you describe your current emotional state?" asked a female reporter from KHON2 News.

Morris rolled down his window.

Alarmed, Hayley reached to stop him. "Sir . . . ?"

To the KHON2 reporter, Morris said, "Actually, it's really difficult to describe what I'm feeling right now."

"Sir, please . . . !" Hayley laid on the horn to clear the path ahead of them, to no avail.

"Perhaps you could try, sir," suggested the redheaded reporter with dazzling white teeth that mesmerized Lachlan Morris, who was verging on tears.

"Sometimes . . . sometimes when you think hope is lost, you learn that not all is as it seems to be."

The words were like a paralyzing gas that temporarily froze the scrum of newspeople gathered outside the window. Hayley, too. For that one impossible moment, she also was similarly immobilized, staring at Morris with dismay.

Then, all hell was loosened upon them.

CHAPTER 27

OFFICE-IN-THE-SKY

Taylor Wilson glanced at his wife and read the expression on her face as if written in Helvetica Bold: **ENOUGH.**

Standing at the police tape barrier outside the mobile command center at Makawao Park with other parents and concerned citizens, they watched police and FBI investigators come and go in their vehicles or converse in tight huddles out of the spectators' earshot. Seventy-six hours had passed since the abduction of the children and their bus driver. As far as Taylor and Janet knew, the authorities had turned up exactly zero clues regarding their disappearance. No idea who had taken the kids. Not an inkling where the hostages were located. Up to this point, the people of Maui's upcountry had received only concerned sympathy and requests for continued patience from the police.

Seventy-six hours.

Fuck patience.

If there was a silver lining to the horror of their sons' abduction, the slow-moving tragedy had papered over the couple's marital problems. In no way had Janet forgiven her husband for his transgressions. But those problems seemed insignificant now. To be sorted out later. The bond forged by their shared parenthood of Bodhi and Finn was as strong as ever, if not more so. Together they had traveled the nerve-racking emotional journey of their sons' disappearance in lockstep.

And now this communal outrage, anger that required a target.

Fifteen minutes past noon on the fourth day of the kidnapping, the upcountry's residents had had enough. If the investigators on the ground couldn't get the job done, it was well past the time to bring in new teams. Maybe there was reason to suspect the motivations of the people at work inside the mobile command center, as some locals suggested. The police detectives and FBI agents—with their impassive faces and methodical diligence—had slowly but surely incurred the community's wrath and suspicions.

"I know," Taylor told her, the first words they had exchanged in the last twenty minutes. They had stood vigil at this place every day since Bodhi and Finn's abduction. Together or taking turns, the Wilsons believed that maintaining a presence at Makawao Park was the very least they could do to participate in the effort to find their children.

Janet, her face gray and wrecked by anxiety, glanced toward her husband with bloodshot eyes. "How can they not have found *something* by now?"

"I'll tell you how," offered a man—Mike Schneider, whose ten-year-old daughter was among the missing kids—standing next to them. "They're part of it."

"Part of what?" asked Taylor warily. Two days earlier, wild rumors swirled that "drug addicts" were responsible for the kidnapping. A small mob gathered at the park in Paia, the site of the island's only homeless encampment. The ensuing altercation drew a police response. Arrests were made on both sides of the battle lines. Taylor was nearly swept up in the mob's passion, fomented around Toohey's outside picnic tables, but the grief-stricken father luckily demurred at the last second. Taylor was more cautious now.

Schneider said, "The kidnapping. Someone told me they saw somebody driving some kids into the complex here late last night."

Taylor was skeptical. "*Some*one saw *some*body?"

Schneider's chest inflated, shoulders drawing back. "You don't care about your kids? Is that your deal?"

The other man's hostility suggested a potential for violence. Janet put a moderating hand on her husband's forearm, but the gesture was unnecessary. Taylor Wilson wanted no beef with his neighbor, a relative newcomer to the island.

Schneider was only getting started. He turned to face the small crowd of locals gathered at the police tape that separated them from the mobile units in the recreation center's parking lot.

"The kids are in there! In those trailers! I've got pictures!"

He held up his phone as if that gesture was proof of his allegation.

Three patrol officers from MPD wandered over, drawn by the mob's increasing agitation. Schneider and other parents pushed against the police tape to vent their outrage on them.

"Calm down! Everyone, take three steps back!" shouted one of the cops.

The crowd moved forward instead, shouting.

Alarmed, Taylor took Janet by the hand. "Let's go."

They pushed through a group of residents behind them, away from the evolving altercation.

The throng refused to be cowed by the police tape and patrol officers. Once they had overrun those two obstacles, nothing stood in their way. From a higher-up vantage point, on the road's shoulder, the Wilsons watched as investigators emerged from their vehicles and trailers to defend themselves. Shoving matches and fistfights erupted throughout the area, with police refraining from deploying more aggressive measures. A single news camera crew hastened to begin recording the mayhem.

Janet's hand went to her mouth. "Oh, my God . . ."

Both Wilsons experienced the same dread. *How can we save our sons when we can't even save ourselves?*

The new Gulfstream G700—with Casablanca marble, black-tinted cabinets, and leather-covered lounges—exuded an understated, elegant vibe that could quickly grow on Joe Gunn. Having been relegated to Oakvale's small, commuter-size Lear on prior business excursions, he was happy to commandeer the only aircraft in the company's fleet capable of flying 2,500 nautical miles to Hawaii. The Gulfstream, sumptuous workhorse that it was, could fly there and back without refueling.

He remained seated in the front cabin, eschewing the rear bedroom with its circadian lighting that imitated daytime across time zones at an accelerated rate. In such a delightful setting, whisked across a sparkling, limitless Pacific Ocean below, it was possible even for a distrustful and hard-nosed man like Gunn to allow his paranoias to subside. Maybe the bitch really *was* dead. Lots of people drown in the waters off Maui. He had looked it up. Twelve to twenty-five per year, with 72 percent of those being visitors to the island . . . just like Anita Fischer.

Gunn had spent the last hour seeking confirmation of Fischer's demise. His preference would be to stay away from Maui entirely. With three hours of flight time remaining, he fervently hoped to receive word before touchdown. That was all he required. Even if the pilot was making his approach to the airport at Kahului, Gunn would cancel landing and return straightaway to California.

He searched for the latest news on his tablet by accessing the Internet via a Ka-band "office-in-the-sky" satellite system. No matter how many times Gunn checked, the news was the same as it had been for the last twenty-four hours: Fischer was presumed drowned, her body yet to be recovered.

The information was the same every time.

Until it wasn't.

Then the news was very different. And Joe Gunn knew that the sleek Gulfstream would be landing at Maui after all.

"That fatuous idiot! What the fuck was he thinking?"

Terry Shaw drove the SUV with alarming speed through the narrow hairpin turns of the mountainside road that led back into town. Next to him, Hayley sat without expression. Of course, rescuing the kidnapped children was of paramount importance; contemplating the tragedy of their deaths was a slithering anxiety at the edges of her consciousness. But Shaw's compulsion to rescue the children was of a whole other order, his urgency to get off the hill bordering on maniacal. Hayley understood the operational necessity of keeping her emotions in check.

Shaw had been in a rage since Hayley dropped off Morris at the bluff-top estate, where the DUSM was waiting. News of the cryptic statement to the KHON2 television reporter—with a corroborating videotape of the short interview—had rocketed around the world in the few minutes it took Hayley to steer the Kia through the mob at the gate and down the long drive to the austere, modernist house. As Hayley pulled up, Shaw had received notification of Morris's gaffe on his phone. Now they were racing back to town. To do what exactly?

Personal failure was not in Hayley's repertoire. Whether earning her blue cord as one of the first women to pass infantry training, going unbeaten as an amateur boxer, or being selected over all other recruits by the deeper state for its first operation, her superpower was to get shit done.

"I'm sorry, Shaw. I tried to stop him. He just . . . blurted it out."

"We need to tell MPD and the bureau what we know. We need to tell them *now*."

"Are we at that point yet?" Off his cutting look, Hayley added, "No one knows what the hell Morris was trying to say back there. He wasn't making any sense."

"He said enough to create doubt that Fischer is actually dead. And that's a green light for these maniacs to start killing kids."

They narrowly avoided clipping a tourist's rental jeep heading up the road in the opposite direction.

Calmly, Hayley asked, "Mind keeping your eyes on the road, Shaw?"

Shaw eased his foot off the accelerator and swerved back into his lane, narrowly avoiding a collision with a second touring jeep.

But his point was well taken. Hayley recognized the paucity of leads available to them. Speculation in the news media regarding Fischer's whereabouts was at a feverish pitch. Time had run out.

She said, "Okay. Let's phone it in."

They had arrived on the outskirts of Kahului, just past the elementary school. Shaw immediately pulled over to the shoulder and stopped.

He didn't care which phone he used anymore. The kidnappers would soon know that the cavalry was coming for them once helicopters, alerted by Shaw's tip, began sweeping Waipio Bay in search of their hideout. The question was, of course, how many children would still be alive when help arrived?

The order to kill the hostages had come five minutes earlier. Like a chef in a Michelin three-star restaurant kitchen, Carranza directed the other men in preparations to close out operations at the house on Honokala Road. Saturnino pulled a small kitchen table into the main room, where he placed it parallel to the much longer dining table.

"*Little kids on this one,*" Oscar Carranza said, gesturing toward the kitchen table. "*The older ones here.*"

Saturnino worked robotically—without words exchanged or show of emotion—and gathered the necessary tools and implements he had purchased at the Walmart store. Chest and dry ice. Two turkey basters and buckets. He placed these items—scissors, knives, and tablespoons—on the floor beside the tables. Time was too short to bother with sheets. Despite the number of hostages, Carranza had ordered them to collect kidneys, eyeballs, and skin.

With two teams working—Javier Suárez and Lozano cutting while Saturnino and Diego assisted—the men hoped to be finished and on their way to the airport in three or four hours. However, their commander hadn't told them all the details of their new orders. Instead, he wanted them to get the business here completed first. Only then would he tell the others what would come next.

Saturnino had heard people in extreme crisis describe an "out-of-body" experience and wondered if that was what he was feeling now. He imagined his younger self standing in the open doorway into the kitchen, watching his older self's preparations to harvest organs from eighteen schoolchildren and their bus driver. Even his repulsion and disgust felt distant and disembodied.

What happened to the world?

How had it become thus so?

Carranza gestured toward Saturnino and Diego and said, *"Bring the first two. I don't give a shit which."*

"Ether? For the hostages?" asked Javier, hurrying to retrieve the plastic jug and cotton cloth from the kitchen counter.

Shaking his head, the former army sergeant said, *"You want to carry them? Fine by me. Or knock them out here at the door before they come inside."*

Both Suárez brothers nodded. The prospect of the task ahead laid heavily upon them, like the wreckage of a collapsed building.

Lozano, however, was impatient to get going. He picked up one of the combat knives and said, *"Quick, cocksuckers. Sometime today, at least."*

―――――

The cut on his face had stopped stinging overnight, its bloody rawness crusted over. The injury hurt when Bodhi smiled, an unlikely event given their present circumstances. After seventy-eight hours in the bomb shelter, a pervasive stink had infused their clothes, hair, and skin. If the bomb shelter possessed a working ventilation system, it was hardly adequate with the room's number of inhabitants. More than one of the child hostages had vomited from the stench, only worsening the problem.

So it was with some relief that the fourteen-year-old heard the padlocks opened outside the door. Whatever was to come next, at least a breath of fresh Maui air would be part of the bargain.

The door pushed open and two men entered with pistols in hand. One of them was Malibu. The other kidnapper was the man the kids called Smile Button.

Bodhi caught the attention of Malibu, whose grim expression communicated all that the teenager needed to know.

Beware.

The situation is dire.

He pivoted to the other kids.

"Move back!"

The children fled toward the room's rear, their screams achieving an ever-higher pitch. Smile Button charged forward, looking over his shoulder and shouting something in Spanish to his fellow kidnapper. Then, shoving the Glock into the front of his waistband, he snagged one of the stragglers—Myles Spenser, as fate would have it—and began to drag him toward the open door.

Bodhi threw himself on the kidnapper, wrapping his arms around his legs. Smile Button responded by hammering the teen in the face with his clenched fist and knocking him out.

Myles wailed.

The older man shouted again at the blond kidnapper in Spanish. Malibu raised his black pistol and vaguely pointed it in the direction of the children. Smile Button had dragged his captive to the doorway, when a tremendous howl erupted from the rear of the bomb shelter.

Bodhi regained consciousness—stars still dazzling in his peripheral vision from the punch he took to the face—in time to see Gilbert Reedy barreling forward, past the startled children and equally immobile Malibu, to the front of the room. He collided with Smile Button with such force that both men and Myles Spenser fell through the door and onto the ground just outside. His caterwauling undiminished, the bus driver scrambled to the supine Smile Button and whipped the pistol from his tormentor's waistband.

A sudden rush of wind and roar washed over the scene from above.

Both men looked up and saw the helicopter, barely one hundred and fifty feet overhead, sweeping past and then banking steeply to return to their location.

In the bomb shelter, Bodhi sat up, and through the doorway saw Gekko on his knees outside, gun in hand and pointed at the kidnapper.

A terrified Myles scrambled away from his captor, back *into* the bomb shelter.

Bodhi felt a presence next to him and turned, face-to-face now with Malibu.

Who was silent.

The fourteen-year-old sensed an object with some weight in his lap. Looking down, he saw a doorstop—metal, with a rubber base—the kidnapper had left behind. When Bodhi lifted his eyes again, Malibu was moving toward the doorway.

Gilbert Reedy stood, waving to the helicopter and shouting hysterically, forgetting the gun in his hand. Malibu stepped outside, into the aircraft's rotor downwash, and pointed his Glock at the bus driver. The other kidnappers poured from the main house, rifles held out before them like a funambulist's balancing pole and charged toward the scene.

The aircraft's engine noise smothered all of the men's voices, but somehow the sirens of approaching police vehicles cut through that racket. In the deepest recesses of his awareness, Gilbert Reedy recognized that salvation had come to him and the other hostages. He stood and gawked at the helicopter, a statue of gratitude and relief.

Bodhi fearlessly emerged from the depths and took Gilbert Reedy by the hand, a boy leading an adult man back through the door and into the bomb shelter. Slamming the door closed, he shoved the chock into the narrow gap between the concrete floor and the metal door. He kicked once and a second time, only harder, wedging the doorstop tightly into that slight fissure.

Reedy caught the boy's gaze. Having lost one ear and some part of his sanity, the bus driver needed just one generosity from Bodhi. One small act of kindness that was not too much to ask.

And Bodhi gave.

"You did good, Gilbert," said the boy. "You did real good."

Racing across the open ground between the main house and bomb shelter, Carranza raised an AK-12 and unloaded a full clip on the chopper overhead. The aircraft retreated, disappearing behind the trees that surrounded the property. Seeing the boy and bus driver withdraw into the shelter and pull the door closed behind them, he gestured to Javier Suárez and Saturnino.

"Kill them! Shoot them all!"

Lozano, who had been on Carranza's heels, raced past his commander and the two other kidnappers, incentivized by the prospect of slaughtering the hostages. He seemed oblivious to that other expectation, the one occupying the thoughts of his cohorts. How soon will the police arrive?

The man known back home in Michoacán as Taliban arrived at the shelter door and, turning the doorknob, leaned his weight against it.

The door held fast.

Lozano pushed again. Nothing.

"Son of a whore!"

He took a step back and then kicked at the door.

The steel door did not budge a fraction of an inch. Designed (but mostly marketed) to withstand a nuclear attack, the door was an impenetrable barrier for cartel gunmen, too.

Police sirens pulsed louder.

Lozano raised his assault rifle to blast away at the immovable obstruction.

"Never mind them!" barked his commander.

Carranza blamed the blond kid and Javier Suárez for the unfolding debacle. He wanted to shoot them both on the spot, but given the present circumstances, the former army sergeant needed guns. The pleasure he would take in killing the two men would have to wait.

He grabbed Lozano by the shirtfront and spun him away from the shelter's door.

They had much to do in the next several minutes.

Terry Shaw sped through Paia, swinging around slower-moving traffic on the two-lane road and heading east toward Waipio Bay. Police sirens echoed across the upcountry, but all were moving in the same direction. More helicopters—commandeered from touring agencies—converged over the north shore east of Haiku.

In the passenger seat, Hayley was on the phone with Andrew Wilde.

"Is Fischer secure?"

"Yes, sir."

"Give me her location."

Hayley could think of no reason not to tell him.

Despite his weaving in and out of the oncoming traffic lane as he took the SUV to speeds that exceeded the posted limit by thirty miles per hour, Shaw glanced her way as Hayley relayed the information to Wilde.

His facial expression read *Is that such a great idea?*

Hayley returned the look with one that read *I know what the fuck I'm doing, thanks.*

"You weren't sent to Maui to rescue a bunch of schoolkids," said Wilde.

As if Hayley needed reminding. She couldn't think of a response that didn't include a particularly virulent expletive.

So she said nothing.

"Go back to the hotel and wait there until USMS has locked down Justice Fischer."

"Copy that," said Hayley, disconnecting the call. Her gaze fixed on the road ahead as the Hana Highway curved past Mama's Fish House and unspooled east. The ocean at Ku'au Cove was visible again, blue to the horizon where clouds collided in a pile. She knew that Fischer's taciturn maintenance man, Jeremiah, was sitting outside the hotel room of the justice-in-hiding. He was, in Hayley's astute opinion, a formidable bodyguard.

"Well?" asked Shaw.

He had a boss, too. Had to make many calls like the one Hayley just concluded.

She was unperturbed. She would see it through to the end.

"Drive," she said.

A traffic jam of police and FBI vehicles clogged Honokala Road a quarter mile from the suspects' location. Shaw considered taking the Ulalena Loop to Hoolawa and approaching the house from the north. But that meant an extra ten minutes driving on Huelo's narrow lanes and he decided hoofing it was a better choice. Shutting down the SUV and hopping out, he and Hayley joined dozens of other responders running up the road, a hovering helicopter their North Star.

Shaw was a little out of breath as they arrived at the house's entry gate, which Hayley didn't overlook. However, she hadn't broken a sweat.

I'm doing better.

Less than forty-eight hours had passed since she quit drinking.

Stopping to watch an MPD SWAT team use a U-shaped tactical gate-pass tool to open the gate's lock, Shaw said to Hayley, "Remember, we're not exactly wanted here."

The gate tool failed to work for unclear reasons. Next, a heavily armed tactical-vest-and-helmet-wearing officer swung again and again with a compact door ram. The gate still held, intact.

Hayley scoffed at the haphazard efforts to breach the residential gate. Though seven feet high and comprised of a steel frame and solid-wood planking, the barrier wasn't hardened.

"What's with these guys?" asked Hayley. Responders were wasting so much time, precious seconds in which the bodies could be piling up.

"Welcome to Maui," said Shaw, adding a sarcastic "*Mahalo.*"

After a minute of trying, the SWAT commander ordered his men to step back and gestured for the team's truck to be deployed as a battering ram.

Maneuvering the armored vehicle into position in the narrow one-and-a-half-lane side road required a three-point turn. Finally, its helmeted driver was in the correct alignment, perpendicular to the gate, and received a go-ahead from his superior. He drove forward, smashed the gate . . . and detonated an explosion that lifted the 17,550-pound Lenco BearCat armored truck into the air and flipped it over onto its roof.

The fiery blast—evidenced not only by the boom but also by a mini mushroom cloud that rose above the trees—was their signal to move out. Hidden from police observers in the three tour helicopters now buzzing over the property by the rain forest's thick canopy, Carranza, Lozano, and Diego Suárez, duffel bags strapped to each of their backs, hauled ass. Jogging along the unmarked property line across two neighboring properties—whoever had selected the house having factored in exactly this exfiltration strategy—the men emerged onto Hoolawa Road, deserted except for Javier and Saturnino waiting for them in the idling Chevrolet Suburban.

They piled into the vehicle and were underway before the onshore winds had dissipated the flammagenitus cloud of smoke and debris over Honokala Road a half mile to the east. A single-lane gravel road linked the Ulalena Loop with Loomis and the gang returned to the Hana Highway a mile from the turnoff farther east, where the authorities were converging.

Oscar Carranza gestured to the older Suárez brother to turn right, back toward Haiku. Not that Javier needed the instructions, but he respectively nodded his acquiescence anyway. Neither the Suárez brothers nor Saturnino was dismayed by the unexpected police raid. Left behind at the safe house on Honokala were the hostages and their precious kidneys, skin, and eyeballs . . . as well as the appalling drudgery of harvesting them.

Their commander's side hustle was his jam, not theirs.

As they drove west on Hana Highway—multiple police vehicles whipping past them on their way to the hostages' presumed location— the Snake Eaters understood they had not yet completed their operation. They knew this because Carranza had received new instructions from their client during their retreat from the safe house. There would be no return to Mexico today.

"We do this last thing, then we go home," he had told them.

Sure, they heard the police sirens. Not too long after that, the explosion as if directly outside the door. Even the concrete floor shook.

Good thing they were in a bomb shelter.

But how secure were they? If the kidnappers had explosives, the chock Bodhi had wedged into the bottom of the door would hardly be protection enough. So they waited, clustered together at the rear of the subterranean shelter and fearing their long ordeal wasn't yet over. That the situation would only get much worse. They thought of their families. Of mothers and fathers. Brothers and sisters. Grandparents. Of favorite pets.

More voices followed earlier ones. No words could be made out, but the language spoken was almost certainly English.

Bodhi couldn't force himself to stand and go to the door.

Then came more shouting. The voices promised that the kids would be okay. To hang in.

Didn't make any difference.

The hostages refused to budge from their refuge in the bomb shelter's deepest recesses.

After many minutes, someone began knocking on the door and attempted to push it open. Too much had transpired in this place for the children—not even the Wilson brothers—to venture forward and open the door to the unknown forces on the other side. Nor did any of them speak. Like Gilbert Reedy, the children from the Sullivan Academy school bus were finished. A collective anxiety had them in its grip. In a moment of harsh irony, their jail cell had become their stronghold.

More banging on the door followed. More voices. More shouting.

And then there was silence. A period of welcome quiet in which the children barely moved a muscle, with no words exchanged between them. Waiting. The half-light from a faulty lamp in the kitchen area at the room's midpoint barely illuminated their faces turned toward the shelter's opposite end. Eyes wide.

"Bodhi? Finn? It's me. It's Dad, guys."

The Wilson brothers slowly reacted to the sound of their father's voice, arms and legs coming to life as if from hibernation. While the other hostages remained in their protective scrum, Bodhi and Finn stood and ventured warily to the room's opposite end. But with a gathering of hope. Tentative yet thrilled. Tempered ecstasy.

"If you've barricaded the door somehow, you can remove it. The police don't want to do anything to get in there that might hurt or scare you," said Taylor Wilson, pausing before he voiced the obvious fear. "If you're *actually* in there, remove the barricade, boys. You're okay now."

They acted with a fervor, kicking at the sides of the doorstop but unable to budge it. Finally, Finn dropped to his knees and attempted to push the metal chock free, still without success.

Bodhi banged on their side of the door.

"Dad! We're in here! We're trying to move this wedge thing to get out!"

"Bodhi! Thank God!" His voice grew fainter as he must have turned away from the door to shout to others behind him. "They're inside! I heard my son!"

Finn stood.

Some of the other kids—but not all—had moved forward and gathered at the door.

Bodhi said, "You kick it on your side and I'll kick on mine. Back and forth. Ready, Finn?"

The ten-year-old nodded. And with that coordinated effort, the brothers slowly—methodically—began to work the chock free.

The door yawned open. Sunlight and fresh air flowed into the fetid shelter. First to greet the Wilson boys was their father, Taylor. Falling to his knees, he took both sons into his embrace.

———————

The children materialized from the bomb shelter, apparition-like. Reduced to the role of spectators, Hayley and Shaw looked on from their vantage point just inside the destroyed gate. Even from that distance, the emotions of the hostages and their rescuers weren't difficult to gauge. Both camps indulged in copious tears of relief. FBI agents in blue windbreakers ushered the children away from the bomb shelter and into waiting vans parked in the driveway. The kidnappers had booby-trapped both the gate and the shelter's entrance, a hastily buried device that required several anxious minutes of attention by the MPD's bomb squad. There was an indisputable motivation to get all hostages and nonessential personnel off the property as quickly as possible.

Hayley tapped Shaw on the shoulder; he seemed wholly engrossed by the children's rescue.

She said, "Let's go."

The USMS deputy was reluctant to leave the scene. Privately, he wondered—and, yes, even worried—if his superiors would ever recognize his and Hayley's contributions.

Fischer and Shaw would be dead if it wasn't for her.

If it weren't for him, the kids would have been killed.

We make a helluva team.

The thought he would never verbalize.

Shaw felt good for the first time in what seemed like an eternity. As relief coursed through his body—the purest of nature's opiates—he turned to follow his unlikely partner back out to the lane.

Hayley registered the ridiculous grin on Shaw's face as they walked quickly up the road toward where they'd left his SUV. She had heard earlier from Andrew Wilde that reinforcements from MPD and USMS had arrived at the hotel. Anita Fischer was secure for the moment. But for how long?

"What're you so happy about?" she asked, a hardness to her voice that took the DUSM by surprise. Not waiting for his stumbling response, Hayley said, "The men who want your protectee dead are still out there somewhere, Shaw. Their job isn't done, so neither is ours."

CHAPTER 28

GOOD GUY

S wapping out their vehicle was the first item on Carranza's mental punch list. Disposal of the Suburban would be a simple matter; given the high cost of spare parts, Maui enjoyed unwelcome notoriety for its illegally dumped vehicles. Set ablaze either for kicks or to obliterate evidence of ownership, the hulks of burned-out vehicles could be found on roadsides from one end of the island to the other. One more derelict wreck would draw minimal attention. To complete their mission the Mexicans would need new wheels to replace the SUV.

Carranza instructed Javier Suárez to pull into the same Walmart in Kahului where Saturnino had secured supplies. As they prowled the parking lot's maze of aisles, the newest recruit played it cool, wisely failing to mention to the others his chaotic effort to secure seizure medication for the infirmed hostage. Beneath his bland expression, however, was a churning worry: Would he be recognized in this return to the scene of a criminal felony?

"We want a Toyota Tacoma. Five or six years old. Four-door obviously," Carranza told his men. *"In the process of parking."*

The Japanese light-duty truck was the most ubiquitous vehicle on

Maui. They were also relatively easy to steal with an electronic device the gunmen brought with them on every mission.

Diego checked behind them. *"One just entered the lot. To your left."*

After the Tacoma's owner parked and walked toward the store's entrance, Carranza dispatched Saturnino to follow the middle-aged gringo wearing a faded Grateful Dead T-shirt into the store. Carrying a small Chinese-made radio device down at his side, an anxious Saturnino caught up with the Tacoma owner as he stopped to browse a display of discounted books just inside the doors. That was close enough for the twelve-dollar radio device to record the vehicle's key fob codes and transmit them to a second radio device that Diego held next to the Tacoma in the parking lot over a thousand feet away. The spoofed code unlocked the vehicle and started the engine without a hitch, as if Diego were holding the OEM fob.

Once the young sicario climbed into the passenger seat, they followed the Suburban out of the Walmart parking lot . . . and Saturnino could breathe again.

Carranza directed Javier Suárez to the mostly undeveloped south shore of the island. Passing in the shadow of Haleakalā, they drove through a verdant, Tolkienesque landscape of lush fields and stone walls. That all changed once the road turned east and—like dropping a new slide into the projector—the scenery turned arid, rocky, and forlorn. The lightly traveled Piilani Highway was barely the width of two passenger cars, hugging the rugged coastline for the entire thirty-five-mile rough-road journey to Hana.

Javier Suárez pulled over at a turnout on a stretch of road that was as lonesome and desolate as the preceding five miles. Nothing lay ahead but more barren landscape and wind. Driving the stolen Tacoma, Diego pulled in behind the Suburban. Saturnino exited to help transfer the duffel bags containing their weapons and bugout kit from the SUV to the smaller pickup truck. Javier climbed out of the Suburban to prepare for its fiery destruction. Carranza stood in the middle of the desolate road while the others worked, reading the latest communication from their client.

The former army sergeant disliked the dynamics of this interminable operation; their client had yet to inform him of its ultimate objective. Throughout the time the Mexicans had worked for the mysterious Joe, their orders—in decent Spanish but clearly not written by a native—had been detailed but frustratingly limited in scope. In Virginia, Joe instructed them to kidnap the mother and two sons and wait for further instructions; the order to kill them was issued two days later. For what purpose, Carranza's client had never bothered to explain.

The same held true in Hawaii. They had only the barest instructions from Joe to kidnap the schoolchildren, without a reason. Then, in time, orders came to kill the kids. Carranza could only guess that their client's objectives were not met on the island. Why else order them to delay their departure and stand by for further directives? When he informed Joe that the hostages may have survived their ordeal after all—reports of the children's status had not yet been released—their client's cryptic response implied a lack of concern.

The former army sergeant's suspicions worked at a high pitch. Survival instincts took precedence over all else.

My destiny is to die here. The bosses in Michoacán have forsaken me.

Carranza's doctors back home repeatedly accused him of paranoia. Friends, family. Fellow soldiers in the army. They all said the same thing. But Carranza knew the truth. They were all out to get him . . . *especially* his bosses in the cartel.

Saturnino was told to gather dry grass and kindling from the hillside next to the turnout, a readily available accelerant on the island's south coast. He piled the tinder in the SUV's passenger compartment, directly under the dash. With a nod from Carranza, Saturnino lit the brush with a cigarette lighter and backed away. Except for Javier Suárez, who remained behind the wheel of the Tacoma, the Mexicans stood in the middle of the road and watched the fire gain momentum. Black smoke began to billow from the Suburban's open windows.

A pickup appeared at the top of a rise one mile east. The gunmen turned their attention from the blossoming car fire to the approaching truck that slowed as it drew nearer. Without haste, the Mexicans moved to the side of the road. No one said a word. Their zombified expressions should have been warning enough. But instead of stepping on the gas and making a run for it, the old gringo behind the wheel of the inevitable Tacoma pickup slowed to a stop next to the sicarios' SUV, now fully engulfed in flames.

Rolling down his window and eyeballing the inferno, he said, "Whoa, Nellie! That's some roaster, isn't it?"

Carranza regarded the elderly driver with mild curiosity as if judging different cuts of meat in a butcher shop. He moved closer to the pickup stopped in the middle of the desolate road.

"Do you speak Spanish, old man?"

The driver grinned sheepishly and said, "Sorry. No Spanish."

"Sadly, today is not your day," said Carranza with insincere compassion. *"Do you prefer one in the heart or between the eyes?"*

"I have a phone if you need one. You want me to call this in for you? Is that it?" asked the Good Samaritan.

Saturnino watched his commander play with the doomed man. Acrid black smoke from the blazing SUV rolled across the road and down the hillside toward the ocean's edge. He could hear the snickering of the Suárez brothers. Even Lozano, seemingly incapable of smiling, was enjoying their commander's cruel performance.

¿Por qué? ¿Cual es el punto?

Saturnino stepped forward, drew a Glock 19 from his waistband, and took aim at the driver's head from point-blank range.

Maui Seaside Hotel's driveway was blocked off by MPD patrol cruisers and unmarked SUVs rented by the newly arrived USMS deputies. Shaw parked a block past the property. They returned on foot, with the DUSM vouching for Hayley when they arrived at the expected cordon of scowling Maui cops. All action, of course, was centered outside the room next to Hayley's, where she had stashed Anita Fischer.

"I will not go anywhere until I've returned to my *home* and seen my *husband*."

Hearing the justice's absolute declaration halfway across the parking lot was a relief. Despite the police presence, Hayley experienced a momentary and irrational dread that her efforts to rescue the kidnapped children had come at a terrible cost. Andrew Wilde was taking no chances. Working from behind the scenes, he had harnessed the full force of the United States Marshals Service to protect Fischer from further threat.

The problem now, apparently, was protecting the USMS from Justice Fischer.

J. P. Stevens, head of USMS's Hawaii district, stood just inside the room with Fischer and her maintenance man, Jeremiah. All other authorities on the scene remained outside, watching the confrontation through the open door.

"Ma'am, my orders are to escort you to the airport right away for a flight on a USMS jet back to the mainland," said Stevens.

Fischer sat on the bed, arms folded across her chest. After twenty-four hours straight in the cramped hotel room, her patience had evaporated.

"I don't give a goddamn what your orders are, Marshal. I'm going home."

She stood up. Stevens remained between her and the doorway, a seemingly immovable obstacle. Jeremiah moved forward from his position, in Stevens's direction.

Fischer waved off the hulking Native Hawaiian. "That's okay, Jeremiah."

Stevens could not disguise his relief. Regarding the maintenance man, he asked, "Does he talk?"

"If he has something to say," said Fischer. "And, I can promise you, when he does talk people listen."

Looking past Stevens, she saw Hayley and Shaw on the walkway with other gawking authorities. "I'd like to speak with Agent Chill," the justice told Stevens.

"Who the hell is Agent *Chill*?"

"That's me, sir."

Hayley took a step forward. Turning around to size her up, Stevens wasn't impressed. He looked to Terry Shaw for clarification.

Shaw said, "From Washington, sir. Sent as part of Justice Fischer's protection detail here on the island. Competent. Highly skilled."

"The swimmer?" asked Stevens derisively.

"Yes, sir," said Shaw. "The swimmer."

Stevens grudgingly stepped aside so that Hayley could enter the room.

"If you don't mind, Marshal?" asked Fischer, most insincerely.

A visibly disgruntled Stevens left the room, with Hayley closing the door behind him.

Sensing her imminent release from the hotel accommodations, Fischer was giddy. She made a face at the door and, in her best version of Tommy Lee Jones, said, "What I want from each and every one of you is a hard-target search of every gas station, residence, warehouse, farmhouse, henhouse, outhouse, and doghouse in that area."

Jeremiah and Hayley exchanged a bewildered look.

Fischer asked, "Tommy Lee Jones? *The Fugitive*? No?"

Her performance was lost on Hayley, who was not much of a fan of the movies cranked out like sausages by Hollywood studios. Jeremiah didn't even own a television.

The justice said, "Never mind. Lachlan and I were just watching it again the other night. One of his favorite movies. I think he can quote even more dialogue than me."

"I'll have to check that one out," said Hayley with little conviction.

Fischer laughed lightly, not fooled.

"How're those schoolkids?" she asked.

"I saw them come out, ma'am. The children are unharmed. Their bus driver, however . . ."

"A brave man," said Fischer, assuming the best and missing by a wide mark.

Hayley wasn't about to tell her what Shaw had already heard about

Gilbert Reedy's conduct during the ordeal, nor would she breathe a word of Lachlan Morris's gaffe that exposed the children to heightened risk.

"You probably should go with the marshal, ma'am. He only wants what's best for your security."

"But you said the children are safe. Coercion has been eliminated as a factor."

"The kidnappers remain at large, ma'am. Plus, I doubt they were the masterminds of the conspiracy. Getting you off Maui to a hard location on the mainland is the right thing to do."

"Married for two days and I've spent more time alone in this crappy hotel room than I have with my new husband. I'm not leaving without Lachlan, Hayley."

Unmarried—and her initial impression of Morris being something less than outstanding—Hayley had difficulty relating to Fischer's adamant declaration.

"Not really for you to judge the merit of the good woman's desires, is it?" asked April Wu.

With a glance toward the bathroom, Hayley saw the ghost of her dead friend sitting on the washbasin, legs dangling. She hadn't noticed her in the hotel room upon entering. Truly, now wasn't the time for debating April. The deeper state operative kept her eyes locked on Fischer to avoid the pesky specter's mocking gaze.

"What if I convince Stevens to hold you in a secure location at the airport until Mr. Morris can meet you there, ma'am? I don't see how that could be a problem. That way, he can join you on the flight."

Fischer seemed pleased with this compromise.

"Agreed."

Hayley nodded, turning to exit the room. She glanced over her shoulder to see April Wu giving her the politest of golf claps.

For fuck's sake!

As the corporate jet cruised at 550 miles per hour, forty minutes out from Kahului, Joe Gunn read the texts from Oscar Carranza twice through, not quite comprehending what had transpired. He had correctly intuited that Shaw had faked Anita Fischer's death. But, with the hostages still in hand, there was yet the opportunity to compel her USMS protector to act. How had the kidnappers' location been found by the authorities? Gunn considered whether or not he should relay these developments to his boss at Oakvale Pharmaceuticals and Carranza's cartel overlords. Doing so, he decided after a few seconds deliberation, would accomplish exactly nothing. Meddling from above would only complicate a situation that was screwed up enough already.

Time was short. USMS would be moving the Supreme Court justice stateside to a security situation immune to his coercive manipulation. No other sitting justice on the Supreme Court fit the same jurisprudent profile required for a decision in Oakvale's favor. Anita Fischer had to go.

As the corporate jet taxied to the terminal for general aviation, Gunn made the first of two calls that required an immediate response. He prayed that both recipients would be available.

If Fischer left Maui in anything other than a box, he was a dead man.

CHAPTER 29

TEMPORAL FOSSA

She was of no further use at the hotel. When it became clear that USMS was moving Fischer to the airport to wait for her husband's arrival, Hayley retrieved her rental car—one of the DUSMs had brought it down from the estate—and drove directly to the hospital, where the hostages were being checked out. As she had been keen to remind Terry Shaw, an unknown number of cartel gunmen were loose on Maui. Hayley was determined to find them, doubly motivated by the ghastly torture dealt Martin Barnes's wife and two sons.

The Maui Memorial Medical Center was less than two miles away. Driving took the six minutes that Hayley needed to suppress a sudden and unsurprising urge to stop for an airline bottle of tequila. Maybe two. In the earliest hours of her recovery, when yearnings were displaced temporarily by Mountain Dew and Snickers bars, she had concluded that the difficulty of quitting booze was overhyped. In the more difficult hours since, however, Hayley had come to appreciate the infamous challenges of quitting alcohol cold turkey.

She considered calling Susan, the schoolteacher from the AA meeting who had recommended a list of recovery supplies.

Cartel gunmen? Kidnapped children? A Supreme Court justice in the crosshairs of remorseless assassins? Sure, these were extreme threats of an unusually violent variety.

But, sweet Jesus, Hayley's skin felt like it was on fire.

I need a drink.

Two minutes from her destination, she found the number on her phone and pushed call.

"Hello?"

Susan's voice was like a balm on Hayley's blistered soul.

"I'm dying. And, without going into a lot of detail, I can't *afford* to die at the present moment."

Of course, Susan knew who was calling. As a member of the AA community for more than twenty years, she had fielded calls like Hayley's frantic cry for help on dozens of occasions.

"I can really identify with that. We all have lives, honey. All of us have people who are counting on us."

"Yes."

"But you have to take care of yourself first. Like on an airplane. 'In the unlikely event of a loss of cabin pressure—'"

"'—secure your own mask first.' Yeah, I got that. But, Susan, I'm just not sure today's the day, if you know what I mean. The timing is very bad."

Driving west on Mahalani Street, Hayley could see the red sign indicating the turn for Maui Memorial Medical Center's emergency facility.

"If you think you can schedule your recovery from an addiction to alcohol like a dental appointment, I can promise you right now that you're going to fail. Strike that. You already *have* failed."

The program was known for its avoidance of sugarcoating reality. Sobriety, a bare-knuckles business, required a direct communication of tried-and-true suggestions and coping tools.

Hayley, the ideal recipient of tough love, put on her turn indicator and slowed her speed.

"I just want to know I can do this, okay?"

Susan was getting home from work. Her day had not been easy, either. But it was another twenty-four hours lived without falling prey to her addiction. Another day of winning.

She said, "One minute at a time. You can do it, Hayley. Not to say that you *will*."

Then, "This might be a good time to pray to whatever god you do or don't believe in."

Susan disconnected the call.

As Hayley parked in the small lot opposite the emergency care entrance, she understood that any dissatisfaction with Susan's response to her cry for help would be childish. The point was connecting with a fellow human being. Of shared experience and community. Family.

Feeling that much stronger—not overcoming a crisis but having held it in check—Hayley exited the rental car and headed for the emergency room entrance, where several law enforcement vehicles were stopped helter-skelter as if in some frozen demolition derby.

Distraught family members waiting for their loved ones jammed the lobby. Tears, smiles, and whoops of joy greeted the emergence of each child through the sliding double doors. But those reunions were taking far too long for parents who had been through four days of unmitigated hell. Their collective tension had not yet been fully eased and it wouldn't be until the missing children were home again.

When Hayley entered the waiting room, medical staff had released only four of the child hostages. The real action was happening on the other side of the electronically controlled double doors, guarded by two MPD patrol officers and uniformed hospital security. Ignoring the disgruntled parents still awaiting their children, Hayley flashed her Publius-fabricated credentials and entered the restricted treatment center.

Every treatment bay was occupied with the influx of so many patients simultaneously. MPD and FBI investigators interviewed the younger kids, who had been the first to be examined by emergency room staff and given clearance for release. Hayley walked the entire circuit of treatment bays to gain an overview of all the victims. Her impression was that the eight-, nine-, and ten-year-olds were too young to be of much use as possible witnesses. She was in search of the bus driver, the sole adult hostage.

Because of the severity of his injuries—an ear loped off and the possibility of infection—Gilbert Reedy was still under the care of emergency room doctors and awaiting test results. Occupied with the youngest children, law enforcement personnel were nowhere in sight when Hayley paused outside Reedy's treatment bay. Medical staff was similarly absent.

She checked a small whiteboard on the wall for his name.

"Mr. Reedy?"

His head now professionally bandaged and frustrated by his doctors' stinginess with pain medication, the bus driver regarded Hayley through eye slits. He wanted them all—cops, kids, gunmen, and doctors—to go away and leave him in miserable peace.

"Mr. Reedy, I'm Special Agent Chill. I'd like to ask you a few questions about the men who abducted you."

The bus driver avoided her gaze and said nothing.

"Did you overhear any of their discussions, sir? The location of a second hideout?" asked Hayley.

The bus driver shook his head.

"Go away."

"Any information you might have can be of help. The smallest detail."

But he had gone mute again.

"Perhaps a description of the kidnappers?"

Nothing.

It dawned on Hayley that the bus driver wasn't destined for any form of redemption. Now what?

"They took off their masks after a while."

The child's voice had come from the next cubicle, where Hayley found two boys—possibly brothers, aged approximately ten and fourteen—sitting on the hospital bed. The older boy, who had spoken up, wore bandages around his head and cheek. The younger one appeared unharmed. Both boys wore the same filthy school clothes they possessed throughout their ordeal.

Hayley glanced at the whiteboard above the bed.

Looking at the older boy, she asked, "Bodhi?"

"That's me." He gestured toward his brother. "This is Finn."

"I see you got a little banged up," said Hayley.

With preternatural calm, Finn said, "Bodhi sustained a fairly significant blow to the temporal fossa, but as of yet hasn't displayed any of the typical symptoms of a concussion, such as headache, ringing in the ears, nausea, vomiting, drowsiness, and blurry vision. The facial laceration is superficial and sutures have been deemed unnecessary."

A good sport, Hayley said, "Okay. Good to hear."

Bodhi said, "Sorry. He 'talks' when he gets nervous."

"That's okay. Very impressive."

Finn was scrutinizing Hayley with a medical professional's focus. "You seem pale. And you're sweating slightly. How are *you* feeling?"

"Knock it off," Bodhi instructed his brother. Looking back to Hayley, he asked, "You're an FBI agent?"

"That's right. You said the kidnappers wore masks initially and then removed them after a while?"

"Yeah. I dunno what I can say specifically about them except for the youngest one. His hair was dyed blond. Couldn't have been much older than twenty-five or so. Looked like the surfers who come over from Mexico."

Confirming the guy who had shot up the Walmart was one of the kidnappers, Hayley wanted more from her teenage witness.

"The other men looked like . . . bad guys?"

"Yeah. Pretty much. Early thirties and late twenties. Normal height and build. Dark hair and eyes. The leader had really bad skin, all pockmarked and stuff."

"Acne vulgaris," interjected Finn.

"Two of the other dudes were pretty obviously brothers. One was a joker, always grinning. The other had long, slicked-back hair. Then there was the Ferret. Thin face, eyes close together. He was the meanest."

While Hayley appreciated the boy's eagerness to help, the information wasn't entirely helpful.

"Vehicles?" she asked.

"Two black Suburbans. New."

Matching the one she observed at Walmart. Both swapped out by now, Hayley guessed.

She asked, "What else? Anything that you think might help in locating them?"

Even with Anita Fischer under blanket protection from fresh USMS deputies and soon to be airlifted off the island, Hayley worried the conspirators would strike again. But how?

Bodhi brooded on the question and came up empty.

"Maybe I'll remember more later? After things kinda calm down," he offered helpfully.

The problem was, of course, that Hayley didn't have the luxury of time.

"Could be early-onset PTSD," suggested his younger brother.

"Shut up, Finn," Hayley and Bodhi said in unison.

A white-coated emergency room doctor stopped by the cubicle, carrying Bodhi's chart. He consulted the papers inside the blue binder.

"All right, Bodhi, it says here you're good to go."

Hayley was reluctant to end the interview. "Okay. Well, thanks, you guys. If you think of anything—"

Interrupting her, Bodhi said, "You should know that the blond one saved our lives."

Hayley reacted with surprise to the teenager's pronouncement. "What?"

"The blond one helped us, like, in a ton of ways. He snuck medication in for Myles's epilepsy. And he slipped me a metal chock that I could use to barricade the door. Without the blond guy, we all would have been killed."

Finn had slid off the hospital bed and pulled on his brother's arm to follow suit.

"C'mon, Bode. I wanna see Mom and Dad."

The ER doctor moved off to attend to other patients. Hayley was processing what Bodhi had just revealed: the youngest kidnapper was working *against* his cohorts.

The fourteen-year-old eased himself off the bed and followed his brother into the hallway, then paused.

To Hayley, he said, "If you catch him—the blond one—remember that he helped us. He's a good guy."

Not a guy that was good, but a *good guy*.

Could such a man have participated in the murder and mutilation of the Barnes's family? Hayley struggled to square contradictory evidence.

She nodded, somber as a black-robed judge.

"I'll remember. That's a promise."

Bodhi Wilson offered a half smile and then, with his younger brother, walked down the wide emergency room corridor toward the double doors. To tears of joy and wide-open arms.

The brothers Wilson were only hours away from their more famous selves. The story of their heroics will rocket around the world, as breaking news, feature articles, in bestselling books, and the inevitable limited series on Netflix. Despite the international attention, Bodhi and Finn will continue to lead their remarkable, idyllic childhood lives. Their parents will ride out the difficulties of their marriage and remold a more durable love for each other, stronger and better as a result of their shared ordeal. Bodhi will mature into a skilled waterman and bypass college to follow his dad into the construction business. Finn, of course, will obtain his D.O. and become an otolaryngologist, as he always said he would. Both Wilson brothers marry—Bodhi and Makana's wedding the upcountry event of the year—and settle on Maui, where they will raise their families in self-built homes within two miles of the house where they grew up.

When he is in his sixties, Bodhi will allow his mind to drift as he sits astride his longboard and waits for the next set at Ho'okipa, a break he has surfed for more than half a century. Gazing at the green hills that bow humbly before the majestic volcano peak, the grown version of his younger self will recall the hard men, the long hours in the bomb shelter at Waipio Bay, and the blond kidnapper's timely assistance. He will remember the FBI agent who interviewed him in the emergency room treatment bay and wonder—given all that will have happened since—if she kept her promise to him.

Despite his years, Bodhi will never lose the grit and unstinting optimism that carried him through his ordeal when he was a fourteen-year-old. For that reason alone, he will decide that Hayley Chill was good as her word.

CHAPTER 30

THE BROTHERS SUÁREZ

Hayley waited with Terry Shaw on the sidewalk in front of the offices for Worldwide Flight Services, a one-story prefab building of unremarkable design that was a stone's throw from the south end of Kahului Airport's main terminal. Away from the general public and well-protected by his deputies, the offices were deemed by Stevens the best possible location to safeguard Anita Fischer while waiting for her new husband to arrive for their flight to the mainland. If the cartel thugs intended to make a move against the Supreme Court justice, they would face a gauntlet of guns.

Like all law enforcement on the scene, Hayley and Shaw wore body armor issued by their respective federal agency. They exchanged few words while scanning the oncoming cars on the one-way Airport Road that looped north, past the terminals, before turning south. A small parking lot and a five-foot wood fence separated the modest office building from the airport access road. Deputies expected Lachlan Morris to arrive at any minute. The USMS jet, parked on the tarmac behind the building, was fueled and prepared for takeoff.

Billowy white clouds galloped across a sharply blue sky. The temperature, as always, was a comfortable seventy-seven degrees. A gentle breeze carried the ocean smell from breakers on the island's north shore a half mile from where they stood. Vehicular traffic was steady, passing the location at a civically measured pace. Situation normal. Still, Hayley felt uneasy, a jitteriness that had nothing to do with her nascent sobriety. Unable to shake the sensation of impending disaster, she was uncharacteristically perplexed.

How could a place of such beauty be a source of such dread?

She glanced to her left and right. Seven deputies stood in a jagged line across the front of the building, not including Shaw. More DUSMs sat inside their vehicles in the parking lot, along with four MPD cruisers. Twin SWAT armored carriers blocked access into the parking lot. Because of the proximity of the active airport runway just behind them, no helicopters buzzed overhead, but patrolled areas to the east and west.

Hayley caught Shaw's anxious expression, one that mirrored her concerns.

"Something stinks," she said.

"Extremely so. These people—if you want to call them that—took nineteen hostages to get what they wanted. They were going to harvest organs from *kids*. I'm thinking they won't give up so easy?"

"If they come, it won't be in a Suburban."

"No."

"The body they found inside the burned-up SUV wasn't one of them."

"No," said Shaw.

"Any missing person reports yet? Would be nice to have a description of the car."

"No," he said with a measure of defeat.

Hayley watched the traffic roll past. The blissful ignorance of those passersby.

It's coming.

To her relief, however, she didn't feel that familiar craving. The woman she once was—before the soul-crushing losses, trauma, and drinking—had returned in a timely fashion. Hayley decided then that the deeper state was her people, a community of shared ideology and purpose. She could do much worse.

"Do you ever get tired of saying no, Shaw?"

The USMS deputy gave it some thought.

"No."

Shaw gazed up the road, hoping to see Lachlan Morris in his car pulling into the checkpoint at the parking lot's entrance.

"Where is this fucking guy?" he asked.

Getting Anita Fischer off his island couldn't happen soon enough.

She sat alone in a small conference room near the rear of the building. Photographic prints of cargo and passenger jet aircraft adorned the walls. In Fischer's opinion, commandeering the local offices of Worldwide Flight Services—a multinational corporation that provided ground services at one hundred sixty-seven airport locations in twenty countries around the world—was a fine example of governmental overkill. As a Supreme Court justice who was truly at the end of her patience, she might have even griped that such measures were unconstitutional. But the WFS manager on Maui was more than accommodating when informed that the disruption wouldn't last longer than an hour. The mention of generous monetary compensation also helped to secure her acquiescence.

Anita Fischer and her USMS protectors had the building to themselves.

Stevens had insisted on keeping her in eyesight when they first arrived, but Fischer eventually shooed him away, preferring time alone to think. Work was out of the question, at least for the time being. She told Lachlan over the phone to pack up all the papers on her desk and bring them along with her laptop. Jeremiah would attend to closing up the house and shipping back her clothes and personal belongings. Fischer hoped to return to the island, perhaps sometime over the summer. Her new husband seemed particularly enamored with Maui and suggested they consider living on the island year-round if she ever decided to retire.

As if *that* was even a consideration.

She considered herself a William O. Douglas–style justice, at least in terms of longevity. With two years on the bench and only forty-five years old, Fischer calculated her chances of beating Douglas's record of 13,358 days in office as better than good. If she was able to avoid being assassinated, of course. Lachlan's comment was a cause of concern, then. Were her friends' fears regarding the rash decision to marry him warranted? Did Lachlan believe she would ever walk away from her seat on the nation's highest court to play golf in Hawaii? He had always been so completely supportive of her and her dedication to the law. Would that sentiment change now that they were married?

My God, what am I thinking?

Buyer's remorse in the earliest days of a marriage, Fischer decided, was only natural. That she was deeply in love with Lachlan Morris was undeniable. And could anyone doubt his love for her after witnessing his heart-wrenching interviews following her presumed drowning? She was certain any differences that might arise between them could be resolved with compassion and understanding. Fischer was grateful for having Lachlan in her life. Those friends who continued to downgrade the newlyweds' prospects were only jealous of her unexpected happiness, resisting her evolution as a human being.

A return to normalcy would be welcome; the wedding and hours since had been a perfect debacle. Once she and Lachlan were settled again at her "embassy-size" home in the gated Georgetown community of Hillandale—his Adams Morgan condo was neither big nor secure enough for their needs—Fischer was convinced any lingering uncertainties and regret would dissipate. They would have people over for dinner, selected from the vast array of intriguing personalities in Washington. She would oversee the house and garden. Resume swimming again at Equinox. And, of course, attend to her duties as an associate justice sitting on the US Supreme Court.

Not a bad life.

Fischer checked her watch. Lachlan should have arrived by now. She reached for her phone—retrieved by Hayley in the earliest hours of their subterfuge—to call him and saw that she had received a text message.

———————

Driving west on Haleakalā, the Suárez brothers stopped at the intersection with Hana Highway. Neither of the men had ever experienced traffic lights so interminable as those on the Hawaiian island. The airport tower was in sight, with passenger jets making their approach across the island's waist from the south and taking off over the ocean to the north. Behind the wheel, Diego was unusually quiet. Javier appreciated this respite from his brother's joke-making and jovial conversation. The guns lay across his lap.

Both men wore ballistic vests and chest pouches, each loaded with six mags.

They had checked the location on Google Maps and accepted that heavily armed US authorities would be guarding the site. If these were their last minutes of life, then so be it. Their families back home would be taken care of by the cartel *if* Diego and Javier performed their tasks well. Their superiors in Mexico would compel Carranza to report all that had transpired during the operation. Every disagreement between members of the team would be revealed. Lozano's beef with the blond kid, Saturnino. The screwup with the hostages. The Snake Eaters' reputation was at risk. The next several minutes were all that mattered now. The Suárez brothers had their job. The others had theirs.

Failure would be worse than death.

Failure was unimaginable.

Javier checked his wristwatch.

"Hurry, brother. Faster."

Without comment, Diego accelerated into the intersection against a red turn arrow. Horns blared and tires screeched, drawing no response from the blank-faced cartel gunmen. A short hop on Hana Highway followed and then a right turn onto Airport Road. The Tacoma's driver's- and passenger-side windows were lowered. Wet, warm Maui air flooded into the passenger compartment and ruffled Javier's hair, despite his generous application of Vitalis Hair Tonic.

The location was only a mile farther, on the right side of the road. Behind the wheel, Diego considered saying something encouraging to his older brother but couldn't find the words. He gave them fifty-fifty odds of surviving. The light traffic they found on the access road to the airport was not a reliable indicator of what lay ahead. The stupid gringos in their stupid cars were destined to be bystanders to a kind of mayhem none had witnessed in their lifetimes.

Glancing to his right, he took in the guns laid across Javier's lap. Loaded magazines were piled on the seat between them or had spilled onto the floor at his brother's feet. Relatively simple machines, the guns were necessary tools of their trade and nothing more. Like a carpenter's hammer. Or a plumber's wrench. As with many of their brethren, the Suárez brothers had no obsession with guns. They didn't fetishize them in the same way the gringos did. Whether a Kalashnikov or AR-15, Browning or Glock, the brothers didn't much care. That they had the correct ammo for whatever gun they possessed—and enough of it—was all that mattered. That the guns were clean and operational was important, too.

"*Are you ready?*" Diego finally asked. Up ahead, on the left side of the road, he saw the modern parking structure that indicated the location's position opposite it.

Javier had emptied his mind of thought. Gone were the images of his wife and children. His favorite dog, Stalin. Of the two-story home in Michoacán that he shared with his brother and his family. Kids' bikes. The smell of sizzling carnitas in a cast-iron pan. Socks folded in their drawer. He had rinsed his mind of all of these things.

"*Yes, brother. I'm ready.*"

Diego nodded and focused his gaze on the road ahead. To the right, he now saw the police cruisers blocking access into the location's parking lot. Police officers stood outside the vehicles. He accelerated, swinging the pickup into the right lane of the one-way airport access road. The curbside terminal drop-off zones were only a hundred yards ahead of the location. Vehicles slowed in preparation for dropping off or picking up passengers.

"*Here! Yes! Here!*" shouted Javier, clutching a long gun. "*Now, brother! Here we go!*"

————————

She saw the truck accelerating and shift over a lane, the silver Tacoma, mud-splattered and battered like so many on the island. Two occupants. Looking to their right. At the building. At Worldwide Flight Services.

No one accelerates here. They slow down approaching the terminals.

Alert now, Hayley crouched and put her hand under her jacket, fingers touching the Glock.

"Shaw—"

Before she could speak further, the Tacoma had stopped in the traffic lane directly in front of their location. Two men—both Latino, approximately thirty years of age—exited from either side of the vehicle and jogged to the wooden fence that separated the parking lot from Airport Road. Both were carrying what Hayley instantly recognized as AKs, weapons that were braced against their shoulders in the firing position.

Military trained.

Hayley went flat to the ground as the gunfire erupted. A barrage of 7.62×39 rounds smashed into the building's front wall, easily piercing its corrugated sheet metal composition.

Full-auto. That's more like drug cartel gunmen.

She looked to her left to see Shaw taking too long to get down . . .

"Shaw!"

Finally, he was flat on his stomach, like her, Glock held out with elbows bracing his stance.

They both held their fire, vehicles in the lot between them and the gunmen blocking target acquisition. Someone on their side of the line was getting shots off, but more fire was coming from the Kalashnikovs. An awful lot more.

Full-auto. Only two of them. Holding their position.

Only two of them.

Full-auto.

Military trained.

Hayley comprehended the gunmen had no intention of pressing their attack on the building.

"Diversion!" she shouted, holstering her weapon.

Despite the gunfire from the road—barely pausing for mag changes—Hayley spun around on her belly and then skittered on all fours to the front door. She reached up—rounds stitching a line across the metal only inches from her fingertips—and turned the knob, pulling the door open.

Inside the building, Hayley saw a USMS deputy on his back and bleeding from a chest wound. Other deputies gave first-aid assistance to their wounded cohort, while still others heroically returned fire through shattered windows despite the apparent danger. Stephens, in charge, was most exposed, carefully drawing aim before taking his shots. The defenders assumed that the attackers would press forward, advancing on the besieged location.

Less than twenty seconds had elapsed since the first gunfire erupted.

Hayley kept close to the floor and crawled across the front reception area, to a corridor that ran directly to the building's rear. Passing offices on either side, she stayed low to the ground as several rounds passed through the building's front wall, down the corridor, and to an office door at the end. Another wounded USMS deputy lay bleeding on the floor there.

Once she turned the hallway's corner, Hayley got to her feet and ran to the windowless conference room. From the doorway, she could see that the room was empty. The only sign of Fischer was her phone on the table.

———————

Between them, they had emptied fourteen magazines, thirty rounds to a mag, laying down four hundred and twenty shots at the building's front wall, the cops standing outside, and the police vehicles blocking the driveway just behind them. That was it. Their role in the operation was over.

Now the escape. The hard road they had before them. Survival.

The Suárez brothers ducked and sprinted for the idling Tacoma, imagining they were dodging the return gunfire from the cops that gathered in tempo and accuracy. That the bullets would never—could never—touch them. Javier barely noticed the acute burning sensation he felt in his right arm. He hopped over the side wall of the pickup's cargo area as his brother dumped himself into the driver's seat, dropped the transmission into drive, and stomped on the accelerator.

A dozen loaded magazines lay scattered across the truck's bed. Grabbing one, Javier flicked the mag release, kicked out the spent mag with the end of the fresh magazine, seated it, and then accessed the charging handle with the same hand. With the stock braced against his shoulder, the gunman's trigger finger and right hand never left the pistol grip during a reload that burned 3.6 seconds. Taking aim on the police vehicles blocking the Worldwide Flight Services parking lot, Javier emptied the thirty-round magazine with rapid-burst fire in approximately six seconds.

Diego steered the speeding Tacoma through the traffic that had slammed to a stop at the first sound of gunfire. People caught on the sidewalk crouched or went flat on the ground, some screaming and others cowering in silence. Javier swapped mags and sprayed the terminal's big windows with gunfire to maximize the terror and confusion. Killing more civilians wouldn't facilitate the brothers' escape, so the sicario aimed high. If bystanders were killed in any case—whether by ricochet or other unintended mishap—that was their bad luck.

As they reached the interisland terminal at the apex of the loop that would return them to Airport Road and diverse routes east, west, and south, Javier began to visualize their successful escape. Their path forward was clear with fewer stopped cars on the road. He watched Diego through the rear window restocking his chest pouch with fresh mags as he drove. Javier retrieved loaded mags from the truck bed and did the same.

Diego steered the pickup right onto Keolani Place, avoiding the police presence at Worldwide Flight Services. In the ninety seconds since they shot up the building, the cartel gunman wagered the cops hadn't the time to regroup and block all roads leading out of the airport area. He bet wrong. Passing a truck rental lot to the right, Diego saw a swarm of police vehicles heading in his direction. He spun the steering wheel and turned left and hard onto Aalele Street, which curved within a few feet of Airport Road.

The gunmen's diminishing options narrowed further when police cruisers and unmarked USMS SUVs swarmed Aalele's terminus at Haleakalā Highway. Diego glanced in the rearview mirror and saw the cop cars he knew would be there. In terms of vehicular escape, they were trapped. Braking, he gripped his rifle and bailed from the truck. Javier, similarly armed, leaped out of the cargo area.

They took a moment to get their bearings. To their left, across the two-lane airport loop road, was the multilevel rental car parking garage. To the west was a single-story commercial building surrounded by a cyclone fence topped with barbed wire. The cavernous parking garage afforded their best chance for evasion and escape.

The brothers needed no discussion of tactics or strategy. Together they had been in fierce battles before, while in the Mexican Army and as cartel gunmen. They were calm, with not a trace of panic or wasted action. They believed God had created them for this moment.

Standing back-to-back, the brothers fired selective bursts at their pursuers speeding toward them from opposite directions, with the expected response: the cops stopped and exited their vehicles. Firing as they walked with a deliberate, not-fast pace, the Suárez brothers moved east, to the narrow grass strip that separated Aalele from Lanui Circle. They were entirely exposed to police return fire, which was mercifully sporadic given the Mexicans' heavy fire and military-grade weapons. Up to this point, the cops possessed only handguns and shotguns that weren't effective at a longer distance.

The clatter of gunfire echoed across the four lanes of roadway, bouncing off the tall parking structure. All civilians had abandoned the scene to the police and the two criminals. Javier and Diego had successfully held off the lightly equipped cops on Aalele Street. Still, their position on the grassy median strip (between two widely distanced palm trees that provided scant cover) was untenable for longer than the thirty seconds that they had made their stand there. An exit from the rental car parking garage onto Lanui Circle was behind them, about fifty yards north. Inside the multilevel structure were innumerable places to hide. Hostages. Unlimited getaway vehicles. Several egresses onto multiple diverse locations.

Inside the rental car parking lot was salvation and escape.

Diego saw the blood seeping through the sleeve covering his brother's right arm at the shoulder, a police round having entered at an angle and finding flesh under the ballistic vest. Javier had forgotten he had been hit and glanced down at the mess. Then, looking to his brother, he shook his head.

Over the racket of his gun, Javier said, "No es nada." He jerked his head in the direction of the parking garage and exit.

Diego grinned and nodded, filled with love for his brother.

Leaving a pile of empty mags and shell casings behind, they turned and jogged for the parking garage exit. God was with them. They would live to see another gunfight. With luck, they might even see their wives and children again.

They took turns firing behind them as they ran. Javier began to feel the pain in his shoulder, cursing his brother under his breath for bringing the injury to his attention. Recoil from the rifle was a particular agony. He fired anyway. Ceasing the covering action was death. Javier faced forward again and saw what had caused his brother to pause and process. Approaching from the north on Lanui Circle was the MPD armored tactical vehicle.

Another twenty-five yards separated the Mexican gunmen from their sanctuary inside the parking structure. The SWAT truck speeding toward them would cut off the Suárez brothers before they got close. Diego spun around and clocked more police cruisers and black SUVs coming up the loop road from the opposite direction. With law enforcement flanking them on Aalele, they were trapped. And one hundred percent exposed to the cops' return fire.

The brothers exchanged a look communicating what they both knew to be undeniable facts.

If they surrendered, the cartel would have them killed no matter where the Americans hid them. Their families—if they were fortunate enough not to be murdered—would get nothing in compensation.

If they fought it out with the gringos—and if their diversionary tactic had been beneficial to the operation—the cartel would support the brothers' wives and children for years to come. Their families would keep the big house in Michoacán. Food would always be on the table. Their kids would continue their studies at the private school.

There was no question what a grinning Diego and bloody Javier would do. It was all written long ago. God knew this to be true.

Swapping spent mags for fresh ones, the brothers Suárez raised their long guns and howled in unison.

CHAPTER 31

MANUAL SAFETY

Leaving her phone on the conference table, Anita Fischer stood and exited the conference room at the sound of automatic gunfire from the street. A USMS deputy was sprawled on the floor at one end of the corridor. She went to the fallen man—undeniably dead, with a bullet wound to the head—and retrieved a Glock 19 from the floor beside him. More rounds from the street traveled the length of the hallway and hit the wall above Fischer's head as she knelt beside the body. Backtracking, she stowed the pistol in a pants pocket and moved quickly to check the three other doors that lined the rear, dead-end hallway.

The first two rooms—a large storage closet and the men's bathroom—were windowless. The last door Fischer tried accessed the company's break room. A small, thirty-six-by-twelve-inch sliding vinyl window situated high on the far wall provided limited natural light from outside. She walked across the room, thumbed the lock, and slid the window open.

Standing on a folding chair, Fischer could angle her body out the narrow opening and pull herself through. She dropped to the sidewalk below the window and paused in a superhero crouch to get her bearings.

The engine roar of a taxiing American Airlines 737 obscured all but a hint of gunfire from the other side of the building. On their odd-looking vehicles, baggage handlers and other ground service personnel trundled past, unaware of the Mexicans' furious assault just seven hundred feet away.

By staying to the rear of Worldwide Flight Services and entering the adjoining UPS offices through a side entrance, Fischer avoided her protectors and the gun battle. Inside, she merged with a large exodus of UPS employees and customers who were fleeing in a panic out the front doors. Once outside, the mob turned away from the gunfire and ran south to Kala Road. Within these earliest moments of the incident, first responders had yet to converge on the airport.

Fischer's best opportunity to evade the police and USMS personnel was now.

Haleakalā Highway began at the underpass with Airport Road. Her beautiful home at Hakuhee Point was eleven miles farther west, but Fischer wasn't headed there. The photograph she had received via text message was unmistakably of Lachlan. Judging by the blood on his face and swollen black eye, he had been beaten. Unseen assailants pressed a gun barrel to his head.

A message that accompanied the text was similarly shocking. The sender said a diversionary attack would be made on her location at the airport in precisely two minutes. Fischer's instructions were to leave her phone behind and exit the building without her protectors noticing. She was to make her way to McGregor Point on the island's south shore and then on foot climb the Lahaina Pali Trail to Kealaloloa Ridge. All within an hour. No cops. No USMS. No FBI. Any deviation from these instructions would result in the summary execution of Lachlan Morris.

She loved Lachlan and could not imagine life without him. Fischer didn't need two minutes to make her decision. She understood the men behind his abduction wanted her dead. That he stood no chance of survival whether or not she followed orders to the letter. The Supreme Court justice knew she was a target the moment she crawled through the narrow rear window at the Worldwide Flight Services offices. But obeying at least the first of the kidnappers' demands gave her one invaluable asset: time.

For the same reason Hayley Chill had faked Fischer's death to delay the children's murders, the justice intended to exploit the allocated sixty minutes to brainstorm an outcome other than hers and Lachlan's deaths. However, without her phone, wallet, and credit cards she was hard-pressed to formulate a plan.

The clatter of gunfire a quarter mile up the road increased in frequency, and Fischer guessed that law enforcement entities had begun to respond to the attackers' diversionary assault. Walking at a fast clip west on Haleakalā, she passed a small independent car rental agency and then an auto repair shop. The roadway next to her was deserted. A blue sky stretched to storm clouds cowering far on the eastern horizon behind her back.

How much time had she already wasted? How many minutes of life did Lachlan have left?

Fischer spied the fourth story of a Courtyard by Marriott visible over the shaggy tops of swaying palm trees that lined the street. The first inklings of a plan began to formulate in her head, emerging only somewhat intact from the clutter of her increasingly scattered and fearful thoughts. She must hijack a car from tourists and drive straight to McGregor Point.

Then what?

Clarity came to her then. She understood why she had abandoned her protection detail. What she needed to do. Armed with the deputy's Glock, she would confront her husband's kidnappers, and the odds of her success be damned. She would fucking shoot them dead if they had harmed her husband. Fischer would shoot until she ran out of ammunition or they killed *her*, whichever came first.

A masonry wall surrounded the hotel, but both the east and west driveways were easily accessible on foot. Fischer entered the property and immediately spied a woman approximately her age—short and slight-framed, wearing business attire—pulling a wheelie carry-on suitcase. She was walking in Fischer's direction, presumably toward her car.

Am I really doing this?

Fischer slid her right hand with difficulty into the right front pants pocket, stretched to capacity by the Glock.

I'll show her I have a gun. Tell her to hand over the car keys and no one will get hurt.

And no one will get hurt. Fischer could scarcely believe that she, an associate justice with the US Supreme Court, could even *think* about saying the hackneyed phrase, let alone utter it while committing a second-degree felony offense. Dressed in Hayley's clothes—cheap khakis and West Virginia Mountaineers T-shirt—was she recognizable? Fischer doubted that shoppers would give Chief Justice John Roberts a second look if he was browsing in the local Whole Foods wearing a gaudy Hawaiian shirt, cargo shorts, and flip-flops. What did her anonymity matter anyway?

Fischer took a step forward to intercept her target. A slight rush of wind and thrum of a car engine over her shoulder announced that a vehicle had entered the lot. Was it now impossible to act? She didn't want to wait for a second possible victim.

"You're not going to try to hijack a car, are you?" asked a female's voice from somewhere behind Fischer.

Failing to find Anita Fischer in the conference room, Hayley checked the three remaining rooms at the rear of the building: a windowless storage room, men's restroom, and cramped break room. All were empty. The small sliding window in the employee break room was open, a folding chair directly under it.

She had watched Fischer swim with limber ease; there was no doubt in Hayley's mind that the Supreme Court justice could get herself out that window. Removing her body armor and standing on the chair, the deeper state operative climbed through the window in less than ten seconds. On the sidewalk outside, she saw planes, flight service trucks, tarmac personnel, and no sign of Anita Fischer in any direction. The gunfire that had been earsplitting while she was inside the building was inaudible outside, masked by the whine of turbine jet engines.

Hauling herself up and through the window from the outside was only somewhat more difficult. Back in the break room, Hayley found Stevens and three USMS deputies waiting for her with weapons drawn.

"Window was open. I didn't see Fischer," she informed them. With a look from Stevens, one of the DUSMs attempted to climb through the window . . . and quickly realized there was no way he was getting through the narrow opening.

"Sorry, sir," he said sheepishly.

Stevens hadn't attained his leadership position in the United States Marshals Service by accident or incompetence. A quarter century with the agency, his career had covered the gamut of its federally mandated responsibilities, whether fugitive apprehension, protection services, or operations with the Witness Protection Program. His only passion outside the job and his wife of twenty-two years was a weekly poker game at the Navy Marine Golf Course a mile from Pearl Harbor. Tall, broad-shouldered, with a craggy facial profile that wouldn't be out of place on Mount Rushmore, Stevens was good law enforcement.

The gunfire from the front of the building had ceased.

"Get everybody saddled up. We do not stop until we find her." Stevens headed back up the corridor toward the front of the building. To one of his deputies, he said, "Tell MPD we need roadblocks on every road out of here. Start with a five-mile radius and work their way out."

Retrieving her body armor and strapping it on, Hayley recalled Fischer's performance of the Tommy Lee Jones speech and decided that she had done a pretty credible job after all. She caught up with Stevens, who had paused at a respectful distance from the dead USMS deputy on the floor where the two hallways met.

"Someone stay with this man!" he ordered before continuing past the body.

Hayley trailed on Stevens's heels as he walked quickly toward the front of the building. Of course, he didn't take her seriously and for the most obvious reason. This wasn't the first (or last) time someone underestimated the young woman with blond hair and powder blue eyes.

"I don't think she was taken against her will, sir," she said to his broad back.

Stevens didn't slow his pace or even look over his shoulder. "What makes you think that? Not all bad guys are big guys."

"It's not the size of the window, sir. Has anyone heard from Lachlan Morris? He was due here ten minutes ago."

Stevens ignored her, apparently uninterested in the young female FBI agent's theories. They arrived in the reception area at the front of the building, where automatic gunfire had nearly destroyed the walls and furnishings. DUSMs attempted to staunch blood loss from gunshot wounds incurred by one of their brethren lying on the floor.

Getting nowhere with the US marshal, Hayley glanced out the blasted-out window and saw one police vehicle after another blow past in the street beyond the parking lot, no doubt in pursuit of the gunmen.

Where's Shaw?

She went to the door—also shot-up and barely attached to its hinges—and looked outside. More deputies huddled over one of their fallen cohorts where she and Terry Shaw had been standing before the gunfire started. Stepping outside confirmed what Hayley already knew to be true. The man down on the sidewalk was Shaw, his pants bloodsopped.

Looking at the DUSM's right leg—intact and with no sign of a compound fracture—Hayley could breathe a sigh of relief. Presumably, the gunmen had loaded their magazines with full-metal-jacketed ammo; soft-nose or hollow point would have caused significantly more damage to the soft tissue in Shaw's thigh. Hitting the femur might have taken the whole leg off.

Shaw locked eyes with Hayley, reading her expression with the ease of a married couple that had long since celebrated their silver anniversary.

"Go get her," he said. "And kill a couple of those fucking guys for me, will ya?"

Hayley nodded, resolute as a Cat 5 hurricane.

The anxiously anticipated ambulance swerved into the parking lot from the street, siren yowling. DUSMs who weren't assisting those injured jogged to their cars as shooting erupted from the other side of the car rental complex, the rapid *tat-tat-tat-tat* of Kalashnikovs as well as more sporadic handgun return fire.

Extracting the Kia Soul—jagged-edged bullet holes stitched across the driver's-side door and rocker panel—was a chore as Hayley joined a traffic jam at the parking lot entrance. The others turned right on the one-way Airport Road—officially Mayor Elmer F. Cravalho Way, but never called such by any local—in the direction of the gun battle playing out a few hundred yards to the northwest. Hayley turned left, speeding up the traffic-free thoroughfare in the wrong direction for a quarter mile, turning right at Hana Highway after flashing her credentials at MPD's first, hastily assembled checkpoint.

Her mind worked the situation, winnowing down possibilities to a most probable scenario. The kidnapping team had contacted Fischer on her private number. How did they have it? Lachlan Morris was taken hostage and gave it to them. In the minutes before the diversionary attack on the location, the kidnappers contacted Fischer. They ordered her to run at the first sound of gunfire. Did they also demand that Fischer leave her phone behind? Or was that her idea because she didn't want the authorities following her, either?

They've got her husband.

She's gone to get him back.

Hayley chided herself for not anticipating Morris's abduction, an obvious soft target who meant everything to their ultimate objective. Dwelling on her failures, however, was a waste of valuable time. Putting herself in the Latinos' shoes, it struck Hayley as unlikely that they would snatch Fischer anywhere near the airport. Too much law enforcement. Conspirators would have ordered her to meet the gunmen elsewhere on the island, away from the action. Undoubtedly, Fischer would've been given a deadline. An hour maybe? The ticking clock would be short enough to prevent law enforcement from mounting an effective search response. But where would Fischer have run? How did she intend to get anywhere without a car, credit cards, or phone?

Hayley's rushed analysis of the situation drew the outlines of what she believed had happened. Still to be determined was Fischer's *present* location. Assuming the justice was on foot, Hayley hadn't seen her on Airport Road. She must have turned west, taking the underpass at the beginnings of the Haleakalā Highway.

Fischer would not be long on foot. In her desperation, Hayley surmised she would act rashly. Having gone this far in the scheme, the justice would do anything if it meant the slightest chance of reuniting with Morris.

Taking a right at Dairy Road, Hayley calculated probabilities with a clear mind. A familiar zealotry had replaced the craving for alcohol. She realized with a jolt that she had found her way home. She once again felt purely alive.

Hayley turned right at Haleakalā, the sprawling Costco big-box store to her right, and sped east on the four-lane thoroughfare. The sight of Anita Fischer—attired in Hayley's ridiculous Mountaineers T-shirt and budget chinos—darting into the Marriott parking lot via the entry drive was utterly unsurprising. Hayley always knew she would find her protectee.

She braked the rental car directly behind Anita Fischer in the hotel parking lot. The Glock was perfectly outlined in the justice's pocket. Given the ill-fitting pants, Hayley was surprised Fischer had managed to fit the gun in there. The woman pulling the wheelie travel bag approached, unaware of Fischer's intention.

"You're not going to try to hijack a car, are you?" she asked through her open window.

Startled, Fischer whirled around and, seeing Hayley, was able to extract the Glock from her pocket with only minimal fuss. Holding the gun with both hands—forward but pointed down—she said, "Yes, as a matter of fact. Step out of your car."

Hayley grimaced at the sight of Fischer's finger curled into the trigger.

"The Glock 19 doesn't have a manual safety like your Sig, ma'am. Index finger outside the trigger guard, please. You see? Like this. Straight along the lower frame, ma'am," she said, helpfully illustrating with her right hand and index finger.

Fischer corrected her grip on the gun, but was grimly steadfast, ignoring Hayley's friendly and casual demeanor.

The woman with the wheelie bag passed the front of Hayley's Kia. Seeing the pistol in Fischer's hands, she yelped with alarm and broke into a frightened trot for her car farther down the parking aisle.

"Just get out of the car."

Hayley remained cool and collected, keeping both hands on the wheel, where Fischer could see them.

"You're not going to shoot me, ma'am."

"Turn on cable news. Stranger things happen all the time." Fischer took a bead on Hayley inside the vehicle. "Out."

Exiting the car, Hayley stepped to the side. She had the skills to take the Glock off Fischer, but couldn't guarantee that the tenacious Supreme Court justice wouldn't shoot herself during the maneuver.

"Have they taken Lachlan?"

Fischer said nothing, her silence confirming Hayley's suspicions.

"Okay. We can do this together, then."

Fischer scowled. "Just like Thelma and Louise, huh?"

The names meant nothing to Hayley. "I guess so, ma'am, if that's what it takes to keep you safe."

"No. Not a chance. I was instructed not to tell you specifically. To leave 'that West Virginia hillbilly out of it.'"

Hayley processed this last statement.

"Ma'am—"

"Enough talk," said Fischer.

Hayley nearly got her foot run over as Fischer sped off in the shot-up Kia.

"Fuck," she said, watching her protectee accelerating through the parking lot toward the opposite exit onto Haleakalā.

She looked across the parking aisle, where the visiting business-woman was cowering inside *her* rental car.

CHAPTER 32

MADAME JUSTICE

*D*rive. Faster!

A call to Andrew Wilde established Fischer's location; Publius had the means to access the GPS in Hayley's rental car that the Supreme Court justice had hijacked. But that took precious minutes that Hayley could ill afford to waste. She was speeding south on Kuihelani Highway, only minutes behind Fischer. Why had the conspirators told the justice that Hayley was to be kept in the dark? That tidbit of information implied there was a mole inside Fischer's circle after all.

The phone vibrated on the seat next to her.

"She's stopped. The parking lot for a hiking trail. In Maalaea," said Wilde without preamble.

He had left his dinner companion—a retired CIA officer whose ass Wilde had saved on more than one occasion during the Iraq War—and retreated to Le Diplomate's bar area for some privacy. Actions on Maui were coming to a head and his beef carpaccio would have to wait. Hayley Chill's sterling performance in the last forty-eight hours had surprised everyone at Publius . . . even Andrew Wilde. Only a certain former president—who had insisted on her staying the course—never lost confidence in the deeper state's first operative in the field.

Glancing down at her phone as she drove, Hayley tapped the screen and brought up a mapping app. "Lahaina Pali Trail?" she asked.

"That's it. I'll get word to USMS. They can put a chopper on the ground there in five minutes."

"Do that and you're signing Lachlan Morris's death warrant."

"Tell me again why I give a goddamn about Lachlan Morris?"

Hayley made the light at Kuihelani's junction with Honoapiilani Highway. She was less than a minute away from the trailhead.

"She's in love with him, sir. Something you might not understand."

"Fuck love. I'm calling in the cavalry."

"No!" Surprising even herself with the stridency of her outburst, Hayley recalibrated. "Sir, I promise you, I'll keep her safe. I can do this."

She hadn't told Wilde that Anita Fischer was armed.

Consulting the mapping app on *his* phone, he said nothing.

Hayley waited him out, letting silence speak for her. Pulling into the tiny parking lot for Lahaina Pali's east trailhead, she saw the Kia Soul. Unoccupied, as she knew it would be.

Wilde said, "The trail appears to climb to a ridge and then drop down to the other side, to Ukumehame."

She was impressed with his proper pronunciation of the Hawaiian place-names.

"Yes, sir. It crosses an access road for the Kaheawa wind farm along the ridge." With confirmation that the Supreme Court justice was on the trail, Hayley had developed a clear understanding of the kidnappers' plan and strategy. "Isolate Fischer. From the ridge, they'll have outstanding surveillance of any approaching law enforcement, including a police helicopter. If they're overmatched, they can withdraw up the ridge and disappear into the West Maui Forest Reserve. Three or four men could hide out for weeks in there."

Wilde asked, "You're thinking they told her to meet them on the wind farm road at the trail's midpoint?"

"Yes, sir."

"What's your plan, Chill?"

Hayley said, "Approach from the west. Get to the top of the ridge before Fischer does and attack from the rear. They won't know what hit them."

"Think you can do that?" Wilde didn't wait for her reply. "Go!"

She disconnected the call. Looking at the map, Hayley estimated Lahaina Pali's west trailhead was a six-minute drive away, five if she pushed it.

Wedged into her pants pocket and inhibiting her gait, the handgun was a heavy, cumbersome thing. But because the trail was so steep and frustratingly rocky, Fischer needed both hands free to brace against falls. Twice already, she had stumbled and bashed the heels of her hands. The sun had long since dropped below the ridge above her, cloaking the trail in the diffuse half-light of dusk. Over her left shoulder, though, the ocean was ablaze with the day's last light. Traffic noise on the highway that connected Maui's waist to its western flank was barely audible. A steady, thick wind came directly from the east, at her back, providing a welcomed extra lift as Fischer climbed the rising path. She had hiked the entirety of the Lahaina Pali Trail a half dozen times and knew its challenges.

In fifteen minutes—half walking and half jogging—she had encountered only one other person on the trail. Keeping her eyes to the ground was a necessity given the preponderance of loose rocks and gravel. She passed the young man without comment. Even as a seasonal resident, Fischer was aware few people ventured out on the route anytime near sundown. Whether they intended to or not, the kidnappers had selected the perfect location for a rendezvous. The wind farm's access road at the trail's midpoint would almost certainly be deserted. From their vantage point atop the ridge, they could observe her approach on foot for a half hour at least. Police backup or surveillance would have been impossible to conceal.

Fischer worried that she wouldn't make the kidnappers' deadline. If they saw her on the trail below, would they allow for some grace period?

She was desperate to see Lachlan alive one last time. She would approach the men with the Glock in the waistband at the small of her back. If her husband was already dead, Fischer would draw on the men and go down blazing. Madame Justice, indeed.

Approximately halfway to her destination, she paused to get her breath and allow her thudding heart to slow. She lifted her eyes to take in the ridge above and the picket line of wind turbines. The swoosh of spinning rotor and blades was audible even at a distance. Fischer saw no sign of the kidnappers or outline of their vehicles on the Kaheawa access road.

———————

Saturnino Valdés Pérez watched Lozano and Carranza among the rocks off the wind farm road, his commander scanning the ridge's eastern flank below them with binoculars. Taliban was armed with an assault rifle, while Carranza wore the mata policía on his hip. They conversed in low voices, seemingly so that Saturnino, standing next to the Tacoma parked away from the road's edge, could not overhear their words. Or maybe he was being paranoid.

Directly overhead, the whirl of wind turbines was shockingly loud. A gusting wind from the east tossed Saturnino's lengthy dyed-blond hair. Paranoid or not, he had decided that Lozano intended to kill him. On more than a few occasions, he had caught the veteran sicario watching him with his predatory stare. Waiting. Obviously, Carranza had ordered his lieutenant to bide his time until their work was completed. Neither man intended to see Saturnino leave the island alive. With the Suárez brothers presumed dead, their allocated shares would go to the surviving operators.

And then, inevitably, three portions would become two.

How would he defend himself when the moment came? Saturnino imagined the scene. Once the gringa was executed, Lozano would turn the AK on him. No doubt, the sadist would attempt only to wound his prey so to extract a more prolonged, excruciating death from Saturnino with a blade. If that were the decision made beforehand, Carranza would be stationed elsewhere—off to the side or in the truck—diminishing the odds for successful, retaliatory action. In the unlikely event that Saturnino killed Lozano, their former sergeant would finish the job. Two parts would become one, helping offset the lost income from the failure to harvest the hostages' body parts.

Why not kill them both now?

The thought struck like a thunderclap. When else will the two other men be grouped as they were presently? With their backs turned to Saturnino, Carranza and Lozano made a seductive target. The AK-12 rested easily in his cradling arms, smelling of the Ballistol oil. With a few seconds' time and minuscule energy, he could send his two compatriots to Hell. The destructive power of modern weaponry! All Saturnino lacked was nerve.

He faced the same problem that had plagued him since arriving on the island. Saturnino Pérez lacked the killer's instinct. Murder repulsed him.

Some assassin I am.

Dejected, he relaxed the index finger of his right hand that had gone rigid across the gun's lower receiver. Saturnino wished he was home at his family dinner table. He longed for the company of his surfing pals. How had he found himself on this ridge, waiting for a doomed woman to offer herself for assassination? Would she fight for her life with more gusto than Carranza anticipated?

Crouched behind a pile of stones, the former army sergeant looked over his shoulder at Saturnino and gestured.

"She's here. Two minutes," he said in a hunter's whisper.

———————

While Fischer ascended Kealaloloa Ridge's eastern flank by fits and starts, Hayley Chill ran up the western approach. Though the wind farm atop the ridge was the midpoint between the east and west trailheads, the path from Ukumehame was a more moderate climb. Nonetheless, ascending the hillside required her absolute focus; turning an ankle on one of the countless rocks littering the route would mean Fischer's death. The sun behind her dropped closer to the ocean horizon. Darkness loomed. Hayley flew past several groups coming down, but overcame none; she and the kidnappers would have the summit to themselves.

Focusing on the path before her—each footfall selected with a split-second decision—was a relief, clearing her mind of useless clutter. Her fitness was nowhere near the level she had maintained while in the army, but Hayley could already feel the benefits of her newfound sobriety. Her heart pounded emphatically. Blood in, blood out. Her breathing was steady and untroubled.

This feels good.

As she ran, Hayley carried the Glock in her right hand for better mobility, ignoring the startled looks of hikers that noticed the weapon as they passed. While a woman alone on the trail armed with a canister of pepper spray was a common practice, a semiautomatic pistol wasn't typically in the nature lover's tool kit. Hayley assumed the hikers would call MPD and report her, but she was unconcerned. Success or failure atop the ridge would be decided long before the cops showed up.

The trail's apex was in sight, approximately two hundred yards ahead. Hayley didn't slow her pace, charging forward. Confident she had outraced Fischer to the kidnappers, the deeper state operative needed time to neutralize all the cartel gunmen. The job would be easier if she had brought a long gun to the fight. Armed with a M110A1 Squad Designated Marksman Rifle—the weapon she had trained on while in the army—Hayley could pick off the sicarios from a distance. The combat dynamic was completely scrambled by the pistol she carried. Getting close without detection was the necessary element for success.

As she drew nearer, Hayley kept her eyes on the ridgeline, where she could see the roof of a truck's cab. Gambling the kidnappers were focused on the trail's eastern approach, she made no effort for concealment. No time for that now.

Her feet barely seemed to touch the ground. A sense of purpose and willpower surged through Hayley. She desperately wanted to prevent the men from harming Lachlan Morris.

The woman deserves that much.

Anyone did.

If one of the kidnappers bothered to check the western side of the ridge, then Hayley would make the long and difficult assault on an elevated fortification. She would fail, but that brutal fight would be her only recourse. At a bare minimum, the ensuing firefight would scare off Anita Fischer.

And I hope like hell it doesn't come to that.

Her luck held. No cry of alarm came from the ridgetop. As Hayley closed the distance to her objective, she veered off the trail, creeping forward through the rocks, outcrops, and high grass. Trade winds swept over the ridge in terrific gusts. Directly overhead now, the big turbines spun at a furious rate. Though she suspected her imagination was only playing games with her, Hayley sensed electricity in the air from the big machines.

The ground flattened out on the ridge, covered by dry grass, dirt, and gravel. Fifty feet to her right, the blond gunman stood next to the unoccupied truck. Hayley didn't see anyone else. Not the other kidnappers. No Morris.

There wasn't a tree or any other possible cover in sight. Hayley was exposed from this point forward. Moving at a slight crouch and with Glock in hand, she kept her eyes riveted on the gunman. He was facing in the other direction, toward the east. The wind carried the sounds of Hayley's advance behind her, away from her target. Fortune may favor the bold, but a little luck didn't hurt. Overhead, the blades turned and turned and turned.

Twenty feet.

She raised her gun, aimed at the back of a head covered with flailing blond hair.

Where are the others?

Hayley swung her focus past the man to the opposite side of the ridge and the rocks there. She thought the figures she saw were more gunmen, but her glance was too fleeting to confirm that alarm. To act on it.

The blond pivoted. His eyes found hers.

CHAPTER 33

ESCARGOTS

Fischer paused to extract the pistol from her waistband as the ground leveled out at the ridgetop. The picket line of wind turbines—like a squadron of alien robotic invaders—were just ahead. She was oblivious to the beauty of the setting and the glorious views in every direction. Instead, Fischer scanned her environs for a sign of the kidnappers—for Lachlan—and saw only dry brown grass and the lonesome piles of volcanic rock.

She knew how to use the gun. Stalked by an ex-boyfriend while in law school, Fischer bought a Sig Sauer and took a series of weapons-training classes. With her cartel adversaries, she shared a dispassionate attitude toward guns. The registered P238 Fischer kept in a small gun safe under her bed back home in Washington was a tool that might be handy in an emergency. Like a windup AM/FM radio or first-aid kit.

The slope eased from her position to the ridgetop, seventy yards distant. Fischer hadn't taken the next step when gunfire from a rocky outcropping above her pulsed and she considered the possibility that she would spectacularly fail at a task for the first time in her life.

The blond kidnapper kept his AK down, cradled in his arms, and shook his head. An inch in one direction, then an inch in the other. Otherwise, the gunman was still, his gaze not daring to leave Hayley.

Her Glock was up, steel sights set on the center of the young sicario's head. From a distance of maybe a dozen feet, Hayley would not miss.

The memory that slammed into her immediate consciousness were the words of the kid from the hospital.

If you catch him—the blond one—remember that he helped us. He's a good guy.

Hayley struggled to imagine the young Latino standing before her being a party to mutilating the policeman's family in Virginia. Her instincts whether he had committed these vile acts or not would govern all her subsequent actions.

Looking into his green eyes, she judged he was innocent.

Hayley thrust her left hand out to take the blond guy's rifle, while keeping him covered with the Glock held in her right hand.

He didn't relinquish his grip on the Kalashnikov, drawing it protectively closer to his chest instead.

A second ticked past. Another and another.

The blond sicario was no threat. Hayley left him behind. Moving forward and low, she led with her pistol.

Forty yards of open ground separated her from the two men. The man with the AK had shouldered the weapon to fire again.

The distance was inside the Glock's effective range. Hayley stopped and took aim on the man with the rifle.

She squeezed the trigger as the men—alerted to her presence—turned. Hayley put two rounds in the center mass of her target and one in his head. The man with the AK dropped.

Hayley ran forward, arm outstretched and shifting her aim to take out the other man. In the split second required for target acquisition, he disappeared behind a pile of rocks. She continued forward, keenly aware of her exposure on the open ground.

———

Hector Lozano was dead. The Scourge of La Tinajas. He whose name must not be spoken.

Dead.

Time took a beat as Carranza stared at his loyal lieutenant lying on his side in the brown grass. A bullet had entered his skull just below the right eye. The Suárez brothers were gone. Now Lozano? Did the woman kill the blond kid, too? Carranza had two or three seconds to register their attacker before he took cover behind the rocks. Armed with only a pistol, she had enjoyed considerable good fortune thus far.

Todo lo bueno se acaba.

Time restarted.

Carranza reached out from behind the rocks and snagged Lozano's AK by its barrel as more gunshots cracked. One of the projectiles grazed the former army sergeant's wrist, nicking his pisiform bone. Carranza felt nothing, pulling the long gun to him and spinning it around, hands finding the correct places. How many times had she fired the handgun? Staying low in his cover, he raised the Kalashnikov and fired three quick bursts in the direction he believed the woman was coming at him.

He listened for the sound of footsteps and heard none. He listened for the sounds of his target's distress—groans or cries of pain—and heard none. He waited. Carranza didn't fear death so much as death at the hands of a woman. Hell had a special place for men who suffered that despised fate.

The former army sergeant listened and heard no footsteps, only the wind turbines. Their ethereal whoosh.

———

Lying on her back, Hayley understood that she had been shot. Not entirely sure, but the deeper state operative believed she had taken the round somewhere in the thorax and that it had hit no major vessels or organs. Ricochet, she assumed, judging by her continued existence. Lucky to be alive. Too bad she had left her armored vest in the car for the dash up Kealaloloa Ridge.

Her hands were empty. What had happened to her Glock?

Where is the fucking thing?

Lifting her head—the only part of her body she could control—Hayley looked for the pistol and saw it on the ground, a few feet from her right hand. It might as well have been a hundred miles.

Nothing happened for how long Hayley wasn't entirely sure. But she knew something *would* happen if she didn't get her ass in gear. Then she saw the man emerge from behind the rocks, pointing the AK at her as he advanced.

Hayley struggled to move—to reach for the Glock on the ground, anything—and made a hash of the heroically doomed attempt.

So, she dropped her head down again and gazed up into the sky. Listening. Soaking in the universe through her ears.

Once he was sure his assailant's weapon was beyond her reach, El Gruñón stood to his full height and walked out from behind the rocks. Approaching her, he considered his next actions. The woman needed to be alive for what he planned to do to her. Breaking both of her arms would be his first order of business, compound fractures and separating humerus bones from the scapula. If the woman kicked at him while he did the other things, then Carranza would break her legs, too. Death would come for her, of course, but not before nightfall.

Who was she? Having no identifying uniform or agency insignia, the woman represented all the people in the world that were out to get Carranza. His superiors and peers in the Mexican Army. The military doctors who tried and failed to dope him with their myriad pills and injections. Former friends and neighbors who secretly talked behind his back. Rival captains in the cartel. All conspired against him. Same as this unidentified assailant, his persecutors were eternally seeking to destroy the former army sergeant. He could count only on his wife and boy for loyalty. His beloved Marlene and darling Hector were Carranza's touchstones in a world of deceit and murderous intent.

He stopped at the woman's feet. She wouldn't even give him the satisfaction of showing him the expected fear in her eyes. Carranza would change that.

"Where's my husband?"

The voice was strident. Carranza knew in an instant its source and spun around with his finger on the AK's trigger.

Of course she would press forward with her Roosevelt-like charge up the hill. More gunfire followed the first bursts, but they sounded different and Fischer entertained the possibility that the police had arrived on the ridgetop ahead of her. That they had engaged the kidnappers in a gun battle and would rescue Lachlan.

Cresting the hill, however, she took in the entire scene at once. She saw the one gunman on the ground, headshot. She saw the unoccupied Tacoma and Hayley Chill lying spread-eagled in the dry grass. Finally, Fischer saw another gunman standing at Hayley's feet, armed with a semiautomatic rifle.

Lachlan was dead. She accepted this as fact and she didn't want to die, too. The turbines overhead spun evermore frantically.

As the gunman turned to face her, Fischer fired.

With night's arrival and a new moon, the beach was dark save for twin portable LED scene lights set up where police had located Lachlan Morris's body. The small parking lot at Haycraft Park on the island's south shore was jammed with law enforcement vehicles, forcing the USMS SUV to discharge its passengers a hundred feet from the entrance.

Anita Fischer was blank-faced as she stepped out of the vehicle, meeting US Marshal J. P. Stevens at the front bumper. They walked up the gravel road toward the parking lot, a deputy illuminating their way with his flashlight. Apart from the circumstances, the night was typically beautiful. Fischer still wore the filthy clothes she had borrowed from Hayley Chill. She and the first responders atop Kealaloloa Ridge—MPD patrol SUVs first, almost immediately followed by FBI and USMS personnel in their unmarked rides—heard the news while Hayley was receiving medical attention in preparation for helicopter transport. Fischer had refused to leave the site until EMS personnel had safely evacuated her injured protector.

One of the DUSMs offered Fischer his phone. Stevens was calling with an update.

That's what he called the news of Lachlan's murder. An "update."

They entered the lot and threaded their way through the jumble of police vehicles, angling toward the beach. Stevens understood he had flubbed the call to the Supreme Court justice and was wary of screwing up again. But he still didn't think Fischer should be here. Homicide detectives from the Maui Police Department were running the scene with agents from the FBI chomping at the bit to get in the game, too. USMS had zero authority here.

"Ma'am, one of the gunmen is still at large. We need to get you off the island immediately."

Fischer did not pause.

"I will see my husband. With my own eyes. Tonight."

Short of placing her in handcuffs, Stevens knew there was no chance of dissuading her. But, as they encountered the different echelons of MPD patrol officers securing the site from the ever-increasing number of lookie-loos gathering on the beach, resistance melted away with one look at her face.

She had been through hell. She had had enough.

Stevens directed Fischer through a maze of police tape. What would have been a two-minute stroll across the strand if walking in a direct line from the parking lot to the site took more than twice that given the serpentine journey. The three of them—Fischer, Stevens, and a flashlight-toting DUSM—walked in silence. Illuminated by the mobile LED scene lights, the body's location was like a nighttime mirage, shimmering in an otherwise black abyss.

Nearing the site, about thirty yards from the water's edge, Fischer recalled their first date. They met for dinner at L'Auberge Chez Francois in Great Falls, Virginia, Fischer driving herself there. A location well outside the District of Columbia and a reservation near closing time were a necessity given the new justice's celebrity single status. Morris, always a stylish dresser, wore a Brioni Sea Island cotton sport coat with a linen shirt and pants. She wore a favorite Celine muted floral cape sleeve dress.

From the first instant, he had been so lighthearted and fun, not the least bit intimidated by the august Supreme Court justice. Unerringly respectful to restaurant staff, quick-witted, always smiling, a human jukebox of spoken word, lovingly inquisitive about *her* and her ideas, Morris made Fischer feel special in a way she had never felt special before. They matched beautifully, without any innumerable tiny frictions that had ultimately halted prior couplings in their tracks. Fischer may have arrived in her car, but she went home in his, Morris playing chauffer to her astonished happiness.

She stopped at the final length of police tape; moving any closer would have put Fischer in the actual crime scene, and, despite her shock, she had no intention of trampling possible evidence. More than anything, Fischer wanted the persons responsible for her husband's death brought to justice . . . if any of them were still alive.

"Do you ever name your escargots?" he had asked her playfully over appetizers.

His body was draped with a white sheet, from under which Morris's bare feet protruded. Stevens waited quietly at Fischer's elbow.

She asked him, "Can they pull back the sheet? I'd like to see his face."

Dissuading her was futile. Stevens gestured to one of the investigators, who immediately recognized the woman standing next to the US marshal, robes or no robes. MPD homicide detective Janice Smith-Archer—mid-forties, on island for a decade, and originally from Detroit—was stunned to see Fischer was still alive. Though details about the incident on Kealaloloa Ridge were scant in these early hours, she had heard the shootout was straight out of an action movie. The on-site investigators had not expected a visit by the murder victim's wife on the beach that night.

Stevens said, "Justice Fischer would like to see her husband, Detective."

Though Smith-Archer had worked dozens of homicides in her tenure as a senior investigator with the Maui Police Department, the detective's heart still ached for the ones left behind to pick up the broken pieces of a shared life. Of a family.

She said, "I'm sorry for your loss, ma'am."

The detective's sincerity and compassion washed over Fischer, producing the first of many tears following Lachlan's death.

Without waiting for a response, Smith-Archer returned to the scene's main stage under the LED lights. "Everybody, take two," she announced.

In unison, the scrum of busily working investigators glanced up from their labors and clocked the victim's famous wife at the police line. Without comment, they dropped whatever they were doing and withdrew into the darkness beyond. Only Smith-Archer remained. She crouched and pulled the sheet to Morris's chest.

His face was unmarred. There was no blood or injury. His expression was of peace and restfulness. As if he were merely asleep, despite the harsh glare of crime scene lights.

Fischer stood still, tears spilling down the slope of her pale cheeks.

"Do you ever name your escargots?"

Never before, but always ever since.

CHAPTER 34

SATURNINO'S STORY

Christmas Day, 2047

I n five days, it will be a quarter century since I first stepped foot on this island. Nearly one week later—as the sun set on the fifth of January—my path turned once more and led to where I am today. My English is pretty good, no? Who says you can't teach an old dog new tricks? Perhaps I wasn't so old when I began a different life here. In those early days, I spoke very little. The less heard and seen of me, the better.

I write these words out by hand. Once I finish telling my story, I will burn the pages and let the winds carry the ash to the ocean. No matter the years that have passed, it's not possible for me to share my origins with the friends I have made here. No one knows the truth. None could understand. They wouldn't recognize the Saturnino of twenty-five years ago, barely a man and one who was caught between two worlds. On the ridge at the other end of this island, he crossed over to a new life by permission of the *rubia* who had gotten the drop on him. She consented to a desire I didn't know that I possessed. Thank God for this woman, whoever she was. Wherever she might be now.

The sound of gunfire between my savior and Carranza was like the starter's pistol in a foot race. Running, I soon abandoned the rifle in my hands. The trees and mountains swallowed me whole, like Jonah into the whale. I hid in that green refuge for I don't know how long. Two weeks? Three? Water was never a problem. Rain fell nearly every day. For sustenance, I ate insects and grubs. Like a chicken. Fires were out of the question, but I was rarely cold. For company, I had the birds, a curious mongoose every once in a while, and God. He was with me always. God was the only way I survived those days in the forest, and I knew He had forgiven me for my sins when I walked out again a different man.

The children we took hostage lived to the north. I walked east along the island's southern shore. Moving only at night and resting during the day, I avoided all human contact. How many pounds did I lose since leaving the others behind? I'm not sure. Believe me, I was skinny! The first person who saw me when I strolled into Hana carrying nothing in my hands but a walking stick screamed in fright. Or perhaps I only imagine that. Dreams of my old life continue to haunt me. Not every night. Only sometimes. The part about the stick is real. How could you forget a time when you owned nothing in the world but a twig of wood and the clothes on your back?

See it there? The stick? Standing in the corner of this house, the length of gnarled wood is the only talisman from my before life.

Once I found work as a handyman, I was able to buy food. For a time, I lived in the garden shed of a house owned by New Yorkers who came to Maui on holidays. For two years, I lived like that. I worked and saved money. People never asked me questions. They didn't care about my origins. How I survived. They only wanted their porches and cars repaired and at a cheap price. I could give them both. I fixed things. I didn't overcharge. As my English improved, the people here began to treat me as if I were something more than a pair of hands they could hire for pennies. I was a human being to them. I became a man of the community.

I didn't pick up a surfboard again until the day I turned thirty. One of my clients was a surfer and gave me one of his old boards as a gift.

Imagine my joy the next morning when I went to Hamoa Beach with my new board. It had been nearly ten years since I had gone into the ocean. Riding a wave once more, I felt as if I were free of my past simultaneously as I reconnected with it. After that first day, I never let another one go by without at least a little time in the ocean. At Koki or Hamoa—or any of the other secret spots on the east coastline around Hana—I found happiness again and many new friends.

After ten years of hard work and saving money, I was able to buy a small house here in Hana and only a stone's throw from the bay. I have a wife who loves me and two sons, eight and nine years old. A day doesn't grow dark without thoughts of the children the same age as my boys when we took them. Every day, I ask God to forgive me. Because I have received so much in the way of His blessings, I have faith that He has absolved me of my sins and continues to do so. His mercy doesn't come without expectations. I live now as a man of God. Through my actions, I strive to show His compassion, love of peace, and kindness.

This is the story of how I came to this place. Only God, the wind, and ocean are witness to the truth that Saturnino Valdés Pérez, a veteran of the Mexican Army's Special Forces Corp, hired gun of the Cartel del Oeste, and former associate of the Snake Eaters, with permission of the blond gringa, abandoned one world and found another in this quiet paradise.

CHAPTER 35

GHOST GUN

H e didn't claw his way to a top position in the pharmaceutical business without learning the value of contingency plans. Two weeks before—and within an hour of receiving news of the operation's utter failure on Maui—David Barrett put his family in a Suburban rented under the name of a rep in the company's sales department and was underway on the road north. His wife, Sandra, and the three kids were presently exploring hiking trails that skirted their decidedly luxurious safe house. The six-bedroom log home sat bull's-eye on twelve hundred acres adjacent to the Grand Teton National Park, at the end of a mile-long gravel road with a secure gate off of Wyoming State Highway 191.

They left all electronic devices behind in Hidden Hills, along with every active bank and credit card. For their immediate needs, Barrett carried a half-million dollars in cash. Long-term needs would be met by the hardware wallet—containing the digital key that would unlock two hundred and fifty million dollars belonging to the Cartel del Oeste—Joe Gunn had delivered three weeks earlier.

New identities were in the process of being created by an ex-

Mossad agent; the layover here in Wyoming was necessitated by the time required to fabricate the new documents. Barrett had told no one about his arrangement with Avi Rokah, not even Joe Gunn. For two hundred grand, the Israeli would provide the Barrett family better services than the United States Marshals Service could offer with their Witness Protection Program.

Rokah advised against hiring security personnel for their remaining days in the United States; the less contact they had with people outside of family, the better. The Barretts had nothing to worry about . . . *if* they followed his instructions. By tomorrow, they would be on their way to a yet-to-be-determined airport for a one-way flight to a yet-to-be-determined country overseas, where they would rebuild their yet-to-be-determined lives.

The kids' young ages had made the upheaval somewhat more manageable. Their oldest, Molly, was eleven and the only child with a phone or social media accounts. Her cooperation proved somewhat challenging, unlike the two younger kids who were convinced the abrupt exodus from California was all part of a grand vacation adventure. Barrett's wife was a tough sell, too, of course. Sandra had had no idea of Joe Gunn's machinations to extricate Oakvale from its legal woes. Relying on more forgivable generalizations, Barrett explained to her that "efforts" to rectify those problems had failed and that he faced a real chance of imprisonment on federal charges if they didn't make a run for it. He said nothing about a special arrangement with the murderous Cartel del Oeste.

After a few days of sulking, Sandra fell once again under her husband's persuasive spell. Indeed, Barrett made the sudden and radical detour in their lives sound exciting. Their vast wealth—the source of which being unmentionable and, therefore, irrelevant—promised a soft landing *somewhere*. On Sandra Barrett's wish list were an ocean view, good private schools, and like-minded expats. A dedicated family man, her husband promised fulfillment of all those demands. By day seven of their new lives, Barrett had convinced them that these big changes were actually *good*. Without the responsibilities of a high-pressure corporate job, he would have nothing but time to spend with his sun-splashed family.

Stepping out of the shower and reentering the bedroom, he was predictably stunned to find a woman sitting in a reading chair by the window, legs crossed and holding a gun pointed at him. With blond hair pulled back in a no-nonsense ponytail and blue eyes that pushed through him to his soul, Hayley Chill was half his age, but seemed to hold within her ten times his gravitas.

The pistol—a 9-millimeter ghost gun—and her blatant disapproval convinced Barrett that his efforts to fall off the radar with new identities had failed miserably.

"How . . . did you find us?"

Hayley had watched Sandra Barrett leave on her walk with the three kids and figured she had thirty minutes at best. She would need only a third of them to do what was necessary here.

"You stopped for gas in Jackson. Your oldest, Molly, borrowed a stranger's phone to reach out to her best friend one last time. That was enough. Since then, we've monitored all of your communications, Mr. Barrett. With the Israeli. Everything."

He regarded the intruder quizzically. She wasn't FBI. But she wasn't cartel, either.

Reading the question in his expression, Hayley said, "I'm the person who took a round from an AK in the chest to prevent you from having an associate justice with the US Supreme Court killed." She paused, her wounds not nearly healed and each breath a trial. "Unfortunately for you, Mr. Barrett, it was a ricochet, or I wouldn't be sitting here."

She had spent five days on the same hospital floor as Terry Shaw, meeting his wife and deepening an unlikely friendship with him. In that time, Publius connected Joe Gunn and Oakvale Pharmaceuticals to the attempt on Anita Fischer's life. The fifth kidnapper, never located, was presumed to have escaped the island. Officials at various agencies and the deeper state allocated resources to find Barrett and his family. All had pinpointed Cartel del Oeste as Oakvale's partner in the scheme. For a time, both the FBI and USMS believed that the Mexicans had disappeared the Barretts. Only the deeper state tracked the CEO to his luxurious lair in Wyoming and uncovered the association with the former Mossad agent.

Wilde gave Hayley the assignment to go after Barrett because she had simultaneously demanded and earned that right. Her injuries still pained her, though the fugitive had no way of knowing it. Barrett confused her occasional wince for a hostile attitude.

"You're going to kill me," he said.

"Somebody will, I can absolutely guarantee it."

Barrett fought the urge to vomit.

Hayley said, "The FBI and cartel can't be too far behind my group, Mr. Barrett. If the FBI gets here first, you'll go to jail for the rest of your life and the money you stole from the cartel will be seized. Deprived of their due, the Mexicans will torture and kill every member of your family. Wife. Children. Your father and mother. If the cartel gets here first? I don't know, maybe they won't kill your parents."

The man began to weep. He was at his bottom and difficult to watch, but Hayley did not avert her gaze, those blue eyes worse than a firing squad.

"Help me," he begged her.

The steam from his shower had fogged the window in the bedroom, only now beginning to clear. Hayley remained seated, gun in hand.

She said, "Something that still bothers me. How Joe Gunn got as far as he did with his scheme. His intelligence during the operation was professional-grade."

Barrett wiped the humiliating tears from his face. "So?"

"The DUSM's phone was compromised with sophisticated malware. We know that. But the way Terry Shaw described Gunn's surveillance, his real-time situational awareness at Fischer's estate, suggests that you had someone on the inside there. Shaw had suspicions at the time, but had little opportunity to pursue those concerns. I have my ideas, too."

The CEO shook his head adamantly. "I didn't involve myself with the details of Gunn's operation."

"You would know this 'detail,' Mr. Barrett, considering its expense. Access like it doesn't come cheap."

He recognized that she was playing with him. That he was subordinate to her. For Barrett, it was a unique experience to submit to someone so young. Words failed.

Hayley leveled her gaze on the CEO, as bracing as a slap across his face.

"When your man, Gunn, called Anita Fischer at the airport, he instructed her to tell no one. He specifically said not to tell 'that West Virginia hillbilly.'"

Barrett stared balefully at his inquisitor, losing the threads of her argument.

Stammering, he said, "I . . . I . . . don't know . . ."

"I didn't tell anyone on the protective detail where I was from, Mr. Barrett. I've learned to speak without an accent to avoid the usual prejudices that a person of my background typically incurs. Justice Fischer is the only person on the island who knew I was born in West Virginia. And I doubt she would be conspiring with her assassins."

Barrett slumped. Of course she knew the answer already. She knew everything.

Hayley waited for him to speak. A confession was required before judgment could be rendered. An admission of guilt was *everything*.

Staring at the floor, Barrett asked rhetorically, "What difference does it make?" He raised his eyes to meet hers. "I mean, he is dead."

Not enough. She remained silent and still. Like Greek mythology's clear-sighted Themis and ancient Rome's Justitia, scales tilting toward a guilty verdict.

Caving to the pressure, the CEO said, "Yes . . . it was Morris."

Hayley showed no emotion having extracted this last unexposed secret of Barrett's despicable conspiracy. She didn't nod or acknowledge his statement in any way. Standing, gun in hand, she said, "'Justice is indiscriminately due to all, without regard to numbers, wealth or rank.' John Jay, the first chief justice of the country, said that. You, Mr. Barrett. Me. Your family. Those kids back on Maui. Their families. We only deserve what's fair and just."

The pharmaceutical executive whimpered, the void opening at his feet and the sight of it terrifying him beyond belief. Would she shoot him here in his bedroom?

Hayley placed the gun on the bed between them, grip toward the quivering man. As if by magic, the hardware wallet materialized in her hand. Barrett's hiding place in one of the shoes in his closet had been less than foolproof.

She said, "Returning the money to the cartel will not be sufficient, Mr. Barrett. Not enough to save the lives of your family. We are all our own best judges. We know what we must do to balance the scales."

The silence that fell between them was broken only by his intermittent sobs.

CHAPTER 36

THE DEVIL YOU KNOW

Two Weeks Earlier

Yesterday the success of Joe Gunn's ambitious plan appeared inevitable. Now all things teetered in the balance. Landing on Maui at two p.m., he had mercifully avoided the airport's shutdown following the assault by the two Mexican gunmen in his employ. A Tesla Model S was waiting for him in the Aloha Air Cargo parking lot.

Gunn had no doubt the entire operation would have ended disastrously if not for his timely arrival on the island. He had managed to extract Anita Fischer from the protective embrace of the US Marshals Service. With luck, she would be dead in the next sixty minutes. In the meantime, Gunn would continue to keep a low profile. He preferred to operate from behind the scenes, and being so close to the action—in this case, within a few miles of what he hoped would be the scheme's final denouement—made him unpleasantly nervous.

His hideout was Haycraft Park, a small unpaved parking lot and three miles of relatively unremarkable (for Maui) beach just west of Kihei. Drawing visitors exclusively from the haphazard clutter of condos and vacation rentals that lined Hauoli Street, the beach was a good location to avoid being seen. He wasn't complaining; Gunn could think of a million worse places than a Maui beach to lie low.

After thirty minutes of sitting on the sand and watching small waves lap against the shore, he had returned to his car for a jacket; with the wind building and the sun getting lower in the sky, his vigil on the beach was becoming chilly. He could see the wind turbines spinning on Keala-loloa Ridge from the parking lot. Would Anita Fischer find some way of arriving there? Gunn didn't doubt her resourcefulness. He counted on the justice's ability to circumvent any obstacles to deliver herself to the Mexican sicarios.

The gamble was on her level of motivation. Did she love Lachlan Morris intensely enough to commit what was, in essence, a suicidal act? By taking advantage of the diversion created by two of the cartel gunmen and escaping from USMS protection, Fischer had more than proven an attachment to her new husband. But, Gunn had to admit, the risk wasn't all that great she would fail to act; he had solid information that the justice, despite her cerebral reputation, was wholly enamored of Morris. Like a schoolgirl, his spy had assured him. Besotted.

Hesitant to jinx his imminent success, Gunn nonetheless analyzed the current situation and liked what he saw. Despite his present fatigue, he felt optimistic. Maybe he'd even have the whole matter wrapped up in time to call home and wish his daughters good night.

Walking from the parking lot and directly to the beach, Gunn trudged across the strand in the direction where his companion was seated a dozen yards from the water's edge.

"Companion" might have been too pretty a word to describe the man. Associate? Co-conspirator? Gunn's scheme to keep Oakvale's case off the Supreme Court's docket would not have been possible without the assistance of an insider. In their dealings—all handled remotely, with today representing their first face-to-face interactions—he had come to have a real appreciation for the dude. Gunn hadn't enjoyed a close friend-ship with another man since college. For this reason alone, he regretted what was to come.

Lachlan Morris, seated on the beach, looked over his shoulder as the corporate security officer for Oakvale Pharmaceuticals drew near. His face showed the rough treatment he had endured at the hands of Gunn, a painful beatdown despite it being completely voluntary. Having kicked off his loafers and never a fan of socks in a tropical setting, Morris was very much in his element on the Hawaiian beach as the sun eased to the horizon. He pushed his toes through the sand as Gunn plopped down next to him.

"You remember doing this when you were a kid? The sheer joy of warm sand coursing between your toes?" he asked Gunn.

Lachlan Morris, Brooklyn-born, was raised in Midwood, a once quiet, middle-class neighborhood fast becoming an enclave of newly arrived immigrants from the Soviet Union, Jamaica, Haiti, and Guyana. Summers were spent at Coney Island, a seventeen-minute trip by subway and graced with a beach liberally sprinkled with cigarette butts, broken glass, and soda can pop-tops. Not that Morris cared at the time. For five consecutive summers, he and his multiethnic gang of Midwood pals contested control of the boardwalk with a handful of like-minded toughs from Sheepshead Bay, Brighton Beach, and Gravesend. Those were glorious days for young Morris, cut short by the thrust of a knife that missed his aorta by a quarter inch.

A different path forward occurred to him in the hospital during his convalescence. Morris had too good a brain to follow his cohorts into the lives of unimaginative mendacity that was their collective destiny. Brooklyn College was the first stop on Morris's transformation, but where he gained much grander ambitions was Princeton University after transferring his sophomore year. The Ivy League and its inhabitants revealed many possibilities for the creatively corrupt that would have been unimaginable in lowly Midwood. Cheating was as reflexive as taking the next breath among a certain crowd on campus.

Having left behind a life where fists, broken bottles, and knives were the usual tools of success, Morris learned to wield a pen and natural charisma as ready weapons. A journalism career was enticing for its possibilities of respectable deception, however low-paying. After J-school at

Columbia and three years slogging at small-market newspapers up and down the East Coast, Morris reported the story of a single mother of four school-age kids who was turning tricks at the Molly Pitcher Service Area on the New Jersey Turnpike. Written for the Gannett-owned *Asbury Park Press*, where Morris was employed, the feature was a sensation reprinted by all of the mass media giant's holdings, including *USA Today*. Only Morris would ever know that he had fabricated the entire narrative.

The "PTA president slash highway hooker" story turbocharged Morris's career. Leaving behind his ink-stained colleagues in the daily newspaper world, he wrote a wildly successful book about the anonymous sex worker and her double-life travails. A string of nonfiction titles followed, but none as successful as *Ms. Doe*. Topics like the sex and bribery scandal that brought down a bishop in the Catholic Church, the Marine officer accused of murder during the Iraq War, and an exposé on the role of "dark money" in the creation of Silicon Valley failed to ignite the buzz surrounding his debut. Morris lost much of his literary zing with his newfound adherence to fact as opposed to the invention of his debut. His residency on the *New York Times* bestseller list proved fleeting. Movie options lapsed without the promised adaptations.

A lifelong bachelor who modeled his approach to romantic commitment on Jack Nicholson's character in *Something's Gotta Give*, pre–Diane Keaton, Morris met Anita Fischer at a party in Washington, DC, hosted by a top editor at the *Washington Post*. For both, the timing was fortuitous. Fischer, newly installed on the Supreme Court, had reached the epitome of the legal profession at the young age of forty-four without much of a life outside that noble pursuit. She was more than ready for the dynamic energy that a well-spoken, worldly, and once-celebrated author could inject into her daily existence. Lachlan Morris, having blown through nearly every dollar he had ever made and suffering stubbornly diminishing sales numbers with every new book, was in dire need of a financial savior. If he was to maintain a lifestyle to which he'd become accustomed, Fischer's wealth—old money always *the best* money—was a godsend.

That is until he received a better offer for his time and energies.

With one-tenth of Morris's joie de vivre and personal dazzle, Joe Gunn found no sensualist appeal in the scrunching of toes in beach sand or other similar bagatelles of life. Though his new pal's influential appeal was undeniable, Gunn had no intention of removing his leather shoes and wool socks. He loathed sand.

"We should have this all wrapped up soon enough," he said by way of non sequitur.

Morris, confident of the mission's outcome, asked, "Mexican cartel types, you say?"

"I didn't say."

"Then a lucky guess, perhaps."

"How're you doing?" asked Gunn, perplexed by his companion's relaxed demeanor.

"Me? How should I be doing? Fine, I suppose."

"You're not . . . remorseful?"

"For assisting you? Perhaps. Somewhat. Sure, why not? Anita is a marvelous woman. She's been ridiculously kind to me in every manner. Shown me the kind of respect that few have in recent years. I do hope I've made her happy in our short time together. But remorseful? I'm not entirely sure. If it hadn't been me, you would've found someone else for the job."

Gunn said, "Marrying her was completely unnecessary, for our purposes at least."

Morris guffawed, ironically indignant.

He asked, "You doubt my motives? I gladly signed a prenup and won't see a penny of her money." He gazed serenely over the gentle waters, the sunlight becoming ever more golden. "Anita wanted marriage. I had no reason to object."

"But you'll get your payday, won't you?" reminded Gunn.

A Cheshire smile broadened across Morris's face. Payday indeed. Life was truly a beautiful thing. He dug his toes into the sand again, searching for warmth under the cooling top layers.

The two men were in weekly contact since Joe Gunn had first approached Morris with a proposed punch list:

1. *Make yourself available to the newly installed Supreme Court justice.*
2. *Romance her, if she proves susceptible.*
3. *Deepen the relationship to the point that Morris would be able to provide meaningful intelligence.*

Fischer's death wasn't considered a foregone conclusion in the early days. That element of the conspiracy only became necessary as the suit against Oakvale Pharmaceuticals wound its way through lower courts. Gunn had to admit that the journalist-turned-author performed magnificently. Why had he never considered a career in Hollywood?

"I'm going to miss this wondrous place," Morris said wistfully, eyes locked on the shimmering line where the ocean met the sky.

Gunn glanced to his right and left. The beach was empty, with not another person in sight. For a Columbia-trained journalist, Morris struck him as painfully naive. Did he expect he would be allowed to live? How could he *not* appreciate the level of scrutiny the murder of a US Supreme Court justice would incur? The man's fate was sealed once the schoolchildren's abduction failed to achieve the desired result, though Lachlan Morris's days were numbered in either case. Joe Gunn would miss their weekly conversations.

He draped his left arm around Morris's shoulders and asked, "Why ever leave?"

Raising his left hand and placing it on the left side of his companion's head, Gunn reached with his right hand to the right side of Morris's jaw. Pushing with both hands in opposite directions, he delivered a sharp kinetic force to the journalist's spinal cord—a sound like popping corn—that destroyed the third and fourth vertebrae.

From experience, Gunn knew that Morris hadn't expired. The actual cause of death, in ninety seconds at the most, would be asphyxiation, brought on by the interruption of instructions between the interconnected neurons in the journalist's brain stem and the different groups of respiratory muscles located in the chest wall, diaphragm, and abdomen. His companion's eyelids fluttered spasmodically as Gunn gently—

almost tenderly—lowered him flat on the sand. The dying man's full white hair caught the failing sunlight that shot through from the west, a halo effect that Gunn failed to notice.

He stood and brushed the devilish sand from his shirt and pants, anticipating the reservoir he would find later in his shoes. Looking up and down the beach, then behind him, across the undeveloped acreage to the north, the corporate security officer felt a swelling of relief.

They were alone, Gunn and the asphyxiating man.

Life is strange.

Lachlan Morris had suggested Haycraft Park as a possible location to lie low while the gunmen did their work. Gunn could not have found a better place to leave a corpse. If any passerby saw the body on the beach from any distance, the natural assumption would be that Morris was drunk, asleep, or both. Alarm wouldn't be raised until midday tomorrow at the earliest.

Gunn bid farewell to his junior partner in the conspiracy with a diffident wave of his hand and trudged across the strand to the postage-stamp parking lot. His watch demanded consultation; the Rolex Submariner's report was not quite half past four. Gunn had decided he would return to the airport and wait for further word from the Mexicans. No amount of forensic analysis, interrogation, or plea bargaining would connect him with Oscar Carranza and his crew. Gunn recalled Rafael Hernández, his contact with the Cartel del Oeste, saying something about the infiltration of an assassin's assassin on the island exactly for that purpose.

Un ajuste de cuentas, or a settling of accounts, would be overseen by higher-ups in the cartel.

In the words of his native country, "not his problem."

———————

Wearing the company coveralls that had been his uniform for the last two weeks, Juan Menotti watched the Gulfstream G700 taxi to the departure end of the runway. The sun had fully set and the sky was deepening blue without a hint of clouds. In the two weeks he had been on Maui, the sicario for the Cartel del Oeste didn't think he had witnessed such a beautiful night. Winds that had blown hard from the east died to nothingness. Menotti would be catching the ferry to Molokai in the morning in anticipation of the Kahului Airport's continued closure at least until then. From Molokai, he would catch a flight with Mokulele Airlines to Oahu and then finally home to Mexico.

Performing the necessary logistical preparations for Oscar Carranza and his crew in Virginia and Hawaii, Menotti knew to remain behind the scenes and avoid contact with the cartel operators. His only interaction with any of the gunmen was when the young blond one had come to pick up their gear on the first evening of the Maui operation. *Nice kid*, thought Menotti. The cartel's operators were accounted for and reported KIA . . . except for Saturnino Valdés Pérez. Menotti hoped the kid had managed to escape the American law enforcement authorities. If police arrested the youngster, a return trip would be required to the island. More cleanup.

Menotti had watched the client—gringo with a round face and attired in the fatuous clothes of a country club golfer—board the Gulfstream forty-five minutes earlier. Sitting astride his cargo tractor, the Mexican with the gold teeth was close enough to perceive the gringo's anxiety and fear. Undoubtedly, he had heard news of the operation's failure. The lady judge was alive. No more men would be coming to take her life. Not long after the round-faced gringo climbed the steps and disappeared inside the corporate jet, the stairs were retracted and the door was closed. With the fast-ascending wail of its twin Rolls-Royce Pearl 700 engines, the aircraft rolled from its parking slot on the tarmac and was underway.

The Gulfstream never paused as it taxied to the end of the runway and accelerated out of its turn. Menotti watched the jet take off, climbing steeply into the darkening sky, quickly a mile offshore and climbing still. He had placed the package inside the aircraft during routine servicing and only activated the bomb after receiving orders from Hernández, five minutes prior to the gringo boarding.

The explosion over the ocean against the gathering night's sky was a beautiful thing of orange and yellow, its thumping report like a thunderclap that blanketed the north shore. Menotti didn't move from his perch on the low-slung tractor until the last of the bomb flash was only a memory. Then he moved quickly. Finally, it was time to go.

Home.

CODA

Now

*H*ell, *I don't believe I've talked half that much my entire life.*
Making speeches. Quoting the Founding Fathers.
Sheesh . . .

Is it a mind cleared of an alcohol fog? Hayley feels different, that much is certain. Changes have come to her life. Recent histories have remolded the refugee from a hard upbringing, devastating losses, and grave responsibilities. Recommitted to the ideals on which Publius was founded, Hayley is a woman reborn. Even Wilde noticed something different in her. The deeper state will make good on its promise to help her brother-in-law and baby nephew. That worry duly shelved, the way ahead is clear for fixing problems of great scope and national necessity.

Safely back in Washington, Anita Fischer deserves the vision of a wondrous love snatched from her at its earliest beginnings. Certainly, Hayley owes the woman that comfort. The truth of Lachlan Morris's horrendous betrayal dies here in this vast and empty space. Hayley needed to know because learning the truth behind the lies is her destiny.

She can ill-afford the delusions that give comfort to those charged with much lesser responsibilities.

She is glad to be clear of the CEO and the ridiculous log mansion erected on what was once the hunting range of the Arapaho and Lakota. The winter air stings her cheeks and reminds Hayley that life is hers to pursue. Walking at a measured pace on the gravel track that meandered to the highway where she left her vehicle, the deeper state operative ruminates on those Native Americans and peoples who followed them. Spanish imperialists. French-Canadian trappers. Desperate settlers who walked across an entire continent to what they hoped would be a future different than their past.

Hayley is a few hundred feet away from the house when she hears the gunshot.

All had come this way and then as quickly were gone again.

ACKNOWLEDGMENTS

I am gratefully indebted to many people who contributed to the creation of this book. JP Stevens offered insights into the world of the US Marshals Service. Don Bentley set me straight regarding a few matters FBI. Mike Hauty and Jackson Hauty were reliably on hand to provide medical advice. Colin Maehler lent an assist on the subject of retail pharmacy practices. Teresa Vandre provided invaluable insights regarding Hayley Chill's addiction struggles. On Maui, Tara Grace and Lydia Hesse were enthusiastic and generous guides. On the Big Island, Misha Hesse and Struan Scott provided unstinting hospitality and the names of their astonishing sons, Bodhi and Finn. Finally, Christie Ciraulo and Tetia Stroud were early eyes on the manuscript. I owe all these folks my most sincere gratitude.

As always, I must offer heartfelt thanks to my editor, Emily Bestler, associate editor Lara Jones, publicist David Brown, and all the other dedicated publishing professionals at Atria Books—I'm looking at you, Dana Trocker, Megan Rudloff, Lisa Sciambra, Libby McGuire, Suzanne Donahue, Sara Kitchen, and James Iacobelli—who helped usher this book into existence. Dan Conaway and Jordan Bayer are the gold standard in the spheres of literary representation and friendship. It bears repeating that I am an extraordinarily fortunate author to have all these talented people in my life.

But, above all else, I must acknowledge you, dear reader. Without your kind attention and imagination, this book cannot come alive. Kudos. Until next time then.